BRUCE GRAY

DISTANT WATER

LIVE OAK

BOOK COMPANY

Distant Water is a work of fiction. The characters, characterizations of historical figures and entities, dialogue, and incidents portrayed are either products of the author's imagination or have been used fictitiously. Any resemblance to actual persons, living or dead, businesses, institutions, governments, events, or locales is entirely coincidental.

Published by Live Oak Book Company
Austin, TX
www.liveoakbookcompany.com

Distributed by Live Oak Book Company

For ordering information or special discounts for bulk purchases, please contact Live Oak Book Company at PO Box 91869, Austin, TX 78709, 512.891.6100.

Design and composition by Greenleaf Book Group LLC
Cover design by Greenleaf Book Group LLC

Publisher's Cataloging-In-Publication Data
(Prepared by The Donohue Group, Inc.)
Gray, Bruce (Bruce Norman), 1947–
   Distant water / Bruce Gray. -- 1st ed.
    p. ; cm.
   Issued also as an ebook.
   ISBN: 978-1-936909-34-6
   1. Lawyers--China--Fiction. 2. Generals--China--Fiction. 3. China--History--1949-1976--Fiction. 4. Family secrets--China--Fiction. 5. Political fiction. I. Title.
PS3607.R29 D57 2012
813/.6   2011945522

First Edition

For my mother, Elinor,
from whose world, sadly, I have faded

THE CHARACTERS

In Hong Kong

BRYAN PATON, American-born lawyer and new hire in Bishops' Estates and Trusts division. A Mandarin speaker and Sinophile.

AH-YEE, Bryan's live-in housekeeper.

AIDAN MACKINNON, Senior Partner at Bishops and social lion.

GLYNIS MACKINNON, Aidan's wife.

MISS CHAO, Aidan MacKinnon's all-knowing secretary.

LI DAK-CHUNG, esteemed Chairman of Nan Hwa Shipping and Adair, Jameson Trading companies.

FIONA LI, socialite daughter of Li Dak-chung.

SIMON LI, son of Li Dak-chung and junior associate at Bishops. Bryan's babysitter at Bishops and close friend of Hugh Highgrove.

LAO MA, the Li family chauffeur.

HUGH HIGHGROVE, First Secretary at the British Embassy in Beijing.

EMMA HIGHGROVE, Hugh's wife and best friend of Fiona Li. Her father is Aidan MacKinnon.

P. F. CHU, *feng shui* master.

HARRY CHEN, powerful Triad gangster. Son of Du Yuesheng, deceased underworld leader of Shanghai's notorious Green Gang.

CAI YIMOU, Foreign Affairs Officer at the Bank of China.

DAI KAI-KUI, Communist union boss with contacts reaching into China.

SIR GEOFFREY LUGARD, Governor of Hong Kong.

In Taiwan

LI GWEI-YU, sister of Li Dak-chung and intimate of Chiang Kai-shek's widow, Song Meiling, and the ruling clique.

In Beijing

GENERAL ZHU FANGGUO, Commander of the Beijing Military Region and former Military Governor of the Northeast Military Region. A nephew of Marshal Zhu De and a Long March Veteran.

COLONEL PENG RUIYI, General Zhu's protégé and closest aide. Grandson of deceased Marshal Peng Dehuai, former Minister of National Defense.

MAJOR WANG CHONGSHI, aide-de-camp to General Zhu.

GENERAL LIANG JUNTAO, Chief of Intelligence of the Beijing Military Region and aide to General Zhu.

PAN BINGQING, China Travel Service guide and Bryan's principal handler in Beijing.

RONG CHENLI, Foreign Affairs Officer at the Ministry of Public Security.

RONG LIAOPING, Agent of the Ministry of Public Security and Chenli's brother.

RONG LINA, member of the PLA's Detachment 8341, assigned to the detail guarding Song Chingling. Married to Rong Liaoping.

JIANG QING, widow of Mao Zedong and leader of the radical faction espousing perpetual revolution.

MARSHAL YE JIANYING, Minister of National Defense and Long Marcher.

GENERAL WANG DONGXING, Commander of People's Liberation Army Detachment 8341.

GENERAL YANG, Chief of Intelligence of the Shanghai Military Region and crony of General Liang.

MAJOR ZHANG, aide to General Liang and executioner.

DR. SONG WENSHU, Administrator and Chief of Surgery at Capital Hospital.

DR. LI ZHISUI, Mao Zedong's personal physician.

KNUD ASCANIUS, First Secretary at the Danish Embassy.

Distant water is of no use if the fire is near at hand.

CHINESE PROVERB

ACKNOWLEDGMENTS

Distant Water had many sources of inspiration. Among them were my mentors in the Foreign Service, Don Anderson and Stape Roy, whose wisdom about all things Chinese was infectious; and the Consulate General Hong Kong and Embassy Beijing families of years ago, whose lifelong friendship provided encouragement and who served as muses for certain of the characters. I thank especially Betty Sher and the late Ron Sher, Lucille Zaelit, Lorraine Takahashi, John and Mary Witt, Lois and Tom Williams and the late George Williams, Danny Chan, Cece Cheung, and the late Blanche Anderson, who, apart from my sister-in-law, was the most enthusiastic reader I have ever known. I owe a particular debt to Lincoln Yung in Hong Kong, whose generosity of spirit sustained me during a difficult time in the progress of my illness and whose continuing concern I treasure. My fondness for Chinese landscape painting and the work of watercolor artist Lo Wai Hin influenced the cover design.

My production helpmates were essential. Foremost among them were my wife, Kaarn, who did most of the heavy editing and, as a Cambridge graduate, kept me straight on matters British; my sister-in-law,

Jan Stout, herself a writer, who provided invaluable critical analysis through several iterations; and Dave King, who edited an early draft and taught me much about technique. I owe special thanks to Carolyn Harris, my professional caregiver, whose assistance was key to the completion of this project.

Finally, I am indebted to the delightful folks at Greenleaf Book Group, specifically Hobbs Allison, Natalie Návar, Jessica Foster, Brian Phillips, Theresa Reding, and Corrin Foster, whose enthusiasm and guidance shepherded *Distant Water* through to its birth.

CHAPTER 1

Thursday, September 9, 1976

Li Zhisui, clad only in pajamas and slippers, ignored the nighttime chill as he sprinted the short distance from his house to the villa. Sentries allowed the familiar figure to enter unhindered. As he stepped into the bedroom, a naked young woman clutching a nightdress to her body withdrew into the shadows. Li went to the massive bed on which his elderly patient lay motionless. Two nurses were already attending the man.

"What is his status?" Li asked.

"He's been unconscious for about five minutes." One of the nurses pointed to the naked, trembling figure in the corner. "She told me the two of them were engaged in vigorous activity when he passed out."

Li placed his stethoscope to the man's chest. "He's still alive, but . . ."

A short older woman strode imperiously into the room. Stocky and rather homely, she wore her short hair bobbed and severely pinned back from her face.

"Several leaders are here to see him. What shall I tell them?" From the corner of her eye she noticed the cowering paramour. "Get out!"

Head bowed, the young woman slowly walked from the room.

The older woman turned back to the doctor. "Well?"

"He is unconscious, and his heartbeat is irregular," Li replied. "Once we restore a normal heart rhythm, he'll need to rest for at least—"

"That's of no consequence," the woman snapped. "He has been that way for months. I'll bring in the leaders once you stabilize him. You are responsible for making that happen before the night is out."

She turned and left the room.

"Doctor," one of the nurses said, "he's having trouble breathing."

For the next two hours, the top medical team in the People's Republic of China struggled to keep the 82-year-old Mao Zedong alive—and failed.

• • •

Fiona Li rolled her eyes upward in derision. *What hocus-pocus gibberish this is.*

"Yes, I think you're right," she said. "The front door is slightly angled in the general direction of the Macau Ferry Terminal. The road curves."

"Hollywood Road. Very auspicious location for an antique shop," the *feng shui* master observed.

"Right in the thick of things," Fiona said.

Fiona Li and Emma Highgrove, friends since before either could remember, had decided three months ago to open an antique shop in Hong Kong. Emma and her husband, Hugh, First Secretary at the British Embassy in Beijing, had been passing through Hong Kong on their way back to the UK for home leave. Emma was despondent that the role of diplomat's wife left her no outlet for her education and interests, and the antique shop seemed the perfect antidote. Even so, the two friends had concluded that Emma could be only a silent partner and adviser. Fiona would run the shop, taking her cues on major inventory and management from Emma in Beijing. And Emma's first management decision had been to insist that any premises she and Fiona rented had to be approved by a *feng shui* master.

It was now early September, and Fiona had not only found a choice location, but, if she caught her train, would be able to stock the shop immediately with the finest antiques to come out of China since 1949. Not bad for the junior partner. It was a pity she had to leave for China just twelve hours before Hugh and Emma were returning to Hong Kong, but her visa stated unequivocally: "Single entry by train from Hong Kong on Thursday, 9 September, 1976." Fiona was determined not to miss her train, which she would do unless this bloody charlatan picked up his pace. She had moved to the front door of the empty shop, but the master was still ruminating at the rear.

With a faintly shrill tone to her voice, she called out, "Almost finished, Mr. Chu?"

"Yes, just a few more minutes. I can't find a rear door or window. Is there one?"

"No, no there isn't. This row of shops is built against a bedrock outcropping of the hillside."

"A-a-ah." Chu walked to the front of the shop, nodding and smiling. When he reached Fiona, he stood with his head bowed, deep in thought. Fiona fidgeted then sighed audibly.

Unperturbed, Chu said, "I recommend placing the sales desk slightly off center and facing northwest. And a mirror should always hang over a potted live evergreen in the front display window."

"That's it?"

"Yes, young lady," Chu said dryly in English. Until now, they had been conversing in Cantonese. Fiona was sure she had heard him stress the word young.

"Thanks ever so much," Fiona said, also in English. "I'll expect your complete written report to arrive at the office of my solicitor, Aidan MacKinnon, by the fifteenth, without fail. Just post it to Bishops, Hutchison House, in Central. Good morning."

Fiona brushed past the bewildered *feng shui* master and out the front door. Chu bolted after her, barely rescuing his overcoat as she slammed the door behind them and threw the dead bolt with the key. She turned, swept past the flustered Chu, and entered the waiting Rolls-Royce, its passenger door held open by her father's chauffeur.

Fiona looked at her watch. Twenty minutes to make it to the Kow-loon-Canton Railway Station in Hung Hom on the Kowloon side of the harbor. There was only one train a day to the Hong Kong–China border crossing point at Lo Wu, and it left promptly at 8:00 a.m.

The limousine sped quietly up Hollywood Road toward the four-lane access way leading to the Cross-Harbor Tunnel. Fortunately, traffic was light. Fiona put on the full-length fur coat that her maid had placed in the car that morning. She had bought it several years ago on a whim after noticing a similarly clad woman strolling on the rue du Faubourg Saint-Honoré and fancying the look. The fur had come in handy on her frequent trips to London and Paris. And now ahead of her was bone-dry, windswept, frigid Beijing. At least she would be warm.

When the limousine emerged from the tunnel on the Kowloon side, Fiona could see the train station in the distance off to the right. She did not relish the trip from Hong Kong to Beijing, nor the four days in Beijing it would take her to close the deal for the consignment of antiques. Precisely who was responsible for the serendipity, or why, did not concern her; but she was eager to surprise her father, Emma, and her older brother, Simon, with this rare good fortune. And so Fiona had told neither her family nor friends that she was going to China. She had simply said that she was going to Macau for a few days and swore the house staff to silence on pain of unemployment.

The chauffeur eased the car to the curb in front of the station, which harbored a maelstrom of activity. When he opened the door, Fiona instinctively recoiled as noise and noxious smells engulfed her. Passengers streamed in every direction throughout the huge open-air station. Most were loaded down with kitchen appliances, TVs, stereos, radios, pots, pans, rice cookers, woks, lanterns, small furniture, or camp stoves, all still new in their boxes and lashed with rope to create a hand-hold. Women carried poles across their shoulders from which bundles wrapped in blankets or sheets were suspended. Squawking ducks and chickens, their feet bound together, dangled upside down from their owners' belts or peeked out from among the bundles. Everyone juggled string bags crammed with canned goods, condiments, vegetables and fruits of every type, sacks of rice, sugar, and flour, and containers of cooking oil.

Hong Kong's largesse was China-bound, borne on the backs of laborers. Most had entered Hong Kong illegally, either in small groups guided by the infamous "snakeheads," or in one of the waves of refugees permitted by the People's Republic of China to overwhelm the border in attempts to humiliate the British. Over the years since 1949, Britain had allowed these refugees to be documented as Hong Kong residents but had steadfastly refused to let their families join them.

A man squatted next to a mound of bundles and string bags a few feet from the open car door. He wore a sweat-stained undershirt, gray cotton shorts, and rubber sandals. His conical reed hat with chinstrap had fallen off his head and was now resting on his back. A small squealing pig, its legs tethered, writhed on the ground next to him.

The man drew deeply on his cigarette as Fiona emerged from the car. The pig was blocking her path. The more she sought to avoid it, the more it seemed to wriggle in front of her. The man dropped his cigarette and leaped up. He and the chauffeur struggled to immobilize the terrified animal as a dismayed Fiona stood teetering above them.

Exasperated, Fiona suddenly darted around the writhing trio. As she dashed forward a stiletto heel caught one of the pig's ears, resulting in even more screeching.

Trembling with embarrassment, Fiona never looked back. Spotting a sign that read "This Way to First Class Waiting Room," she burst through the crowd of gawkers that had gathered and, like a crane amidst a flock of chickens, strode regally in the direction of the sign.

On the train, Fiona fidgeted in her seat as the New Territories countryside rushed past the window. She seldom traveled by train, and never outside of Europe. Even though they had departed Kowloon almost an hour ago, she could not seem to get comfortable. The cars were open, without compartments, and the seats were in groups of four, two on either side of a table. When she had boarded, roughly half her fellow passengers had been Hong Kong Chinese. As the train made more stops in Kowloon and the New Territories, these suburban commuters got off. Now, less than fifteen minutes from Lo Wu and the border, Fiona and two men were the only Chinese among fifty or so European tourists on their way to China. The two Chinese men wore boxy, ill-fitting government-issue suits that stamped them as PRC officials.

"The Rome-Milan bullet train it's not," Fiona mumbled.

"I'm sorry. Did you say something?" asked the woman sitting across the table.

"Huh? Oh . . . no, sorry. Just thinking out loud," Fiona said.

"Are you a Chinese government official? We're Swedish, on a one-month world peace and friendship study tour to China. We get a government stipend every three years for a study tour abroad. There are twenty-four of us. My name is Bodil, and this is my husband, Gunnar. We're both schoolteachers from Stockholm . . . well, not Stockholm exactly, but a town near Stockholm. But nobody knows where Ekeby is, so we just say Stockholm. Gunnar, isn't that a beautiful fur coat? Did you buy your coat in China? Oh, I can't wait to see your Great Wall. Look, we've arrived at Lo Wu. Gunnar, get out the passports."

Fiona marveled at the woman's respiratory capacity.

After clearing Hong Kong immigration, Fiona and the other passengers walked across the Lo Wu Bridge to the PRC side. There they were directed to a building where they were to undergo Chinese customs and immigration inspection.

Fiona dreaded the coming three-hour train ride to Guangzhou in the company of Bodil, Gunnar, and their tour group. She would have to elude them in the customs hall and then board a different car from theirs. It was easy to track the group's location because their leader guided them by holding aloft a small flag bearing the tour company's logo.

Fiona entered the customs building well behind the tour group but noticed that each of them was carrying a grease-stained box that doubtless contained a lunch. It was nearly noon, and Fiona was ravenous. Hunger always made her irritable. She had skipped breakfast that morning because of the *feng shui* master's early arrival. She resolved to sit down to a leisurely lunch in the station restaurant after passing through Chinese customs and immigration.

"Li Guangmei? . . . Who is Li Guangmei?" a girl shouted in Mandarin from the center of the entry hall. She wore green cotton pants and shirt, white plastic sandals, and a green cotton Mao-style cap bearing a red plastic star. Her shirt, worn out over her trousers, had red epaulets and accents that resembled those worn by soldiers in the People's Liberation Army. She stood next to a handcart on which were stacked Fiona's three pieces of Louis Vuitton luggage.

The girl scowled and looked down at a list she was holding. She raised her head and bellowed in irritation, this time in English, "Who is Fiona Li?" She pronounced the "Fi" in Fiona like "fie."

Fiona bellowed back at the girl, "It's Fee-ona. And by the way, my

Mandarin is rusty. I speak Cantonese, English, and some French. Take your pick."

The girl stared, mouth agape. Then her face flushed red, and she began to giggle with embarrassment. When she regained her composure, she said in English in a barely audible voice, "I regret return to Motherland make unpleasant by me not speak Cantonese. I from Shandong province. Only speak Putonghua. How you say . . . Mandarin? And a little English."

"Then why on earth are you working in Guangdong province?" Fiona asked.

The girl straightened as she solemnly recited in Mandarin, "I am a Red Guard. I hold high the teachings of our Great Leader, Comrade Mao Zedong." Her voice becoming increasingly shrill, she went on. "In 1967, I was elected by the other students to be provincial leader of the Shandong Red Guards. We vigorously smashed the remnants of capitalist, counterrevolutionary culture and the supporters of Deng Xiaoping. We smashed our school, the university, then the libraries and museums. We traveled all over the province to carry out fully the teachings of our beloved Chairman Mao. We dealt severely with those who opposed us and defeated the putrid relics of Confucianism. When our work was finished, Chairman Mao sent soldiers to replace us so we could go back to school. But I was twenty and too old. So the Party assigned me here, to this highly prized position."

"And that would be . . . ?" Fiona asked, her stomach groaning from hunger.

The girl appeared deflated. "What did you say?"

"And your position is . . . ?"

"Oh. My position is China International Travel Service worker."

"Well, let's actually work a little then, shall we?" Fiona said while inspecting the name tags on the bags on the cart. "Yes, these three are mine. Now, can we move along before all the seats in the restaurant are taken?" Fiona turned and began walking toward the door marked "Foreigners."

"Miss Li. Over here, please. You pass through customs and immigration this way." The girl gestured toward a door marked "Chinese Citizens." Fiona spotted the man with the tethered pig squatting just inside.

"No, that's not right. I'm British. Well, Hong Kong British." Fiona imagined the restaurant filling up.

"That's right. You're from Hong Kong, and you're Chinese. So you're a Chinese citizen. Please, this way," the girl insisted.

Fiona batted at the flies and mosquitoes that were bedeviling her. Sweat beaded on her forehead and upper lip. She bristled, "Look, I have a Hong Kong–British passport, so I'm a British subject. And I'm damn well not—"

"You're not going to what?"

A People's Liberation Army officer stepped from behind the two-way mirror before which Fiona and others, unaware of the officer's presence on the other side, had occasionally preened themselves. His uniform was crisply pressed, and he was strapping, even muscular. The travel service girl lowered her head and took a step backward. The three were alone, the other passengers, railway staff, and officials having already gone through one of the two doors.

"What is it you won't do, Li Guangmei?" the officer repeated in nearly unaccented English as he slowly walked around to stand behind her.

Temporizing, Fiona took off her fur coat and laid it carefully across her forearm. She had never before heard the Mandarin pronunciation for the characters of her Chinese name. Now she had heard them three times in the last thirty minutes. And they had never sounded so menacing.

"Surely you were not going to say that a Chinese citizen need not obey Chinese law," the officer said.

"No. No, of course not," Fiona said, her head crooked awkwardly over her shoulder. Although born in China, Fiona had left in 1949 at the age of one year, along with her father, mother, and two-year-old brother. She had not been back since. "It's just that I hold a Hong Kong–British pass—"

"Li Guangmei!" the officer shouted. Fiona flinched and felt the muscles tighten in her neck. "Where were you born?"

"Shanghai."

The officer walked around to face Fiona and stood a half step too close for her comfort. He continued in a much softened and cadenced voice. "Possibly, but suffice it to say that you were born Chinese. It follows, therefore, that you are a Chinese citizen and subject to the laws of China. Many Hong Kong compatriots are confused about this. This is the legacy of colonialism and imperialism."

"I apologize," Fiona said, "but I've always steered clear of politics."

"Ah. A word to the wise. With a name like yours, it would be most prudent that you proceed with caution while in China,"—he stepped even closer to Fiona and lowered his voice so only she could hear— "especially in these dangerous times."

• • •

The train was still about two hours from Guangzhou. Rice paddies, made verdant by the abundant but malodorous night-soil fertilizer, stretched as far as the eye could see on both sides of the track. It was early afternoon, and except for the occasional laborer trudging along a dusty lane, the farm workers had all taken shelter from the unforgiving sun in the mud huts that lined the lanes. Even the swallows that habitually darted over the paddies, devouring the rich harvest of insects, had gone to roost.

Fiona stared out the window, her mind still reeling from what the PLA officer had said. The officer seemed to know something about her. Assuredly, her father, Li Dak-chung, was prominent; but the family had never mixed in politics. And it was hardly news that these were . . . what were his words? *Dangerous times.* She slipped off her high heels and raised her feet onto the empty seat beside her. *If I could only relax for the rest of the trip.*

When at last the train pulled into Guangzhou station, the passengers began making preparations for arrival. The girl who had helped Fiona at Lo Wu had said that another China Travel Service guide would meet her in Guangzhou. The train to Beijing did not leave until the next morning, so arrangements had been made for an overnight stay at the Dong Fang Hotel. Fiona had heard horror stories about Guangzhou's premier hostelry, but, given the trying day, she was prepared to suffer any privation for a bath and a night's rest.

The train stopped, and the passengers loaded down with their cargoes poured out onto the platform. Because of her encounter at the Hong Kong border, Fiona had been obliged to board the last car of a very long, fully booked train. She had no interest now in coping with the mob making its way down the platform. She was being met, and her bags had been checked through. She decided to sit tight until the crowd thinned out.

Soon the clamor and bustle ceased—odd for the busiest station in southern China. She alit to an eerie sight. On her platform, on the adjacent platforms, and in the waiting trains, there was not a soul to be seen. All of the normally ubiquitous railway service staff and the hawkers selling newspapers and sandwiches had vanished. The ticket-checker's booth was empty.

Fiona pulled her fur close around her. Far down the platform, under the station's massive curved superstructure, she could make out three figures running toward her, pistols drawn.

CHAPTER 2

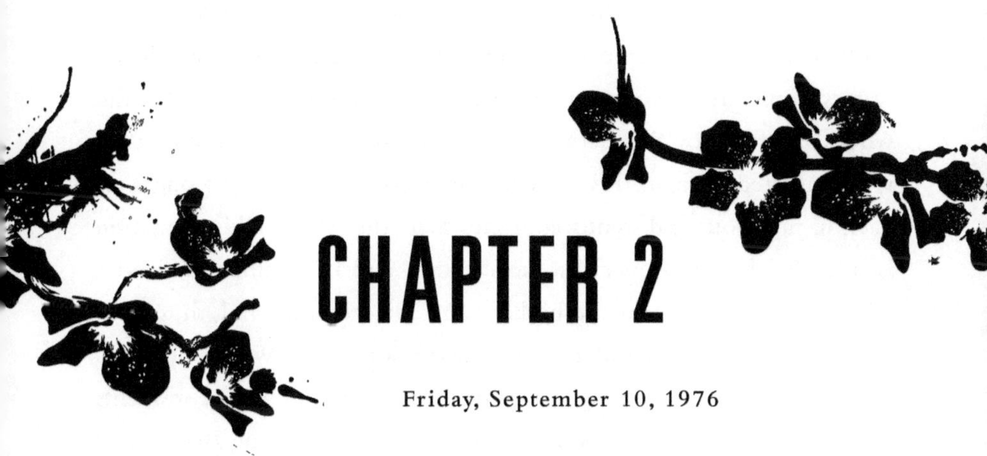

Friday, September 10, 1976

The Royal Hong Kong Police launch was on routine night patrol in the Pearl River Delta southeast of Lantau Island. As the launch commander Lt. Ng Kwok-Fai would later reconstruct from his log, he had been scrupulous in keeping within Hong Kong's territorial waters. In the fast-waning moonlight, the launch lookout, scanning with binoculars, spotted what looked like a body floating in the water roughly in the direction of the PRC island of Dawanshan.

Ng immediately ordered, "Full stop!" and directed the launch's searchlight toward the body. He was determined that no illegal immigrant would mar his spotless record by swimming ashore during his watch. He knew that, if unable to land on one of Hong Kong's small outlying islands, PRC snakeheads often forced their luckless clients overboard.

A lifeless naked body floated on its back about fifty yards off the bow. The body was in PRC waters, but the current was bearing it toward the launch. Ng decided to wait. No sense risking an international incident for the body of yet another Cultural Revolution victim.

For the last ten years, victims of China's Great Proletarian Cultural Revolution had floated down the Pearl River from Guangzhou. Most washed out to sea, but occasionally a body surfaced in Hong Kong waters. Some Hong Kong papers then reported every grisly detail of the wounds suffered by the victim and speculated salaciously on how they were inflicted. The six PRC-owned newspapers in Hong Kong shot back in pompous and stentorian tones that "the whole Chinese nation is offended by the imperialist lackey press and its attempt to slander China" and insisted that the bodies were Triad killings and, thus, irrefutable proof of the decadence and corruption of the West. There was always a call for Hong Kong's more than four million Chinese residents to "throw off the yoke of America's capitalist running dog Britain and return Hong Kong to the Motherland" or to "paint Hong Kong red from the earth to the sky."

The launch swayed gently at anchor in the still, now moonless night. Ng and his crew rested while awaiting the corpse's approach. Only their running lights and the searchlight that Ng periodically switched on to check the body's position established the launch's location. Ng again checked his instruments to confirm that the launch was still in Hong Kong waters and entered the coordinates in the ship's log.

Suddenly a boat's engine roared to life in the distance, and two searchlights darted forth like the eyes of a cat converging on its prey. The corpse was now about fifteen yards from the police launch.

"Lieutenant!" the lookout cried. "PLA Navy cutter at eight o'clock, 500 yards out, advancing full speed toward us!"

Instinctively, Ng shouted to his crew, "Life jackets on! Prepare to be rammed amidships!"

The cutter drew down on the launch, and Ng braced for impact. But twenty yards out the cutter suddenly swerved parallel to the launch, cut its engine, and switched on all its deck lights. Its wake nearly cap-sized the launch, and Ng was thrown to the deck as water poured over him. He clambered to his feet only to see a machine gun trained on his deck and several of the cutter's crew members struggling to pluck the corpse from the water. On the cutter's bow, illuminated in the glow of a searchlight, was the flag of the People's Republic of China.

Ng quickly counted his crew. *Thank God, nobody went overboard.* At that moment, the cutter's crew landed the corpse on deck, and the engine roared to life again. Then the cutter turned and, at a fast but not reckless speed, disappeared in the direction of the Mainland.

The entire incident had lasted less than five minutes.

· · ·

The wallah-wallah bobbed and swayed on its short journey across Victoria Harbor from Kowloon to Hong Kong Island. Propelled swiftly and effortlessly by a Hakka woman, the long black fringe on her hat pulsing in cadence with the strokes of her oars, the small boat was the only direct transport back to the island after the Star Ferry stopped running at 1:00 a.m.

I slumped back on my haunches in the bottom of the boat and blinked. My eyes were flooded with light from the stories-high neon advertisements blanketing the buildings of the business districts on both sides of the harbor. On the island, the twinkling lights from apartment blocks resembled star garlands ascending Victoria Peak. Hong Kong had no need of moon or stars. The city created for itself what it needed to survive.

The twenty-minute crossing completed, I strolled past the deserted ferry terminal and on through the pedestrian underpass to the side of Chater Garden facing the venerable, old Honk Kong and Shanghai Bank, or "Honkers and Shankers" as it was irreverently nicknamed. I crossed Des Voeux Road and rested for a moment on the stone steps of the bank building.

A jarring noise suddenly assaulted my ears: the clack-clacking of bamboo poles mixed with hundreds of voices speaking rapid-fire Cantonese. One voice was amplified over a loudspeaker. My weary mind searched for the origin even as I struggled to shut out the sound. Curiosity overcame me. Pulling myself up on one of the two massive bronze lions that guarded the Hong Kong and Shanghai Bank entrance, I turned in the direction of the noise.

The imposing Bank of China, floodlit in the darkness, stood across Queen's Road from the Hilton Hotel. Dozens of high-wire artisans were girdling the Bank's buff-colored stone façade with bamboo scaffolding. With lashing strips clenched in their teeth and new poles balanced on their shoulders, those below ferried supplies to their topmost brethren. Still others draped the borders of the completed scaffolding in black crepe and made ready to unroll a billboard-sized portrait of the kind that was a Communist signature. Ornate red-and-gold lanterns with braided black silk lanyards completed the tableau's perimeter.

I climbed off my perch and walked down Queen's Road to join the crowd gathered in front of the nearby Bank of China. They were all dressed alike, with white button shirts or blouses, open at the neck and worn out over gray slacks. Each wore sandals: white plastic for most, black leather distinguishing the senior cadres. Younger women wore their hair in braids; the older, in short bobs. The men wore their hair unfashionably short, making them easily identifiable as mainland Chinese in sophisticated Hong Kong.

"What's going on?" I asked a young female cadre in front of me.

She turned, tears streaming down her face, and answered in impeccable English as if reading from a prepared text, "It is announced in Beijing that Our Great Leader, Chairman Mao Zedong, has died."

So another imperial reign had ended. I could only imagine what the division of spoils would mean for China—and for Hong Kong.

. . .

Later that morning the familiar caw-caws of sulfur-crested cockatoos floated up from the canyon below my apartment on May Road, halfway up Victoria Peak. I walked out on the balcony to one of the world's great vistas: downtown Hong Kong and the harbor below, with Kowloon peninsula and the New Territories in the distance. Indeed, from my vantage point I could survey, on a clear day, upwards of 70 percent of the British Crown Colony of Hong Kong and see nearly as far as the border with China. But for a Friday morning, the city, normally bustling, was eerily still.

My apartment was also unusually quiet. Ah-yee, the live-in housekeeper who had come with it, normally filled the air with Chinese folk melodies, which she would occasionally challenge me to translate. "Make better your Chinese," she would say in quite serviceable English.

About sixty years old, Ah-yee fled to Hong Kong from Shanghai in 1949 just before the Communists overran the city. She learned English as a girl when she attended an American missionary school in her native Nanjing. I had managed to pry that much out of her in three months, but like most Chinese of her generation not native to Hong Kong, she believed it vital that her past remain vague. To her, China's civil war, even as late as 1976, was not yet over; and the ultimate victor would surely wreak a frightful revenge on those known to sympathize with the vanquished.

I pushed open the kitchen door expecting to see Ah-yee, cheerful and clad, as always, in a white tunic fastened by a row of frog closures, black silk pants, and black cotton shoes, her hair tightly combed back into a bun held by a mesh snood. Instead, I found uncharacteristic chaos. Unwashed dishes littered the sink. A pot of cold coffee, a basket of lukewarm toast, a plate of melting butter, and an open jar of jam were on a tray on the counter. The refrigerator door stood open. On the terrazzo floor in front of it, illuminated by a wedge of light, was a broken jar of Devon cream, its contents faintly rancid. Ah-yee's prized portable radio was on the windowsill broadcasting, at an almost imperceptible volume, the BBC's Cantonese-language news.

I started toward the closed door leading to Ah-yee's rooms when I heard the back door swing open, soft shoes being wiped on the mat, and key and chain securing the door. Ah-yee was mumbling. I heard footsteps coming toward the door that separated us. When Ah-yee pushed it open and saw me, she abruptly stopped.

Excitedly she blurted, "Oh, Mr. Paton, I so sorry! Mo Zak-dong die. I very afraid. *Hou ging.* This year, moon month have double very bad luck, bad joss. First Tangshan—how you say, earthquack? Now this! This morning I hear radio, I must *zek-hak* go temple pray, light joss stick. Then go fortune teller tell fortune. I very sorry. *Hou deui m'jyuh.*" As if blurting this out re-trued her psychic gyroscope, she then switched off the radio, closed the refrigerator door, and began restoring order to her realm.

"Not to worry," I said.

"Mr. Paton, you eat now?"

I thought a moment. "No," I answered, "I have to go out."

• • •

Half an hour later I was on the Peak Tram heading toward downtown. I patted myself on the back for understanding Ah-yee's concern. To the Chinese, a lunar calendar year containing an extra "leap" month is a year fraught with potential for natural disasters and political upheaval. 1976 was such a year. Mao's death on Thursday, following the catastrophic late-July earthquake in the Chinese city of Tangshan, had only con-firmed Ah-yee's sense of foreboding. To her way of thinking, she had done the only prudent thing: visit a temple to immunize herself, then consult with her fortune teller to confirm her immunity.

When the Peak Tram reached its downtown terminus, I hopped off and rushed out to Garden Road. Further down the hill I could see a huge crowd in front of the Bank of China, filling the intersection of Garden Road and Queen's Road Central. I could vaguely make out a voice speaking by microphone at the memorial ceremony for Mao. I longed with every fiber of my being to attend the ceremony.

But duty called. I was late for my lunch with Simon Li, the lawyer at Bishops who had been assigned to babysit me pending Aidan MacKin-non's return. The more I got to know Simon, the more I realized that he was the one in need of mentoring. The son of Li Dak-chung, Simon had grown up in the public eye as his father's business success both paralleled and came to symbolize Hong Kong's emergence as an eco-nomic power and the growing influence of Hong Kong Chinese over the colony's commercial life. Simon and his younger sister, Fiona, had enjoyed the best of both Hong Kong and Britain but seemed to belong wholly to neither.

I continued along Lower Albert Road to the nearly vertical stairway descending to Wyndham Street and finally reached level ground at car-and-pedestrian-choked Queen's Road Central. I dodged and veered my way across Queen's and Des Voeux Roads, slipped into the Mandarin Hotel by the back door, and made a quick left into the hotel's elegant coffee shop.

Simon was seated at our usual table with a man and woman whom I didn't recognize. He had neglected to mention, of course, that we would be four. The three were chatting and gesturing as I approached. Simon spotted me and stood.

"Bryan, old boy, you made it. I was beginning to think that rabble down the road had blocked your path. May I introduce Hugh and Emma Highgrove of Beijing, London, and Pitlochry. Hugh and Emma, this is the American chap I was telling you about, Bryan Paton."

Hugh stood to shake my hand. Although he did not match Aidan MacKinnon's lofty height, he was still taller than me at over six feet. When the three of us were seated, Emma said with a broad grin, "Simon's been telling us about your wardrobe."

On my first day in the office back in June, Simon had taken one look at my threadbare "best" suit and instantly whisked me in his silver Jaguar convertible to his personal tailor.

"Only the best for a Bishops lawyer," Simon said. "Now if I could just convince him to get rid of that bloody embarrassing car of his."

"Yes, Simon's taste in clothes is impeccable," I replied. Sensing that the Highgroves knew Simon well, I took a chance. "But he's an insufferable snob about everything else."

First Emma, then Hugh, burst into laughter as Simon's face turned bright red. Hugh mussed Simon's hair as Emma got up, went around the table, and kissed Simon on the cheek.

The ice broken, we fell into easy conversation over lunch, much of it a nostalgic history of the friendship that linked the three of them. Hugh and Simon had known each other since they were students together at Harrow. Simon had come to Harrow knowing no one and self-conscious about his distinctively Asian features. Slight of build and bookish, he was unprepared to parry the schoolboy taunts and jibes to which he was easy prey. Hugh, on the other hand, was athletic and, so Simon said, something of a bully. The only child of a wealthy London barrister and a Harley Street obstetrician, Hugh had manifested his loneliness by rebelling.

Improbably, and to the delight of their parents, Hugh and Simon became fast friends. They alternated school holidays in London and Hong Kong, and Hugh went on to study Chinese history at Cambridge.

Simon's record at Harrow was not good enough to qualify him for entry to Cambridge. His father would not countenance the suggestion that he arrange a gift to Cambridge to smooth the way, so Simon entered the red-brick University of Sussex. In 1972, he finally scraped out a law degree and returned to Hong Kong.

Emma met Hugh at Cambridge, where she studied archaeology and anthropology and developed an interest in Chinese antiquities. A month after graduation, the two were married in the garden of Emma's grandmother's home in Pitlochry, Scotland. Simon was best man. Hugh entered the British diplomatic service and was assigned first to the British High Commission in Singapore, where he and Emma lived for four years. In 1974, Hugh was posted to the British Embassy, Beijing, as First Secretary. The two were now in Hong Kong for ten days on their way back to Beijing after their annual ten weeks of required home leave, which they had spent with their respective parents in London and Pitlochry.

After lunch, we adjourned to the lobby lounge for tea and coffee. A torrential tropical downpour was inundating the streets.

"Tell me, Emma," I said, "how does a Pitlochry lass come by her interest in Chinese antiquities?"

"A natural progression, I suppose. What with being born and raised in Hong Kong . . ."

"Sorry, I'd just assumed you were Scotland born and bred."

"No . . . uh . . ." Emma shot an irritated look at Simon.

"Uh . . . sorry, I forgot to mention it to him." Simon turned to me. "Emma's maiden name is MacKinnon. She's the boss's daughter. Oh, and by the way, you're having dinner at the MacKinnons' tomorrow night. Black tie."

It was futile being angry with Simon over his thoughtlessness. The more you complained, the more he pled to being an indolent wastrel, as I saw once again when he gave me a ride home that afternoon in the pelting rain.

"Honestly, Bryan, I can't imagine why I forgot to give you the invitation. Miss Chao gave it to me weeks ago. I remember slipping it into the breast pocket of my suit coat and, well . . ."

"They do know I'm coming, don't they?"

"Yes. Yes, of course. I told Miss Chao when she gave me the invitation to mark you down as accepting. You don't have other plans, do you?"

"Fortunately . . . no."

"I agree. Bloody lucky that, especially considering my disgraceful behavior. Bollocks! The least I can do is to give you a lift tomorrow evening."

CHAPTER 3

I was still fuming about Simon's failures as I struggled with my bow tie. I had turned down his offer of a ride. Lack of punctuality was another of his charms, and I was determined not to be late for so important an occasion. I was grateful, however, that I had let him talk me into having his tailor fit me for a tuxedo. "Dear boy, whatever would you wear if visiting royalty had a do?" His utterly sincere pomposity made me grin, then grimace at the bow tie's refusal to behave.

"Mr. Paton, I tie for you?"

I started at the sound of Ah-yee's voice. She was standing in the doorway of my bedroom, a basket of clean folded laundry balanced on her hip.

"Uh . . . oh . . . yes, please. Sorry, didn't hear you singing."

"Bad joss. Not sing until Mao in ground. Bad joss."

With a few twists and a decisive finishing tug, the bow tie submitted to Ah-yee's skilled hands. She abruptly turned away but could not hide that she had been crying. I did not pry.

"Thank you," I said.

She was in my closet sorting the basket's contents, her back to me. She did not turn around but waved a "don't mention it" in my direction. I could hear her quietly sobbing. I picked my coat off the bed and left.

Soon I was steering my dilapidated Volvo up Victoria Peak on sinuous, congested Magazine Gap Road. A rivulet of sweat running down my back made me realize that the air-conditioning had failed. The car shuddered and balked, and I felt it begin to slow.

Come on, come on, at least make it to the Barker Road turn. The driver behind me honked—more than once. I glanced in the rearview mirror. A line of at least twenty cars trailed down the hill behind me. Sweat now soaked my shirt.

Come on, come on. I rocked back and forth, as if doing so would replenish the car's ebbing horsepower. The road leveled out a bit, and the car, as if suddenly revived, lunged forward. I reached level grade at the Peak Road turn, where the setting sun blinded me. Fortunately, the Barker Road turnoff was only about thirty feet farther on.

As I rounded the turn, a sickening shudder shook the car, and an acrid black plume of smoke issued from the exhaust pipe. The engine stopped, and the car began rolling backward toward busy Peak Road. I pulled the parking brake. Fortunately it held.

I was on a lightly traveled side street but dangerously close to the corner. Drivers coming up Magazine Gap Road and making what amounted to the elongated U-turn onto Peak Road and then onto Barker could not see me. I got out and leaned against the car to weigh my options. I was sweaty; and the oily smoke, still lingering in the windless tropical air from the car's blown head gasket, stained my shirt. It was 7:25. The invitation said 7:30 for 8:00, so technically I had 35 minutes before the party sat down to dinner. *But a new hire missing cocktails with the boss?*

I groaned. I would never make it in time. Even if I jogged the half mile down Barker Road to the MacKinnons', I would look and smell as if I had changed the oil. Just then a car, its tires squealing, hurtled around the Peak Road corner and onto Barker. The driver jammed on his brakes and only by inches stopped short of my car's rear bumper.

"Bloody hell, you can't stop here!" the driver shouted as he jumped from his car. "Bryan! What the—" It was Simon.

"Well, you got your wish. My car just gave up the ghost," I said. "But look, can you help me get to the MacKinnons'?"

Laughing, he said, "Of course. But dear boy, you look a sight. I was just on my way home to change. You can clean up at my place and wear one of my tuxedos. It's just there, where that car's pulling into the road. Pop must already be on his way."

About a hundred yards farther on, a chauffeur-driven black Rolls-Royce was pulling out of a gated driveway and turning in the direction of the MacKinnons'. I suddenly felt embarrassed for having turned down Simon's frequent invitations "to come to my place for a dip, or maybe some tennis." His irritating habits had caused me to hold him at arm's length, but he was beginning to demonstrate the qualities of a loyal friend.

"I'll ask one of the servants to sort out your car." Chuckling, he added, "What should I tell him to do with it? How about if I just quote the TV anti-littering advertisement: 'Put it in the bin!'"

• • •

"She's *where*?" Emma was in the vestibule of the MacKinnon home greeting latecomers, that is, Simon and me, while her parents joined their other guests for cocktails. We had actually managed to arrive at

8:10—late, but not unconscionably so. Emma had heard Simon correctly but could not believe that Fiona would go off to Macau on the very day that she and Hugh returned to Hong Kong.

"I suspect Fiona is exhausted from the toil and strife of finding digs for the antique shop," Simon said sardonically. "But my lips are sealed. I promised her I wouldn't tell you the details. She'll be back in four days, revived after being pampered at the Pousada de Sao Tiago!"

"Ha! She's just lucky Hugh and I will still be here. Otherwise, I'd rip the *vinho verde* out of her carefully manicured hands and dragoon her back to Hong Kong faster than you could say 'hover ferry.'"

Emma took my arm and began guiding me to the living room. "Come on, Bryan, I'll introduce you to Li Dak-chung. Fiona and Simon are the exceptions that prove the rule 'the fruit doesn't fall far from the tree.' They fell so far, you honestly wouldn't believe that Mr. Li could ever be their father. He's not only thoughtful, but also gracious, punctual, modest, thrifty—there he is."

Emma led me to two older men who stood deep in conversation. I recognized Run Run Shaw from the newspapers and television. Li Dak-chung was a small gray-haired man with a dignified demeanor and kind eyes. Momentarily I visualized him in Chinese robes, bearded and mustached, sitting on a mat in the manner of the seven ancient scholars ubiquitously depicted in Chinese painting. I knew that he was a widower. Simon had told me that his mother died of tuberculosis in 1957.

"Mr. Li, Mr. Shaw," Emma said, "may I present Bryan Paton? Bryan has just joined my father at Bishops." We shook hands, and Run Run Shaw excused himself to join his wife.

"Well, young man," Li said, "Aidan and Simon are both very high on you. I hope you'll enjoy working with the family."

"Thank you, sir. I'll try to live up to the billing."

"Too bad Fiona isn't here. She's off to Macau on one of her beauty trips, you know. She is one busy young lady, what with the new shop and keeping up appearances," Li chuckled.

"I look forward to meeting her, sir. I hope that you and I can meet soon as well to discuss how you envision my being of service to the family."

"Yes, yes. All in good time," Li said. "Shall we go in? I think Glynis is beckoning."

"Well, here is our handsome, young gentleman guest," Glynis MacKinnon said as we entered the living room.

She spoke with a distinct brogue, but a stout Scots matron she was not. She was clad in a full-length navy silk *chih-pao* that clung to her tall, slender frame. Her gold-streaked brown hair was piled high on top of her head, and dangling sapphire-and-diamond earrings drew attention to the part of her long neck that was not covered by the *chih-pao*'s high Mandarin collar. Her resemblance to her daughter was striking. All eyes turned to her as she spoke, as I imagine happened in every room she entered.

"Let's all go in to dinner, shall we?" She took my arm and led me forward. "I'm Glynis MacKinnon. And you must be Bryan Paton. My, but that's a fine Scottish name. Clans MacDonald and MacLean, isn't it?"

Glynis MacKinnon was not the only woman who caught my attention that evening. The physician-turned-writer Han Suyin was there. Han was responsible, through her four-volume autobiography, for explaining more to me about the travails of modern China than any other person. The daughter of a Chinese railway official and his Belgian wife, Han led a life that both paralleled and symbolized the forces and torments that forged the People's Republic of China. Throughout her life, she endured the stigma of being Eurasian in a Chinese culture where racial homogeneity is sacrosanct. Trapped in an abusive marriage to a Kuomintang general who was then killed in 1947 during China's civil war, she later became a friend to Zhou Enlai and other senior

Chinese Communist officials. I thought she had a wonderful face—strong with a hint of sadness—born, no doubt, of a life of struggle.

When we were seated, Aidan MacKinnon stood. "I want to say a few words about a subject that has been very much on the minds of all of us, and much of the world, since Thursday afternoon. Regardless of how each of us may have viewed Mao Zedong, I think all of us can agree that a giant of Chinese history has died. 1976 has already been a momentous year for China. Indeed, some have even gone so far as to speculate that the prophetic events of the last nine months confirm that the Communist Party has lost the fabled Mandate of Heaven, the traditional source of the right to govern China. Throughout Chinese history, such a loss has always been a harbinger of upheaval. Please join me in a toast to the Chinese people. May they be spared further violence and suffering."

As we rose and joined MacKinnon in the toast, I thought of Ah-yee's tears. I was wrong to assume that she, nonpolitical if not anti-Communist, in some way mourned Mao's passing. I now realized that she feared the kind of brutal chaos whose potential victims were ordinary Chinese like herself.

We began chatting as the MacKinnons' Filipina servants served the soup. Strains of a traditional Chinese orchestra floated softly in the air, and savory scents of food emanated from the kitchen. As the somber mood eased, the murmur of conversation became punctuated by laughter.

"Aidan, dear friend, you're more Chinese than I am," Li said.

"You've been a patient and forgiving mentor, Dak-chung. I'm merely a student of China, with much more to learn."

"Have you two known each other long?" asked Sally Welles, the Australian Consul General.

"Only about ten years, since I—" MacKinnon began.

"—since Aidan's legal alchemy turned a sow's ear owned by Mr. Li into a silk purse," Dr. Han finished.

From a magazine article I had read, I knew that Li and Han had never met, although both were public figures and obviously knew each other by reputation. MacKinnon knew both well, but I sensed that he had underestimated their mutual antipathy. I suspected that Welles, like any good diplomat, had studied both Han and Li, as well as Li's company, Nan Hwa Shipping, and its startlingly swift takeover of Adair, Jameson. There were still many questions regarding that deal that governments desperately sought to have answered. Welles diligently sipped her soup while listening intently.

"Tell me, Mr. Li," Han said, "how does a bankrupt company like Nan Hwa Shipping raise sufficient capital to take over so large and influential—and consummately British—a conglomerate as Adair, Jameson? Or should I direct that question to your sister in Taipei and her Kuomintang banker friends?"

"Dr. Han," Li said, "you are a daughter of China and a daughter of Europe. Which is speaking now?"

"My heart is always with oppressed people, wherever they may reside."

"I am confused, Dr. Han. Do you include the Chinese in your classification of oppressed people?"

"Of course I do."

"Oppressed by whom?"

"By the Europeans and the Japanese who would dismember and colonize China. And by an inherently oppressive imperial system that left China weak and supine prey for them."

"And you do not consider China's present government equally or more oppressive?" Li asked.

"The evolution of socialist democracy inevitably entails a period of unsettling, even radical, transition from feudal ways," Han replied.

"How facile, Dr. Han, to label the murder of millions of Chinese and the destruction of Confucianism 'unsettling.' Perhaps you consider this justified in order to achieve what you call 'socialist democracy,' which isn't really democracy at all. But enough. Suffice it to say that my purchase of Adair, Jameson is a matter of record. Have you no pride in the fact that it's now owned by a Chinese?"

"I deeply resent your—"

Li turned suddenly to Ms. Welles. "Where in beautiful Australia do you call home?"

Caught off balance by Li's abrupt shift, Welles managed to answer, "Why only the loveliest village in New South Wales. It's called Berrima."

• • •

Aidan MacKinnon motioned me out to the balcony. During after-dinner drinks, he had asked me to stay behind. I had just said good-bye to Run Run Shaw and his wife, who had invited Simon, the Highgroves, and me to their estate at Sai Kung on Thursday evening for a private screening of the newest Shaw Brothers *kung fu* film, *The Oily Maniac*. Except for Hugh and Emma, who were staying with the MacKinnons, Simon and I were the last of the guests.

The MacKinnons' palatial home, at the end of a long winding driveway high above Barker Road, was two-and-a-half terraced stories that projected eastward from the spine of a hill. All levels commanded breathtaking vistas, north over downtown Hong Kong, Kowloon, and the harbor, and south over Repulse Bay, Lamma Island, and the South China Sea. The balcony was a vast expanse that extended outward from the first level and appeared to float on its concrete stilts. Simon and MacKinnon were chatting when I joined them outside.

MacKinnon looked over his shoulder as I approached. "Simon, would you excuse us for a while?"

After Simon had gone, MacKinnon said, "Cigar, my boy?" He was holding a half-smoked Montecristo, the brand with the easily recogniz-able ring that Clancy, my parents' boarder back in San Francisco, had always smoked on special occasions. The aroma reminded me of the Clement Street world that I had left almost four years ago.

"No, thank you," I said.

"I hope you enjoyed yourself this evening."

"Very much so, thank you. I particularly enjoyed meeting Dr. Han and Mr. Li."

MacKinnon grimaced. "You had never met Li Dak-chung? Where are Simon's manners? I particularly asked that rascal to look after you until I got back."

"It's entirely my fault. If anything, Simon's been overly solicitous. I'm afraid I avoided him at first."

"Ah . . . well then. He's a good heart and comes from damned fine stock. At least you've met Fiona."

"Only once—in passing. We bumped into each other at Bishops just after I came on board. Actually, I'd be hard-pressed to pick her out in a lineup today."

Had I just implied that Fiona was forgettable? Anything but; she exuded the self-confidence that accompanies great beauty and a vitality that showed in her eyes and her step.

"I understand she's in Macau for a few days," I added lamely.

"I wondered why she didn't come tonight. Bloody flighty, that one. By the way, what did you make of that dustup Dak-chung had with Han Suyin at the dinner table?"

The question was that of someone who wanted to find out how much I had understood. *My first test.*

"I suppose first and foremost that passions still run high almost thirty years after the putative end of China's civil war. And I'm familiar with Dr. Han's political bent. But beyond that, there seems to be quite a bit of bad blood between the two of them over the Adair, Jameson takeover." I was pretty sure there was something else on MacKinnon's mind, but I wasn't sure what he was driving at.

"There's nothing personal between them over the Adair deal per se. I was referring to Han's mention of Dak-chung's sister in Taipei, Gwei-yu. You know her, of course."

"No . . . I mean, yes, but not well. I only met her once. She's very old-school Kuomintang, isn't she?"

"Do I detect a bias?" MacKinnon said, with a twinkle in his eye.

"Not at all. I just meant that she spoke about the KMT's return to the Mainland and establishing so strong a foothold here in the Colony that the PRC could never swallow it up or the UK give it back. All very pie-in-the-sky, I thought. Of course, I didn't say so."

"Well, she's quite high on you, my boy. So high, in fact, that she's the reason I hired you." MacKinnon paused, apparently noticing my surprise. "Best fill you in. You see, Nan Hwa was, and is, a family business. Before the war, Dak-chung and Gwei-yu's father saw to it that, in the event of his death, each of his children would inherit half of Nan Hwa. Very progressive was old man Li to provide for his daughter, and very un-Chinese. But between the wars there were many Shanghainese who admired and emulated Western legal concepts."

MacKinnon took out another cigar, clipped off the tip, and rolled the other end over the flame of a match he had lit. When he had drawn about an inch of ash, he said, "So, in '45, when old man Li died, Nan Hwa passed in equal shares to Dak-chung and Gwei-yu. When Shanghai fell in '49, Gwei-yu fled to Taiwan with Chiang Kai-shek, and Dak-chung came to Hong Kong and reconstituted the family business. I honestly don't know why they went separate ways, but perhaps it had to do with the Chinese family's primordial need to have an escape route on either side of a conflict."

MacKinnon drew deeply several times on his cigar. "Gwei-yu enjoyed a favored position in Taipei as a close confidante of Madame Chiang Kai-shek. Gwei-yu could be trusted to toe the KMT line, so she was *enabled*, shall we say, to build a newspaper and media empire.

She was also enabled to participate as an investor when Madame built the Grand Hotel in Taipei."

I knew the Grand Hotel. Taipei had long needed an international-class hotel. Rumor had it that Madame Chiang Kai-shek was the only person with enough clout to finagle the choice site, and enough money to get the hotel constructed. The Grand, built in opulent pagoda style, now reposed on a hillside overlooking Songshan International Airport and downtown Taipei. *But what did all this have to do with me?*

"Oh, nearly forgot the punch line, dear boy," MacKinnon said. "Gwei-yu's empire includes the small but very profitable Taiwan Institute of Foreign Languages."

• • •

Sensing that I wanted to think, Simon avoided his usual banter as he drove me home. Little had I known that he had an aunt in Taipei, much less that she was my former employer. And I certainly had no inkling that she was so well connected to Madame Chiang and the ruling clique. Although the Generalissimo had been dead for eighteen months, his son Chiang Ching-kuo had succeeded his father as Taiwan's ruler. Madame Chiang, edged aside by her stepson, had moved to her family's estate in New York, but she was still powerful in Taiwan and pivotal in relations with Taiwan's only important remaining international backer, the United States.

I remembered well the Institute's twenty-fourth anniversary celebration at the Grand Hotel. Orders had come from on high that all Institute staff members were to attend. I had shaken hands and chatted with Li Gwei-yu. She had shown considerable interest in my background, and it now seemed that the encounter had led to MacKinnon's offer of a position with Bishops. The offer had come unexpectedly after the Hong Kong dragon boat races in May. The Chinese University boat, on which I crewed, had won a photo-finish upset victory over the favored Chuen Gwok Rowing Club boat. That night the race sponsors held a charity ball at the Repulse Bay Hotel on the south side of Hong Kong Island. A must-event for the colony's officials and *taipans*, it marked the end of the social season before the wealthy and powerful—Chinese and British alike—retreated to their castles or cottages in the British Isles for the summer.

Not five minutes into the festivities, the University's president approached me and whispered that Aidan MacKinnon wanted to meet with me. I was to go immediately to the hotel's Sovereign Suite. I was dumbfounded and a little unnerved. Aidan MacKinnon, senior partner of the Hong Kong office of Bishops, Britain's most prestigious international law firm, was not only a lion of the legal profession but a genuine celebrity. A beefy man with a ruddy complexion, he bore an uncanny resemblance to Peter Ustinov. At 6 feet 4 inches, he literally stood above most of his contemporaries. And with his commanding voice and manner and attractive wife, Glynis, on his arm, he was guaranteed paparazzi interest wherever he went.

MacKinnon had rocketed to fame years earlier when he and Li Dakchung, then the little-known owner of the nearly bankrupt Nan Hwa Shipping Company, engineered Nan Hwa's takeover of the giant Hong Kong–based British trading conglomerate Adair, Jameson. Cloaked in intrigue when it was consummated a quarter century ago, the deal had rocked the financial world and sent the pound into a weeklong nosedive. Adair, Jameson had a hammerlock on the Colony's economy, and its abrupt takeover by a non-British owner had sent shock waves through the world's markets. The deal made Li and MacKinnon famous and both of them millionaires.

MacKinnon had gone on to cement the respect and affection of all Hong Kong Chinese by winning a civil judgment for millions of dollars against a Macau casino long known to be owned by the Triads. His pro bono client was a five-year-old orphaned Hong Kong girl who had witnessed from beneath her bed the grisly Triad-ordered murder of her mother, her grandmother, her four sisters, and her father, a small-time loan shark. The trial riveted Hong Kong for months. The climax came on the trial's final day when MacKinnon put the trembling five-year-old on the stand and led her, with avuncular tenderness and in flawless Cantonese, through what she had seen that day when five Triad gang members hacked her family to death.

My conversation with MacKinnon had lasted barely five minutes. He was blunt and direct, not too surprising in a man with his gifts. He wanted me to accept a position at Bishops in their Estates and Trusts Department to undertake, he said, "a particularly challenging assignment for which others insist you are eminently qualified." As the conversation progressed, it became clear to me that MacKinnon had no intention of telling me who these "others" were.

My Cantonese program at Chinese University was ending in ten days; the Volvo needed more work than I had anticipated; and my savings, if not replenished, would last only a few more months. I had struggled for some time over what I would do next. At a minimum, the job at Bishops would buy me additional time. But more than anything, it was the mystery and the challenge that had made me accept MacKinnon's offer on the spot. I thought about our intriguing encounter for the rest of that day and resolved to learn who or what had motivated Bishops to pursue me. But when I called Bishops the next morning, MacKinnon's secretary, Miss Chao, told me that Mr. and Mrs. MacKinnon had left for Scotland that morning and would not return to Hong Kong until September, more than three long months away.

When I accepted MacKinnon's offer, I had insisted that I be told the whole story of Nan Hwa's takeover of Adair, Jameson. I could not function as legal adviser to a company if I was ignorant of the pivotal event in the company's past. I was being asked to handle legal affairs for one of the commercial pillars of Hong Kong, as well as the Colony's foremost private fortune. Taking on such a responsibility would immediately propel me into the public eye. Journalists and diplomats would be buttonholing me everywhere I went. I had to know the whole story, if only to know what *not* to say. MacKinnon had remained noncommittal, saying only that he would talk to Li Dak-chung. The takeover was clearly still a proprietary subject for the two of them.

I left the MacKinnon estate still uncertain of my place and mission at Bishops. *Exactly what had I been hired to do?*

CHAPTER 4

Monday, September 13, 1976

General Zhu Fangguo closed his office door as he did for an hour each afternoon. He had instructed his secretary to schedule only the most urgent appointments during that hour. It was not easy for the military governor of the Northeast Region—China's most strategic, industrialized, and resource-rich—to carve out free time. Zhu told his staff that he wanted the hour free to study the thoughts of Chairman Mao, and he kept a well-thumbed copy of the *Little Red Book* prominently in view on his desk. He found that it conferred on him a kind of immunity, intimidating the potentially traitorous, and amused those few who understood his true purpose.

Zhu alone knew that his copy had not been opened since 1970, four years after the beginning of the Cultural Revolution. That was the year when the sanctimonious Red Guards had found him of sufficient rectitude to allow him to resume his army career. Or, in Red Guard parlance, his thoughts were *not anti-socialist and free of Confucianism, capitalism, and bourgeois revisionism.* The Cultural Revolution had meant three years of having his regiment run by a committee of four teenagers while he and his staff officers dutifully recited Mao's thoughts. But he had survived.

In fact, Zhu used his private hour each day to "daydream," a word he had heard in an American film. Foreign films were not publicly screened in China, but he was able to view them as a privilege of his general-officer rank. Even then Zhu saw them only within the relative safety of the villa his uncle Marshal Zhu De maintained in Diaoyutai, the manicured Beijing enclave of Western-style villas reserved for visiting heads of state and the most favored retired senior Communist Party and PLA officials. The film's subtitle translated *daydream* as "free thinking during daytime." Zhu had been captivated by the idea and since then had reserved one precious hour for free thinking during daytime. He found it enormously liberating, the perfect antidote for the pervasive monotony of Communist China's public discourse.

Not that he was turning anti-Communist—far from it. He was a devout Communist and the nephew of the second most revered figure in the PRC's pantheon of heroes. Zhu had learned about Marx even before he had learned to hold chopsticks. He graduated first in his class from Whampoa Military Academy, where he learned tactics and strategy from Zhou Enlai, at that time Whampoa's political director.

In 1934, Zhu accompanied Zhou, his uncle, Mao, and Deng Xiaoping on the Long March, during which he met his future wife, Ye Guangrong. Over the next fourteen years, he moved up from a posting as Zhou's military aide-de-camp to Deng's deputy political commissar of the PLA Second Field Army and then up to battalion commander in the PLA Eighth Route Army under his uncle, Zhu De. After Zhu De became PLA commander-in-chief in 1946, his nephew was assigned to Mao's personal staff in Yenan, where he served as liaison to Liu Shaoqi, the future president of the PRC. That same year he married Ye Guangrong. In 1947 they had a son and, in the following year, a daughter.

After that, Zhu Fangguo's personal interests and family life faded into the background, as befitted a senior government, Party, and military official.

At his desk, Zhu hung his head in disgust and regret. The plan that seemed so innocuous a month ago now exposed two people he cared about to unimaginable danger. *Damn. How could he have been so foolish? Well, thank heaven the situation might still be remedied.* Remedied? Salvaged was more like it, but it would take all the power of his position. He hoped he was not too late.

Zhu rose and walked to the window. Since the Cultural Revolution began, PLA headquarters in all of China's twenty-six provinces had, by decree from Beijing, been moved into Communist Party headquarters in each provincial capital. Zhu's office was in the center of Shenyang, the capital of Liaoning province. From his window, Zhu stared at the massive, copper-colored statue of a striding Mao that dominated Shenyang's main square. It had been a favorite Red Guard rallying point. Its shadow darkened even the adjacent Liaoning Guest House, the white Victorian-style showplace hotel that the Japanese had built when Shenyang, then Mukden, was the capital of their puppet state of Manchukuo.

"Well, now you're gone, my old friend," Zhu said to the statue, "and the fat's in the fire. Where will it end? Where will it end?"

That morning Zhu had put all forces under his command on alert, something he had not done when Zhou Enlai died in January or when his uncle died in July. Zhou's and his uncle's deaths were occasions for sincere grief and tranquil reflection among all Chinese. Mao's death was like the firing of a starter pistol, signaling the race for the succession. Zhu knew whom he favored, but he also understood the strength of his adversaries and the mortal danger of losing. A war for China's future was a terrible prospect, and bravery would be needed to vouchsafe that future into the right hands.

This would be a time for the settling of accounts, no matter how old. Warlordism was centuries older than Communism and far more ingrained; and the chaos that followed an emperor's death afforded cover for exacting cold revenge. One had to act quickly or one would become prey. Emperor Mao was dead, and now he himself was forced to become predator. This was the time to avenge the murder of twenty-seven years ago.

Someone knocked on the office door.

"Come," Zhu said.

"I'm sorry, sir," Major Wang, his young aide-de-camp said, "but it's five past four. I have important news. I hope I didn't interrupt you."

"Major Wang, I know it's been ten years since we last saluted or acknowledged rank, but those snot-nosed teenagers have gone back to their classrooms. I'd like you to observe military courtesy before giving me your message."

"Yes, sir, sorry, sir." Wang snapped to attention.

Zhu really could not fault Wang Chongshi, who had come into the PLA in 1967, just after the start of the Cultural Revolution. The military had not been immune to political pressures. Indeed, the PLA had been forced into an unwanted and unwelcome role, first as a model for the Red Guards, then as the guards' nanny and enforcer, and finally, as their master. China had lost a whole generation of scholars, professionals, and leaders since then. Zhu knew that if the radicals came to power in Beijing, such losses would continue. Even if the moderates won, China would need another generation just to recover from the damage.

"Thank you for humoring this old guerrilla fighter, Major," Zhu said without sarcasm. "I learned to stand at attention for Zhou Enlai at Whampoa, and old habits are difficult to break."

Wang suddenly laughed.

"Is something funny, Major?" Zhu asked.

"I just remembered the story you tell about the time when you and Premier Zhou met with Khrushchev in Moscow." Wang could not help chuckling a second time.

Zhu smiled at the memory of Khrushchev's crass attempt to embarrass Zhou. Khrushchev had said that he himself had been born a peasant, while Zhou had been born into a wealthy landlord family. The nimble Chinese patrician had shot back, "Yes, and we are both traitors to our class."

"Never forget it," Zhu said. "That story teaches more Communism than ten manifestos from Moscow. Now, what's that you have there, Major?"

"Oh, yes, sir, your orders, sir, transferring you to Beijing, sir."

Zhu smiled at Wang's eagerness. They did, after all, live in a system in which power always trumped competence; and Wang knew that he was now irrevocably stamped as one of Zhu's protégés. As Zhu's star rose or fell, so did his own.

"No need to overdo it, Major," Zhu said.

Wang handed Zhu the orders and a second piece of paper on which a phone message had been scribbled. Zhu glanced at his orders then set them aside and began reading the message. His hand began to tremble, and he had to summon all of his military training to retain his composure in front of his subordinate.

"I see Colonel Peng called," Zhu said. "Did he say what he wanted?"

"Unfortunately the phone connection was so bad that I couldn't understand a word," Wang said, "but it sounded like he was calling long-distance. Could that be right, sir?"

"I'm sure I don't know," Zhu said. "But Major, just to be safe, better interrupt me if he calls back."

• • •

Miss Chao sounded uncharacteristically strident on the phone. Normally unfailingly polite, she practically demanded that I come to Aidan MacKinnon's office immediately. From her tone it was clear that she, and by implication MacKinnon, would tolerate no delay.

Bishops consumed three floors of Hutchison House, an elegant new high-rise on Harcourt Road in the heart of Hong Kong's Central District. I was fortunate to have an office on the same floor as MacKinnon's, although mine faced east over Wanchai and his faced the harbor and Kowloon beyond. When I arrived at MacKinnon's office, Miss Chao was less agitated than morose. She was talking in a low voice in Cantonese with one of the other secretaries, who glanced at me but kept talking—something about a murder—until Miss Chao shushed her.

"Tammy, we mustn't be so rude as to forget that Mr. Paton speaks Cantonese," Miss Chao said. "Mr. Paton, this is Tammy Lau, one of the secretaries in the Criminal Law Division."

"Hello," I said, nodding in Miss Lau's direction. "Did I just hear you say murder?"

"Yes, but . . . uh . . . no," Miss Chao said, obviously disturbed that I had overheard. "Perhaps you'd better go right in. He's waiting for you with Mr. Highgrove and Mr. Li."

At last, the promised meeting with Li Dak-chung. Maybe now I'd get some answers about why I was hired.

MacKinnon was staring out the window, his back to me. Li, ashen, his mouth in a tight line, was sitting in one of two wing chairs flanking a sofa and coffee table. Hugh, on the sofa, looked grim. Against the wall behind the sofa was a massive bookcase with numerous lighted chambers that contained Chinese porcelains and carved jade figures. MacKinnon's desk, an oversize, freestanding table, stood at the far end of the room in front of a credenza that held framed photographs and other mementos. The room was opulent and tasteful but filled with an almost palpable air of gloom.

"Come in, dear boy, and take a seat," MacKinnon said without turning around.

Li nodded but did not speak. He sat erect in his seat, his wiry frame conditioned by ascetic habits and the daily tai chi exercises that he had practiced every morning for the last forty years. Trying to seem more confident than I felt, I joined Hugh on the sofa. MacKinnon turned, crossed the room, and sat in the wing chair nearest to me.

"I'm afraid we've had the worst possible news concerning Fiona," he said. "It seems she's met with a horrible accident. Somewhere in China, of all places." MacKinnon paused then added, almost as an afterthought, "I'm afraid she's dead."

I felt cold, so cold. For a moment I couldn't speak. Then, gathering myself, I said, "But surely she's still in Macau."

"Unfortunately she was never in Macau," MacKinnon said. "The Portuguese police assured me yesterday that Fiona never entered Macau on Thursday, or on any other day, for that matter. Apparently her body was found somewhere in southern China. She . . . it . . . her body has, for some reason that still hasn't been explained, been transported to Beijing."

Li groaned, his stoic demeanor crumbling. He began to tremble with what I believed was rage, as if the recognition of what had happened to his daughter had at last overwhelmed him.

"I know who is behind the murder of my daughter, and that person must pay," he said. "But first I want Fiona's body brought back to Hong Kong for burial. That's your responsibility, Aidan, and yours, Bryan. Then I will deal with the murderer myself, in my own way."

As if calmed by having assigned responsibility for coping with his daughter's death, Li sipped tea from a cup on the table and sat back in his chair. The strain that he had been under seemed to have dissipated, his expression transformed into a look of iron resolve.

"Dak-chung," MacKinnon said, "we don't yet know the circumstances surrounding Fiona's death. There is no reason to believe she was murdered. Bryan and I will attend to the details and pass on any information as soon as it comes to light. Why don't you go home and get some rest."

"Perhaps . . . in a while. First I need to be sure that Bryan is clear concerning the danger he faces in Beijing. In those shallow waters, even shrimp can make fools of dragons."

Beijing? Danger? Just how far did Bishops and Li expect my commitment to extend? I felt weak. "But I've never even—"

"We're aware you've never been to China, my boy," MacKinnon said. "But the Li family have absolute confidence in your ability to handle this mission. And so do I."

MacKinnon paused for my reaction. I had agreed to manage the Li family's business affairs on condition that I would be briefed on their personal affairs as well. I never imagined that I would have to plunge into unfamiliar waters so soon. Still, this is what I had signed on to do. I nodded.

"Good. Now, let's get to specifics."

MacKinnon explained that the government of the People's Republic of China had never recognized British sovereignty over Hong Kong and so considered all Hong Kong Chinese to be citizens of China, not Britain. They would not tolerate any involvement by the British Embassy in Fiona's case.

Hugh said that he and Emma were nonetheless prepared to assist me informally and that they were moving up their departure for Beijing in order to accompany me. My own status there would be, essentially, that of a nonperson. Not only was I representing a Chinese citizen in China, which the Chinese authorities would consider a deliberate affront, but I was also a citizen of a country with which the People's Republic of China had no diplomatic relations.

On this last point, Hugh was deliberately blunt. "There is no American Embassy in Beijing. If you get into trouble, there's no consul to bail you out. There is a small, unofficial liaison office, but the Chinese keep it on a very tight leash."

Hugh explained that the Communist Chinese ordered the world on a simple scale, from friend to foe. All things flowed from where you fell on the scale. The top rank was reserved for Albania and Romania, Communist countries whose maverick pro-China foreign policies irritated the Soviet Union. The Soviets were positioned far to the "foe" end of the scale. Even further toward "foe" was the United States, which not only did not recognize the People's Republic of China but also maintained an embassy on Taiwan.

"And we British fare little better than you Americans," Hugh added. "Our presence in Hong Kong really rubs them raw."

For a moment I thought of suggesting that I might not be the best man for the job. But I was so captivated by the prospect of visiting Beijing, even under sad and possibly dangerous circumstances, that I decided to keep silent.

Complicating our plans was the death of Mao Zedong, a subject on which Li was surprisingly well informed. Mao's death would be the occasion for nationwide memorial ceremonies and the closure of Chinese government offices—offices I would need in order to handle what Li forecast would be reams of paperwork and mind-numbing bureaucracy.

Then there was the matter of the succession. As Mao's health began to decline in recent years, two factions plotted to fill the void he was creating, inadvertently or deliberately, by his failure to choose a successor. Mao's wife, Jiang Qing, led the radical faction. Based in Shanghai, the radicals supported the Maoist version of perpetual revolution, the concept behind the convulsive Cultural Revolution, which they fomented and applauded. The moderates, on the other hand, advocated a more gradual, planned evolution of Chinese socialism. Currently in considerable disarray, the moderates had no clear leader. Their ranks had been decimated during the Cultural Revolution by the murders of Mao's handpicked successor, President Liu Shaoqi, as well as Minister of National Defense Peng Dehuai, and other prominent figures.

Premier Zhou Enlai, who had died of cancer nine months before Mao's death, Deng Xiaoping, Field Marshal Zhu De, and current Minister of National Defense Ye Jianying had at that time barely escaped with their lives only because they and other Long March veterans had been Mao's fellow Communists and comrades-in-arms for more than fifty years.

Mao was believed to have favored the radical faction over the moderates. There was no doubt that now—with his death—the two rival camps would swing into action. This struggle would play out simultaneously with the funeral and national period of mourning.

Li grimaced. "And now Mao's Shanghai trollop of a wife wants to throw China once again to the dogs. If Jiang Qing wins, her reign of terror will make the Communist victory in '49 look like a dress rehearsal. Except now her victims will be her fellow Communists. People who want to end the madness, people like Deng, will all disappear in the dead of night. And so will the innocents. All those innocent Chinese . . ."

Li's voice weakened, and he began to weep unashamedly. MacKinnon went to his side to comfort him. After a few minutes, Li wiped his eyes dry with his handkerchief and resumed his stoic demeanor.

"Thank you, Aidan," he whispered.

"Dak-chung," MacKinnon said gently, "why don't you go home?"

"Yes, I believe I will," Li replied. "May I ask that Bryan stop by the house later today?"

"Of course I will," I said.

My opinion of Li, already high, had increased immeasurably during the last two hours. I had also arrived at a new appreciation of the deep and genuine friendship between him and MacKinnon. Like many, I had assumed it was based on business necessity or professional affiliation. After all, both were famous throughout the Orient—Li for having single-handedly amassed the greatest of Hong Kong's great fortunes and MacKinnon for his legal acumen. It was natural that they would gravitate toward one another.

In some circles Li and MacKinnon were vilified for their seemingly unbreakable bond of mutual trust and loyalty. Most of their detractors assumed that this bond was born of Nan Hwa's takeover of the fabled and oh-so-British *hong*, Adair, Jameson. The criticism was always tainted with the acrid odor of racism and not a little hint that the takeover could only have resulted from criminality. I had not been entirely unaffected by the gossip, and I still had many unanswered questions about the takeover and the origins of the Li family fortune. But at least I now knew their friendship to be sincere. And I recognized that now was not the time to insist on the promised briefing.

• • •

Hugh gave me a ride to the Li estate on Barker Road later that afternoon. A large group of reporters and photographers were camped outside the gate. Word had already leaked that something was amiss with the Li family. The press had not yet discovered the specifics, but it was only a matter of time.

Li's security guard, sitting in a booth just inside the gate, recognized Hugh's car and opened the gate as we approached. Six Hong Kong police constables held the press at bay, enabling Hugh to gun our car through to the compound.

A distraught Simon greeted us at the door. Gone was all of his brash good humor. In its place, I found a man struggling with a tragedy with which his life thus far had not prepared him to cope.

"Thanks, both of you, for coming," he said. "Pop's on the phone, but he'll be right along. He has the documents you came for."

"Documents?" I asked as Simon showed us into the main reception hall.

"Fiona's birth certificate and whatnot. In case you need them in Beijing."

In contrast to its Western exterior, the interior of the Li home was laid out and furnished like a traditional Chinese home, a replica of which I had seen at the National Palace Museum in Taipei. In the large, high-ceilinged main reception hall, there were four low-slung over-stuffed chairs. In front of each stood a low Blackwood table carved with a traditional Chinese motif. Around the room's periphery sat eight matching straight-backed Blackwood chairs with carvings mirroring that of the small tables. On one wall four scrolls hung over an altar table. The inner two bore grass-style calligraphy; the outer two, traditional landscapes. A yellow bowl—probably Ming—decorated with green dragons sat in the center of the altar table. Another wall was dominated by a large, hexagonal window, its opaque glass covered by wood lattice-work. The remaining walls were covered with polished rosewood panel-ing. A very fine rose, beige, and pale-green wool Tianjin carpet covered the burled mahogany parquet floor. Several orchid plants bloomed in their pots, and a rosemary bush trained to resemble a windswept cypress scented the room.

Simon rang a bell to summon a servant then asked, "What can I get you two?"

"Uh, tea will be fine for me, please," I replied.

"I'll have the same," Hugh said.

"Is Pu Erh okay?" Simon asked.

"Whatever you're having is fine, Simon," Hugh replied. I nodded.

"Well, I'm feeling a bit peckish." Turning to the Filipina servant who had materialized, Simon said, "High tea for three, please, Ramona, with the Pu Erh. Oh, and a pot of Pop's Mao Jian as well."

"Yes, sir," Ramona replied.

I was relieved that Simon had an appetite. He looked pale, and his sunken, bloodshot eyes testified that he had been crying.

"I'm deeply grateful to you two and Emma for doing this for our family," Simon said. "I begged Pop to let me go to Beijing, but he wouldn't hear of it. Said it's far too dangerous. I told him that if it's too dangerous for me, it's certainly too dangerous for anyone else. Well, there you are." His voice trailed off.

"We're glad to do it," I said.

"Of course we are," Hugh said. "And as for danger, rest assured that Bryan will be in and out of China before any harm comes his way."

I appreciated Hugh's attempt to reassure Simon, but his words rang hollow after Li's comments that morning.

Li came through the door shaking his head. When he saw Hugh and me, he held out his hand. "Hugh. Bryan. I trust Simon has made you comfortable."

"Yes, very," Hugh said. I nodded.

"I was on the phone with the governor just now." Li settled into one of the overstuffed chairs. "He's heard the rumors, and his office is being besieged by the press. I felt I owed it to him to tell him about Fiona. Needless to say, he was appalled, and very gracious in offering his condolences."

The room fell silent when Ramona entered carrying a large tray laden with our tea. She proceeded to lay out plates and cups.

"Shall I pour, sir?" she asked Li.

"No thank you, Ramona. Simon will do it."

After she left, Li continued. "The governor didn't say it in so many words, but he was clearly nervous that something major was in the offing regarding Adair, Jameson or Nan Hwa. I must admit, I hadn't thought about the financial implications of rumors about the family; but from his perspective, he's quite right to be concerned." Then Li turned to me, and I sat a little straighter. "Bryan, after we're finished here, you'd better make a brief statement to the press at the bottom of the drive. No details. Just say that Fiona died in an accident while traveling abroad. Funeral arrangements are pending. Say nothing about where she died or about your going to China. We don't want to rile the Chinese authorities, do we, particularly in this uncertain period following the death of Mao."

"Nor give them any reason to be concerned about Hong Kong's stability," Hugh said.

"Oh, yes. Heaven forbid that Jiang Qing and her cronies should see this as an opportunity to pounce. Hasn't that shrew done enough damage already?" Li said acidly.

I was shocked at the venom which came from the stoical Li. And this was the second time I had heard him associate China's power struggle with Fiona's death. I began to suspect that the association was not an accident.

Hugh looked pained that he had inadvertently irritated such a gentle man. "I'm so sorry, Mr. Li."

Li slumped in his chair. "Oh no, dear Hugh, I'm just a little edgy. Think nothing of it."

"Edgy about what, Pop?" Simon asked.

"Nothing. Let's drop it." Li started to hand me Fiona's documents.

Simon abruptly stood, took the documents from his father's outstretched hand, and passed them to me. His move was dismissive rather than polite. "No, Pop. No more changing the subject." Simon went down on one knee in front of his father. "Pop, I know you're hurting, but please, don't shut me out. Don't shut Bryan and Hugh out either. They're our friends. Please, tell us what's haunting you."

Li stared into his son's eyes. Then he stared at me, then at Hugh, then back at Simon. Finally, he rose from his chair and walked slowly, with shoulders hunched and head bowed, toward the door. He turned and, with a sad look on his face, said, "Bryan, until you make it back to Hong Kong, stay in close touch with Hugh and Emma. There will be many in

Beijing who will wish you ill only because you're in my employ. Keep your enemies close by."

• • •

The motorcade carrying Taiwan's intelligence chief, General Shen Chen-kwei, to the residence of Madame Li Gwei-yu in the exclusive suburb of Yangmingshan was bogged down in Taipei's notorious traffic. Shen had won his plum post by ingratiating himself with Generalissimo Chiang Kai-shek, whose speedy exit to Taiwan he had arranged. He had also been a protégé of the infamous Chen Yi, whose brutal put-down of a rebellion of native Taiwanese in 1947 led to the death of thousands and, eventually, to Chen's own execution. With these connections well-known, Shen quickly became one of the most feared and despised men on the island.

The general ordered his driver to radio ahead saying that he had been delayed. He could not afford to alienate the second most power-ful woman in KMT politics. He was, however, prepared for the inevit-able scolding.

When he arrived at the compound, Li Gwei-yu informed him that she had an appointment with the hairdresser. "You're late!" she snapped. "What do you have for me? And be quick about it."

Over the next half hour, Shen told her what his agents in Guang-dong had learned about what had befallen her niece on the Mainland.

"Do nothing," she said. "Do you understand? Nothing. I'll han-dle this."

CHAPTER 5

Tuesday, September 14, 1976

Fiona's death was on the front page of every morning newspaper in Hong Kong. All but the Communist papers carried a front-page photograph of me making the announcement the previous afternoon.

The tabloids speculated wildly on where and how Fiona had died, and even whether she was dead at all:

> Sources close to the Li family yesterday told our reporter that Fiona Li is in hiding in Switzerland pending the birth of her baby, fathered by wealthy Welsh jockey and international playboy Llewellyn Owain. Mr. Owain was Miss Li's escort last June to the Dragon Boat Regatta Charity Ball held at the exclusive Repulse Bay Hotel. Over subsequent days and nights, the pair was photographed at several Kowloon nightspots, riding at Fanling, and romping and cuddling

aboard the Li family's luxurious junk Phoenix while it anchored in Silvermine Bay. On the morning of Mr. Owain's departure for Melbourne to ride in the Australian circuit, the two were discovered having an embarrassingly early breakfast in the lobby of the Peninsula Hotel.

Because horse racing—or, more precisely, betting on horse racing—is Hong Kong's preeminent sport, this tabloid version enjoyed the most currency among Hong Kong's citizens. Extrapolating from this gossamer wisp of upper-crust scandal, some tabloids even wafted the innuendo that Owain had had Fiona murdered.

The English-language *South China Morning Post* was characteristically succinct, offering only the fact of Fiona's death. It did, however, speculate on the implications for Hong Kong of anything that could compromise the stability of Nan Hwa and Adair, Jameson, *which together constitute 22.99 percent of the Gross Domestic Product of the British Crown Colony of Hong Kong and employ 3.6 percent of the workforce.*

The Communist-controlled newspapers were, not surprisingly, fixed on Mao's death. Among their pages of lockstep eulogies and paeans to Mao's glory was a small back-page article condemning the stranglehold over Hong Kong's economy exercised by the *lackey Li and his octopus of companies.*" The final sentence mentioned Fiona, but only as "*the late daughter of the bourgeois capitalist criminal Li Dak-chung.*

I put aside the stack of papers that Ah-yee had bought for me. My blissful anonymity had ended. Now known as the *mouthpiece and hired gun of the Li family*, as one paper characterized me, I felt violated. Fleetingly I thought of the trip to China as a kind of reprieve, a notion quickly dispelled by recalling Li's chilling admonition. Was it prophecy, or merely caution? Why should I be wary of enemies in Beijing?

"Unless somebody's holding out on me," I said aloud.

I pushed my chair away from the dining table and tilted it back on two legs, as if my balancing act would restore the equilibrium that had been snatched away the previous day. I suddenly felt unsafe in my own home.

"Somebody is holding out on me," I repeated even louder.

I nearly toppled backward when Ah-yee pushed open the swinging door that led from the kitchen. "Mr. Paton, you call me? Want more coffee? Toast?"

"No. No thank you, Ah-yee." I brought my chair back to earth. "I was just thinking out loud."

"Mr. Paton, you feel okay? You very pale."

"Yes, thanks, I'm fine. I just got a start when you came through the door."

"You very famous now," Ah-yee said with a mischievous grin as she began clearing my breakfast dishes. "Picture in papers. Radio say your name many times. Always mispronounce your last name. Say like American general, not *Payton*. So many Scotland people in Hong Kong. Think they get it right. *Sei lo!*"

I smiled. Ah-yee continued to amaze me with her knowledge of things beyond China. She had picked up on the fact that, from the European perspective, Hong Kong's history and commercial vitality was largely a creation not of the English but of the Scots. Scottish surnames like Hutchison, Jardine, Matheson, Adair, and Jameson were foremost in the European saga of Hong Kong. I had no doubt that the name Mac-Kinnon would join that illustrious group.

Her arms full of dishes, she added, "Ah-yee get much face working for you. Very happy. Thank you."

Her eyes glowed and, beaming, she swept regally through the kitchen door.

• • •

Ah-yee's confidence notwithstanding, I still could not shake the feeling of vulnerability. And the taxi driver was not helping.

We careered around the Magazine Gap roundabout and hurtled down the Garden Road hill toward the American Consulate General. I had to get a second U.S. passport in order to travel to the PRC because my current passport had a Taiwan visa. The two warring sides refused to accept any passport that bore a visa issued by the other.

"Uh . . . I'm in no hurry," I said cheerily in Cantonese.

"Yeah, but I am," the driver said. "Damn petrol price keeps goin' through the roof. How's a person s'pose ta live? Huh? Can you answer me that?" He turned toward me to drive his point home then did a double take.

"Hey, aren't you that guy works for Li Dak-chung? Picture's in all the morning papers. See?" He held up a crumpled Chinese-language tabloid with my picture on the front page. The taxi continued to hurtle down the hill.

"Eyes on the road," I said. My knuckles were white from gripping the overhead handhold.

The driver turned his face back to the front just in time to steer the taxi into the lay-by taxi queue in front of the St. John's Building, across the street from the Consulate General. I nearly slid off the seat as the driver jammed on the brakes.

"Thought I recognized you. Imagine that, in my hack. Hey, this one's on the house. You work for Li Dak-chung, you're okay by me! And hey, twist the tails of those snooty English that's jealous of Li and MacKinnon. Serve 'em right! And hey, for my money, that Li girl was done in by that jockey fella—whatshisname."

He was still talking even after I got out of the taxi and his next customer had entered and slammed the door. As they drove away, I could hear the driver. "You'll never guess who that guy is . . ."

Although it was not yet 9:00 a.m., the tropical sun and humidity were pitiless. I loosened my tie and draped my suit coat over my arm. Across the road, the Consulate General's Visa Section and American Citizen Services Section were about to open for the day. The line of several hundred applicants already stretched up the Garden Road hill. I wasn't worried about the crowd. I had called ahead to let the Consul General, Walter Anderson, know that I was coming and why. I had met him at the MacKinnons' dinner party and welcomed his offer of help if I ever needed it.

I decided to stop at the flower stand next to the St. John's Building to buy bouquets to send to the Lis and MacKinnons. By the time I finished, the applicant line had diminished to about a dozen. I crossed the road and entered the Consulate General. The process was gratefully swift, and I was back in the taxi queue across the road inside of an hour with the new second passport in my pocket.

When I arrived at my desk at Bishops, there was an envelope leaning against a teacup. Marked "Urgent and Confidential," it was postmarked Friday afternoon from Kowloon and was addressed to "Miss Fiona Li, c/o Mr. Aidan MacKinnon, Esq., Bishops, Hutchison House, Central." It bore no return address.

"What can I do for you?" Miss Chao said from my office doorway. "Mr. MacKinnon said I was to give you all necessary assistance to expedite your departure for China."

"Uh . . . well . . . I scarcely know where to start," I said, putting the envelope aside.

"Yes, that's why Mr. MacKinnon wanted me involved. I arrange all the MacKinnons' travel. He wouldn't know how to phone for a taxi without my help." She sat down in one of the two visitor chairs facing my desk and opened her steno notebook to a page filled with Chinese characters, English words, and numbers. "Why don't I start by telling you what I've already done? Then you can tell me what more you need."

"That sounds fine. And thank you," I replied, much relieved.

For the next twenty minutes, Miss Chao dazzled me with the extent of her preparations on my behalf. She had sent a messenger to the China Travel Service office to obtain the forms I needed to complete for my Chinese visa. She had also filled in the forms except for the passport details.

"I'm afraid you'll need a new passport because you've lived in Taiwan," she said. "Even if I were willing to stand in that hot line at the Consulate, which I'm not, I can't apply for a passport for you. You'll have to go yourself."

She looked back at her notebook and ran her finger down the page, scanning for the next subject she wanted to brief. With all the nonchalance I could muster, and realizing this was probably the one and only time I would ever best this efficiency automaton, I placed my new passport in front of her.

"But . . . oh . . . oh yes! This is a new one! Well done, Mr. Paton." Miss Chao actually gave me a girlish giggle. "I like a gentleman who comes prepared for any eventuality."

She then proceeded to brief me on travel reservations and itinerary, which were the same as the Highgroves'. We were booked on the daily train to Lo Wu on Friday morning, then by Chinese train to Guangzhou. There I would have an obligatory overnight stay at the Dong Fang Hotel. "China's tourism bureaucracy operates on the principle of 'fleece the foreigner' before they let you travel to your next China stop," Miss Chao noted wryly.

On Saturday we would proceed by CAAC Ilyushin jet to Beijing, a four-hour nonstop flight. "You're lucky! On Mondays, Thursdays, and Fridays, the daily flight takes up to nine-and-a-half hours. It meanders through Hangzhou, Changsha, Wuhan, and Shanghai before finally making it to Beijing in the dead of night—that is, if the pilot doesn't wander off course and park your jet against a mountainside." This time,

Miss Chao was deadly serious, and once again, I was reminded of what I was up against.

"And when you arrive in Beijing," she went on, "you will be met by a guide from the China International Travel Service who will inform you of the date and time of your appointment to . . . uh . . . see Miss Li." Miss Chao looked down at her notes and swallowed hard.

After she had finished, I asked her to make two phone calls for me. The first was to Run Run Shaw to apologize for having to miss the film showing Thursday evening. The second was to ask Ah-yee to begin packing a suitcase for me.

"Of course." Having regained her composure, Miss Chao rose to go. "Anything else?"

"No thanks. I think that's everything for now."

"Well, if you think of something, just pucker up your lips and whistle. I always dreamed of being Miss Moneypenny for a handsome man." She was out the door before I had a chance to react.

I had never thought of Miss Chao as anything other than the boss's very efficient executive assistant. She was the one at Bishops who knew everyone's birthday and saw to it that each received a card from MacKinnon. She considered it her responsibility to know all the office relationships and gossip and to keep the detritus from spilling onto MacKinnon's desk. But a coquette and a flirt? She was certainly attractive enough and always impeccably groomed. Complementing her office uniform of straight black skirt, low-heeled shoes, and crisp white blouse clasped at the neck with an old-fashioned cameo brooch, she wore her long black hair smoothly tied back at the nape of her neck. But that prim aspect was startlingly relieved by long manicured fingernails covered in bright red polish. She obviously had a sense of adventure. *Move aside, Moneypenny.*

I turned my attention to the unopened envelope addressed to Fiona, slit it open, and removed the contents. The cover letter, dated Friday,

September 10, was from a P. F. Chu, whom the letterhead identified as a *feng shui* master with an office in Hankow Road, Kowloon. It read:

> This letter transmits herewith the results of my September 9 inspection of the Hollywood Road premises in which you propose to conduct the business of selling Chinese antiques.
>
> As we agreed at the premises yesterday morning, I am posting this report to your solicitor, Mr. Aidan MacKinnon, Esq.

I sat bolt upright in my chair. Fiona had been here in Hong Kong as late as last Thursday morning. And I had a witness. Was Chu involved with Fiona's disappearance? No. He would hardly send the letter to Bishops if he were involved. Unless the letter was a subterfuge, a ruse of normalcy meant to conceal his participation.

Were the Triads involved? I could not rule it out. Fiona would be an irresistible target for a kidnapping and hostage-for-ransom plot. They might even have snatched Fiona on the other side of the border where they could hold her until a ransom was paid. They were well-known to have connections with their brethren inside China who had survived the Communist victory. Originally a Chinese nationalist, anti-foreign fraternity, the Triads eventually turned to crime under the guise of providing security; and, in Hong Kong, they had either slid into, or been taken over by, organized crime. Although kidnapping was not a routine Triad method—they usually stuck to loan-sharking, prostitution, and gambling—it was possible that a rogue splinter gang wanting to establish their financial independence had resorted to a one-off ransom scam. Had they snared Chu into acting as bait, or was he a Triad shill, identifying potential targets of opportunity? Perhaps Fiona had been killed trying to escape, or by a nervous, trigger-happy gang member. It would be easy to disguise her body as that of one more Cultural Revolution victim, another bit of flotsam jettisoned by China's ten-year reign of terror.

Whatever the case, I had to start by getting as much information as I could out of Chu. I picked up the phone and dialed the number on the letterhead. No answer. I decided to go to Kowloon. I owed it to Mr. Li to learn everything I could about Fiona's last hours.

• • •

Hankow Road is in the Tsimshatsui section of Kowloon, directly across the harbor from Hong Kong Island. Ordinarily I would have taken the Star Ferry to Kowloon, but my newfound notoriety made me cautious. I decided instead to use one of the Bishops Mercedes. I drove through the Cross-Harbor Tunnel, parked in the public car park on the roof of the Ocean Terminal, and walked the few blocks to Hankow Road.

Chu's office was a nondescript storefront on the left side of the street, almost to Haiphong Road and near Kowloon Park. A sign on the door in Chinese and English said "Please Come Again After Lunch." It was nearly noon, so I decided to have a Reuben and cheesecake at Lindy's a few blocks away.

When I returned to Chu's office around one o'clock, the door was standing open and the latest Sam Hui pop hit was blaring from a radio inside. I entered the darkened storefront and let my eyes adjust. An older Chinese man in shirtsleeves and loosened tie sat half-asleep, swaying contentedly in sync with the radio. A fan, positioned so that it blew directly into the man's face, whirred on the table behind the radio. An empty bottle of Schweppes Bitter Lemon sat perilously close to the drowsing man's elbow. Somehow this was not how I pictured a practitioner of ancient Chinese spirituality.

"Ahem."

The man stirred then reached for the radio's on-off switch. In doing so, he upset the bottle, which tilted, then wobbled off the table. I reached out and grabbed it just before it crashed to the bare concrete floor.

"*M'goisai neih ah*," the man said sleepily in Cantonese. "*Yau mat gwai gon ah?*"

When his eyes adjusted to the light and he saw that I was a Westerner, he said, "Oh, sorry. Thank you very much. My name is P. F. Chu." He rose from his chair and shook my outstretched hand. "How may I be of service?"

"Hello, Mr. Chu. My name is Bryan Paton and I represent—"

"Say, aren't you that lawyer whose picture is in all the morning papers?" Chu said. "Works for Li Dak-chung?"

"Yes. Yes, I am. The reason I wanted to—"

"Thought I recognized you. Terrible thing that . . . about his daughter and all. Can I offer you some tea?"

Chu plugged in an electric kettle and scooped some loose tea from a canister into an egg-shaped tea ball. He closed the tea ball and suspended it by its hook and chain inside his oversize tea mug.

"No, thank you. Actually, Fiona Li is the reason I wanted to—"

"Are you sure? It's Long Jing tea. Very refreshing. A gift from a wealthy client."

I was tiring of Chu's interruptions. Then I realized that he had guessed why I had come and needed a modicum of social lubrication in order to feel comfortable talking to me. The path of least resistance was to accept the tea and chat until Chu was ready to discuss Fiona.

"Actually, Mr. Chu, I'd love some tea."

"Ah, that's good. I think you'll feel much better after just a few sips. We Chinese think of tea as the perfect coolant on a hot day. It's supposed to drive out the heat. Make you sweat. Never believed it myself, but by the time I was old enough to realize it was poppycock, I was hooked on tea!"

He chuckled at his own joke as he puttered among his tea balls and mugs. Despite the urgency of my errand, a feeling of contentment over-whelmed me. Perhaps he was right about the tea. I tossed my suit coat over the back of an extra chair and sat down.

I said in Cantonese, "Long Jing tea. From which province?"

"You speak Cantonese so fluently," Chen said. "Very few foreigners in Hong Kong ever bother, what with English so widely spoken. Where did you pick it up?"

"At the Chinese University. I took a six-month immersion course."

"Ah, a scholar! Well, allow this old fool to add to your wealth of knowledge of Chinese culture. Long Jing tea is grown near the famous West Lake in Zhejiang province. It is highly prized among Chinese. It is even rumored to be . . . uh . . . to have been Mao Zedong's preferred tea."

"Are you saddened by Mao's death?"

"Of course. All Chinese, regardless of their political views, are sad. Whatever his crimes, and there were many, he at least made China stand on her own two feet. He made Japan and the West fear and respect China for the first time in our history. But now—"

He handed me a mug of tea with a matching porcelain lid and sat down. We sipped our tea in silence, accompanied only by the street noise coming through the open front door and the whir of the fan.

"But now," Chu continued after an especially long draught, "I fear that China will again slip into civil war. Mao left no clear successor, and his wife is a savage, power-hungry predator."

"Mr. Chu," I ventured, "I have come to see you about Fiona Li, since you were one of the last persons to see her. I must go to China on Friday. Fiona died there, and her father asked me to bring her remains back to Hong Kong for burial."

"I thought as much," Chu said.

"But how did you—"

"Oh, just the suspicion of an old geomancer that Miss Li was des-tined for China. She was very much in a hurry, and I saw a fur coat on the seat when the chauffeur opened the car door for her. Nobody wears a fur in this heat unless they're on their way abroad."

"Did you say chauffeur?"

"Yes, he took Miss Li away in a black Rolls-Royce limousine. I assumed the car was Li Dak-chung's."

"Yes, I think you're right. Thank you, Mr. Chu."

• • •

I went directly from Chu's office back to Hong Kong Island and, without stopping at Bishops, to the Li family estate in Barker Road. I had to talk to Lao Ma while his memory was still fresh.

Simon had once told me that Lao Ma had been his father's chauffeur for over thirty years. Originally hired by Li in Shanghai in early 1946, Lao Ma was now more a family member than an employee. He had doted on Simon and Fiona when they were children, often taking them to see Chinese opera or sneaking them warm *baozi* on nights when they were confined to their rooms without dinner after some mischief. It was inconceivable to me that this adoring avuncular figure could be involved in Fiona's death. But he certainly could provide information about where he took her last Thursday and why.

When I arrived at the Lis', the guard recognized me and opened the gate as my car approached. Yesterday's gaggle of reporters had dwindled to about a dozen, but there were still enough of them to crowd around the car as I slowed to turn into the driveway. A few shouted questions, and some flashbulbs popped near my open window as the car slid through the gate. The long driveway up to the house was lined with several dozen citrus jasmine trees, each in its own massive clay container. The intoxicating perfume from the small white blossoms induced in me an almost overpowering languor.

I drove past the house and the guest car park and turned off on the small slip road that led to the garages and staff quarters. Lao Ma, clad in slacks, undershirt, and suspenders, was in the large asphalt oval in front of the garages polishing the Rolls. He was tall and heavy for a Chinese, characteristic of his Manchu origin. I had no doubt that, despite his sweet and gentle disposition, if someone tried to attack Fiona, Lao Ma would be more than capable of defending her or at least raising the alarm.

I parked and got out of my car. Lao Ma, intently buffing a fender, raised his head at the sound of my door closing.

"Hello, Lao Ma," I said. "My name is Bryan Paton. I'm the new lawyer representing the Li family."

"Yes, I recognize you from the papers."

For once my fame was working in my favor. "I'd like to ask you a few questions about Fiona if you don't mind."

Lao Ma's massive frame sagged, and he seemed to age suddenly well beyond his fifty-eight years. "Do you mind if we sit down?"

"No, of course not."

He went into the garage and brought out two folding chairs, which he set up in the shade of a bauhinia tree at the edge of the oval.

"I told Mr. Li everything I know last night, just as soon as I heard she was dead. If only I had told him earlier, she might still be alive."

"You can't blame yourself."

"She was like a daughter to me, and I failed her when she needed me most."

We sat a while in silence. Lao Ma was hunched over, his forehead in his hands. I gave him time, waiting until he lifted his head.

"I suppose the best place to start is with what you told Mr. Li last night," I said.

"I first took Miss Li from here to Hollywood Road—to the shop that she and Mrs. Highgrove wanted to lease for their antique shop. She said she had an appointment with a Mr. Chu. Something about *feng shui*."

"Yes, I talked to Mr. Chu earlier this afternoon. Tell me about where you went after that appointment."

"Well, Miss Li was in a hurry, always looking at her watch. After we left Hollywood Road, she told me to take her to the Hung Hom train station. That morning, her maid and I loaded three pieces of Miss Li's luggage into the car. Oh, and the maid also put Miss Li's fur coat in the car. I just assumed Miss Li was catching the train to China."

"Did anyone join Miss Li at the train station?"

"Not to my knowledge. After she entered the station and I put her luggage on a porter's trolley, I didn't see her again."

"Did you see anyone speak to her?" I asked.

"No. There was a fellow squatting in the way when I opened the door for her. His pig set up an unholy row, but the man didn't say anything to Miss Li. It was over in a second. She headed straight for the waiting room." He shook his head. "Last I saw of her."

"Is there anything else you can think of that might shed light on why she turned up dead in China?" I asked.

"No, nothing, except that she did make me promise not to tell anyone about where I took her Thursday morning. I don't think that's of much help."

"Why?"

"Why what?"

"Why was it so important to her that nobody knew where she was going?" I asked.

"I really don't know. She never said."

. . .

After I left Lao Ma, I went back to Bishops. It was almost 7:00 p.m., but I needed to jot down a few notes on what Chu and Lao Ma had told me. Fortunately, Miss Chao was still in the office, so I dictated the notes to her and asked her to pass a copy to MacKinnon in the morning. When I finished dictating, Miss Chao handed me a manila envelope containing my itinerary, tickets, ten U.S. $100 bills, and my new passport with the Chinese visa stamped inside. *Well done, Miss Moneypenny. And almost two days before I leave.*

"Are you sure U.S. dollars are accepted in China?"

"Not to worry, the mighty greenback is the Chinese government's preferred foreign currency. They may be Communists, but they're not stupid." Miss Chao gave a wry chuckle. "I think you'll find my fellow countrymen to be the world's most instinctive capitalists, even—no, make that especially—the Communists. It's in our genes."

"Do tell."

"Oh, by the way, I was asked to give you two messages. Mr. MacKinnon said you were to feel free to use a Bishops car until you leave for China. And Hugh Highgrove asks that you meet Emma and him for dinner at 8:30 at the Red Pepper Szechwan Restaurant in Causeway Bay."

"If I miss dinner Ah-yee will strangle me."

Miss Chao was already out my office door when she called out, "Not to worry. I already phoned Ah-yee to let her know you wouldn't be home for dinner."

• • •

I drove to Causeway Bay, parked in front of the Lee Gardens Hotel, and walked the two blocks to the Red Pepper. The restaurant was packed with Chinese diners, but I spotted Hugh and Emma just being seated. I crossed the room and joined them.

"Hello, old chap," Hugh said, gesturing toward a chair. Emma nodded. She appeared distracted, and I doubted that she wanted to be there.

After we had ordered, I asked Emma, "Are you aware of any reason why Fiona wouldn't want anyone to know she was going to China?"

"None whatsoever. You mean she didn't even tell Simon or her father?"

"No, she didn't. I suspect that if she had told Mr. Li, he'd have reacted the same way he did when Simon wanted to go."

"How so?" Emma asked.

"Apparently, as if someone had poked a stick down a badger hole. When Simon brought up the notion of his accompanying me, Mr. Li adamantly opposed the idea."

Hugh nodded. "His father forbade him to go to China. He said it was far too dangerous."

"Maybe Mr. Li is concerned about the situation right now," Emma said. "What with Mao dying and all, China is bound to get dicey, for the next few weeks at least."

"Well, that's the thing I can't figure out," I said. "Mr. Li keeps waltzing up to the notion that Fiona's death is somehow tied in with China's developing power struggle. When I think he's on the verge of explaining himself, he turns irascible and descends into a rambling fume about Jiang Qing."

"I agree," Hugh said. "I really don't know what to make of his behavior . . . unless, of course, there is some connection."

After the hot and sour soup arrived, I turned to Emma. "How are you bearing up?"

A forced smile flickered across her face as tears welled up. All right, she nodded silently, mopping her eyes with her napkin.

"Tell me about Fiona," I said. "I only saw her just the one time."

"She was my best friend. We met in the first form at St. Paul's Convent School and were close from then on. Like me, she played sports, badminton and table tennis, mostly. At my urging she took tennis lessons and progressed quickly. I could never beat her. We spent a fair amount of time in the early years devising pranks to play on our teachers—notes saying they needed to be somewhere they didn't, loose chair legs, that sort of thing. Fi was the ringleader and was summoned to the headmistress's office much more frequently than I. We both sang in the school choir. Fi had a lovely clear soprano that I thought she should have trained; but, as with most things, she rejected the discipline it would have required.

"After A levels, we saw each other whenever we could. It never occurred to her to pursue a degree. She was happy with the path expected of one with her social position. It did not hurt that she was a beauty, full of energy, and had a sparkling personality to match. When I first went up to Cambridge, Fi joined me from one of her routine visits to Switzerland, France, and Italy. And, of course, she was part of the wedding party when Hugh and I married in Scotland. She stayed with us for a month in Singapore when Hugh was posted to the High Commission there. Then when Hugh was transferred to Beijing we were able to see each other more frequently, and the notion of the antique shop took form. She was so excited about it. I think she was happy to find something steady to which she could devote herself and call all her own." Emma's voice cracked.

"I'm sorry . . . I—," Emma said as she rose and hurried off in the direction of the ladies' room.

"I'm worried about her," Hugh said. She hasn't been eating, and tonight she barely touched the crispy duck or the pork and *zha cai*, two of her favorites. I don't know how she will handle the formalities in Beijing."

My fear exactly.

• • •

Li Dak-chung had just settled into his favorite armchair near the window in his study when the phone rang. Ramona appeared in the doorway. "It's Madame Li calling from Taiwan, sir."

Li sighed and closed the open photograph album on his lap. "Thank you, Ramona. I'll take it."

"Elder Brother?" said the slightly shrill voice on the line. She used the customary form of address among Chinese siblings. "Are you there?"

"Yes, Gwei-yu."

"I'm calling to tell you how shocked I was to hear about Fiona. What did she get herself into? I want you to know that my newspapers are reporting just the facts. You can count on me to protect the family."

"And why would you feel it necessary to do that?" Li felt the heat rise, and his heart started to pound.

"Well, you know Fiona's reputation."

"And what was that precisely?" Now he was furious.

"Well, she should never have been involved with that fast racing crowd, especially that jockey fellow."

"Don't believe everything you read in the newspapers," Li said. He doubted she would grasp the irony. "I suppose you would want me to convey your condolences to Simon?"

"Yes, yes, of course. I won't be able to come for the burial."

"I didn't expect you would," Li replied acidly. "Busy are you?" He opened the photograph album and began to leaf through the pages. *Simon and Fiona as babies among their toys at the Cameron Road flat in mid-levels.*

"Oh yes. There is really so much still yet to do. Ching-kuo is quite a handful." *Fiona on her mother's lap at the Dragon Boat races.*

"How is Song Meiling?" *Fiona aged eight, a pout on her face, in her school uniform.*

"She's well. I ring her every week. You know I went with her to New York last year to help her get settled."

"I saw it in the papers. So she's finally abandoned Taiwan . . . or been ushered out by her stepson." *At Fanling, holding the reins of the pony, Simon and Fiona atop. Fiona on her sixteenth birthday.* He closed the album.

"Never! She'll be back. When the time is right. I tried to convince her to relocate to Hong Kong. We could use her there."

"What influence could she or your KMT friends possibly have on Hong Kong?" Li was instantly sorry he had asked.

"Well, we could tell people what those Communists are like—what's in store if they continue to let them worm their way in. *You* certainly haven't been doing it."

Li yawned into the phone. He was tired, and this was tiresome.

"And that wife of Mao's," Gwei-yu droned on. "She's dangerous."

"I can agree with you on that point, Gwei-yu. And now I must—"

"She'll force another flight of millions. We would welcome them here, of course, but I'm sure you don't want another wave of poor refugees emptying the public purse. Hong Kong should join with us. We're the only bulwark left against those criminals."

Li had had enough. "I appreciate your call, Gwei-yu," he said softly. "Now I must rest. You will understand that these are difficult days."

"Just remember what I have said. Good-bye, Elder Brother."

CHAPTER 6

Wednesday, September 15, 1976

The plane that brought General Zhu and his aide-de-camp from Shenyang to Beijing had arrived nearly an hour ago at the Lantianchang Military Airfield on the northeastern edge of China's teeming, dusty capital. And the car sent to pick them up had not yet appeared.

"Not an auspicious beginning for the new commanding officer," Major Wang said.

"Major!" Zhu said. "Be patient, please. After all, the founder of socialism in China has just died. One must be circumspect in troubled times such as these . . . for the sake of China's future, if not for your own."

"Yes, sir."

An orderly entered the waiting room and saluted. "General, your limousine has arrived."

The Red Flag limousine sped the new commander of the Beijing Military Region and his aide through the capital's bicycle-choked

streets. Shielded from onlookers by dingy, sun-faded beige window curtains, they were headed toward Zhu's new quarters at the Ministry of
National Defense.

The Ministry was located in central Beijing on the northwestern
edge of the Forbidden City. A wall separated it from Beihai and from
Zhongnanhai, the compound reserved for the homes and offices of only
the most senior officials of the Party and government, including Mao
and his wife, Jiang Qing. Zhongnanhai was protected by Detachment
8341, an elite regiment of bodyguards and soldiers commanded by
General Wang Dongxing, a longtime confidant of Mao and a member
of the Politburo whose villa was also in Zhongnanhai. Staffed by the
People's Liberation Army and therefore ostensibly under the Ministry
of National Defense, Detachment 8341 was, in fact, a force unto itself.
Its writ covered all of China, and it was the Chinese leadership's last line
of defense in the event of domestic upheaval or a coup d'état.

The driver eased the limousine up to the senior officials' private
entrance. An honor guard and dozens of generals and senior colonels
were waiting to welcome their new commander. The driver stopped
the car, and a guard opened the door for General Zhu. The vice commander, General Kang, saluted. "Welcome to the Ministry, General."

"Thank you, General Kang. Good to be here."

"May I present your senior staff?"

Zhu nodded and received them quickly while Major Wang chatted with junior officers near the entrance. The death of Mao dictated a
more subdued and informal ceremony than would ordinarily have been
the case.

After Zhu had finished with the last officer in the line, General
Kang said, "You must be tired from your journey. May I escort you to
your private apartment?"

"No, General Kang, I'd like to go directly to my office."

"Yes, sir. Right this way," Kang said then whispered, "I'm terribly sorry about your car being late. We had an unscheduled demand from Zhongnanhai for a limousine."

"I quite understand. Marshal Ye asked me to meet with him right away. When is that appointment?"

"At three o'clock, sir."

Zhu looked at his watch. It was just after one o'clock, sufficient time to have Major Wang try to locate his daughter and Colonel Peng.

• • •

The Minister of National Defense, Marshal Ye Jianying, was a legendary veteran of the Long March and a survivor of many Party battles. Now seventy-seven and still a devout Communist, Ye began his association with Zhou Enlai while working for Zhou as an instructor at the Whampoa Military Academy in the 1920s. He remained a protégé and loyal supporter of Zhou throughout his life.

Ye survived the Cultural Revolution because of one seminal event. During the Long March, he sniffed out a plot by a rival to Mao to seize control of the fledgling Chinese Communist army and movement. He warned Mao in time, and this crucial act ensured Ye of Mao's personal protection during the late 1960s when the radical faction, under the guise of the Cultural Revolution, was savagely attacking and murdering prominent Communist moderates.

General Zhu arrived at Marshal Ye's office promptly at 3:00 p.m. He was eager not only to see his old Whampoa instructor and Long March mentor again but also to learn why Ye had abruptly ordered his transfer to Beijing. Why not wait until the confusion accompanying Mao's death and funeral was over?

"Is something wrong, General Zhu?" Ye's secretary asked.

"Pardon me?" Zhu said.

"You were grimacing and shaking your head."

"Oh, no, nothing's wrong. Thank you for asking."

"Minister Ye shouldn't be too much longer. Can I get you some tea?"

"No, no thank you." Zhu would have liked tea, but he particularly needed this meeting to remain focused.

The door to Ye's office opened, and chatting amiably, the Minister and several PLA officers emerged. Like Deng Xiaoping, his close friend and political ally of more than half a century, Ye was short in stature. Also like Deng, Ye had a placid demeanor that caused some to make the fatal mistake of assuming that he was less than the hardened guerrilla fighter he was.

"Dear friend, so sorry to keep you waiting," Ye said after showing his other guests out.

"Marshal Ye, I am honored to see you again and to have the good fortune to serve under you."

"Let's go into my office and catch up." Ye turned to his secretary. "Could you please bring us some tea?"

Ah, well. Tea would be nice.

The two went into Ye's private office and settled into adjacent easy chairs. There was a massive oil painting on one wall depicting, in heroic fashion, the Red Army crossing the towering Snowy Mountains of Sichuan province on the Long March. Both Ye and Zhu were survivors of the treacherous crossing. Zhu remembered it as a cold, wet miserable time.

After his secretary brought the tea and closed the door behind her, Ye said, "Dear friend, we need your help."

"Yes, of course."

"Without hearing the purpose? Do you really trust me so completely?" Ye smiled as he reached for his tea. "You are not gullible, and you certainly aren't a fool, so you must be that rarest of persons, a loyal comrade dedicated to preserving socialism in China."

"Such people are not that rare, I think," Zhu said. "All they need is a leader who won't betray them."

Zhu was certain of Ye's political leanings. What he was not sure of was whether Ye was disposed to serve as the nucleus around which the moderates could rally. Their mutual friend, Zhou Enlai, had been the natural choice; but since his death no other moderate of sufficient stature had yet risen to challenge Jiang Qing and her cabal of radicals for control of China. And time was now perilously short.

Ye paused for a moment. "Jiang Qing must be stopped. If we don't act, she'll murder us all. And it won't be a swift death either. It'll be like President Liu's—slow and lingering and painful. And she won't stop with us. She'll have to eliminate our families, our subordinates, our supporters. It will be a bloodbath."

Zhu was instantly filled with fear for the safety of his daughter. She had been so tiny, so fragile, so helpless the last time he saw her. He longed to explain.

The sudden crackle of gunfire so close on such thoughts paralyzed Zhu. The teacup and saucer balanced on his knee crashed to the floor.

"Did I startle you?" Ye said. "Or was it the rifles?

"Some of both, actually. What are—?"

"That's just the ceremonial rifle squad firing blanks to practice for a ceremony for Mao. In any case, you're quite right to be concerned."

Zhu leaned over to gather up the shards of the shattered porcelain. It gave him a moment to digest what Ye had said.

"Leave that. Someone will see to it later," Ye said. "Do you agree with me? About Jiang Qing, I mean. Please be frank. We've been through too much together over the last fifty years to start playing games now."

Zhu was relieved to concentrate on how to prevent Jiang Qing from seizing power. It temporarily took his mind off his daughter.

"I couldn't agree more," he said. "My only hope is that having acknowledged the danger, you're prepared to lead us. With Zhou and my uncle dead, you're the only hope we have."

"Have you ever known me to be timid or reluctant? I wouldn't be much of a leader if I hadn't thought through very carefully my tactics and strategy. Remember what Zhou always said: 'All warfare is deception.' Well, I'll add to Comrade Zhou's dictum by saying that luck is the residue of planning."

Zhu laughed. "So, to give you time to plan, you've been deceiving our enemies."

Ye smiled, "Exactly. Now you know why you were my favorite student at Whampoa. It was because you had uncanny perceptiveness. Sometimes it seemed you were reading my thoughts."

The two old comrades—Ye almost seventy-seven, Zhu just past sixty-nine—shared a moment of laughter. By Chinese reckoning, they were just entering their most intellectually mature, professionally successful, emotionally stable years. Moreover, their mutual tribulations had conditioned them to survive privation. Even now, both were vigorous, vital, even virile, and more than equal to the perilous task they were plotting.

"Seriously," Ye said presently. "I have been thinking about these matters a great deal. The hardest part has been paying lip service to that viper, but at least it has kept her off my trail—that, and my saving Mao's hide during that dustup during the Long March. Mao's lingering for so many years and his frequent ups and downs lulled us into assuming that last Thursday evening's episode was nothing more than just another step in his never-ending medical decline. When it became clear just how serious it was, I rushed to his bedside. That shrew was there, too, taunting and goading and baiting, as usual—so much so, in fact, that I let down my guard and had a go at her. It was nothing of any consequence, at least as far as I was concerned. But that's when it jelled. I realized I'd have to step forward and lead the fight against her."

"I must say I'm relieved," Zhu said. "May I ask who else is with us?"

"So far, I'm certain of Li Xiannian and Wang Dongxing. No one has yet approached Hua Guofeng. He's the crucial unknown right now."

Premier only since Zhou Enlai's death in January, Hua Guofeng was a little-known and unheralded senior Party leader when Mao plucked him from obscurity and designated him as his own titular successor. Hua had little following in either the Party or the military, and it was widely assumed that he would serve only as caretaker until the real post-Mao leadership sorted itself out. Hua was, in fact, so lacking in gravitas that the Party erected huge billboards on street corners across China showing Mao and Hua sitting side by side with Mao saying, "With you in charge, I'll rest easy." But, as irrelevant as Hua might appear, he still had to be reckoned with, particularly because he had not yet tipped his hand.

"We have to either ease him aside or neutralize him," Zhu said.

"When push comes to shove, I think Hua will be with us," Ye said, "especially when he sees the majority of the military united against the radicals. Distant water is of no use if the fire is near at hand. That's why I transferred you here so quickly. It would be folly to have gone ahead without the Beijing Military Region commander supporting me. After your forces seal the city, we'll move in and arrest Jiang Qing and her supporters."

• • •

With a sense of excitement tempered by apprehension, Zhu hurried back to his office. When he arrived, Major Wang informed him that Colonel Peng had called twice.

"I've never heard the Colonel sound so frantic," Wang added.

"Get him back on the line immediately," Zhu said.

Zhu waited at his desk. When Wang had Peng on the phone, Zhu motioned to Wang to close his office door.

"Where's my daughter? Is she safe?" Zhu said into the phone.

"I . . . I . . . I'm afraid I don't know, sir."

"What do you mean you don't know? Isn't she with you?"

"No, sir. I really don't know exactly where—"

"She isn't with you?" Zhu shouted into the phone.

"No, sir. No, she's not. I'm afraid she's been kidnapped."

CHAPTER 7

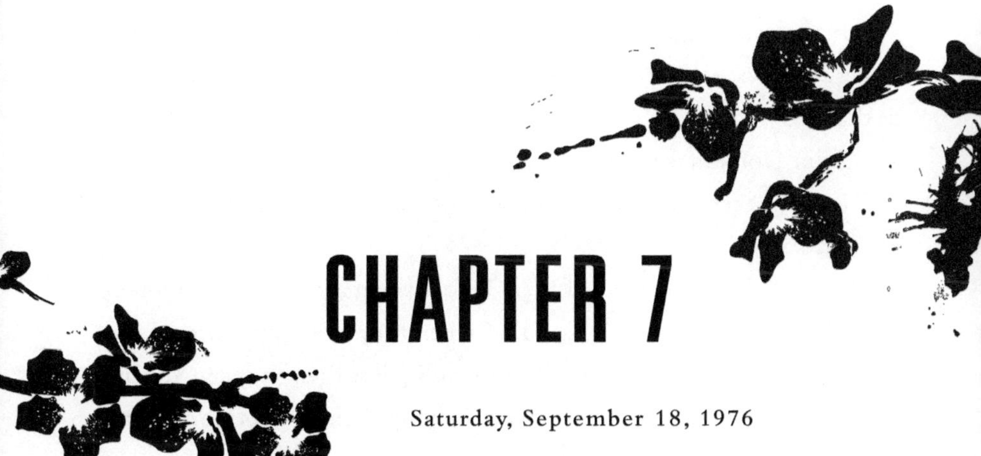

Saturday, September 18, 1976

My stomach groaned with hunger. We had been delayed in Guangzhou for five hours by mechanical difficulties. The terminal at Guangzhou's White Cloud Airport had neither restaurant nor snack bar nor shop. I could see why. Ours was the only plane on the tarmac, and there were few other passengers in the terminal.

Three hours into our wait, a surly CAAC employee trundled out several cases of unrefrigerated Chinese cola. He would accept only U.S. dollars, Hong Kong dollars, German marks, or Swiss francs, much to the frustration of the other foreigners who had deliberately bought Chinese *yuan* before departing Hong Kong. I made a mental note to thank Miss Chao for my cache of U.S. currency.

When we were finally airborne, I eagerly awaited what I naively assumed would be a sumptuous Chinese meal that would welcome a planeload of foreigners to the homeland of that matchless cuisine. Instead, women in boxy, ill-fitting cotton slacks and shirts slung into our laps a scrawny apple and a sandwich consisting of two slices of dried-out white bread and, upon close inspection, a sliver of gristle-streaked ham. There were no beverages available except for water.

Hugh leaned across the aisle, half-eaten apple in hand. "There's something I've been meaning to ask you, old boy. How did you come to the law?"

"Aunt Doris Nakamura."

Hugh cocked his head. "You will not convince me that you are Scots-Japanese."

"No, no. Aunt Doris, an Ikehara before she married, is my mother's best friend. She married Uncle Yukio when they were both interned in a camp in Utah during the war. Both families lost their property during the internment, and my parents were helping them file for compensation. I thought that I would one day study law so that I could help; I was eight years old."

"And you never once wavered?" asked Emma, leaning across Hugh from her window seat.

"Well, I got some reinforcement during my last year at Berkeley when I faced the prospects for a history major with a specialty in Tudor and Stuart Britain."

"Mmm . . . a closet Anglophile," said Emma. "But Simon said you never practiced until his aunt discovered you in Taiwan. What were you doing there?"

"Teaching at Madame Li's Language Institute. You see, I was bitten by the China bug. It was Nixon's fault. His visit to Beijing and Shanghai in February 1972 started it. With six months to go at Columbia Law School, I signed up for a college-level Chinese history course and a three-hour-a-night immersion course in Mandarin. I devoured everything written about China, attended lectures, went to museums, and wandered New York's Chinatown on my rare free Sundays.

"My full scholarship paid the bills, and my associate editorship of the law review meant that no one was inclined to question my abysmal class attendance during those months. When I graduated in June, I went home to California to take the bar exam. I had promised my father that his only child would not squander three years at Columbia without at least banking bar membership. And I had the thought of trying to combine law with my interest in China."

"Your father is an attorney?" asked Hugh.

"No. My parents have a fruit and vegetable market in San Francisco. They would not approve of that apple you're eating."

"Go on with your story," Emma said.

"While awaiting the results of the bar exam, I resumed Mandarin classes and hired a private tutor, Miss Liu, for conversation and calligraphy. Just after the news came that I had passed the bar, Miss Liu gave me an ad she had clipped from the newspaper recruiting English teachers for the Taiwan Institute of Foreign Languages with, it said, branches in Taipei, Kaohsiung, and Taichung. It was irresistible. I went for an interview and, within a week, was on a plane to Taipei."

"Did you enjoy Taiwan?" Emma asked. "I've heard it's provincial and boring."

"Not true. Anyway, you find what you want to find. I spent three idyllic years down island in Taichung. I had a two-story house on a quiet dead-end lane. There was a huge mango tree in the back. I could pick the fruit from my second-floor balcony. Better yet, from that balcony my friends and I could watch evening baseball games on the lighted diamond that abutted my back wall. After the games we would walk a quarter mile or so down a dirt lane to a Mongolian barbecue restaurant surrounded by rice paddies. We spent many a night there drinking Chinese beer, talking and laughing, much to the improvement of my colloquial Mandarin."

"So what prompted you to leave, old boy?" Hugh asked.

"Well, after three years, my Mandarin was fluent and my bank account flush. I decided that I wanted to be closer to the Mainland now that the PRC seemed to be taking steps toward an opening to the West. I arrived in Hong Kong in January, two days after Zhou Enlai's death. With my academic record and years of teaching in Taiwan, I qualified for admission to the Yale-in-China Chinese Language Center of the Chinese University of Hong Kong. I took a room in a student hostel and bought a twelve-year-old right-hand-drive Volvo. And, well, you know the rest."

Hugh sat up straight and gripped his seat. The Ilyushin passenger jet was descending much too steeply. I had been on too many jets, both in the States and during my time in East Asia, not to recognize that something was wrong. I shot a frightened look across the aisle at Hugh and Emma.

"If you think this is white-knuckle flying," Emma said ruefully, "just wait until we come in for final approach."

"CAAC pilots are all active-duty Chinese Air Force pilots," Hugh added, a grim look on his face. "Frustrated stick jockeys, one and all."

As we approached Beijing's Capital Airport, the pilot abruptly veered left, then right, then reversed the engines momentarily, throwing the jet into what seemed like an uncontrolled dive. The wings shuddered, and the airframe groaned as the jet hurtled earthward. Several overhead compartments popped open, dumping their contents onto the heads of terrified passengers. The mounds of bundles, coats, and boxes piled in front of each emergency exit rolled into, then down, the aisle. A woman several rows in front of me began shrieking.

"That's the runway there," Emma said nonchalantly.

It was just past 9:00 p.m. and pitch-dark outside. Although we were over one of China's largest metropolises, few lights were visible on the ground. Hugh's eyes were fixed on the opposite window, staring blankly into the void. The color had drained from his face, and his hands had a death grip on the armrests.

"Where?" I craned my neck left and right to see out the window. "I can't see any lights."

"Keep looking," she said. "Watch that long black empty space."

"But we're much too low and must be right over it!"

Two strings of pearly lights suddenly appeared in the black void, and the airport control tower sped past the window. The plane was flying just above treetop level. The pilot maneuvered it into a steep left bank. Any second I expected to hear the left wingtip scrape the ground. After executing a U-turn, the pilot dropped the jet onto the middle of the runway and jammed on the brakes. I was thrown so far forward that I thought the seat belt would cut me in half. Once the plane stopped, the runway lights were turned off.

"They do that to save electricity," Emma said.

Hugh's color had returned, and he was opening and closing his hands to restore flexibility. The woman who had shrieked began crying and laughing simultaneously. One of the women who had served our apple and sandwich announced via the plane's sound system, "This is Beijing. Exit the plane promptly."

As we walked down the mobile staircase to the tarmac, an acrid plume of black smoke welled up from under the plane. We had blown a tire on landing. I looked around. We were the only passengers in the airport, and as at Guangzhou, ours was the only plane. We walked the thirty or so floodlit yards to the terminal, a single beige sandstone box that had all the charm of a derelict tenement. Once inside we were required to present our passports to assure that we had internal visas permitting us to be in Beijing.

A Chinese woman poked at my elbow. "You are the American Bryan Paton? Come this way. The car is waiting."

I had been saying good-bye to Hugh and Emma, who had a British Embassy car and driver waiting to take them to their apartment in the enclave of diplomatic housing in the eastern district of Jianguomenwai.

The Chinese government had prohibited me from accepting the High-groves' invitation to stay in their spare room, no doubt so they could charge me for a hotel stay.

I broke off my conversation with Hugh and Emma and turned to face the woman. She was a few inches taller than average and, as far as I could tell, somewhere around my age. While not beautiful, her face, devoid of makeup, was rather handsome, with strong well-balanced features and large bright eyes. She wore the unvarying attire of virtually every citizen of the People's Republic of China—faded blue cotton pants and shirt and, in the crisp autumn Beijing weather, padded jacket and a cotton cap pulled down over her mid-length bobbed hair. Clearly cold, she constantly rubbed her bare hands together.

"I'm sorry. I didn't hear what you said."

"I am China International Travel Service guide Pan Bingqing. You are the American Bryan Paton? Come. It's cold."

She started walking toward the door and swung her arm in a circle behind her, motioning me to follow. She was clearly annoyed that my plane had delayed her well into the brisk north China evening. I waved to the Highgroves as I hurried out the terminal door held open by Miss Pan. A cold biting wind funneled through the open door. Emma called out behind me, "We'll meet you at the hotel for breakfast in the morning."

I emerged from the terminal to find a driver, dressed exactly as Miss Pan, holding open the passenger door of what appeared to be a 1949 Ford. Clancy had a framed photograph on his dresser back in San Francisco showing him holding me, at that time a two-year-old child, in front of his new '49 Ford parked at Fisherman's Wharf. I paused momentarily to look at the car. It had a fastback body style like an overturned bathtub, tires as big as a bus's, and wide whitewalls, just like in Clancy's photograph. Sensing Miss Pan fuming behind me in the cold, I abandoned my reverie and got inside.

"The driver already has your luggage in the trunk," she said.

The five-mile asphalt road from the airport to the city was two lanes and flanked by pear orchards. At infrequent intervals there were cross-roads, no more than dirt lanes, down which I could make out darkened mud-hut villages. The road was dimly lit by numerous streetlights under which sat groups of villagers playing cards or chatting. They did not move as our car approached. The driver simply veered wide into the oncoming lane to avoid them, a maneuver made possible by the absence of any other vehicle on the road in either direction.

"The peasants are recreating," Miss Pan said knowledgeably.

"I certainly hope their *recreation* doesn't result in tragedy," I said.

"Yes, you are quite correct. Taking their recreation in this manner does expose them to significant peril."

She was clearly quick on the uptake.

"Your English is excellent, Miss Pan," I said.

"Oh, I have only mastered one or two sentences," she responded with a girlish giggle. "I still must study more."

I recognized this as the standard response to the standard language compliment. It was one of the first things I had learned to say in Mandarin and Cantonese, and I had taught my students to say it in English at the Institute in Taichung.

"Miss Pan, I've noticed this car's interior is newly refurbished. Who did such a marvelous job?"

"Why, this car is new," she said, implying that I had suddenly taken leave of my senses.

"So it's not a 1949 Ford?"

"Of course not. It's a brand-new Shanghai. We make them here in China." Miss Pan continued in a monotone, "Chairman Mao made China self-sufficient. We have no need to import technology from the West."

Rehearsed phrases, I knew, were developed to avoid any freelancing by the guides. I wondered if the driver understood English and whether he and Miss Pan were each required to report on the conduct of the other.

As we entered the built-up area of the city, the cold wind produced little funnels of dust in the dimly lit empty streets. The only signs were huge exhortatory billboards saying "Long live the People's Republic of China" or portraying Mao's faith in Hua Guofeng. Not a soul was on the sidewalks, nor were there any vehicles on the streets. Our driver slowed, but did not stop, at red lights. There were no trees, grass, flowers, or bushes. The berm was of hard-packed mud, like adobe. The houses and shops, mostly single story, were also constructed of mud. The occasional two-story structure was made of wood.

Miss Pan volunteered, again in a monotone, "Beijing lies atop an active earthquake zone. We are required to build with seismological conditions in mind." She said "seismological" slowly, syllable by syllable. I wondered how that translated into mud huts and rickety wooden structures, but I just nodded.

The city changed when we turned onto Chang An Jie, Beijing's principal thoroughfare. From the map I had studied before coming, I knew that Chang An Jie ran east to west past the diplomatic enclave of Jianguomenwai, the Beijing Hotel, and the northern edge of the old, and now abandoned, Legation Quarter. In spite of its prominence, Chang An Jie was illuminated only by pallid yellow streetlights that cast more shadows than they dispelled. I could only assume that this was to save electricity. There was no danger, however, of the lack of light contributing to nighttime traffic accidents because, as with the other streets we drove along, we had it to ourselves.

Our driver coasted through the red light at the intersection of Chang An Jie and Wang Fu Jing Street and up a ramp to the entrance to the Beijing Hotel. It was nearly 11:00 p.m., and I could think of nothing but a hot shower and ordering something—anything—to eat from room service.

I got out of the car. The entrance and porte cochere were still draped in black crepe in tribute to Mao, whose public memorial service had been held several days previous, a week after his death. A dark, narrow anteroom, just inside the hotel's three main double doors, ran the length of the entryway. As I entered, suffocating heat from a hissing radiator and the nauseating smell of stale cigarette smoke, sweat, and garlic nearly overpowered me. At one end two men, bundled against the cold, dozed on the floor. At the other end, a sleeping man sat in a chair, his head on a small wooden table and cradled in his crossed arms. His hand held a smoldering cigarette, the end of which had scorched its shape onto the tabletop next to an overflowing ashtray filled with butts. The table also held a telephone and a tall lidded tea mug.

Just past the anteroom was a cavernous, two-story-high lobby about half the size of a football field. To the right was an L-shaped wooden reception counter next to two curtained glass doors and a bronze plaque that said, in English and Chinese, "Dining Room." To the left was a sitting room furnished with sofas and easy chairs. The three large rooms were dimly lighted by a single floor lamp behind the reception counter.

There was no one in the lobby area except a woman in pigtails. Dressed like Miss Pan, she was slumped over asleep at a desk behind the reception counter. The driver came in carrying my suitcase, followed by Miss Pan.

Miss Pan took one look at the sleeping woman and let out a "*Wei!*" in a voice resembling the caw of a raven.

The woman slowly roused, in no rush to greet the most recent customer of China's premier hostelry. With a face like a fist, she grumbled to Miss Pan in Mandarin, which neither of them yet knew I understood. I saw an opportunity to escape, at least temporarily, the yoke of for-foreigners-ears-only rehearsed dialogue. Besides, I sensed two extraordinarily strong personalities about to meet. *This could be entertaining.*

"Hold your tongue. You'll wake the dead," the woman said to Miss Pan.

"Yes, well, I certainly woke you, and you're apparently dead between the ears."

The woman bristled, then squared her shoulders and straightened her blouse. With her arms rigid and straight, she put both hands on the counter and cocked her head to one side. "Just who do you think you are, talking to a Red Guard like that?"

"Former Red Guard," Miss Pan said. "Thank the Army for putting a stop to that nonsense. A foreign guest arrives, and you're asleep on the job. What kind of impression do you think that creates?"

"Mao taught all Chinese not to cower before foreigners. Or maybe you need a dose of struggle and re-education? I could easily—"

"Mao never taught us to be discourteous," Miss Pan said in a softer tone. "Look, it's late. Let's let Mr. Paton go to his room so we can all get some sleep."

"Miss Pan," I said, hoping the interruption would end the fireworks, "when will I be seeing Fiona Li?"

"You have an appointment at 9:00 a.m. on Monday at Capital Hospital. Dr. Song, the hospital's administrator, will see you. Don't be late."

As the woman turned in my direction she grumbled under her breath, "Yeah, well, Jiang Qing will continue the anti-Confucian struggle."

Miss Pan handed me her business card, and we said our good-byes. After I registered, I asked the woman if room service was still available.

"Sorry, no room service," the woman said.

"Is there anywhere to get a bite to eat? A candy bar? A bag of potato chips?"

"No." The woman's defensiveness confirmed that she had been asked this many times before.

Now beginning to feel faint from lack of food, I trudged toward the elevator bank.

"Oh, Mr. Paton," the woman called out after me, "your room charge includes all meals. If you miss a meal, there is no rebate."

"Thank you. I assure you I won't miss breakfast."

CHAPTER 8

Sunday, September 19, 1976

I awoke before sunrise, and in spite of feeling famished, neglected, abused, and insulted, I lay in bed relishing the moment. I was finally in China. I resolved to put politics out of my mind and concentrate on getting the most out of the precious hours not spent seeing to Fiona's remains.

I sat up and took my first good look around the room. It was of adequate size but not for the oversize blond wood furniture that took up most of the space. There were two single beds with brownish maroon coverlets separated by a nightstand containing a built-in radio. Emerging from the back of the nightstand was an incongruously thick electrical cord at least an inch and a half in diameter. I wondered about its purpose. A large bureau opposite the beds supported a black-and-white television, and against the same wall stood a desk with a lamp and telephone. In front of the sliding glass doors which led to a narrow balcony sat two very large overstuffed armchairs with covers matching those on the beds and doilies on their backs and arms. A brown rug completed the drab décor.

It was just before 7:00 a.m. Since the dining room did not open until 8:00, I decided to take a short walk. I got up and went out on the balcony to orient myself, guidebook in hand. The sky above was clear and blue, but the city was blanketed by thick smog from the coal and wood fires used for cooking and heating. I gasped for breath and felt my throat constrict.

The hotel was on the northwest corner of Chang An Jie and Wang Fu Jing Street. Directly across, on the north edge of the old Legation Quarter, was the six-story brick and masonry headquarters of the China International Travel Service, with red lightbulbs on its roof spelling out "Long Live the Glorious Chinese Communist Party." Visible in the Legation Quarter and among the many trees, I could see European-style buildings, including a church with two steeples. One of the steeples had a cross dangling precariously, someone obviously having tried to knock it down. In the near distance to the right, I could see the vast expanse of Tiananmen Square, bordered on one side by the Great Hall of the People and on the other by the Museum of the History of the Revolution.

After a shower and shave, I dressed and left the hotel. There were no cars, but the streets teemed with people on foot or riding bicycles. Every few minutes a packed city bus lumbered past. A policeman stood on a yellow circular platform in the center of the intersection attempting, for the most part unsuccessfully, to direct the stream of pedestrians walking and crossing at random as they hurried on their morning business. Occasionally I saw the policeman deliver a stern lecture to a luckless miscreant who actually surrendered to his command to approach the platform. The other pedestrians continued to cross helter-skelter, secure in the knowledge that the policeman had snared a sacrificial lamb.

As I turned onto Wang Fu Jing, I was greeted by a rich tableau of daily life. The sidewalks were crowded with people in the now familiar blue cotton garb, some with mufflers over noses and mouths to defend against the cold and smog. Shops were open or opening, and some of the combinations were odd, indeed. One offered pots, woks, and delicate artisan paper cuttings. Another featured soap, toothpaste, and pickled cabbage. And there was a shop selling only rubber boots and toilet paper. I passed a lane leading to a courtyard in which perhaps a dozen people were silently intent on the graceful flowing moves of tai chi. Just beyond I stopped in a large bookstore—Hugh later told me it was Beijing's only—and bought three copies of Chairman Mao's plastic-covered *Little Red Book*. I thought it a fitting memento of the times. Further on at a small open green space, a toddler bent over the low metal railing to reach for a flower. An intentional split in the back of his pants exposed his bottom to the world, useful I discovered a block or two later for satisfying urgent needs. But what made me catch my breath was a symbol of old China: a small gray-haired old woman with a cane, hunched over, inching her way down the bustling sidewalk on her tiny bound feet.

After my walk I met Hugh and Emma at 8:30 in the hotel lobby, and we went into the dining room for breakfast. The dining room was as cavernous as the lobby but twice its size. The feeling that one was eating in a gymnasium was exacerbated by the lack of a carpet: every footstep on the wood floor echoed throughout the hall. This feeling was relieved somewhat by cotton tablecloths and napkins, as well as by small vases of flowers on each table.

After we ordered, Hugh said, "Well, Bryan, any first impressions?"

"I knew Beijing would be different from Taipei or Hong Kong, but I clearly underestimated the extent of the difference. China seems to be locked in a time capsule. It's like a giant 1949 theme park."

"Very perceptive," Hugh said. "It's a complicated situation, and they're facing some difficult choices."

"Ugh," Emma said. "Save that diplomatic mumbo jumbo for your next dispatch to London. Full marks, Bryan. It is like living in a museum."

"Emma's nothing if not refreshingly plainspoken," Hugh chided. "That's why I cherish her. She keeps my thinking on an even keel."

"But seriously, darling, the Chinese born since '49 don't know anything about the world outside China. Those who do don't dare let on lest they be hounded and shut up for being anti-Communist or some such rubbish. It's a massive conspiracy and fraud, not a complicated situation."

"See what I mean?" Hugh said to me with a broad grin. "Darling, it's not whether I may or may not agree with you. For the most part, I do. But my official position means I simply have to be more circumspect. God forbid I should say something that the bugs pick up or my tail overhears. It could easily spin out of control and result in another 1967, especially in the current climate. Nobody wants that."

"Wait a minute, Hugh," I said. "Let me catch up. Bugs and your tail? And what happened in 1967?"

"Ah, brutish reality confronts the starry-eyed China aficionado." Hugh gave a wry chuckle. "Not to worry, Bryan. It happens to us all sooner or later. I'm frankly amazed that your epiphany came so early. Only in Emma's case have I seen it come sooner."

"And I'm not so sure yours has come even yet," Emma joked. She reached across the table and patted Hugh on the cheek.

The server arrived with our breakfast. Hugh fell silent until she had gone then said, "The inescapable reality in Communist China is that a foreigner is never alone. Just try to get lost. Somebody will step out of the shadows and get you back on the correct path."

"Otherwise you might actually meet and befriend ordinary Chinese," Emma said.

"Emma and I are now so accustomed to our tail that I'm thinking we must be obligated to remember him at Christmas—like the char and one's newsagent. Hmm . . . What does one give the perfect Public Security gumshoe who follows you everywhere?"

"New sneakers?" I said. "But what's this about bugs?"

"As foreigners and diplomats," Hugh said, "we assume that everywhere we're allowed to live and work has Chinese listening devices. It's a simple commonsense precaution."

"When we first arrived in Beijing," Emma said, "our embassy apartment wasn't immediately ready for us, so they put us in this very hotel for six weeks. The first day, I noticed a cigar butt on our balcony, presumably left by a previous guest. Well, when we were about to move out, I went out on the balcony to snap some photos, and the disgusting thing was still there. I went back into the room and said to Hugh, loudly, 'Have you seen that filthy cigar butt on our balcony? It's been there for six weeks.' We went down to lunch and were gone only about an hour. When we came back to the room, I went back out on the balcony to take some final photographs—and I swear by all that's holy—the cigar butt had disappeared, and the balcony had been swept spotless." Emma and I laughed while Hugh hummed the theme song from *The Twilight Zone*.

"Oh, and by the way, old chap," Hugh said, "that nightstand between the beds? Have you tried to move it or noticed the fat cord growing out of the back? That's where the spy works live."

After breakfast, Hugh and Emma offered to take me on a drive around Beijing.

"You're sure it's no bother?" I said.

"Of course not," Emma replied, "it's Sunday, and the car is right out front. Where would you like to go first?"

"I suppose I ought to find out where Capital Hospital is," I said. "That's where we go tomorrow to identify Fiona's remains."

"It's barely two blocks from the hotel," Hugh said. "Why don't we walk to the hospital, then come back and pick up the car."

"Besides, walking will test how well you remember hopscotch," Emma added with an impish grin.

Hugh furrowed his brow and shot her a questioning look.

"You know," Emma said, "the state of the footpaths and the level of public hygiene."

Hugh's frown turned to a scowl. "Ah, yes," Hugh said. "One of our pet peeves. Some Chinese have no reluctance in clearing their throats and spitting phlegm anywhere they please."

"More overly scrupulous circumspection from our man in Beijing," Emma said. "The footpath will be wall-to-wall spit. Not to worry, Bryan. I'll hold onto your arm until you get your sea legs. If I don't, you're in danger of glissando-ing away from us. In the meantime, you'll have to step like a butterfly with sore feet."

"So I noticed on my walk this morning," I said. "But Hugh, you still haven't told me what happened in 1967."

During the short walk to Capital Hospital, Hugh explained that in that year the British Embassy in Beijing was besieged, sacked, and burned by Red Guards. "They were enraged over the detention in Hong Kong of several Communist journalists who had led mobs through Hong Kong's streets. We were forced to take decisive action to stop China's then-nascent Cultural Revolution from spilling over into the Colony."

"That must have been dicey," I said.

"It required deft diplomacy, indeed," Hugh replied as we reached Capital Hospital, located three streets up from Chang An Jie and down a dusty lane off Wang Fu Jing.

Architecturally, the hospital was a combination of Chinese pagoda and Victoriana. Through the metal vehicle gate I could see that the large, three-story building was constructed around a central courtyard. The entrance was at the top of a curved staircase leading from the courtyard to the second floor. A PLA sentry with a rifle slung over his shoulder guarded the entrance. The sentry seemed extremely nervous, eyeing us warily as we approached.

"You lot are responsible for all this." Hugh pointed through the gate at the hospital.

"Americans? How so?"

"It was built by the Rockefeller Foundation in 1921," Hugh said. "It used to be known as Peking Union Medical College. It was one of the first and, even today, remains one of the largest of the overseas programs undertaken by the Foundation."

"Quite a pedigree," I said.

"Yes," Hugh replied, "but sadly, since 1949 the government has let the bloodline decay. As you Americans say, 'this dog won't hunt.' What was once the finest hospital in China, and one of the best in Asia, is now just a pale shadow of its former self."

"Could we walk to the Forbidden City?" I asked.

"Certainly," Hugh replied. "Cars aren't allowed in Tiananmen in any case."

For years the Forbidden City had fascinated me. It was a symbol of the grandeur of a millennia-old civilization; but more important, it was an ageless rebuke to those both inside and outside China who focused only on Communism when judging the worth of Chinese culture. It was unthinkable that the radicals had launched the Cultural Revolution, with the Red Guards as their unwitting tool, to destroy that culture.

"If Jiang Qing takes power, the City might not survive long enough for me to make another trip to Beijing," I added, only half joking.

"No risk there," Emma said. "Besides being right next to their bolt-hole, Zhongnanhai, the Communists have co-opted the Forbidden City as their symbol of legitimacy. Just look at the first stamps they issued in '49 and '50."

We walked along Chang An Jie west toward the Forbidden City in the brisk mid-September weather. The prevailing winds had failed to disperse the smoky haze that blanketed the city, and yellow dust was blowing in from the Gobi Desert. Gradually, almost imperceptibly, a crowd gathered around us as we walked. As we continued on our way, this circle of curious Chinese moved with us, those in our path simply walking backward. Some were eating popsicles or apples. They chattered, giggled, or pointed out oddities of our dress or physical features. The majority were young adults who likely had experienced little, if any, contact with non-Chinese in their lifetimes. Hugh and Emma appeared oblivious to the crowd.

"Seems we've acquired an audience," I said.

"You'll get used to it," Hugh said offhandedly. "Another result of their being cut off from the outside world for so long."

"Another diplomat at the embassy and his wife have two blond children, ages three and four," Emma said as we crossed Chang An Jie to Tiananmen Square. "They stopped taking them out because the Chinese walked up to the children and rubbed their hair. Some asked if it were real; others, if it were gold. It terrified the children."

Our host of observers accompanied us lockstep across the boulevard and into Tiananmen. Four massive eye-level portraits of Marx, Engels, Lenin, and Stalin faced Chang An Jie on the north edge of the square. As we approached Marx, a dour, stone-faced soldier, his hands overlapped at the back of his waist, stepped from behind the billboard. Like a subtle change in the temperature, the crowd sensed his presence and began melting away. After the last onlooker had gone, the soldier glared at us with soulless, unblinking eyes, his hands still behind him. I noticed that he had a holster and pistol strapped around his waist. Finally, the soldier executed an about-face and strode away.

I felt my jaw relax. I saw that there were about thirty such soldiers strolling about. The chill wind sent up dust from their every step in the vast expanse of the square.

"Bryan, are you all right?" Emma asked.

"Would you like to sit down, old bean?" Hugh added.

"No, I'm okay."

"Let's walk down the left side of the square as far as the old American Legation," Hugh said, "and then up the other side past the Great Hall of the People to Zhongnanhai. The Forbidden City is still shut in commemoration of Mao's death."

As we walked past the neo-Stalinist Museum of the History of the Revolution, closed to all but a select few senior officials, Hugh began a soliloquy as encyclopedic as it was enthralling. "The museum sits in the space formerly occupied by buildings housing the Board of the Imperial Family, the Ministry of the Interior, the Ministry of Finance, and the Board of Ceremonies. That building there is the former French Hospital of St. Michel, on the north side of the small street now called East Qiao Min Lane. The American Legation guard barracks was on the south side of the lane and visible from Tiananmen. The old American Legation, a complex of several Federal-style buildings, was just east of the barracks.

"The French hospital and the former American compound mark the westernmost extension of what was, between 1900 and 1942, the self-governing Legation Quarter. As you must know, the Boxers laid siege to the quarter in 1900. By the time foreign military forces intervened, the Chinese imperial government was so weakened that it had no choice but to accede to the foreign powers' demand for sovereignty over the quarter."

"Yes, it's no wonder that the Chinese are wary of foreigners," I said.

"Quite. In its heyday, the quarter housed thirteen foreign legations, guard facilities, and parade grounds, as well as several banks, hotels, and foreign post offices. There were also two hospitals and a self-contained transportation and municipal facilities system. The quarter had such amenities as the Peking Club and the French-built Catholic Church of St. Michel. East Qiao Min Lane was the quarter's east-west artery. I'm afraid I haven't yet discovered its former name."

"Oh, dear," Emma shouted in mock surprise. "That just won't do! No dessert and no bedtime story for you tonight."

Suddenly, we heard the sound of boots on the paving stones. A soldier, pistol drawn, was running toward us. Then a man wearing a topcoat and hat stepped from the shade of a tree in front of the Museum of the History of the Revolution and held his hand up, blocking the soldier's path. The soldier shouted something at the man and attempted to wave him away. The man held his ground, his right hand now firmly planted against the soldier's chest.

The two engaged in a heated exchange until the man pulled a card from his inside vest pocket. When he saw the card, the soldier put the pistol back in its holster, locked his heels, then took a step back and saluted. The man turned and, with his head tilted down so that the brim of his hat obscured his face, returned to the shade from which he had come. The soldier executed a crisp about-face, marched a few paces, and then resumed a normal stride in the direction of the center of Tiananmen.

"I wish I could have heard that," I said.

Hugh smiled. "I think the danger has passed. Fortunately we were on foot and not in the car. He might have sprayed the car with bullets before my tail had a chance to tell him we're foreigners."

"Darling," Emma said, "you really must remember him at Christmas."

CHAPTER 9

Monday, September 20, 1976

In the early morning Emma and I went to Capital Hospital to identify Fiona's remains and arrange to have them shipped to Hong Kong. The Bank of China's foreign affairs officer in Hong Kong had told Miss Chao that China would tolerate no involvement by the British Embassy in Beijing. Emphasizing that I had only seen Fiona once and that Miss Li's closest friend was, coincidentally, the wife of a British diplomat posted there, Miss Chao had asked that Emma be allowed to accompany me to confirm the identification.

"I will convey your request to Beijing," he had replied, "but the death of Li Guangmei is China's internal affair. Mr. Paton must obey Chinese law." We had heard nothing further.

We arrived at the hospital promptly at 9:00 a.m. As Emma and I waited for Dr. Song in the reception area, the main door abruptly swung open, and Miss Pan shot through the entrance. She had a distraught, desperate look on her face. Her head twisted left and right as she willed her frantically searching eyes to adjust from sunlight to the darker interior. Her eyes narrowed furtively and locked on their target—me.

"Mr. Paton," she warbled in a high-pitched tone of disdain, "what are you doing here?"

"Why . . . I was . . . it's just that . . . you knew I had an appointment with Dr. Song this morning."

"Of course I did," Pan said testily, "but you shouldn't have left the hotel alone."

"He didn't," Emma said. "He was with me. I'm Emma Highgrove. My husband works at the British Embassy. I live in Beijing. There was no danger of Mr. Paton getting lost."

"In any case, Mr. Paton," Pan said, glaring at Emma, "you're paying for a car, driver, and me." She turned to face me. "Serious consequences would result if . . . if anything should happen to you. Please, applicable regulations require that I accompany you to every work unit you visit." *No doubt serious consequences would be visited on her, too, if I wandered alone into a restricted area.*

Presently, a somewhat portly gray-haired man wearing a long white coat entered the reception area and introduced himself as Dr. Song Wenshu, Administrator and Chief of Surgery. He showed us into the hospital proper and down a high-ceilinged hallway with a concrete floor. The hallway was easily twice as high and wide as those in modern hospitals. Doors to individual rooms stood open the length of the hall. The rooms were unoccupied, though each was made up; and the light from their windows provided the only illumination as we walked. We met no one, neither patients nor hospital staff.

Dr. Song led us to a small door at the end of the hall that opened onto a narrow, unlighted staircase. As we descended the stairs, the air grew colder. At the bottom, Song took a key from the pocket of his smock, unlocked a metal door facing us, and hefted it open.

Chill, damp air and the sound of dripping water enveloped us. Song reached through the door and switched on a light within. The void receded as we passed through the door and our eyes adjusted. A single bulb hanging at the end of its cord revealed eight doors, four on each side of a low central passageway about a hundred feet long. The walls were sweating and appeared to have been roughly hewn from the soil beneath the hospital.

"I can't bear the thought of Fiona lying in this ghastly dungeon," Emma said. "Bryan, please, we have to get her out of here—*now.*"

"We will, we will, just as soon as possible."

Dr. Song turned and said in a genuinely apologetic tone, "China is a poor country. I, too, am troubled that our facilities are not equal to those in the West."

"China has nothing to apologize for," Miss Pan said. "Besides, the British Embassy was expressly forbidden to send a representative to this procedure. You must leave, Mrs. Highgrove."

"It's not a 'procedure,' and I'm not representing anybody. I am here for my dearest friend of more than twenty years," Emma said, her eyes beginning to fill with tears.

"Nonetheless, you must leave." Turning to Song, Miss Pan said in Mandarin through gritted teeth, "We must be very careful, Doctor, to assure that our foreign guests take away a favorable judgment of China. Applicable regulations require it. Understood?"

Song's nostrils flared. He replied curtly in Mandarin, "Understood."

Miss Pan was still unaware that I spoke Mandarin. Dr. Song looked beaten, his professionalism sullied by Miss Pan's authoritarian rectitude. The calm, assured physician who had greeted us upstairs had, below stairs, been forced by Miss Pan to assume the mantle of Party sycophant. It hung loose and tattered around his slumped shoulders.

Miss Pan stepped back to the stairway door and held it open. "Mrs. Highgrove," she said in English to Emma, her other hand pointing to the stairs. Emma did not move.

"Please," Miss Pan said, "I'm sure you'll find the reception room warmer and less damp." Her voice commanded rather than cajoled. It was clear she would brook no refusal. Emma hesitated then walked to the door and up the stairs.

Song walked to the second door on the left, took another key from his smock, and unlocked the padlock. The room inside looked like pictures I had seen of early 1900s meat lockers.

"Shall we go in?" Song said with a quick disgusted glance at Miss Pan.

Miss Pan started toward the door after me. Song held his hand up, blocking her path.

"I'm sorry, next-of-kin or legal representative only. Regulations," Song said, a faint smirk creasing his mouth.

Miss Pan momentarily looked puzzled. More than most Chinese, she knew that there were no regulations at all. The thing that dictated the course of events in the People's Republic of China was whatever the most powerful person in the room held to be the truth. But here she was willing to concede. "I had no intention of entering, Doctor." She left the room and closed the door behind her.

• • •

When I emerged about half an hour later, Miss Pan was waiting. We rejoined Emma in the hospital reception room.

Emma bolted from her chair. "Well?"

"I'm not sure," I said.

"What do you mean you're not sure?"

"The body was too badly—" I searched for a word that would not horrify Emma. "—too badly damaged to permit a positive identification."

The reality was that by the time a Chinese cutter fished it out of the South China Sea, the corpse had been mauled by sharks. That, plus the effect of saltwater and time of exposure had rendered it nearly unrecognizable as a human being. There was not enough of the head left intact to establish eye or hair color. Based on the existence of an epicanthic fold on the uneaten flesh of one eye socket, the Chinese authorities concluded that the person was Asian. Because the corpse was found in Chinese waters, they assumed that it was Chinese. There was enough left of the genital organs to determine gender.

"Then how can they possibly claim it is Fiona?" Emma asked.

"That's what I asked as well. Dr. Song said that is a question only the Ministry of Public Security can answer."

"The relevant organizations and offices have issued a conclusive ruling," Miss Pan said. "You may be confident that this is Li Guangmei. The People's Government has many years of experience processing dead bodies." She said this matter-of-factly, with no apparent inkling of its irony.

"I have no doubt of the government's ability to issue such a ruling," I said, "but I have to be sure." I couldn't risk a confrontation at this early stage, and I was grateful when Dr. Song entered the room.

"We were able," Song said, "to get an imprint from three fingers and the thumb of the right hand. The fingerprints are not complete. Several of the surviving fingers on that hand sustained damage, but I think they will be sufficient to permit the Hong Kong authorities to make a positive identification."

"Doctor," Miss Pan said, "the relevant government organizations have already concluded the matter. The body is Li Guangmei. There is no need to refer anything to Hong Kong."

Dr. Song's patience was clearly wearing thin. "Comrade Pan," Song said, "your participation is not—"

"It's entirely my fault," I interrupted. I still needed both of them to complete my mission. "Dr. Song made precisely those points downstairs. But I'm afraid Hong Kong law requires fingerprint identification."

Miss Pan appeared relieved that Song was toeing the line.

"Well, in that case," she said, "we'll speak to the Ministry of Public Security about forwarding the fingerprints to the Bank of China in Hong Kong. Please wait while I telephone ahead."

It seemed I was learning to cope.

• • •

Miss Pan, Emma, and I went directly from Capital Hospital to the Ministry of Public Security. Hugh had told me that the Ministry was located in the Legation Quarter behind the Museum of the History of the Revolution on the grounds of the former British Legation. Its entrance sat where there had once been a small, exquisite Anglican church opposite the British Minister's residence. The architecture of the quarter's remaining buildings was a compendium of turn-of-the-century design: American Federalist, Japanese, Dutch, Russian, Chinese, British, Italian, Mexican, French, German, Austro-Hungarian, Portuguese, Spanish, and Flemish. The windows of the buildings had been bricked-up; the doors, locked and chained. The Chinese government used the former Church of St. Michel, the one with the dangling cross I had seen from my hotel balcony, as a grain warehouse.

According to Hugh, ordinary Chinese never entered the former Legation Quarter. To do so would render them susceptible to the charge of idolizing foreign things, the most heinous crime in the Chinese Communist legal lexicon. As a consequence, the quarter was always eerily deserted.

Miss Pan wanted us to use the car assigned to me to go to the Ministry, but Emma and I elected to walk. Miss Pan disapproved and was doubly horrified when we decided to walk through the Legation Quarter instead of taking Chang An Jie.

"Exactly the same distance," Emma said.

"Yes, but your route takes you into feudal times and past China's shame." Miss Pan's observation was unscripted and downright poetic.

Miss Pan, the driver, and the '49 Ford knockoff tailed Emma and me as we walked south on Wang Fu Jing Street below Chang An Jie, past the St. Michel church, and west along East Qiao Min Lane. Our route took us past the bricked-up French, German, Japanese, and Spanish legations and the still architecturally elegant Hotel des Wagons-Lits. The old *grand dame,* now shuttered and locked, still presided majestically over the heart of the Legation Quarter.

"A shame, really," I said. "Don't the Chinese realize that foreign tourists would pay any price to stay in a hotel like that if they maintained it?"

"I'm afraid it's just as Miss Pan said. For all Chinese, and not just the Communists, all of this is just a painful reminder of when the West and Japan put a boot on their necks when they were starving and defenseless."

"No wonder we haven't seen any Chinese," I said.

"Maybe someday," Emma said, "when China's national nightmare is over and the Chinese learn to trust us again . . ."

After crossing a narrow green space and an open sewer line improbably known as Jade Canal, we passed the former Russian Legation, its sign still there on the gate.

"Are you sure you won't drive?" Miss Pan called from the car.

"We'll be fine," Emma said. "We're almost there."

We turned north onto a narrow lane that led directly to the Ministry. The access was heavily guarded, and the soldiers on duty were shocked to see us approach on foot. One of them stepped into our path.

"Entry is not permitted," the guard said.

Miss Pan jumped from the car and approached at a run. Between gasps for breath she said, "These foreigners don't speak Mandarin. They're my responsibility. I called the Ministry's Foreign Affairs Office. We have an appointment."

I was gratified that she had called ahead. For all her brusque defensiveness, Miss Pan was invaluable at bullying those in authority who had set up roadblocks for me. She pulled a card from her pocket and showed it to the soldier. I wondered whether it was identical to the card Hugh and Emma's tail flashed at the soldier yesterday in Tiananmen. *Was Miss Pan a Public Security agent?* The soldier checked his log then opened the vehicle gate for the car and driver. The three of us followed the car through the gate.

The Foreign Affairs Office was just inside the main door of the building. The lobby was dark and dingy and smelled of the same malodorous brew of dust, sweat, and garlic that pervaded every building I had been in except for the hospital. *Was this building like Moscow's infamous Lubyanka? Did Chinese enter never to leave?* The Chinese government had long staged public executions in packed soccer stadiums, afterward billing the impoverished families of the condemned for the cost of the bullets. They cited this as the ultimate deterrence for crimes against the State. I suppose it was, not only for murderers, rapists, and thieves, but also for recalcitrant critics, obdurate scholars, and irredeemable partisans of democracy. I felt a chill, and temperature was not the cause.

A Foreign Affairs officer greeted us warmly with a broad smile. "Welcome to the Ministry," he said in English. "My name is Rong Chenli."

He was perhaps in his late thirties or early forties and wore black horn-rimmed glasses. His well-tailored charcoal-gray Mao suit and polished leather shoes testified to his rank. Like all Chinese officialdom, including Miss Pan, he wore a black armband in memory of Mao.

Rong ushered us into a small room fitted out with a sofa, four huge overstuffed chairs, and a large coffee table. Each chair was covered in beige cotton and had three matching doilies—one on each arm and a larger one across the back. A painting of Red Army soldiers crossing a mountain snowfield covered one entire wall. I recognized the painting and furniture as identical to those in the hospital's reception room.

"You are seeking information about the tragic death of Chinese citizen Li Guangmei? Is that accurate?" Rong asked after we were seated.

His English was virtually unaccented, better even than Miss Pan's. He smiled constantly, but the effect was to soothe rather than to convey sincerity. Here was a consummate barbarian handler—a well-mannered, impeccably groomed front man whose purpose was to put the supplicant off the scent of his mission. I glanced at Emma, who looked ill. In contrast, Miss Pan beamed admiringly at him, apparently content with his unctuous deportment.

"Yes, that's right," I said. "We're particularly interested in knowing why you are certain that the body is, in fact, that of Fiona Li."

"The relevant organization has issued a certificate to that effect." Rong prepared to rise, as though this statement concluded the matter.

"What did the forensics show?" I probed.

"I can assure you that the relevant organization followed correct procedure in reaching its conclusion."

A smoldering Emma ignited, and she shot to her feet. "Listen, you're not dealing with just anybody."

Both Rong and Miss Pan appeared genuinely shocked. This evidently happened only rarely. I leapt to my feet and placed myself between Rong and Emma.

"Mrs. Highgrove," I said, "is under a great deal of strain. Her friend has died, and we just want to verify identity and transport the remains to Hong Kong for burial."

"Then she has only to accept the Chinese government's decision that identity *has* been verified," Rong said. "I must make clear that China will not be browbeaten or coerced. The whole Chinese nation categorically rejects the use of force or threats of force. China joins the oppressed peoples of the world in condemning imperialism, colonialism, bourgeois revisionism, capitalism, and hegemonic militarism."

We suffered Rong's gratuitous diatribe in silence. I felt Emma tense on my arm. I guided her back to her seat and returned to mine. I moved slowly, consciously trying to ease the tension in the room and resist the urge to follow Emma's lead and strangle the officer and his chirping acolyte.

I decided to try another tack. Given the condition of the body, the Ministry must have based its identification on the effects found with it.

"Can you tell us where we can collect Miss Li's luggage and effects?"

"I'm afraid these are not available," Rong said. "Li Guangmei was a Chinese citizen. Her property reverts to the State. There is nothing more to report."

Rong and Miss Pan stood up. Rong kept his eyes on the floor, consciously avoiding eye contact with Emma or me. Miss Pan self-consciously straightened her light cotton coat. Rong patted his hair in place and yawned while he stuck his free hand in his pants pocket. Emma and I, both still seated, did not budge.

"Look," I said, "We accept that the . . . uh . . . relevant organization is satisfied that the body is Fiona Li's, but I can't take it back without fingerprint identification. Hong Kong law requires it, and Customs will not admit the body without it."

Emma began to sob. "You must help us with this. The Li family has a right to know. Simple humanity demands it."

Rong glanced at Emma then looked back at me. "You are wrong. China *must* do absolutely nothing. Nothing!"

Emma stared blankly, sullen and detached. Miss Pan said something to Rong, and they chatted quietly but volubly in a Chinese dialect unintelligible to me. Then Rong's demeanor suddenly changed. There was a look of pity in his eyes. He looked at us and, with head slightly bowed, said in a soft voice, "The Chinese people are a good people, an honorable people. Be patient, be patient." He turned and strode out of the room.

I suspected we had won.

• • •

Later, traveling east on Chang An Jie toward Jianguomenwai, Emma had regained her composure but not her usual cheery mood. Miss Pan, like Emma, was pensive. I was thinking about my next move. At a minimum, I owed MacKinnon a phone call. We had agreed that I would pass on anything significant for him to relay to Li Dak-chung. I also needed to pick his brain on how to proceed from here.

Miss Pan, in the front seat, swung around to face Emma and me. In an ostentatious, almost comical manner, she said, "Mr. Paton, this is a good time to see Ri Tan Park. It's in Jianguomenwai district, only a few blocks from Mrs. Highgrove's apartment building. You did say you wanted to see it, didn't you?"

I had learned enough to realize this melodrama was for the benefit of the driver. I had not asked to see the park. *Why did Miss Pan want to speak to me alone?* It seemed best to trust her.

"Yes, thank you," I said.

The car turned left onto a side street, then right into the guarded Jianguomenwai diplomatic apartment compound. Miss Pan showed her card, and the soldier at the gate waved the car through.

"You must feel safe living here," I said to Emma.

"Huh? Not likely," Emma said. "The guard is there to keep ordinary Chinese out. The government doesn't want foreigners polluting them with subversive ideas like democracy and human rights. And they're absolutely apoplectic at the thought of a Chinese Cardinal Mindszenty or an Andrei Sakharov taking up residence in one of our apartments."

I saw the driver glaring at Emma in the rearview mirror as the car rolled to a stop. Clearly he understood English. And I was sure now that he was reporting our activities.

The Jianguomenwai compound consisted of three brown-stucco apartment blocks separated by hard-packed dirt parking lots interspersed with heavily cracked and eroded concrete. Several non-Chinese children were playing outside. The driver had to use the horn to avoid hitting them. There were no flowers, grass, or trees. The overall impression was of a grim, Soviet-style tenement.

I saw Emma to her apartment. The elevator was out of order. "As usual," Emma said. So we walked up three flights to the apartment. On the second-floor landing, we had to skirt an African woman who had just slaughtered a chicken in the stairwell. Hordes of cockroaches and flies had already converged on the blood, and entrails spattered the stairs and walls.

"If a country recognizes the PRC but can't afford the cost of an embassy or housing," Emma explained, "then the PRC foots the bill. Taiwan does the same thing. Both are desperate for international recognition. But here, it's meager rations."

When I returned to the parking lot, the driver was gesticulating at Miss Pan. At one point, he jabbed a finger against her shoulder. As I came within earshot, they abruptly broke off their exchange. Miss Pan's face was flushed and red. *Interesting.*

We drove the few blocks to Ri Tan Park in silence. I busied myself by reading the names of the embassies from the placards on the sentry huts outside each compound. The British Embassy was less than a block from the park.

We parked at the Guanghua Road entrance. Miss Pan and I got out and walked toward a flagstone square in the center of the small park. A restaurant resembling a one-story Chinese cottage was on the far side of the square; several foreign families were inside.

A Chinese puppet show was under way in the square. A red banner over the stage proclaimed in Chinese "Long live Comrade Kim Il Sung and the Democratic People's Republic of Korea!" A second banner read "Resolutely defeat American imperialism!" Several hundred Chinese children, all wearing the red kerchief of the Communist Party's Young Pioneers, sat clapping, laughing, and gesturing excitedly in front of the puppet stage. The children's parents milled about on the periphery. Numerous older Chinese men and women were strolling by or playing Chinese chess at masonry tables dotted around the square.

Miss Pan gestured toward a retaining wall supporting a flower bed and sat down. I sat next to her. We were on the edge of the square, near enough to the stage to observe the show and the children, but distant enough from both to talk without being overheard.

"We haven't much time," Miss Pan said.

I clapped and laughed along with the children without looking at Miss Pan. "Go ahead."

"Rong, the officer at the Ministry," Miss Pan said while looking at the stage and clapping, "is from my native village, Guangan, in Sichuan province. Do you know it?"

"No. Should I?"

"It is also the native village of the most powerful man in China, a man called Deng Xiaoping. Have you heard of him in the West?"

"Of course, but isn't he under house arrest?"

"Yes, but he has many supporters who—"

A roar and applause from the children drowned her voice. On the stage, a puppet version of an American F-86 Saber jet fighter crashed near a painted city labeled "Pyongyang." A red flashlight bobbing from below the stage represented the jet in flames.

"I couldn't hear you," I said. "What has Deng Xiaoping got to do with Fiona Li?"

"It's complicated. The main thing is that Li Guangmei's file has been withdrawn from the Ministry of Public Security on the personal order of Premier Hua Guofeng. Hua used to be Minister of Public Security. He has many friends there who owe their jobs to him."

"How did you find all this out?"

"Rong told me at the Ministry."

"Why should he tell you?"

For the first time since we sat down, she looked straight at me. The puppet show had just ended, and the children were beginning to stand and search for their parents. Miss Pan turned back to face the stage.

"It's not important. I've already said too much. Enough to get me and my family killed."

She stood and started walking toward the path leading out of the park. I followed, and we were soon part of the crowd streaming toward Guanghua Road. When I caught up with her, she turned abruptly and pulled me to the edge of the crowd. We were still some distance from the road. She waited until the crowd thinned out.

"You must never speak of this around any Chinese, especially your driver," she said.

"I already gathered that."

"Rong will find out what he can about what happened to Li Guangmei. I will tell you what he discovers."

She began walking, then said, "Oh, and don't speak of this with the Highgroves or on the phone. It would be extremely dangerous if you did."

• • •

That night I placed a call to MacKinnon from my room. It took over three hours to get an international long distance line, but shortly before midnight the hotel operator put me through.

"Dear boy, what news?" MacKinnon said.

"I'm afraid not much. We've hit several snags."

"Please explain."

"The body was apparently in salt water for some time before it was found. Sharks pretty much decimated it. There wasn't enough of the face left to compare to the photographs Fiona's father gave me."

"Can't my daughter be of assistance? She's been Fiona's friend for some twenty years."

"Emma was with me at the hospital this morning, but they wouldn't let her view the body. She was, and still is, extremely distraught."

"I'll try to call her tomorrow," he said. "What possible reason could they give for excluding her?"

"They're extraordinarily sensitive about British Embassy involvement."

"But Hugh's the diplomat, not Emma."

"Nonetheless, they almost physically barred her."

"Hmm. That's a new wrinkle. Only a short time ago Emma was able to attend an event that Hugh and other accredited Western diplomats could not. Something's definitely amiss."

I heard a suspicious clicking noise on the line and remembered Miss Pan's admonition against discussing sensitive subjects on the phone.

"Bryan, are you still there?" MacKinnon asked. "I thought I heard you ring off just now."

"I'm still here," I said. "It's probably static on the line at my end."

"Yes. How did they decide the body was Fiona's?"

"My guess is that they still haven't."

I heard the click again.

"What did you say?" MacKinnon's irritation was now obvious.

"I said I'm not sure that they've made a positive ID. I think they've agreed to send the salvageable fingerprints to Hong Kong for comparison with Fiona's."

"Where did she die?"

I decided to test the clicking noise with a statement I knew would be provocative. That might confirm whether somebody was listening and taping.

"They don't know—" I said and paused.

There was another pronounced click on the line. Before MacKinnon could react, I hastily added, "—or at least they're not telling me."

MacKinnon was silent for a few seconds. "My boy, . . ." he began. I could almost hear him deliberating what to say next. He was aware of our audience. "Listen," he said, "it's still early days, much too soon to have anything useful to report to Li Dak-chung. Just tell me how they're transmitting the fingerprints. I'll have the authorities here pull Fiona's records and have them at the ready. That should reduce turnaround time."

"They're coming through the Bank of China."

"I was afraid of that," he said. "Well, we'll just have to work with them when the prints arrive."

Click. *The Chinese really ought to buy some up-to-date bugging equipment.*

"They've also confiscated her luggage," I said. "They say she was a Chinese citizen so all her property reverts to the State."

"I think Li Dak-chung can live with that," he said, "unless, of course, they count Fiona's share in Nan Hwa and Adair, Jameson."

Click.

• • •

I turned over and looked at the alarm clock on the nightstand. Ten past three. I had been unable to sleep since talking to MacKinnon earlier that night. So Fiona had a share in Nan Hwa and Adair, Jameson. If she had a share, who would inherit? Simon? Or would Fiona's share revert to her father? Had she even made a will? I was confident that MacKinnon, as the previous Li family attorney, would have seen to that. But not knowing for certain was eating at me. And what about Simon? Did he also have a share?

Suddenly, my failure to get an in-depth briefing on the Li family's legal affairs took on a new and ominous dimension. Whoever controlled Nan Hwa and Adair, Jameson had a stranglehold on Hong Kong. If those two *hongs* slipped into the wrong hands, the resulting financial tsunami could have worldwide repercussions. Surely the authorities here wouldn't try to get their hands on Fiona's property in Hong Kong. Or would they?

A chill ran down my spine. I got out of bed, opened the drapes, and stared out the window. In the distance, across the city skyline stretching from east to west, stood a row of six new twelve-story apartment buildings. Lights were on in several apartments, but only as far as the second floor in each building. Were the apartments on the first two floors the only ones finished? Or did they rent those apartments only to night owls? Maybe they had only enough power for two floors.

I laughed at my lame attempt to take my mind off the knot in my stomach. What Miss Pan had left unsaid was gnawing at me. What did Deng Xiaoping have to do with all of this, and what was the Premier of the People's Republic doing with Fiona's file?

I had to talk to Hugh.

CHAPTER 10

Tuesday, September 21, 1976

I batted sleepily at my alarm clock. The ringing did not stop. I batted again, this time sending the clock crashing to the floor. *Damn.* I sat up on the edge of the bed, grabbed the clock off the floor, pushed the off button, and started to lie back down. The ringing continued. *Damn again.* This time it was the phone. I got up and answered it.

"Bryan? Hugh, here. You up? It's after eleven."

"I just got up. How's Emma?"

"I'm afraid she's still shaken," Hugh said. "Her father's call this morning pepped her up somewhat, but she's never before encountered the kind of official callousness she suffered yesterday."

Emma and Hugh's opinion would change if they knew how much Rong and Miss Pan were risking by trying to get more information.

"Yes," I said, "there's no excuse for how we were treated. The sad thing is that they will probably be commended."

"I understand you phoned Aidan last night. Did he have any ideas on how to proceed?"

"He seems content to wait until the Bank of China verifies the fingerprints. As for the details of Fiona's death and the return of her property, I'm afraid we'll get no satisfaction on those issues."

Click.

"You sound tired."

"I didn't get much sleep last night. The call to MacKinnon didn't end until almost one. Then I tossed and turned for hours. I don't know when I finally dropped off."

"In that case, I won't keep you. I just wanted to check on your day yesterday. It sounds like a waiting game until we hear from the Bank of China."

"Look, Hugh, I have to talk to you."

"How about dinner? I'll check with Emma and give you a tinkle."

We said good-bye and hung up. I had barely put down the receiver when the phone rang again. It was Miss Pan.

"Mr. Paton, I was concerned that you'd gone out without me," she said. "Do you still want to go to the Temple of Heaven?"

"What? Oh . . . yes, just as we planned." I now realized that it was safest for Miss Pan if we talked at an outdoor tourist site.

"Good," she said. "Tomorrow, then. Oh, and by the way, I got hold of that information you were curious about. You know, about how the temple was built."

Click.

• • •

General Zhu fidgeted then took a long drink of tea. Briefings were an inevitable regimen for a new commander, but this one seemed interminable.

"... and so, in conclusion," the briefer droned, "the forces of the Beijing Military Region are ideologically prepared to fight a guerilla campaign against the Soviet hegemonic invaders should they undertake such a reckless adventure."

Zhu got up, and the other generals on his senior staff rose and stood at attention.

"Thank you, Colonel," Zhu said to the briefer. "Your techniques of socialist indoctrination are impressive." He turned to the generals. "Any questions or comments?"

Hearing none, Zhu strode toward the door Major Wang was holding open for him.

"Is he here?" Zhu asked as he approached Wang.

"Yes, sir, in your apartment, as you ordered," Wang replied.

"Is anyone with him?"

"No, sir."

General Zhu had sent Wang to the Beijing train station that morning to meet the train carrying his senior aide, Colonel Peng Ruiyi. Zhu had known Peng for nineteen years, ever since the colonel's grandfather, Peng Dehuai, had recommended him as a promising young officer. Zhu himself had been the beneficiary of such patronage when his own uncle had recommended him to Deng Xiaoping. Besides, it was not possible to spurn the grandson of a Long March veteran, one of only ten marshals ever in the PLA, and the then Minister of National Defense.

Peng, in classic skip-a-generation fashion, was as rough-hewn and blunt as his grandfather. At fifteen he had foregone a privileged billet at the Hunan Military Academy in favor of work repairing railroad tracks in his native Hunan province. After three years of backbreaking labor, Peng gave in to his mother's pleas and volunteered for the Red Army. Much to the dismay of his commanders, who wanted to curry favor with the old marshal, he would accept conscription only as a private in the infantry. His grandfather was delighted. Peng earned a battlefield officer's commission during the Korean War when, after their commander was killed, he led his company in taking a key bridge near Seoul during the Chinese Communist Volunteer Army's re-capture of that city.

Along with Peng's peerless Communist and military pedigree, Zhu valued him for his loyalty, integrity, and plainspoken nature. That was why he had entrusted to Peng the most dangerous and risky mission he had ever conceived: the protection of his daughter. And now it had ended badly. Well, there was nothing for it but to find out what had happened and go from there.

Major Wang opened the door to General Zhu's apartment. Zhu waved away the servant who had hurried to the door, tossed his hat on a chair, and went directly to his study.

"I'm not to be disturbed for any reason," he said to Wang as he closed the study door. Colonel Peng stood at attention.

"Please sit down, Colonel, and tell me what happened," Zhu said.

"Thank you, sir. I located your daughter just as you instructed and assumed custody of her. We then boarded—"

"How did you find her? And where?"

"Well, I found out that she never made it from the train station to the airport in Guangzhou, and Customs said they had not processed her in. Assuming she had been taken right from the train, Customs contacted Lo Wu to give them a description, then turned the matter over to the police. The police posted notices about a well-dressed unauthorized compatriot, but it was the neighborhood warden system that came through with a critical lead. The police eventually found her alone and locked up in the back of a medicine shop with just a fur coat. I assume the police are still looking for the men who took her. She said there were three of them and described them to the officers."

"Go on," Zhu said.

"After she had something to eat, we boarded the night train to Beijing. We were asleep when three soldiers, guns drawn, burst into our compartment. They woke us and demanded that I turn your daughter over to them. I refused, but they threatened to harm her if I interfered."

"I'm sure you did what you could. What happened then?"

"Seconds after they left our compartment, I went to the window. The sign on the platform said 'Lingkou.' Five soldiers were on the platform with your daughter. I assume that the other two had boarded the train earlier to delay it while the three dealt with us. Since there was nothing I could do without endangering your daughter further, I continued on to Beijing."

"Quite right. Where is Lingkou?" Zhu asked.

"Between Nanjing and Shanghai," Peng replied.

Zhu stood up, went to the door, and called to Major Wang, "Could you please get me a map of the Nanjing-Shanghai corridor."

"Yes, sir."

Zhu closed the door and sat down. "You're sure that the men who took her were soldiers?"

"Yes . . . well, no. That still bothers me. It could have been a masquerade."

"What was the condition of my daughter when you last saw her?"

"Excellent, sir."

"Is she . . . is she . . . I mean, what did she—"

"Is she pretty?" Peng offered.

Embarrassed, Zhu simply nodded.

"Yes, sir," Peng said.

"It's just that—" There was a knock on the study door. "Come."

"Your map, sir," Wang said.

"Thank you, Major." Zhu spread the map out on his desk. "Show me where Lingkou is."

"It's here," Peng said, "next to the Grand Canal, about 200 kilometers northwest of Shanghai and about 100 kilometers east of Nanjing, and—"

"—and only about 30 kilometers from the Yangtze River," Zhu finished. "Colonel, this was an extremely well-planned and executed abduction. They could have taken her anywhere. Down the Yangtze and out to sea, into Nanjing or Shanghai, even by barge up or down the Grand Canal."

"Or to a thousand other cities and villages in the Yangtze River delta."

"Yes, to a thousand other cities and villages in the Yangtze River delta." Zhu paced the room, trying to fathom the motives of his daughter's abductors.

"General," Peng said, "her abductors would see that she's fragile and probably couldn't endure an arduous journey. That argues for a site in or near Lingkou village. That doesn't give us much, but it does narrow the possibilities somewhat."

"Yes, but it still leaves us with all of Jiangsu province—and Shanghai. Shanghai is the radicals' home base, and this could be their handiwork. They might have assumed by now that I can't support Jiang Qing and are holding my daughter as leverage. But how on earth did they find out? Colonel, go back over the *Internal Intelligence Digest* reports for the last three months. Look for any mention of me, no matter how seemingly insignificant."

The *Digest* was the daily intelligence briefing for senior Chinese Communist Party officials. It was compiled from the thousands of daily reports Chinese intelligence operatives at home and abroad were required to submit to Beijing. It was considered so sensitive and its distribution was so restricted that even foreign intelligence services were not aware of its existence.

"And of your daughter, sir?" Peng asked.

"Huh? I'm sorry, what did you say?"

"Should I also look for any reference to your daughter?"

"Yes . . . no . . . why would she be mentioned?"

"Sir, with all due respect, I've been operating in the dark so far. At some point, you must confide in me about your daughter if I'm to be effective."

Peng's frank assessment was right on the mark, and Zhu knew it. He thought of the two women, one loved, one hated, at the center of his life and of the two tasks—the rescue of his daughter and the plot to seize power—that were now inextricably linked. The innocuous plan of a lonely father to see his daughter had been conceived when Mao was still alive. Mao's death had plunged him into the middle of the struggle that all Chinese dreaded, and his daughter was now a pawn in that struggle. It was time Peng knew the truth, especially if he were to ask his trusted associate to risk his life.

"You're right," Zhu said. "You're absolutely right."

For the next hour, Zhu told Peng the story of his infant daughter and of the moderates' plot, led by Ye Jianying and Wang Dongxing, to arrest Jiang Qing and her three key supporters before they could launch their coup d'état.

When Zhu finished, Peng said, "Well, sir. Jiang Qing is almost certainly involved in your daughter's disappearance."

"Colonel," Zhu said, "I want my daughter found. Are you willing to go back to Lingkou? As a member of my personal staff, you have greater latitude to operate than would an officer on my military region staff."

"Yes, sir. But this time I'd like to take a few troops with me. I have some good men whom I can trust to keep their mouths shut."

"Of course. And check with General Liang. His colleagues in Shanghai will know the area. Just don't tell them why you're there."

"No, sir. How much time do I have?"

"We plan to arrest all four radical leaders on October 1. I have to know she's safe by then."

"Yes, sir, but why National Day?"

"That afternoon the leadership will give the usual reception for the diplomatic corps in the Great Hall of the People where my troops are in charge of security. There will be a Politburo meeting immediately before the reception, which means that Jiang and her three henchmen will be together in one place. The troops will isolate central Beijing and arrest them at the meeting."

"An excellent plan, sir."

"Marshal Ye set it up. He and Wang Dongxing are still recruiting others in the leadership. He also convinced the Politburo yesterday to name Premier Hua as Chairman of the Party. That keeps Mao's most powerful position from going to his grieving widow, who will shed crocodile tears only as long as it takes to gain the power necessary to launch a reign of terror."

"The post of Chairman would have given Jiang all the power she would need to checkmate the moderate leadership before they could mobilize to stop her," Peng said.

"Exactly. What's more, as of yesterday's meeting, we're now pretty confident of victory. When the dust settles, we'll use the Party propaganda machinery to rehabilitate Deng Xiaoping."

"October 1," Peng said. "Only ten more days. That makes my task all the more immediate."

"Yes, but please be clear about one thing. I won't commit my troops until I know my daughter is safe."

"But sir, you can't mean—"

"I do, Colonel."

Peng seemed to shrink back on himself. "Please excuse my outburst, sir."

"Of course. The political situation has all of us on edge. I've never avoided a challenge. Now I'm confronted with the two most serious of my life. With your help, I intend to engage them both head-on."

"Yes, sir." Peng stood and started for the door. Abruptly he turned. "General, do Minister Ye and the others know about your daughter? Do they know you won't deploy your forces if I don't find her?"

"No, they don't. And they need never know. I have full confidence you'll succeed."

"Thank you, sir."

"And Colonel Peng," Zhu said, "no one other than you and I knows about my daughter. You must operate in complete secrecy."

. . .

That afternoon, Peng re-read the last three months of the *Internal Intelligence Digest*. He had read them before, but only as part of his daily routine, highlighting for General Zhu those entries that had military significance and discarding the merely salacious or titillating. In doing so, he had developed a practiced eye for recognizing and skipping over the dross. But now he had to read carefully every entry. There was no way to predict which, if any, contained the precious nugget that could provide a lead and shorten the time needed to find and rescue Zhu's daughter. And Peng desperately needed every minute of the next ten days. He pored over the breathless account of what the bug heard in the boudoir of the French president's mistress; the gruesome secret transcript, purloined by China's operative in Santiago, of the torture and death of a leftist student by Pinochet's secret police; a nauseating account of Idi Amin's cannibalistic preference for young children; and on and on. He found nothing even vaguely connected to Zhu or the girl.

Peng hated to come up empty-handed, particularly where his boss was concerned. He remembered clearly those dangerous days in 1959 when Zhu had protected him, then a young lieutenant on his staff. At a leadership conference in Lushan, his grandfather had criticized the Great Leap Forward, Mao's deeply flawed attempt to industrial-ize China's agrarian economy virtually overnight. Mao lashed out furiously at Peng Dehuai, dismissing him not only from his post as Minister of National Defense but from the Party as well. Mao had made support for the Great Leap Forward the litmus test of sup-port for himself, and no one else in the leadership dared to acknowl-edge what they all knew to be true—that Mao's policy was a great leap backward.

In 1966, during the early days of the Cultural Revolution, Jiang Qing found Peng Dehuai easy pickings. She dispatched her Red Guards to make an example of the aging warrior. They tortured and beat him so severely that his internal organs were crushed and his spine shattered. But he never gave in. After one particularly severe beating, he was said to have pounded on a table so ferociously that the cell walls shook while he shouted at his torturers, "I fear nothing! Your days are numbered!" Peng Dehuai eventually paid with his life for speaking truth to power.

Peng shuddered as he recalled those painful memories. He had idol-ized his grandfather, and Zhu had put himself in considerable danger by protecting him, both in 1959 and in 1966. He was damned if he was going to let Jiang get away with blackmail now.

Peng rose from his desk and began pacing his small office. He grabbed the stack of papers in his in-box and began reading the first one, the *Internal Intelligence Digest* for today, Tuesday, September 21. The lead entry immediately caught his eye:

THE FABLE ON KEEPING ONE'S WORD

Zeng Zi was Confucius's disciple. He was widely known for his filial obedience.

One time his wife had to go to market in a hurry. Her child wanted to go along and clung fast to her.

"Listen to me," she coaxed the little boy. "I shan't be

long. When I get back, we'll kill the pig for dinner."

When his wife returned home, Zeng Zi sharpened his knife and set about to kill the pig.

His wife immediately stopped him. "Don't take it seriously! I was just soothing the child."

Zeng Zi quickly drew his wife aside. "We must keep our word, even with little children. Children don't know much. They learn from their parents and listen to what their parents teach them. If you lie to him now, you're teaching him to lie later. And once you've lied to him, he will never believe you again. This is not the proper way to teach a child."

Having said this, Zeng Zi killed the pig for dinner.

All of this was intriguing, but what really caught Peng's eye was the note appended to the bottom:

Who among us is the New Zeng Zi, and why has he betrayed New China and his own New Daughter by lying to both? (Source: ZNHP401)

That was it. The appearance of the fable, even in the secret *I.I.D.*, was the beginning of a campaign to discredit his boss, or worse. He was sickened by the thought.

But then there was the source code. They were usually easy to figure out. "BK44," for example, meant that an agent number 44 in Bangkok had submitted the entry. But "ZNHP401"? Peng realized he would have to check the *I.I.D.* manual, which was kept in the arms vault of the Beijing Military Region commander. Only General Zhu was authorized to have the vault's combination, but he had insisted that Peng also be cleared to enter the vault. The Ministry of Public Security had raised a stink but gave in when Zhu sent them a tartly worded memorandum saying that he had already given the combination to Peng. The Ministry had sent Zhu an equally tart reply noting his "obstinate attitude" and informing him that his confidential personnel folder had been amended accordingly.

Peng went through to Zhu's office. The entrance to the vault was located in a false closet specifically designed as a cover. Peng rotated the dial for the combination, depressed the lever, and pulled open the heavy bombproof door. Along one wall was a locked rifle case containing ten Kalashnikovs. Below the case, a shelf contained stacked ammunition boxes and rifle-cleaning equipment. On the opposite wall were gas masks, first-aid kits, and other survival paraphernalia. At the rear stood four file cabinets. Peng opened the first cabinet and took out the *I.I.D.* manual. He opened it to the source-code section and ran his finger down the list: "ZNHP401" was not there. There was, however, a footnote at the bottom of the last page that read "For codes ending in 'P,' consult the leadership appendix."

Peng had heard about but never seen the leadership appendix, which contained personal data on the senior echelon. Unauthorized use of the appendix carried severe penalties. General Zhu would incur the penalties as well, and the Ministry of Public Security would relish the retribution they would be obliged to visit on his boss. Should he ask General Zhu before consulting it? No, he knew what Zhu would tell him.

He pulled the appendix out of the file cabinet and opened it to the source-code section. According to the first paragraph, "ZNHP" referred to a Politburo member residing in Zhongnanhai. But who was "401"? Peng leafed through the manual. His hand began to tremble as he ran his finger down the page labeled "300–400." A drop of sweat landed on 401 at the same time that his finger reached it. He coursed horizontally to the name bearing *I.I.D.* code 401.

He froze. Code 401 was assigned to the former Minister of Public Security, now Premier and Chairman of the Chinese Communist Party, Hua Guofeng.

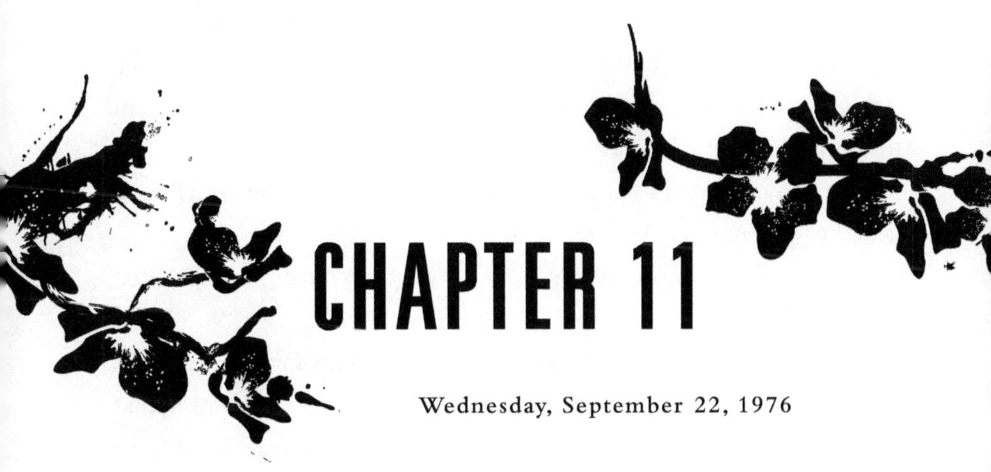

CHAPTER 11

Wednesday, September 22, 1976

After finally grabbing a seat on the crowded rush-hour bus, Peng glanced through the window, as if doing so would erase what he had just seen in the *People's Daily*. The person next to him was, coincidentally, reading the same article.

He looked back at his newspaper. There it was: "The Fable on Keeping One's Word," the same fable that had appeared in the *Internal Intelligence Digest* the day before. Except that now it was no longer secret. All of China was reading between the lines to determine which senior official was under attack. The article seared his eyes.

He had to warn General Zhu. He rose from his seat to get off at the next stop and return to the Ministry. As he stepped into the crowded aisle, a placid-faced elderly woman with bound feet lunged for his seat, elbowing out of the way a brawny teenager who also wanted it. He fought his way to the door, exited, and walked the short distance to the Ministry.

Peng went directly to General Zhu's apartment. One of the servants admitted him and directed him to the study. Peng tapped lightly at the study door.

"Come." Zhu was sitting at the map table, the *People's Daily* spread out in front of him. A bottle of Scotch, a half-filled whiskey glass, and a pack of cigarettes sat on the table. A half-smoked cigarette smoldered in the cradle of a crystal ashtray.

"Ah, Colonel Peng," Zhu said, "I thought that might be you. Please, sit down. I assume you've seen today's paper."

Peng sat down in one of the chairs at the map table. "Yes, sir. What do you make of it?"

"It's worrying, I grant you that. But what I find most revealing is that it doesn't include the footnote you saw in the *I.I.D.* You know, that sentence at the bottom about the New Zeng Zi betraying New China and lying to his New Daughter?"

"Yes, sir, but what does publication of the fable mean? Can it mean that the Premier isn't with us? Is it possible that he's holding your daughter hostage?"

"I'm not sure," Zhu said, "but it appears certain that whoever is ultimately responsible for this article also has my daughter and is using her in order to secure my allegiance. By going public with the fable, that person has upped the ante—and underestimated me."

Zhu sipped his whiskey and drew several times on his cigarette. Peng knew to remain silent.

"Frankly," Zhu said at last, "I'd be willing to say it's not Hua Guofeng. He hasn't got the balls. No, there's only one person capable of this level of audacity."

"Jiang Qing?" Peng said.

Zhu nodded. "Jiang Qing."

• • •

Located at the eastern end of Eurasia, China is prey to winds that blow thousands of miles across the Russian steppes and Siberia. By the time they reach China, they are cruelly frigid and stripped of most of their moisture. The desiccated wind turns skin into parchment and slices surgically through garments in a frenzied and invariably successful search for bone. In 1976, winter on the north China plain arrived early. By the last week of September, the citizens of Beijing were shivering as if it were already January.

Anticipating a short stay, I had not brought winter clothing, and there was nothing available in Beijing without a ration card. I wore the only jacket I had.

"You're dressed much too lightly," Miss Pan deadpanned as she greeted me in the hotel lobby. The driver was standing a few paces behind her.

"This jacket is the warmest thing I have with me," I said. "I'll be okay. I have a wool sweater on underneath."

"At least you have gloves."

The only reason I had gloves, or the wool sweater for that matter, was that Ah-yee had tucked them in my suitcase. She obviously knew better than I what weather I would face.

As we drove to the Temple of Heaven, south of Tiananmen Square, I scanned the guidebook entry. The Temple was surrounded by a park many times the size of the square. This lent even more majesty to what was already one of the most impressive structures in China. The Temple's massive triple conical roofs were covered in deep blue tiles, each topped with a gold-plated knob. Its traditional Chinese architecture made it the symbol of ancient Beijing.

The driver dropped Miss Pan and me on the edge of the park just south of the Museum of Natural Science. The contrast between the overheated car and the glacial Beijing gale was stark.

"Invigorating," Miss Pan said as we exited the car.

"Not the word I'd have chosen."

Miss Pan was about to reply when her cotton cap blew into a crowd waiting at a bus stop. It flew into the chest of a girl who held it fast as Miss Pan scurried toward her to retrieve it. They giggled and exchanged pleasantries. Determined to avoid another similar mishap, Miss Pan wrapped her muffler around her head and tied it securely under her chin.

We walked toward the Temple in silence. I assumed that Miss Pan wanted to get beyond the busy street and the park entrance before she started to talk. It was a Wednesday morning, and there were few people in the Temple grounds. The wind created whirlwinds on the dusty path, and the sun struggled to glimmer through the city haze.

"Rong says he's very nervous about the case of Li Guangmei," Miss Pan said as we emerged from the park onto the cement-tiled square immediately surrounding the Temple. We were still a good fifty yards from the Temple itself. "He says he is now certain someone very high in the government is monitoring the case."

"But . . . why?"

Miss Pan stopped abruptly and turned to face me. "Please, Mr. Paton, lower your voice. This square is famous for its ability to carry sound great distances."

Just then a large crowd of foreigners led by a Chinese woman holding aloft a small flag entered the square from behind one of the Temple outbuildings and walked en masse in our direction. As they neared our position, I heard the Chinese woman droning in English, "At the northern end is the main Temple hall, the Hall of Prayer for Good Harvests, which has a history dating back over 500 years. It was here that the Emperor prayed in person for abundant crops."

We did not speak until the group was well into the park. Once we were alone, Miss Pan said only, "We will now move on to visit the Temple itself."

When we reached the marble platform on which the Temple stood, she made a pretense of explaining a feature on the platform's marble railing.

"We can talk here without being overheard," she said, pointing at some decorative doodad.

I nodded admiringly. "Could you please tell me what Mr. Rong said?"

"I'm afraid the case of Li Guangmei is far more complex, far more serious than Rong thought." She trembled, in spite of the fact that the Temple now sheltered us from the strongest wind. "He advised very strongly that you accept the conclusion that the body you saw at the hospital is Li Guangmei's and take it back to Hong Kong. A senior leader has taken an interest in her case. Rong said it could be dangerous for you to remain in Beijing any longer. I agree."

I was stunned. I had been prepared for bad news, but this amounted to a threat against my life. I bristled at the thought of a macabre tug-of-war over Fiona's remains.

"No," I said. "I refuse."

"What?"

"I won't be intimidated. I refuse to go back to Hong Kong until I have a positive fingerprint identification. We've been through this before."

"Mr. Paton, you are a guest here. You have no choice but to obey the laws of the People's Republic of China," Miss Pan said in exasperation.

Suddenly, out of the corner of my eye, I saw the shadow of a person move across the Temple's façade. I turned. Our driver, hands behind his back, was strolling along the platform. Miss Pan had seen him over my shoulder. As the driver came abreast of us, he nodded "hello."

"Now, if that's perfectly clear," Miss Pan said, "I suggest we continue our tour inside the Temple."

The driver strolled on around the circular temple and out of view.

Miss Pan pointed to the Temple door. "That way."

I followed her. Inside it was dark, but I could discern that we were alone.

"We can talk here," Miss Pan said softly, "but please keep your voice low."

"Who is this senior leader who's interested in Fiona's case? Do you mean Premier Hua? You already told me he had her file." I was eager to finally get the information before we were interrupted yet again.

"No, it's someone else, someone extremely powerful. Premier Hua summoned Li Guangmei's file on the leader's behalf so that the leader could remain . . . uh . . . anon . . . anon . . ."

"Anonymous," I finished. "It means unknown—behind the scenes. But who is it?"

"Chairman Mao's widow, Jiang Qing. Jiang Qing is the one who needs to remain anonymous."

• • •

That night I had dinner with Hugh and Emma at their apartment, and afterward I helped them wash up. I was eager to discuss with them all that Miss Pan had told me, but I did not dare risk speaking inside.

"After we finish here," I said, "let's stretch our legs a bit."

"What a good idea," Emma said.

We put on our jackets and went out. There was a harvest moon glimmering through the ubiquitous haze. The wind was still frigid, and the air was laden with grit as fine as face powder that I tasted whenever I spoke.

"The wind is coming off the Gobi tonight," Emma said, "and bringing part of the desert with it. It wreaks havoc with delicate equipment like stereos."

We strolled north in the general direction of Ri Tan Park and the British Embassy. Unlike the rest of Beijing, Jianguomenwai was well lighted by numerous streetlights. There was no one out except the PLA guards stationed in front of each embassy compound.

"Hugh," I said after we had walked a while, "can you think of any reason why Hua Guofeng and Jiang Qing would be interested in Fiona?"

"What?" Hugh and Emma said simultaneously.

We were near the gate of the Polish Embassy compound. The PLA guard at the entrance turned to look at us. After he assured himself that nothing was amiss, he resumed staring straight ahead. Hugh, obviously shaken, motioned us to walk on out of earshot of the guard. We stopped in the shadow of a tree.

"Where did you hear that?" Hugh asked in a tone of grave concern. I could see by the look of distress in Emma's eyes that she was unnerved as well.

"From Miss Pan . . . today, at the Temple of Heaven. She said Rong told her. He's the fellow Emma and I met with at the Ministry of Public Security."

"Bryan," Hugh said, "you must tell me all that transpired between you and Miss Pan. And please be careful to differentiate between what Miss Pan personally knows and what this Rong fellow told her."

For the next hour, as we strolled through Ri Tan Park, I related the complete story. When I finished, Hugh asked if I had read that morning's *People's Daily*. I had not.

"There was an article," Hugh explained, "in the form of a fable. It marks the start of a campaign to destroy someone. We haven't yet figured out who is being targeted, and neither have the analysts in London."

"What's the fable got to do with Fiona?" I asked.

"Well," Hugh continued, "the leadership of the Party propaganda apparatus—it publishes all newspapers in China—are allies of Jiang Qing. Anything major that appears in the *People's Daily* has to have her personal approval. The fable is targeting someone who is threatening to her, almost certainly someone in the moderate camp. Your information that Jiang has Fiona's file leads me to suspect that Fiona's case is somehow tied to the power struggle. Nothing in China ever occurs in a vacuum."

"Miss Pan volunteered that both she and Rong come from Deng Xiaoping's native village. She didn't explain why she wanted me to know that, but it must be that she and Rong—"

"—are in the moderate camp," Hugh finished. "That's why they're willing to help you. They are not isolationists. Bryan, you must be much more careful until we find out how Fiona fits into all of this. You don't want to anger the likes of Jiang Qing or her supporters. And believe me, she has many. For the next few days, I suggest you stay close to the hotel and don't contact Miss Pan or anyone else. In the meantime, I'll report everything to London and Hong Kong and ask for instructions."

"What should I do if the Bank of China in Hong Kong replies on the fingerprints?"

"Unless I miss my guess," Hugh replied, "I very much doubt that you'll have an answer any time soon. If, as I suspect, Fiona's remains are key to a larger scenario, then the radicals will want to delay."

"But can they reach into the Bank?"

"Both the radicals and the moderates have henchmen in every institution. And both know that, this time, if they lose, they're dead."

CHAPTER 12

Friday, September 24, 1976

Aidan MacKinnon was famously slow to anger. "He has the patience of Job" Miss Chao was fond of saying, and not always in admiration. She thought that obstreperous subordinates and taunting opponents should feel the full force of MacKinnon's rhetorical wrath. And she was about to get her wish.

"Miss Chao," MacKinnon bellowed through the closed door to his office, "get me Cai Yimou at the Bank of China—again."

When Miss Chao had the Bank's Foreign Affairs Officer on the phone, she transferred the call to MacKinnon.

"Mr. Cai?" he said with forced cheerfulness. "Aidan MacKinnon, here. Listen, I just wanted to—"

"Mr. MacKinnon. How is your good self this afternoon?" Cai knew very well that MacKinnon was angry. When they spoke earlier that morning, Cai said that the fingerprints had arrived from Beijing late Thursday afternoon and would probably be transferred to the Royal

Hong Kong Police Department's Fingerprint Bureau today. MacKinnon had just heard from the Bureau that they still had not arrived. Cai had to have known.

"Very well, thank you," MacKinnon replied. "Mr. Cai, I will be sending a messenger to collect the fingerprints and take them to the police department. This will expedite things as well as assist you at the Bank. He will be there within ten minutes."

"Your offer is very kind, indeed," Cai said, "but as I told you this morning, the relevant Bank departments must review the case before taking any further action."

MacKinnon had grown weary of the Chinese Communist penchant for redressing more than a century of grievances by being bloody-minded. He decided to try one more tack. If it did not produce results, he would have done with Cai and the Bank of China and try another avenue to expedite identification of Fiona's remains.

"Mr. Cai," MacKinnon said, "you're doubtless aware of the magnitude of the tragedy that has befallen the Li family. Li Dak-chung has lost his only daughter. I appeal to your sense of—"

"Mr. MacKinnon, Li Guangmei was a Chinese citizen. Do not make hollow appeals based on bourgeois sentimentality. Her case will be handled consistent with—"

MacKinnon slammed the phone down. Cai had jerked his chain once too often. MacKinnon knew he had few options. In the ordinary course of events, it was simply a matter of deducing what a person like Cai was really after and providing it. MacKinnon was a master at making such deductions. Indeed, he had built an extremely successful and lucrative career on doing so. For MacKinnon, the key to life was negotiation and compromise, but he now realized that he would have to circumvent Cai and the Bank.

He could do it. He had encountered a broad spectrum of people during his more than three decades in Hong Kong. He was a personal friend of the governor as well as of the English matrons who enforced a rigid village morality on Hong Kong's tiny but powerful expatriate community. He was equally conversant, however, with Wanchai bar girls, Triad chieftains, and Communist labor union bosses.

Ordinarily MacKinnon was loath to call on his questionable contacts. Such a call invariably involved an obligation to repay the favor. He had never turned his back on such an obligation, nor had he ever done anything illegal in repaying one. But convincing Cai to be compassionate might entail methods the details of which he did not wish to know.

MacKinnon rolled his chair to the credenza and opened the doors. He took from inside the telephone he used for confidential calls, those which Miss Chao did not monitor or transcribe. He picked up the receiver and dialed Dai Kai-kui.

CHAPTER 13

Saturday, September 25, 1976

Today was the start of the horse racing season at Happy Valley. MacKinnon was a member of the Board of Directors of the Royal Hong Kong
Jockey Club and owned a luxury box atop the racecourse. He took seriously his role as a director, and he and Glynis never missed opening day.
This year, as usual, they had invited a cross section of local luminaries to
join them in their box for a day of punting and for feasting on a lavish
catered buffet and bar. As at Ascot and Churchill Downs, opening day at
Happy Valley was a semiformal occasion.

Aidan and Glynis MacKinnon exited their limousine in the relative
security of the private directors' entrance. Barely ten feet from them but
separated by a chain-link fence, hordes of punters streamed toward the
public gates. The weather was typically subtropical, overcast with stifling
heat and humidity.

"Looks like the relentless afternoon downpour won't grant us a
day's reprieve," Glynis said with grim resolve. She loved her life in Hong

Kong, but nowhere else with a similar climate held the least attraction for her.

"Yes, I dare say you're right," Aidan replied.

He put his arm around his wife's waist as they walked down the hallway under the grandstand toward the elevators. A uniformed page held open for them the elevator door marked, in Chinese and English, "Lift Reserved for Grandstand Box Patrons." Another uniformed page greeted them as they emerged from the elevator into the air-conditioned splendor of a wide high-ceilinged hallway carpeted in navy blue. To the right, on the racecourse side of the hallway, were doors to individual boxes. On the opposite side, next to the elevators, was a large glass-and-metal enclosure with six betting windows. Each window was staffed by an employee wearing a uniform identical to those worn by the pages.

The MacKinnons entered their box, which was more than three times the size of the average first-class hotel room. The Jockey Club catering staff had already provisioned the bar and set up the buffet table, which featured an ice sculpture of a galloping horse and jockey. Chairs and tables with starched linens dotted the large room. A bright red carpet with gold medallions covered the floor. The wall facing the racecourse was floor-to-ceiling glass, except for a door at the far right, which led outside to thirty-six stadium-style seats in three tiered rows covered by the extended roof of the grandstand. The seat cushions and padded backs matched the interior carpet. The MacKinnons' guests arrived, appropriate speeches were delivered, and the governor declared the 127th Happy Valley racing season under way.

After the third race and following lunch, all settled down outside with their drinks for the remainder of the afternoon's races. Waiters ferried refills, and pages scurried back and forth to the betting kiosk to place bets for the guests.

MacKinnon enjoyed the betting process, so he normally placed his bets and collected his winnings himself. He went out into the elevator lobby and started toward the kiosk. A dozen or more people were walking to or from the betting windows or standing around in groups chatting. A woman who appeared drunk, her purple-flowered hat askew, was arguing loudly with a man in one of the kiosks.

A man wearing a metallic-gray sharkskin suit with matching paisley silk tie and breast-pocket handkerchief approached and laid his hand on MacKinnon's arm.

"Hello, Aidan," he said. "I thought you'd be here today."

MacKinnon stopped and turned to face the man. He was squat and overfed. His heavily pomaded hair fit him like a cap, and a gold tooth flashed when he spoke. They were in the middle of the lobby. Two other men had followed the man into the hallway and stood a short distance behind him.

"Kindly take your hand off me," MacKinnon said evenly.

The man quickly removed his hand. "Do you remember me?"

"Yes. You're Harry Chen, the owner of that Macau casino. I really have nothing to say to you." Mackinnon thought Chen looked like a caricature of one of Run Run Shaw's movie gangsters. *Was it intentional or in his genes?* He turned and walked away.

"I really think you'll want to hear me out," Chen called out. "It's about Fiona Li."

MacKinnon walked back to Chen. "Kindly lower your voice and leash your hounds. What about Fiona Li?"

"Actually," Chen said, "I had hoped Li Dak-chung would be here today so I could talk to him directly."

"Understandably, he's secluded at home until he finds out what happened to his daughter."

"Well, I think I can help him," Chen said. "Certain people have contacted me with information. And a certain person has asked for my help. With respect, it would be a mistake for you and Li to reject my offer."

"If you're in any way involved with Fiona's death," MacKinnon said, "I shall personally—"

The two men behind Chen stiffened and reached inside their suit coats. "Calm down, MacKinnon," Chen interrupted.

"Is this your perverse idea of getting revenge against me for suing your casino? Because if it is, you've made a serious mistake."

Chen looked smug, then narrowed his eyes and whispered through clenched teeth, "If I ever wanted to retaliate against you—and I don't— believe me, you and you alone would feel it. I would never, *never*, punish a fellow Chinese like Li Dak-chung for your bad deeds." Chen adjusted his tie and his sleeves so that his gaudy diamond-and-ruby cuff links were visible. "I have information for Li Dak-chung about Miss Li. Will you arrange a meeting?"

"I will advise my client of your offer."

"That's fine . . . very fine." Chen smiled broadly. "Now then, Aidan . . . uh . . . may I call you by your first name?"

"No."

"Mr. MacKinnon it is, then. May I invite you to my box for some refreshment?"

"What box?"

"Ah, the gods have seen fit to grant my business ventures good fortune this year. I just purchased a Jockey Club membership."

"We'll see about that," MacKinnon said. "Your sort isn't welcome here."

"Because I'm Chinese?"

"I won't dignify that comment with a reply. You're a two-bit gangster, exactly like your father."

MacKinnon knew a good deal about Chen's heritage. His father, Du Yuesheng, nicknamed "the Triad King," had been leader of Shanghai's infamous Green Gang from the early 1920s until the Communist victory in 1949, when he fled to Hong Kong. The Green Gang ruled the Shanghai underworld with an iron fist, principally because one of Du's top lieutenants, Huang "Pockmarked" Jinrong, was also the chief of detectives in Shanghai's French Concession. The gang controlled the gamut of lucrative criminal enterprises—opium dens, brothels, hired killers, the slave-girl trade, protection rackets, and gold smuggling. They also controlled several key trade unions. The opium trade, in particular, accorded the gang enormous power; and Shanghai's French Concession soon had a monopoly on opium throughout China.

In 1927 Du ordered his Green Gang thugs to support Chiang Kai-shek and the KMT in brutally suppressing the Communists and expelling them from Shanghai. In the course of the fighting, Chiang's troops and their Green Gang allies killed more than five thousand. At the time, the KMT was allied with the Communists to try to bring some semblance of order to post-imperial, warlord-ravaged China. Chiang's betrayal of his Communist partners precipitated China's civil war.

Harry Chen was born in Shanghai in 1949, shortly before Du fled to Hong Kong with his family and transferred his Triad operation there. Chen was raised in the British Crown Colony in ostentatious opulence, a lifestyle that continued even after his father died in 1951. But it was not a happy childhood. His mother was shunned by the English and Chinese matrons who served as gatekeepers to respectable society. As a result of this ostracism, Chen was tutored at home rather than attending one of the Colony's exclusive private schools. As part of his tutelage, he was groomed by his godfather to take over the Du family business. In the process, he acquired a character of hale and well-met greasiness with a thinly coated patina of British refinement.

MacKinnon saw that his remark about Du had hit home. Chen was furious and hiding it badly.

"If you'll give me your home phone number, I'll call you in the morning to find out where to meet you and Li Dak-chung," Chen said.

"I'll be in my office after ten. Call me there."

MacKinnon turned and walked away. *Harry Chen. Good God.* He was still trying to buy his way into society. And now he was somehow involved in Fiona's disappearance. Whatever that might mean, it did not bode well.

CHAPTER 14

Sunday, September 26, 1976

MacKinnon rose before dawn and went to the small greenhouse in the garden of his house to tend his collection of orchids. A little more than two hours later, he drove to Central for early Sunday services at St. John's Cathedral. He parked in the multistory car park between St. John's and the Hilton Hotel. After the service, he strolled down to the Hilton for breakfast. Typhoon Iris had grazed Hong Kong six days earlier. The Colony's superb typhoon tracking system had given ample warning of Iris's approach so that only a dozen or so people were injured by flying debris from the 95-kilometer winds. The thrashing rain and lightning, some of it horizontal across the harbor, had scrubbed the air clean of city and factory fumes.

After breakfast, MacKinnon set out to walk the three or so blocks to Hutchison House. Thanks to the typhoon, the morning was uncharacteristically cool, with a sea breeze that swept away, if only temporarily, the blanket of humidity that usually cosseted the city. Rather than take the overhead pedestrian walkway direct from the Hilton to Hutchison House, he detoured across Chater Garden to the waterfront and Queen's Pier. Dozens of Filipina maids had already collected in the garden, a number that would swell to several thousand by midday as they gathered on their day off for conversation and mutual support.

When he reached Queen's Pier, MacKinnon stopped and gazed across the harbor to Kowloon. It was not quite 9:00 a.m., and the air, though still fresh, was warming rapidly. He turned toward City Hall. About a dozen or so people were standing in the square between the modern structure and the harbor practicing tai chi with ballet-like synchronicity. He watched as they finished "Grasping the Sparrow's Tail" and flowed into "Waving at the Clouds." As the group broke up, one of them waved at MacKinnon and walked toward him.

"What a pleasure to see you out and about," MacKinnon said.

"I couldn't waste this rare and beautiful autumn morning," Li Dakchung replied. "I suspected that this view and the companionship of my old exercise group would raise my spirits."

"Right you are." MacKinnon took out a cigar, clipped the end, and lit it. "There's been a development I think you should consider. Not about Fiona's remains, unfortunately, but about getting information on how she died."

"You know that I will go to any lengths to discover how my daughter was murdered."

"I'm afraid this involves a rather unsavory character whose motives may be entirely mercenary."

"I'm quite prepared to pay his price if his information is credible," Li replied. "Who is this person?"

"Harry Chen."

A look of disgust clouded Li's face.

"Yes, I know," MacKinnon said. "I ran into him yesterday at Happy Valley. He wouldn't tell me what he knows. He insists on telling you himself. I distrust his motives, but there's no denying his ability to extract information from across the Bamboo Curtain."

"When do I meet with him?" Li asked.

MacKinnon was surprised by how quickly Li had accepted Chen's demand for a meeting. Still, he had a duty to client and friend.

"Dak-chung, let me meet with him first and tell him—"

"Aidan. I know all about Harry Chen and his Triad operation. But if he has information about Fiona, then I must meet with him."

"As you will," MacKinnon said. "He is supposed to call me at my office at ten this morning. Running into you saves me calling you at home. May I suggest we meet him at the office as soon as he can get there?"

"I agree," Li said. "Aidan, I know you disapprove of my meeting with Chen." Li thought a while, then spoke again, "Do you mind if we walk to Hutchison House? I have a story I want to tell you."

"No, of course not."

"Good," Li said. "Just let me tell Lao Ma to go on ahead with the car."

Li and MacKinnon strolled past HMS *Tamar*, the headquarters of British Forces Hong Kong, and up Murray Road toward Hutchison House.

"You know," Li said, "in Shanghai, when Gwei-yu and I were young, our father taught us many outdoor games, which we played for hours in the garden of our house. He knew that children love games, but he also wanted to instill in us Confucian values. So every game he devised also illustrated an ancient Chinese precept.

"After an afternoon of play and then dinner, Gwei-yu and I were exhausted—but not too exhausted for our favorite part of the day. After we washed up and got in bed, our father would come to our room and tell us a story. We didn't realize it at the time, but every story drew on the game we'd played that day.

"Our favorite game was Lure the Swallow from her Nest. We never tired of it. My father was pleased that it was our favorite because he considered the precept it taught—blunt an opponent's advance by luring him into emptiness—to be extremely important."

"I think I see."

"Luring Fiona's murderer off safe ground and into unfamiliar territory will give me enormous advantage," Li said. "I do not have eyes to see inside China. So I must deal with a person like Harry Chen, who does have such eyes."

• • •

Harry Chen arrived at Hutchison House shortly after eleven. He ordered his bodyguards to wait in the Bull and Bear pub on the ground floor while he went up to Bishops. Miss Chao, who was in the office catching up on filing, opened the main door for him.

"Mr. MacKinnon and Mr. Li are waiting for you," she said, while trying to avoid staring at Chen's white patent-leather oxfords. "Right this way."

MacKinnon and Li stood when Miss Chao and Chen entered MacKinnon's office. MacKinnon took a few steps toward Chen. "Hello, Mr. Chen." Turning his head toward Li, he said, "Harry Chen, may I introduce Li Dak-chung." Chen extended his hand to Li. Li hesitated then shook it perfunctorily and quickly sat down, as did Chen and MacKinnon.

Miss Chao broke the frosty silence by asking whether anyone wanted some refreshment. MacKinnon and Li declined, but Chen, obviously uneasy, asked for coffee. "White, please." Miss Chao left to fetch it.

"Mr. Chen," Li said, "what information—"

"Call me Harry, please."

Chen leaned back in the wing chair and grinned broadly at Li, revealing teeth heavily yellowed by years of two-pack-a-day nicotine addiction. He pulled out Lucky Strikes and offered them to Li and MacKinnon. Both declined.

"Mind if I smoke?" he asked.

MacKinnon shook his head "no" and pushed a large ashtray across the coffee table to Chen. It nearly slid off. Chen grabbed it and laughed nervously. MacKinnon and Li remained expressionless. Chen took a Zippo lighter from the outside pocket of his sport coat and lit a cigarette. In spite of the heavy air-conditioning, beads of sweat appeared on his upper lip and trickled from his forehead down the sides of his face.

Li cleared his throat, "Mr. Chen, what information do you possess about the murder of my daughter?"

Chen shifted in his seat and crossed one leg over the other. "I . . . uh . . . someone has contacted me regarding your . . . uh . . . case. I . . . I simply want to be of help. That's all, I swear." He held the smoldering cigarette between the tips of two fingers and used the side of his hand to wipe away the sweat trickling down his face.

"Did you have anything—?" Li began.

"Who contacted—?" MacKinnon said at the same time then deferred to Li.

"Mr. Chen, did you have anything to do with the murder of my daughter?"

"No."

Li sighed.

"I swear!" Chen shouted.

"Mr. Chen," MacKinnon said, "please calm down. We're not accusing you of anything. We're just gathering information."

"Then you've come to the right place. But I will be treated with respect. That's the least I demand if your family expects me to help."

"Is that your only price?" Li asked. "Our respect?"

Chen stubbed out his cigarette and immediately lit another. MacKinnon noticed that the fingers where Chen held his cigarettes were stained yellow.

"My price, as you call it," Chen said, "is not to be treated like a rabid dog afflicted with mange."

"Don't talk rot," MacKinnon said. "No one's treated you with anything but the utmost courtesy. We can't be faulted on that account. We are under a great deal of stress from being unable to get a positive identification of Fiona Li's remains."

"Well," Chen said, "it just so happens I can be of help on that score as well. I've heard through the grapevine—never mind how—that a fellow named Cai at the Bank of China is being, shall we say, uncooperative. As a symbol of my sincerity, Aidan, you have my personal guarantee that Mr. Cai will call you tomorrow morning to say that the problem has been resolved."

"How on earth—"

"—did I know about Cai?" Chen said. "Let's just say my sources are many and varied. They're the lifeblood of a man in my line of work."

MacKinnon thought back to the call he had made the previous Friday afternoon to Dai Kai-kui, head of Hong Kong's most powerful Communist labor union. He had met Dai years earlier when the governor asked MacKinnon to mediate a particularly acrimonious labor dispute. MacKinnon was successful and, in the process, earned the respect and gratitude of both business and labor. Although their politics were decidedly different, over the years both Dai and MacKinnon had made a point of keeping in touch and, occasionally, did the odd favor for one another.

Bloody hell. Had Dai used Chen to get to Cai? He would never have suspected Dai to be mixed up with the likes of Harry Chen. But then, who would have thought he himself would have dealings with either of them?

"You mentioned a moment ago," he now said aloud, "that someone had contacted you about the case. Who?"

Chen raised his eyebrows and looked at MacKinnon, then at Li, then back at MacKinnon. "You mean you don't know?" His disbelief seemed genuine.

"Obviously not." Li glared at Chen.

"No. Sorry. I just thought you knew, that's all. Why, last week your sister called me from Taipei."

"I don't believe you," Li said. "Why would my sister contact you?"

"Damned if I know. She said she'd heard about me from her friends in Taipei and wanted my help in finding out what had happened to her niece. That's all, I swear."

"I still don't believe you. Unless . . ." His voice trailed off and he fell silent. He looked as if he were solving a complex mathematical equation in his head.

"Dak-chung, unless what?" MacKinnon said.

Li shook his head. "Never mind." He paused. "Is that all she said?"

"Yes, except to offer to cover my expenses and any fee I named," Chen replied. "I told her I'm glad to be of service. On the house." With a lit cigarette still between two fingers, he nervously twirled the enormous ruby-and-diamond ring on the other hand.

"Ever been to Taiwan?" Li asked.

"Sure, many times," Chen said. "I have a house in Taipei. Spend about half my time there."

"Have you ever met my sister?" Li's tone slipped from inquiry to interrogation.

"No, I swear. But everybody in Taiwan knows the name Li Gwei-yu. She's as powerful as anybody except for Madame Chiang herself."

"Then how did she get your name?"

"I told you. I don't know. But I'd be a damn fool to turn her down."

* * *

The meeting over and Chen having made his unctuous good-byes, MacKinnon turned to Li. "Would your sister make such a contact?"

"I don't know," Li replied. "I'll call her later to find out. I suspect it's tied to what Taiwan's intelligence agents on the Mainland have picked up in recent days."

"Would your sister have access to that information?"

"Yes, she would," Li said. "You look surprised. Aidan, my father was a major financial backer of Chiang Kai-shek, as was I. When the Generalissimo and Madame Chiang fled to Taiwan, I supported Gwei-yu's decision to go with them. The KMT clique in Taiwan watch out for each other."

"Did you and Gwei-yu know Du Yuesheng?" MacKinnon asked.

"I didn't." Li fell silent and looked at the floor. "I can't speak for Gwei-yu."

Li got up, put his hands in the pockets of his slacks and walked to the window, where he stood looking out at the harbor.

"In those days, everyone in Shanghai knew the name Du Yuesheng. He flaunted his power and wealth. Poor children wanted to be just like him when they grew up. That's where his Green Gang got its recruits. Even the foreigners who governed most of Shanghai in the '20s and '30s didn't dare tangle with Du."

Li turned and faced MacKinnon. "Cross Du, and you wouldn't see daybreak. Survival—nothing more. Everyone just wanted to survive."

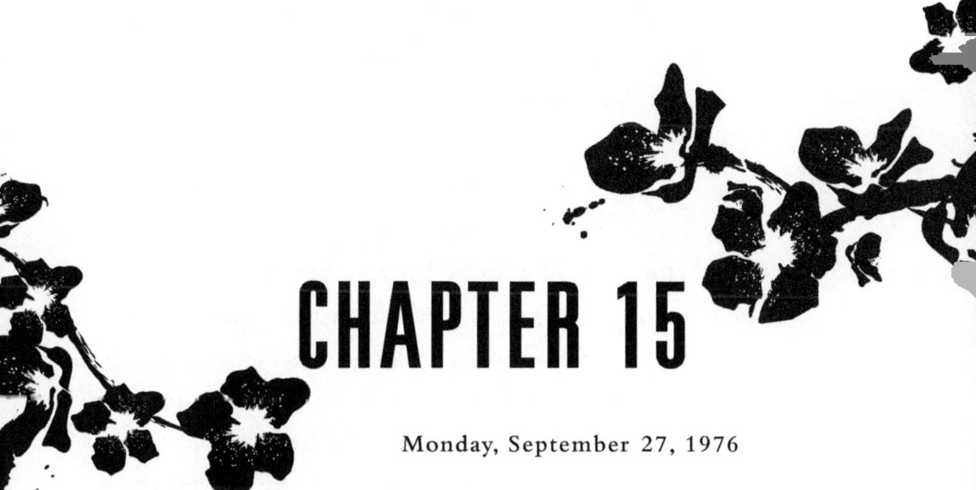

CHAPTER 15

Monday, September 27, 1976

MacKinnon was in the office early. As usual, Miss Chao was in before him. She had a sixth sense for when her boss would need her.

"Good morning," Miss Chao said. "You're in early today."

"Good morning," MacKinnon replied. "Yes, I'm expecting a call. I didn't want to miss it."

"As a matter of fact, you had a call already this morning," Miss Chao said, "from Mr. Cai at the Bank of China. He sounded distraught. Anyway, he asked me to tell you that the fingerprint results came in and were forwarded to Beijing."

MacKinnon scowled. "Did he say anything else? Did he say if the results confirmed identity?"

"No, sir, nothing else. Only that he had to ring off because he had some urgent business. His voice was quavering, almost like something had just frightened him. Very odd."

"Please see if you can get him back on the line." MacKinnon turned and went into his office. His intercom buzzed a few minutes later.

"Mr. MacKinnon," Miss Chao said, her voice trembling so much that she could hardly form the words, "I'm afraid Mr. Cai isn't . . . is no longer . . . available. They're saying he's dead."

• • •

I had spent the better part of a week hanging around the hotel, as Hugh suggested when we last had dinner. Emma had loaned me several mysteries as well as the week-old London papers that the Foreign Office courier brought in on his regular run. I also managed about an hour a night in front of the black-and-white TV in my room before the monotonous drivel of news acceptable to the Party and programs extolling the virtues of the leadership deadened my mind. Boredom was making me irritable. I was overjoyed when MacKinnon finally called.

"Bryan!" MacKinnon sounded surprised to hear my voice. "I was just about to hang up again. I've called four times in the past two hours."

"I'm afraid I dawdled over dinner. Any news?"

"Much. The Bank sent the results to Beijing today. And Bryan, the body isn't Fiona's. Quite simply, the prints don't match. The Hong Kong police told me this afternoon that the fingerprints from your body don't even resemble Fiona's prints on record here."

Click.

"Somehow that doesn't surprise me. Have you told Li Dak-chung?"

"Yes, this afternoon."

"What was his reaction?"

"I wouldn't have thought it possible, but he wasn't surprised either. He advised me to get you out of China as quickly as possible."

Click.

"I understand," I said. "I'll ask my China Travel Service guide to make arrangements for me to return to Hong Kong as soon as possible. But what about the body? The Chinese authorities are insistent that I take it with me."

"Dak-chung says you're not to accept the body. The Hong Kong government won't permit an unidentified corpse to enter the Colony."

I knew MacKinnon was now speaking to the bug on our phone line. If I was to have any chance of getting out of China without the body, I had to be able to say that the British would not allow it into Hong Kong.

"And, by the way," MacKinnon replied, "congratulations on a successful trip."

Click.

· · ·

Good. Now I did not have to wait for the Chinese authorities to notify me formally about the body. They knew that I knew the truth. Or at least they should, if the bug was worth the effort. But before leaving, I wanted to learn as much as I could about what really *had* happened to Fiona Li.

I reviewed what I knew for certain about the case: On the morning of Thursday, September 9, Fiona met the *feng shui* master, Mr. Chu, at the antique-shop location in Hollywood Road. She then used her father's car and driver to go directly to the Kowloon train station in Hung Hom. Lao Ma took Fiona's luggage to the waiting room and left it on a cart beside her seat, but he did not actually see Fiona board the train to Lo Wu. Fiona had told her maid that she was going to Macau for a few days, but she had taken her fur coat, implying a colder destination. Then on Sunday, September 12, the Chinese authorities notified Li Dak-chung that his daughter had been found dead in China and that her body had been taken to Beijing. That same day, the Macau police told MacKinnon that Fiona had never disembarked there. Fingerprint analysis subsequently proved that the body lying in Capital Hospital is not Fiona's. Jiang Qing has the file on Fiona's case, and Miss Pan and Rong are being helpful because they are Deng Xiaoping supporters. For unknown reasons, Fiona is a subject of interest in the leadership power struggle. She may or may not be alive. If she is, she is probably in danger as, perhaps, am I.

My mind spinning, I picked up the last of Emma's mysteries, read a few pages, then threw it on the bed. I looked at the TV. Unfortunately the night's fare was to be an hour-long program on increasing millet production and a soap opera about workers in a sandal factory. I thought a London *Times* crossword, also from Emma, might lull me to sleep. That too failed to divert my attention from the dangerous road I still had to travel.

I was going stir-crazy. In spite of Hugh's admonition to stay in the hotel, I decided to take a walk. Even the smoggy Beijing night air was better than the four walls of my room. I put on my jacket and took the elevator to the lobby. The same night clerk was on duty, haranguing a pair of elderly and thoroughly bewildered foreigners.

I exited the hotel through the main door and knew immediately that someone was following me. *Had I suddenly become important enough to warrant a tail of my own? Or had I always had one?* In spite of the flush of vanity, I did not relish being singled out, and certainly not by the Chinese secret police.

I walked down the hotel's sloping circular driveway. The only person there was a tall Chinese man walking toward the hotel parking lot. He was dressed like one of the taxi drivers, but there was something out of place about him. Unlike typical drivers, his clothes were not rumpled, and he carried himself ramrod straight, almost proudly. There was an air of orderliness and calm about him. I watched as he strolled up to a Red Flag limousine. He knew I was staring at him. He leaned against the limousine then took out a cigarette and lit it. He tried to hide his face by averting his gaze downward. I continued to stare at him while he smoked about half of his cigarette.

His face showed briefly from beneath the brim of his cap when he glanced to see whether I had continued on my way. He was clean shaven and probably in his thirties. Eventually I tired of this *kabuki*. He was probably just the driver of some high Communist official who was having a tryst in the hotel.

I turned and continued walking to the corner, crossed Chang An Jie, and headed south toward the Legation Quarter. The lights around the hotel entrance quickly faded into the enveloping gloom of the abandoned quarter. No lights shone from windows, and the trees were etched in black against the charcoal sky. My footsteps echoed eerily on the sidewalk.

Just before the Church of St. Michel, I turned left onto an even darker side street. It led me past the old Austro-Hungarian Legation, a resplendent white Viennese mansion set well back from the street. I managed to make out its shape through the seven-foot black metal spike fence that surrounded the compound. A sudden gust of wind rustled through the trees and created a groaning, metal-on-metal noise a few feet from me. An irrational terror seized me. Every shadow became a specter, every noise a wail. After a moment, I realized that the creaking noise I had heard was the ornate compound gate swaying in the wind. My heart stopped pounding in my throat, and I let out a breath.

Suddenly I heard the faint but growing sound of a car approaching on the street behind me. I knew the buildings were all abandoned. So who, I asked myself, could possibly be driving in the quarter this late at night? I could not see my watch, but I knew that I had left the hotel around midnight. I turned. The sound was growing louder. The headlights were off, but I could just make out the shape of the car about fifty yards away. *Why didn't he turn his lights on?*

When the car was no more than twenty yards from me, I saw the driver's face in the light from the car's instrument panel. A split-second later, he saw me. The headlights suddenly blinded me as the car's engine gunned and its tires screamed. I crossed my arms in front of my face and backed up against the gate. I realized that I had nowhere to go.

Quicker than a flash of lightning, an arm from inside the gate grabbed me, pulled me inside the compound, and threw me on the grass beside the driveway. The car hit the gate and its masonry pillar with bone-crushing force where I had been standing just a half-second before. As the driver slammed the car into reverse, I heard the clang of metal falling to the ground. After he disengaged from the gate and pillar, he slammed the car into first gear, swung the car into the street, and sped off.

For a brief moment, the car's headlights flashed past the face of my savior while I was still on my back on the grass. It was the man I had seen earlier that night in the hotel parking lot. He walked a few paces and bent down to pick up something. He held it close to his face. Apparently satisfied that he had correctly identified the object, he tossed it onto my chest and said casually, "Souvenir."

Still dazed and terrified, I clutched the object and struggled to my feet. The man had disappeared. I ran my fingers over the object until it revealed its unmistakable identity: a Mercedes-Benz hood ornament. And then it occurred to me. The man had spoken to me in Mandarin.

CHAPTER 16

Tuesday, September 28, 1976

National Day was four days away. General Zhu could breathe more easily now that the plans of the moderates had finally begun to coalesce. He had always been confident that his troops were prepared, and he had called in each of his key commanders for frank one-on-one conversations in his apartment. Having the chats there instead of in his office underscored that everything said was off the record. He offered each the opportunity for an immediate transfer if he preferred not to take part. All he asked was that they remain neutral, and he promised there would be no reprisals after the moderates seized power. To a man, the commanders were with him.

Zhu knew that they would be. After all, he had handpicked most of them. The others he and Marshal Ye had carefully reviewed. Ye could personally vouch for every one of them. What Zhu was not sure of was the political leadership, particularly those who did not have a strong military background. Like all soldiers, he was suspicious of politicians, in particular the Premier and new Chairman of the Chinese Communist Party, Hua Guofeng. In recent days, moderate-faction intelligence had picked up indications that Hua was making overtures to Jiang Qing. This was proof to Zhu of Hua's weakness and, more worrying, his unreliability. Hua could never be a particularly influential ally, but his opposition was an obstacle that Zhu would rather eliminate before his troops raised their rifles.

Zhu had talked to Ye about gaining leverage over Hua. They had assigned a trio of loyal officers to scour Hua's personal life to uncover something—anything—they could use to exact his cooperation, or at least his neutrality. The trio had found nothing in Hua's stolid, unremarkable *apparatchik* past. It left Hua an unpredictable factor, and that was unsettling.

Zhu reached for the telephone on his desk then stopped. Best to wait for the meeting. Marshal Ye had mandated a gathering of the moderate leaders to review and approve the final plans developed for the National Day assault at the Great Hall of the People. Ye, Zhu himself, Wang Dongxing, and Vice Premier Li Xiannian would be there as well as a representative of the consensus leader of the moderates, Deng Xiaoping. Deng himself was still in Guangzhou under house arrest, which had been imposed by Mao before his death and enforced by the radicals in the three weeks since.

Major Wang stuck his head through the door of Zhu's office and said, "Sir, meeting in fifteen minutes."

Wang had been energized and enthusiastic ever since Zhu informed him of the plans to arrest Jiang Qing and her cabal and free Deng Xiaoping. Zhu found Wang's youthful optimism invigorating, but he winced as the image of his missing daughter flashed before his mind's eye. Zhu started to get up from his desk when the phone rang. It was Colonel Peng.

"General, have you seen the morning paper?"

"No, not yet."

"On page one," Peng continued, "there's a new diatribe questioning the loyalty of the 'New Zeng Zi' and demanding that he be put on trial."

Zhu's blood ran cold. In the split-second it took Peng to utter those words, the old warrior, hardened guerrilla fighter, ardent Communist, and protégé of Deng and Mao knew he was a marked man. He knew from experience the uses of show trials. The KGB had taught the Party to favor them as a means of disgracing and eliminating popular officials or public personalities. An unknown person could simply be tortured, brutalized, or shot and his organs harvested for profit. But the well-known, and particularly those whom the Party had lionized and permitted to travel abroad, had to be so thoroughly discredited that the public would clamor for their execution—and the execution of their families as well, more often than not.

"Please wait while I get the paper." Zhu put his hand over the phone's mouthpiece and called through the open office door, "Major Wang, please bring me this morning's *People's Daily*." After Wang brought it, Zhu motioned to him to close the door.

Zhu spread open the paper on his desk. There, above the fold in the space reserved for important Party pronouncements, in bold type, was the headline: "Should the Masses Demand That the New Zeng Zi Be Put on Trial?" The article began:

> The traitor masquerading as the New Zeng Zi is a poisonous stinking weed who steadfastly rejects the demand of the Party and the masses that he abandon his bourgeois, anti-socialist thoughts and actions. The Party and the masses have grown weary of his obstinate refusal to struggle and to resolutely study the teachings of Comrade Mao Zedong. The Party unswervingly unites with the masses and steadfastly

supports the demand that the stinking weed New Zeng Zi be pulled out by the roots, removed from his positions, put on trial, and made to suffer the verdict of the masses. His pernicious seed should be eradicated so that it never again germinates.

The article went on to catalog the New Zeng Zi's ideological sins, which it said constituted "*an insidious counterrevolutionary plot to overthrow the Party and the masses and, with the assistance of foreign powers, subjugate China to a capitalist bourgeoisie.*"

It also condemned the New Zeng Zi for "*arrogant commandism and splitism*" vis-à-vis the PLA. In support of this accusation, the author cited no less an authority than Mao himself when he wrote:

Some comrades in the army have become arrogant and high-handed in their behavior toward the soldiers, the people, the government, and the Party, always blaming the comrades doing local work but never themselves; always seeing their own achievements but never their own shortcomings; and always welcoming flattery but never criticism. The army must endeavor to eradicate such faults.

"General," Peng said, "are you still there? Did you find the article?"

"Yes. I am reading it now." Zhu kept reading and re-reading the reference to eradicating the new Zeng Zi's "pernicious seed." He knew it was a direct reference to his daughter. "What else could it be?" he muttered.

"Sorry, General," Peng said, "I didn't catch that. Say again, please."

"The reference to Zeng Zi and his pernicious seed . . . What else could it be but an attack on me and my daughter?"

"Nothing else, sir. I'm afraid you are correct."

"I was just thinking that this article may give us the leverage we need over Hua."

"You mean," Peng said, "the divisiveness that a show trial would cause at so difficult a time for the nation?"

"Exactly," Zhu said. "Hua wouldn't want anything to precipitate a crisis so soon after Mao's death. And we can use that."

• • •

My encounter at the Austro-Hungarian Legation had left me bruised and exhausted and had given me a splitting headache. I lifted my head slowly from the pillow and was relieved that the aspirin I had taken before falling into bed the night before had done the trick.

After I showered and dressed, I went to the dining room. There were no Chinese among the several hundred foreigners having lunch in the cavernous room. Hugh was there with a lunch partner and waved me over.

"Hello, Bryan," Hugh said. "May I introduce you to Knud Ascanius, my counterpart from the Danish Embassy? Knud, this is Bryan Paton, the American I was telling you about."

Knud and I shook hands, and we all sat down. I immediately liked Knud, who seemed quick-witted and intelligent. His meaty hands and arms and his barrel chest made him appear more like a Copenhagen fishmonger than a well-educated diplomat. Like most northern Europeans I had encountered, he spoke nearly unaccented English. I soon learned that his easy smile complemented a wry sense of humor.

"We've just ordered masses of Chinese food," Hugh said. "Care to add a bowl of rice and take potluck?"

"It sounds ideal."

"Bryan," Hugh said, "you look exhausted. What on earth have you been doing? I thought you were staying close to the hotel until we heard something."

"I had a sudden encounter with the front end of a Mercedes–Benz in the Legation Quarter at midnight last night."

"There are certainly not many of those around," Knud said.

Hugh looked grim. "Bryan, why were you in the Legation Quarter at all, not to mention at midnight?"

"I couldn't sleep," I said a bit too defensively. I was ashamed at having done something so patently reckless, something that Hugh had warned me not to do.

"It's just not on," Hugh said. "One doesn't wander about willy-nilly in a police state. And certainly not at midnight!

"I'm fascinated to hear the details," Knud said, rescuing me from the dressing-down I knew I deserved. "Come on, Bryan, fess up."

"Yes," Hugh said dryly, "fess up."

As we ate, I recounted what had happened the night before. When I described being pulled from harm's way by a stranger and the matter of the hood ornament, Hugh and Knud put down their chopsticks and stared at me.

"Precious few people," Knud said, "have access to a Mercedes. As a matter of fact, I've only seen one. It was in May of last year, when our prime minister visited China. His meeting with Zhou Enlai was inside Zhongnanhai. Zhou was ferried from his residence to the meeting in a Red Flag limousine, but several of his hangers-on arrived in a black Mercedes."

"Yes," Hugh said, "I've seen that one, too, but only inside Zhongnanhai where it's safely out of public view. No Chinese official would be caught in public in anything but a Red Flag."

"I imagine it could be dangerous even to use it in Zhongnanhai," Knud said. "One could be tarred as 'a lover of foreign things.' Fatal."

Hugh pinched his lower lip as he thought. Then he roused, placed both elbows on the table, and spoke volubly to Knud while pointing a finger at him for emphasis.

"Precisely. No official would dare use a Mercedes, except someone who is untouchable—someone safely above the fray or too powerful for anyone even to contemplate retaliation."

"Well, Mao and Zhou Enlai are dead," Knud said. "That leaves only . . ."

Knud looked at Hugh. Hugh smiled, took a piece of paper from his pocket, and wrote so that Knud and I could see: "Jiang Qing." Hugh added in a low voice barely perceptible above the din of the lunch crowd, "She's long been rumored to favor expensive Hong Kong beauty products and such decidedly un-Communist frills like jewelry and silk scarves. Mind you, all in the privacy of her villa in Zhongnanhai. Why not a Mercedes?"

"But why Bryan?" Knud said. "With all due respect, I honestly think the Red Widow has bigger fish to fry—or murder—than a Hong Kong lawyer."

Hugh shot me a look that had "best keep quiet" written all over it. He had not mentioned to Knud what I was doing in Beijing, and he obviously did not want to broach the subject. The signal did not escape Knud's notice.

"What? Is there something more, something I don't know? Are you two holding out on me?"

"Red Widow?" Hugh said. "How'd you come up with that one?"

Knud beamed. "You've heard of the black widow spider? Well, Jiang Qing is venomous, and she's a Communist, and now she's a widow."

"Full marks," Hugh said.

I nodded. "It suits her to a tee."

"And full marks for trying to distract me," Knud said. "Now, why would the Red Widow try to murder Bryan? Come on, out with it. I need something juicy for my weekly cable to Copenhagen."

Fortunately for Hugh, he did not have a chance to reply. I saw a Chinese man enter the dining room and begin carefully examining each table in sequence. By the time the man's eyes reached our table, I had recognized him, leapt to my feet, and begun striding toward him. He recognized me, too, and turned and bolted back out the entrance. I quickened my pace then broke into a full run when it appeared that he might elude me. Startled diners stopped and stared. I ran through the dining room entrance, nearly bowling over a middle-aged Japanese couple, and out into the lobby. I looked left and right and straight ahead into the lounge. The man had vanished.

Hugh and Knud came up behind me. "Bryan," Hugh said, "what on earth was that?"

"Are you okay?" Knud asked. "Did you catch him? Who was he?"

I was still looking around the lobby, watching to see if a curtain twitched or a door creaked. The man was nowhere to be seen.

"Bryan," Hugh said, "do you realize that you very nearly knocked over the Japanese ambassador and his wife? Knud and I had to apologize."

"I'm sorry," I said, "but that's the guy—"

"—who tried to kill you last night?" Knud asked.

Distracted, I did not focus on what Hugh and Knud were saying. I could not conceive of how the man had managed to escape so quickly. I walked over to the reception counter. The clerk on duty was the same one on duty the night I arrived.

"Excuse me," I said in as pleasant a tone as I could muster. "Did you see where that man went just now? He just ran out of the restaurant."

"What man?" she snapped, glaring at me.

"He was Chinese, and he just this second ran out of—"

"Impossible! No Chinese are allowed in the hotel."

I was as exasperated as she was surly. "Were you on duty just now?"

"Mr. Paton, I have been on duty since 7:00 a.m. and standing where you see me now for forty-five minutes. No Chinese man entered or exited the restaurant." She squared her shoulders to lend force to the pronouncement she was about to make: "NO . . . CHINESE . . . ARE . . . ALLOWED . . . IN . . . THE . . . HOTEL!" She then did an abrupt about-face and disappeared into the off-limits area behind the reception area.

Okay, she was lying. No doubt the man had eluded me by slipping into the off-limits area and, in all likelihood, made good his escape via a staff-only route. There was no point in searching further.

I had not noticed that Hugh and Knud were standing behind me. When I turned, Hugh said with forced politeness, "If you're quite finished terrorizing the hotel for now, would you bloody well care to explain what that was all about?"

"I recognized that guy from last night," I said. "He saved my life. I just wanted to thank him. And also find out why he's following me, and on whose orders."

Knud had to get back to the Danish Embassy. This suited Hugh's purposes because he needed to tell me in confidence what instructions he had received from the Foreign Office in London. We strolled north on Wang Fu Jing Street.

"Bryan, the analysts in London think you had best leave China at once. That will come as no surprise to you."

"No. MacKinnon and I had already concluded that."

"Fair enough," Hugh said. "But what will come as a shock is what the Hong Kong political adviser had to say in his cable." Hugh glanced left and right and then behind, looking for anyone close enough to overhear us. "No one. Only my faithful tail about fifty meters behind us," he grinned. He became serious again. "What I'm about to tell you is very highly classified. You must agree not to discuss it with anyone."

"I understand."

"Let's get past this crowd first," Hugh said.

We were approaching the *People's Daily* office building. Each day the newspaper posted the pages of that day's edition on about a dozen glass-covered bulletin boards that lined the narrow sidewalk. Those who could not afford or did not have access to the paper could read it here. At any time of the day or night there were at least a few avid readers. Today, however, the crowd was unusually large, which meant the newspaper had published something of momentous importance. As we picked our way through the crowd, I found out what that something was. It seemed that every other reader was asking those to the right or left of them who the "New Zeng Zi" could be.

After we passed the crowd, Hugh said, "Aidan turned up evidence that the Triads may be involved in Fiona's disappearance."

"That possibility crossed my mind at the beginning. Why does he think so?"

"Aidan's contact at the Bank of China was murdered under circumstances that suggest a Triad hit. Aidan had contacted an old Communist labor-union acquaintance to intervene with the Bank to speed up release of the fingerprint results. Then a notorious Triad guy turned up who knew about Aidan's contact and promised to goose the Bank to cough up the report. It's the stuff of mystery novels, eh? The governor ordered the Hong Kong police to turn the whole bloody business over to Special Branch for investigation.

"And there's more. Once the Hong Kong police determined that Fiona was not lying dead in Capital Hospital, they launched an investigation. It seems that she did board the train at Lo Wu but never passed through Customs at Guangzhou. The thinking is that she is being held somewhere in Guangdong province. The police have contacted their Chinese counterparts for assistance."

"But Hugh, that doesn't explain the Jiang Qing angle."

"No, but what it does do is make your immediate departure from China far more compelling. Your work here is finished, Bryan. Look,

I'm sorry to be so cross, but Emma's been deeply shaken by Fiona's disappearance. Your almost being murdered last night . . . well, the whole thing has become much too dangerous."

"I'm sorry. I've been focusing on what happened to Fiona and not nearly enough on the danger the search for her entails."

"Look, you're not British, and even if you were, the British Embassy has no power to order you to leave China. All we can do is explain the danger to you and—"

"Hey, that's coals to Newcastle, especially after last night. The minute I get back to the hotel, I'll call Miss Pan to make arrangements for immediate departure."

"I think that's best," Hugh said with obvious relief. "You've done yeoman's labor here for the Li family."

Hugh was soft-soaping me. By any measure, I had not accomplished much of anything on my foray into China. I was no nearer now to finding Fiona than when I arrived ten days ago. But Hugh was correct on one point: my presence in Beijing was endangering too many people. It was time to go.

• • •

When we parted at the hotel, Hugh and I agreed that I would call him as soon as I had talked to Miss Pan. She seemed relieved to hear my voice when I phoned her minutes later. We agreed to meet in the lobby lounge in a quarter of an hour. I went directly to the lobby, expecting to have to wait. She was already there.

"You're certainly prompt," I said as I sat down in the easy chair next to hers. I realized I had no idea where she worked. "By the way, Miss Pan, where is your office?"

She tensed, "Why do you need to know?"

"I don't need to know. Just passing interest, that's all."

"Please confine your interest to the purpose for which you came to the People's Republic of China."

I was momentarily flummoxed by her officiousness until I remembered her abrupt change of behavior at the Temple of Heaven when she spotted the driver over my shoulder. We were being watched, perhaps even overheard. I had ignored one of the rules I should have learned since coming to Beijing: Never let down your guard.

"Now." Miss Pan flipped through her notepad looking for a clean page. "When do you propose to depart Beijing and by what means?"

"As soon as possible and by whichever means is quickest. I assume that would be by air."

"Not necessarily. It could be by train to Guangzhou if the plane is full. You will be booked on whatever is available."

Well played, Miss Pan. Nothing like a little condescension to keep the foreigner in his place.

"Whatever is best," I said. "You're the boss."

A hint of a smile lilted around the corners of her mouth. She bent lower over her notepad, apparently to keep from erupting in laughter. More than anything else I had experienced in China, this moment of unspoken communication between us reassured me that personality could survive even the most draconian system of mind control.

"I think I have everything," she said after a moment. "I'll need your passport to arrange your boarding passes."

I reached into the inside pocket of my sport coat, retrieved my passport, and handed it to her. She put the passport and her notepad into an oversize black plastic pouch that bore a mostly illegible logo in faded gold. She struggled with the pouch's balky rusting zipper before abandoning it midway at a frayed thread blocking the track. During this process, she maintained the appropriate official decorum, which, judging from the expression on her face, I took to be grim and businesslike.

She rose abruptly from her chair and issued a brisk, "Good day, Mr.

Paton. I will inform you soon about when and how you will depart Beijing." She then strode grandly from the lobby with head held high and pouch secured under her arm against the predations of highwaymen, vagabonds, and other plunderers of travel service paraphernalia.

Greta Garbo, eat your heart out.

• • •

I went immediately to my room and called Hugh at the British Embassy. The switchboard put me through to his office, and in spite of the numerous annoying clicks on the line, I conveyed the substance of my conversation with Miss Pan. I yearned to regale him with a description of Miss Pan's Oscar-caliber performance, but if I did, she would no doubt suffer for it. Tales truthfully told would have to await my return to Hong Kong.

After I put the receiver down, I did not know what to do with myself. Until now, I had a purpose. With that purpose now frustrated, I was at loose ends.

I decided to start packing. While I was at it, my mind wandered back to the night outside the former Austro-Hungarian Legation. The man who saved my life had used Mandarin when he said "souvenir" and tossed me the limousine's hood ornament. How had he known that I speak Mandarin? Perhaps he didn't know. It could be that Mandarin is all he speaks. On the other hand, maybe there was a file on me somewhere, and he had access to it. Okay, language was a piece of the puzzle, but it was not the key. More important, why had he followed me from the hotel parking lot last night and at whose behest? And why had he shown up in the hotel restaurant today?

I put down the sweater I was folding and went out onto the balcony for some air. Beijing's pallid afternoon sunlight was waning.

The man obviously had permission to be in the hotel. Or maybe he did not need permission. Only the Chinese secret police had the unquestioned right to go anywhere in China. That meant that the man who pulled me from the limousine's path was almost certainly one of them. If so, it would explain how he knew that I spoke Mandarin, a fact that I still had not revealed to anyone in Beijing. He would have access to whatever file the Ministry of Public Security kept on me. I was reasonably certain that China's agents in Hong Kong and Taiwan had compiled a complete dossier. After all, how many American lawyers who speak Mandarin and Cantonese and who represent Li Dak-chung apply for visas to visit the People's Republic?

A gust of wind pierced my thin cotton shirt. As I hurried indoors, my phone rang.

"Hello."

"This is Pan." It was her officious voice, which I took to be for the benefit of whoever was listening. "Mr. Paton, this telephone call constitutes formal notification that the Ministry of Public Security of the People's Republic of China has barred you from traveling beyond a radius of five kilometers from Tiananmen Square. A courier will momentarily deliver written confirmation to you."

Click.

It seemed I wasn't leaving immediately after all. But on whose orders? And why?

. . .

General Zhu slumped into an easy chair in his office. It had been a long, productive meeting, and he was exhausted.

Major Wang appeared at the door. "General, can I get you some tea?"

"Yes, please," Zhu said, "and ask General Liang to step in for a moment."

"Yes, sir," Wang said.

General Liang Juntao was head of the intelligence staff for the Beijing Military Region and one of Zhu's closest aides. When Zhu arrived in Beijing, Liang was serving in one of the PLA's most sensitive assignments, head of the intelligence staff for the Guangzhou Military Region. In that post, Liang had acquitted himself superbly. Zhu arranged to have him transferred to Beijing, ostensibly for his talent but also for another reason Zhu had been careful not to reveal: Liang knew everything there was to know about the border with Hong Kong—who and what crossed it, in both directions, either legally or surreptitiously.

"General," Zhu said as Liang entered, "good of you to come. I hope I didn't interrupt anything important."

"No, sir," Liang replied.

"Good, good," Zhu said. "Please, sit."

After Liang had settled into an easy chair, Zhu said, "General, I wanted to give you a readout on today's meeting, and then, if there is time, I want to discuss another matter." Zhu shifted in his chair and found a comfortable position. "The meeting went well. Deng is now fully engaged, and his representative delivered a brilliant analysis of the plan. Deng wrote the presentation himself. For security reasons, there was only one copy, which was burned before we adjourned."

"Sir," Liang asked, "how can we be certain that Deng wrote it?"

"An excellent question. The document was passed around at the meeting, and those of us who had worked for Deng recognized it immediately as his handwriting."

"I must say, sir, I'm relieved."

"Frankly, I am too. We then went over in detail the order of battle for the operation at the Great Hall of the People Friday evening. We made only minor changes; the order remains essentially as I laid it out previously to you and the other commanders. I've asked Major Wang to make the changes and distribute the revised order to all of you no later than 6:00 p.m. today."

"Sir, will Deng make an appearance at the National Day reception after we arrest Jiang and the other radicals?"

"We debated that, but ultimately we decided against it. We could break the house arrest, but the foremost concern is that something might still go wrong. If he were to emerge prematurely, he'd be lost to us. He is far too valuable a leader for us to take that risk."

Zhu paused, suddenly paralyzed by the fear that he and Peng might not locate his daughter in the three days remaining before National Day.

"General Zhu," Liang said, "is something wrong?"

"No, I was just thinking about a related matter. Where was I? Oh, yes. The other reason Deng shouldn't appear at the reception is that first we have to engineer his rehabilitation. That requires the Party propaganda apparatus, and it's still under Jiang's control."

"Quite so, sir. By the way, did you read the article in today's *People's Daily* about a New Zeng Zi being put on trial?"

Zhu flinched but was careful not to reveal his suspicion that the New Zeng Zi was he himself.

"Yes, I did read it. In fact, I raised the subject at the meeting. I think the article gives us leverage to persuade Hua into finally committing to us."

"I'm afraid I don't follow, sir, especially since Hua's not that crucial."

"He's not, but it's in our interest to prevent him from joining Jiang's camp by default. The spectacle of the trial of a revered Long Marcher and military leader would be a national catastrophe, and Hua knows it."

"So . . . it becomes Hua's patriotic duty to oppose what the article advocates, and that means opposing Jiang because she and her toadies at the *People's Daily* are behind it. Brilliant. But sir, how exactly is Hua to be brought around?"

"*Was* brought around. Deng agreed that Hua should be invited to the meeting. After Hua was apprised of the facts, the Premier pronounced himself firmly in the moderate camp."

"Deng is nothing if not quick and decisive, sir."

"I agree. It's a relief having him in charge." Zhu paused for a moment then said, "General, I know you know a lot about the border with Hong Kong—what's brought across it and so forth. Very soon we'll need evidence to use against Jiang Qing. You know the sort of thing, her voracious appetite for foreign finery—perfume, dresses, scarves. Now, we all know she has those things secretly shipped in from Hong Kong. What we need to do is to parade that stuff in front of the masses. Support for her will collapse. That's where you and your operatives come in. We'll need proof—"

"General Zhu—"

Zhu stared at him. Liang had never interrupted him before. "—I know it will sound preposterous, so preposterous in fact that I shouldn't really bring it up . . ."

"General Liang," Zhu said, "please make your point."

"Well, in the course of routine intelligence inquiries relevant to the National Day operation, I discovered, purely by chance, mind you, that you have a daughter."

CHAPTER 17

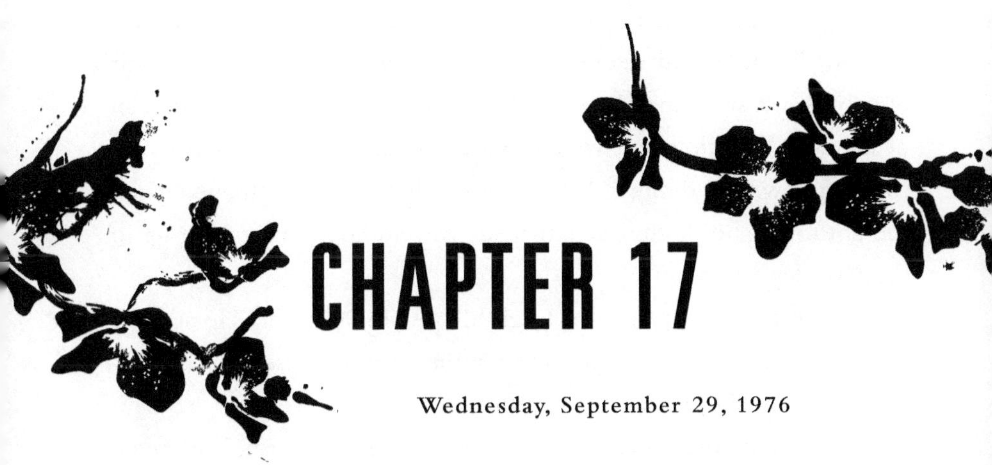

Wednesday, September 29, 1976

Five kilometers. How much is that in miles? Let's see, multiply by 0.625 . . . My head would not stop buzzing with the terms of my confinement to central Beijing. The more I tried to fall asleep, the more the whole sorry mess grated on my frazzled nerves. I rolled over in bed and squinted at the fluorescent hands on my clock: 3:15 a.m. *Lord, give me strength.* I rolled onto my back. My eyes now wide open, I stared at the ceiling of my darkened room.

Shouting and the sound of running feet suddenly shattered the tomb-like silence. *At least two people.* I heard the door creak as if someone were leaning against it. I leapt out of bed when I heard the sound of paper sliding under my door. Someone was shouting in Mandarin, "You there, stop! What are you doing? Stop that!" I recognized the voice of one of our hall monitors-cum-Public Security agents. One of them was always on duty in a closet-sized station on each floor of the hotel.

As I reached down to pick up the piece of paper, I heard the person who delivered it begin to run.

"Stop! You can't go there! STOP!"

I slipped the piece of paper into the breast pocket of my pajamas, opened the door, and stepped out into the hallway. The service stair door was just swinging closed, and the out-of-breath hall monitor, an overweight, middle-aged woman with hair cut comically short, was running down the dimly lit hallway in my direction. She stopped when she got to me, no doubt aware that she had no hope of catching up to the intruder.

"Mr. Paton," she gasped in English, "are you all right? He actually tried to break into your room." Then, remembering herself and her station, she growled, "Return to your room, please."

Brashly confident that she did not understand German, I muttered under my breath, "*Jawohl, Frau Obersturmbahnfuhrer.*" I re-entered my room and closed the door.

I waited a few minutes before turning on the small lamp on the desk. I retrieved the note from my pocket and spread it in the dim circle of light. It was in Chinese:

> I have information about Li Guangmei. Meet me in
> Tiananmen near the museum at noon today. Do not
> approach me. I will watch the square. If it's safe, I will
> approach you. Immediately destroy this message.

The note had to be from the man who saved me outside the Austro-Hungarian Legation. My earlier suspicion that he knew I spoke and read Mandarin had been right on the mark. Why else would he have used Chinese characters to write his message?

I shuddered as a thought crossed my mind: how was I going to shake my tail? Surveillance would be even more intense now that my movements had been restricted. The writer of the message could not possibly have known about that development. Well, I'd just have to find a way.

I went into the bathroom and, without turning on the light, tore up the note and flushed it down the toilet. I turned off the desk lamp and got back into bed. I was finally dropping off to sleep when another unsettling thought roused me. Hugh would go ballistic if he found out I was mixing in again. I was reluctant to put Hugh, and by extension Emma, through any more trauma. Moreover, if my Tiananmen encounter should land me in hot water, they could not come to my aid. Even if the British Ambassador were disposed to risk letting Hugh intervene on my behalf, unlikely in the extreme, the Chinese authorities would turn a deaf ear.

But what about Li Dak-chung and Simon? Hadn't they sent me to Beijing specifically to find out what had happened to Fiona? Failing to meet with someone who possessed information about her was tantamount to resigning as the Li family attorney. I certainly had no intention of doing that. They were counting on me.

I lay awake struggling with my conscience for another hour or so before I finally arrived at a compromise. I would not worry Hugh and Emma by telling them in advance about the Tiananmen meeting but would promptly divulge all the details immediately following the meeting. I would then cease all involvement in Fiona's case as long as I was still in China.

I slept only fitfully the rest of the night and was grateful at last to spot sunlight at the margins of the drapes. Groggy from lack of rest, I willed my body out of bed.

During morning ablutions and breakfast, I studiously avoided thinking about how I would get out of the hotel without being seen. When I walked out of the dining room a little after 9:00 a.m., I still had the better part of three hours to come up with a plan. I strolled across the lobby to the lounge and sat in an easy chair. Feigning boredom, I picked up a copy of the English-language version of *China Pictorial* and opened it on my lap. Except for the clerk dawdling behind the reception counter, the lobby and lounge were deserted. Nonetheless, I was certain that I was being watched, as I would be whenever I attempted to leave the hotel.

A ruckus broke out in the taxi drivers' anteroom at the front entrance of the hotel. Several of the drivers were using a wadded-up ball of paper as a soccer ball and competing at kicking penalty shots into an imaginary goal. Slow day. I went back to flipping the pages of the magazine on my lap. Then it dawned on me: what better way to leave than in plain sight in a taxi? I could ask the driver to take me past the sights and end up two hours later in Tiananmen where I would simply pay the fare and release the taxi. *Damn. I might even shake my tail.*

As I approached the taxi stand, the drivers abruptly broke off the pick-up soccer match and eyed me warily. Okay, so they'd been briefed on me. Did I really think it would have been otherwise? I made my way through the stench of sweat, garlic, and ashtrays that had not been emptied in days to the table where the taxi dispatcher reigned. Stifling heat from the radiator threatened to suck the breath from my lungs.

The dispatcher drew hard on the butt of a too-short unfiltered cigarette and blinked back tears when the smoke irritated his eyes. "Where you go, Mr. Paton?"

I smiled and tried to look like the stereotypical rube tourist. "I'd like to see the sights of Beijing. Can one of your drivers take me?"

A clutch of drivers had by then crowded uncomfortably close around me, alternately giggling and whispering like the crowd that had surrounded the Highgroves and me on Chang An Jie on my first day in Beijing. The dispatcher stared. "What you want see?"

"I don't know," I said. "What would you recommend for a business-man about to leave your lovely city?"

The dispatcher smirked. "Recommend? I have no recommendation." His English suddenly was textbook perfect, a sure sign he had switched to the canned phrases. "Mr. Paton, please tell me precisely where you want to go, and one of my drivers will take you there."

I tried to look stumped. "Uh, I really don't know. I forgot my guidebook, and I haven't any—"

"Well, perhaps you'd first care to retrieve it from your room."

"What?"

"Your Beijing guidebook." His tone had softened. It was now encouraging, mentoring, comforting. I was genuinely surprised. "Perhaps you'd better get it before setting out." At the gaggle of drivers at my elbows he shouted in Mandarin, "Shut your traps and get lost!"

He turned back to me. "Now, wouldn't you like to get your guidebook . . . and perhaps a jacket? It's very cold outside. Oh, and don't forget your camera. You might like to take some photographs."

Feeling like a child being readied by his mother to play in the snow, I nodded, left the anteroom, and crossed the lobby to the elevator bank. On the way to my room, I wondered whether I was being stupid. I shouldn't be skulking around in the shadows. I tried to shake the feeling of being involved in—what? Treachery? Espionage? Murder? Whatever it was, it was damned unpleasant. I longed to leave the Communist dictatorship that bred such crimes and resume my life in Hong Kong.

The elevator bounced to a halt on my floor, and I got out. As I rounded the corner, I saw that the door to my room was being held ajar with a bucket of cleaning supplies and dirty rags. This surprised me because no one had been in to clean my room for a week. I walked to the door and abruptly pushed it open. The hall monitor was rifling through a desk drawer. She quickly closed it and pretended to be dusting, but not before I saw her slip something into the pocket of her smock.

"Mr. Paton," she said a shade too cheerfully, "I thought you'd gone out. I'm just finishing with your room."

"Don't mind me. I just came up to use the bathroom and get my things. Then I'm off for some last-minute sightseeing."

The woman quickly finished the feigned dusting and scurried to the door, dipping to snag the bucket handle and slamming the door behind her. It was a well-practiced maneuver born of frequent execution under pressure. I went to the desk and opened the drawer. I wanted to know what she had pocketed, although I already knew.

Yep. She'd taken the hood ornament.

A few minutes later with jacket, camera, and guidebook in hand, I returned to the taxi station. The dispatcher was busy herding a Swedish tour group onto a bus. After they departed, he returned to the anteroom and assigned a taxi and driver to take me on a tour of the city.

We proceeded east on Chang An Jie past the Observatory. My guidebook claimed it was built by Italian Jesuits in the seventeenth century and had been left derelict by the Communist government since 1949 because it was a hated "foreign thing" undeserving of preservation. The book said there were numerous antique European scientific instruments decaying on the roof. It actually sounded quite interesting. Besides, I might arrive at Tiananmen too early. I told the driver to stop. He reacted as if stung by a swarm of hornets. "Strictly forbidden, strictly forbidden," he said as he gunned the car until the Observatory was out of sight.

By this time, he had intimidated me into keeping quiet. I let him choose those sights that would not subject me, or him, to reprimand. Unfortunately this category included such gray neo-Stalinist monoliths as the Worker's Stadium, the Beijing Exhibition Hall, and Beijing Central Train Station. As we drove past each, the driver waxed eloquent on the virtues of what he called "socialist modernization transforming China's corrupt bourgeois imperial cultural legacy." I got the impression that he did not appreciate the Forbidden City.

I glanced at my watch: 11:45. I interrupted the driver's soliloquy to remind him that I wanted to arrive at Tiananmen about noon. He sneered a "humph" but nonetheless turned east onto Chang An Jie.

He pulled over in front of the billboard portrait of Lenin, on the Great Hall side of the square, a few minutes after 12:00. I paid him off, collected my things, and hopped out of the taxi. The sky was cloudless, and a freezing wind had whipped up. Except for the ubiquitous PLA soldiers, there were only a few people in the square. I zipped my jacket, slung my camera strap over my shoulder, and with hands already growing numb with cold, opened the guidebook.

The Museum of the History of the Chinese Revolution was opposite the Great Hall. I strolled across the square, stopped midway, and made a pretense of studying the museum's architecture. A figure lounging near the Museum's entrance began walking toward me. I could not make out who it was, but I knew by the man's clothing that he was not one of the soldiers.

Footsteps approaching me from behind startled me, and the guidebook tumbled from my freezing fingers. A soldier bent to pick it up. As he did so, I glanced toward the distant figure. He abruptly shifted direction and, almost imperceptibly, thrust his chin toward the Tiananmen Gate, the main entrance to the Forbidden City complex, across Chang An Jie. The soldier handed me the guidebook with a tourist-friendly smile. I mumbled "shay-shay," attempting to imitate how a tourist would say thank you if he had learned his Mandarin from the book's "Useful Phrases" section. The soldier said "*bu kechi*" and walked away.

My palms were sweating and my heart was pounding in my throat. I thrust my hands and the guidebook into my jacket pockets and turned to face the Tiananmen Gate entrance. The figure had crossed Chang An Jie and was sitting on a bench near the entrance with his elbows on his knees staring at me. I looked away and angled toward the crosswalk. After crossing the boulevard, I strolled toward the entrance. As I neared the bench, I recognized that the figure was, as I suspected, my savior from two nights ago.

The man lowered his head as I came abreast of him and stage-whispered in English, "Meet me at the nine dragons, through the gate." I kept walking and passed through the Tiananmen Gate into the Forbidden City proper, the rectangular 178-acre complex of palaces; throne halls; courtier, eunuch, and servant quarters; and sundry outbuildings of China's Ming and Qing dynasty emperors. I continued due north a few minutes through the Meridian Gate, where I stopped.

Nine dragons *what*? Temple? Gate? I consulted the guidebook, which had a map of the complex. I ran my finger down the "J's" in the map index, searching for *jiulong*—nine dragons. How bizarre, I thought. The American has to translate the Chinese man's English back into Chinese to discover the meaning. I found a listing for "Nine Dragons Screen." "Bingo!" I shouted.

A screech at my feet made me jump. I had not noticed that a child, having no doubt encountered her first Westerner, had planted herself directly in front of me and was gaping at me with mouth wide-open. When I shouted, the child screamed in terror and ran wailing into the outstretched arms of her mother. Out of the corner of my eye, I caught sight of a person dodging the child to avoid a collision. It was the man I was about to meet. He laughed as he sidestepped the tot and, without looking at me, whispered in English, "Hurry." He continued walking and, bearing left, passed over one of the five bridges in front of the Gate of Supreme Harmony and out of sight.

I smiled, nodded "sorry" to the woman holding the whimpering child, and bore right through the Zhao De Gate in the direction of the screen. As I passed the Archery Pavilion, I glanced west. The man was standing at the corner of the massive Hall of Preserving Harmony, nearly half the way across the complex from me. He looked back and, apparently satisfied he had not been followed, started walking toward me. I turned right, walked the short distance to the screen, and guide-book held in front of me, feigned studying the tile and masonry object.

He came up behind me. "Beautiful, isn't it?"

"Extraordinary . . . absolutely extraordinary," I said, playing along. "Can you tell me how they got those brilliant colors so many centuries ago?"

"I know a lot about the Forbidden City but, unfortunately, not everything."

"Maybe you can tell me which of these thousands of palaces and buildings I should see first. I'm leaving Beijing in a few days and don't have much time."

"That's difficult, but if I had to choose, I'd recommend the Pavilion of 10,000 Spring Seasons in the Imperial Garden. Perhaps you'd like me to show you the way."

We were deep within the complex, and I had not seen a soul except for the child and her mother. The frigid wind was blowing in gusts and swirls along the cobblestone pathways between the many structures. We walked along a pathway leading north while he kept up a chatter of trivia about the complex.

"The Forbidden City was laid out on a north-south axis and faces south—" He took my arm and stopped. "This will be fine. We won't be observed here."

We had reached the north wall of the complex and were near its rear gate, the Gate of Divine Prowess. The massive 33-foot-high red wall afforded us maximum privacy. There were few buildings along the pathway leading to the gate. Only the two, 3-story pagoda-style turrets at the east and west corners of the wall oversaw our location. Just to be safe, he guided me into the lee of the shorter Imperial Garden wall.

"Listen," I whispered.

He was craning his neck left and right, and appeared to focus on the two turrets as sites of possible surveillance.

"Listen," I said in a slightly louder voice, "since yesterday I've been followed everywhere."

"No, you haven't," he said, stifling a laugh.

"Yes I have. Yesterday someone from the secret police delivered—"

"—to your hotel room a notice confining you to a radius of five kilometers from Tiananmen Square. I wish you'd looked up at me when I dropped the damned thing off. It would've made today a hell of a lot easier."

"What? How did you—?"

"I've been following you since the day you got off the plane. How stupid do you think we are? Do you really think we'd let the attorney for the man who controls Hong Kong's economy just trot around anywhere he wants?"

His statement jolted me. So he was my tail. That certainly explained my rescue that night in the Legation Quarter and his loitering around the hotel. It suddenly dawned on me that he must know who tried to run me down—and why.

"Just who are you?"

"My name is Rong Liaoping," he said. "I'm with the Ministry of Public Security. Oh, and by the way, you can relax. There are no other Ministry agents scheduled for this sector today."

Now that I could get a good look at him, I realized that he was as tall as any Chinese man I had ever seen. And even his dull clothing could not disguise his athletic frame and good looks.

"I believe," he said, "you've met my older brother, Rong Chenli. He also works at the Ministry, as a Foreign Affairs Officer."

Now, at long last, the fog was dissipating. If this fellow was Rong's brother, then he must know Miss Pan. And all three of them must be part of the moderate faction working ultimately for Deng Xiaoping.

"Your note said that you know something about Fiona Li," I said. "Tell me, and we can part company."

"Who?" Rong said. "Oh, you mean Li Guangmei. Yes, I do."

He turned his head and looked warily at the western turret. A sound like someone snapping his fingers had attracted his attention. I had heard it, too, but thought nothing of it. Just then, a flock of birds rose from the turret and took flight.

Rong turned his head back to face me, his sense of relief obvious. "I thought I heard something. It was just birds." He laughed a nervous laugh and rubbed his hands together. "Well, concerning Miss Li, when I—"

A flash from the turret momentarily blinded me and, instinctively, I lowered my head. A deafening crack struck my eardrums. The bricks in the wall directly behind me shattered, and red dust sprayed on the back of my head. Rong flung himself on top of me, and we fell to the ground as a second crack sounded. My brain caught up with events. Someone was shooting at us from the turret. A second shot ricocheted off the wall. I felt Rong go limp, and his full weight pressed down on my chest. I struggled to lift him as a third, then a fourth crack sounded. Dust kicked up from the ground and the wall behind. We were pinned down.

Suddenly the shooting stopped. I could hear at least two people, maybe more, running down the stairs of the turret. Just then I felt a tug on my shoulder and someone behind me said, "Come this way. Carry him." I was stunned and, for a split second, hesitated. I turned my head and looked at the person who spoke. It was the woman with the crying child whom she now held in her arms. There was a terrified look in the child's eyes but nary a whimper from her mouth. The woman frantically waved an arm and shouted, "Hurry! Follow me!" She ran down the pathway and disappeared around the corner of the Imperial Garden wall.

I hefted Rong up and half-dragged, half-carried him down the pathway. When I reached the corner, the woman was waiting for me. She motioned me on and darted through a gate into the garden. I followed her as fast as I could, one arm around Rong's waist, his limp body slung over my shoulder. I could hear several people talking excitedly in Mandarin around the corner from where we had just escaped.

I dragged Rong through the gate into the garden and looked around for the woman. She was nowhere to be seen. I rested Rong against a boulder and looked for a gunshot wound. His forehead was badly bruised and swollen, and blood trickled from a gash on his right temple, but as far as I could tell, he was breathing steadily.

Voices on the pathway just outside the garden wall were growing louder. I heard one of them shout, "Search the garden!" *Shit. Damn the woman.* I lifted Rong's unconscious body and started toward the nearest of the dozen or so palaces and pavilions.

"No, not that way. Over here . . . hurry!" It was the woman, the child still cradled in her arms. She was standing across the garden in a darkened doorway that appeared to lead under one of the palaces. She turned and disappeared into the void.

I shifted my grip on Rong and stumbled toward the darkened doorway. A dense stand of bamboo screened us from the gate, but I could hear several male Chinese voices growing louder. I hurriedly dragged Rong through the doorway and, as quickly and silently as I could, moved the massive door closed with my foot.

Inside, the darkness was absolute, but the silence was reassuring. I felt exhaustion so overwhelming that my body weakened, and Rong slipped from my grasp to the floor. He groaned, but I was too weary to care. After a few seconds I heard one of our pursuers say from near the doorway, "They're not over here." I suspected that he would soon push the door open to check. I bent down and groped for Rong. He groaned again as I lifted him. Summoning as much will as I had left, I plunged blindly forward down the dark hallway.

Then something tripped me up. Fortunately I was dragging Rong slightly behind me so that his weight acted as an anchor on both of us.

I wound up sitting on what I discovered was the top step of a stone staircase. Rong, splayed out behind me in the hallway, was now moaning more frequently and appeared to be coming to.

From somewhere beneath me came a distant whisper. "This way, down the stairs." I recognized the woman's voice.

Once again I lifted the half-conscious Rong and began feeling my way with my foot down the uneven, slippery stone steps. The staircase wound downward and, after seemingly a hundred steps, bottomed out into what I sensed from the echo of my footsteps was a long narrow hallway. A bright light at the far end of the passage flashed on, momentarily blinding me and triggering a response in Rong, who abruptly came to in a state of groggy half-life. He haltingly struggled to his feet then quickly collapsed. He remained conscious, although still not fully alert.

"Where are we?" he asked, shielding his eyes from the light.

"Damned if I know," I muttered.

The woman, the light behind her, ran toward us. "Quickly, you can rest when we're behind the security door."

She put the child down then grabbed Rong by his armpits and helped him stand. Together, we supported him down the hallway to a door that stood open. Once through the door, the woman signaled to me to sit Rong down against the wall. She quickly ran back for the child and, in one swift motion, snatched her up from the floor. Once back inside the heavy metal door, she slammed it shut and threw the bolt. We were now safe from our pursuers.

Rong was again losing consciousness and slowly sliding to the right against the wall. I sat down close beside him, propping him up with my shoulder. The woman carried the child to the other side of him, set her on the floor, and began doing what she could for Rong.

For the first time, I was able to look closely at her. She appeared to be in her twenties. Her long jet-black hair was twisted at the back of her head and pinned casually, if not haphazardly, with a barrette run through with a pointed stick. The smudges and scratches on her hands and face caused by the day's events and her drab cotton clothing could not mask her snow-white, almost transparent skin. She was, quite simply, one of the most beautiful women I had ever seen. And I had a strong impression of having seen her somewhere before.

"Thank you," the woman said after she had done as much as she could for the unconscious Rong. "You've saved my husband's life."

"He's your—?"

"That's right. Rong Liaoping is my husband. And this is our daughter, Liming."

"And bright and beautiful she is, indeed," I said while looking at the child.

"Ah, you speak Mandarin. Then you'll also be able to translate my name, Lina."

"Let's see, 'Li' means *beautiful* and 'Na' means—" I paused, searching for the best English translation.

"*Graceful*," Lina said. "In choosing a name for me, my stepfather was definitely an optimist. Unfortunately I'm not the least bit graceful."

I thought I heard something farther down the hallway. "Don't you think we had better get moving?"

"That is not necessary. The soldiers will be here soon."

"Soldiers?"

"That's right," Lina said. "This tunnel leads to the Ministry of National Defense. It's part of the system of underground passageways that the Emperors built over the centuries for one reason or another. These old tunnels honeycomb the Forbidden City and Zhongnanhai. They even extend beneath Chang An Jie into Tiananmen. The minute I slammed the door closed, an alarm went off in the Ministry signaling a security breach in the tunnel. Don't worry, help is on the way."

"I sure hope they get here before the soldiers on the other side of the door bash it down," I said.

"They're not soldiers!"

Lina looked at Liming, who was now resting her head on her father's arm, then continued in a soft voice, "I mean they're not *regular* PLA. The Army would never tolerate in the fighting ranks toadies like the men who shot at you. And you can rest assured that they won't come near that door. They're too afraid to tangle with real soldiers."

"Who are they?"

Lina turned her head and looked down the tunnel toward the Ministry. Our rescuers were running toward us, the sound of the taps on their boots echoing off the walls. Lina turned back to me. "They're Red Army political commissars."

• • •

General Liang, accompanied by an aide, marched toward the garrison holding facility. He was furious. As intelligence chief, overall security of the Ministry of National Defense installation was one of his responsibilities. Now, just three days from National Day, not only had there been a massive breakdown in security, but the perpetrators had nearly penetrated the Ministry building itself. And one of those involved was a foreigner—an American, no less.

Liang knew that there would be hell to pay. Jiang Qing would be overjoyed to learn that Zhu and his subordinates had been so incompetent as to allow an American spy to penetrate the Ministry of National Defense. She would not even need a show trial in order to have them all summarily executed. He had to devise a way to keep the incident quiet, at least until after the National Day operation was completed. Then, if Deng and the moderates were successful, a breach of security at the

Ministry would be lost in the shuffle. If they were not, and Jiang and the radicals survived, well, they would all be dead anyway.

Of immediate importance was reporting the matter to General Zhu, who had ordered that anything out of the ordinary be promptly relayed to him. But first he had to be clear on the details. That meant personally interrogating the criminals.

• • •

A man in a general's uniform which bore one star stormed past the guards and into the room where the soldiers had brought Liaoping, Lina, me, and the child. He was wiry and not particularly tall with the obviously dyed black hair so common among Chinese officials in their late fifties and beyond. Even discounting the scowl, he was unattractive. His lips were too thin and his nose too large to suit his face. He wasted no time.

"What were you doing leading an American spy into the Ministry?" he said to Liaoping and Lina in a menacing tone.

Lina maintained a grim-faced silence that only infuriated the general more. For the first time since my encounter with Liming at the Meridian Gate, the child, seated on the floor between her mother and father, began to wail uncontrollably.

"Give me your identity documents." The general turned to one of the guards, "And get that child out of here. Perhaps that will loosen the tongues of these traitors and their American lackey."

One of the guards brusquely snatched Liming off the floor. Lina sprang from her chair and grabbed his arm. Another guard wrestled Lina back to her chair and held her there while the wailing Liming was carried out of the room. The door slammed shut, intensifying Liming's screams and her mother's anxiety. Liaoping, groggy from his wounds, roused slightly when he heard his daughter's howls.

The general stood by calmly while this scene played out. "Now that I have your full attention, if you ever want to see your daughter alive again, you will answer my questions. If you do not, the State will execute both of you and turn your daughter over to an orphanage for the children of traitors. When she reaches the age of sixteen, she will incur a debt to the State equal to the cost of the bullets used to execute you as well as the surgery necessary to extract your organs. Do I make myself clear? Oh, and the American spy will be shot today. His organs will yield a handsome profit for the Party." I tried to keep from shaking with terror by thinking of Ah-yee and my warm, safe flat in Hong Kong.

The general glared directly at Lina while delivering this monologue and waited for a moment for the impact of his statement to sink in. "Give me your identity documents."

Lina still looked relatively calm, which gave me some hope. She reached into the breast pocket of her blouse and retrieved her ID card, then reached across and pulled her husband's card from his shirt pocket. She handed both to a guard who passed them to the general.

After he had spent an inordinate amount of time studying the cards, the general finally turned to Lina. "How long have you been with Detachment 8341?"

"You know that I am prohibited from answering that question."

The general stiffened then swung around and shouted at one of the guards, "Get me the child!"

"Wait!" Lina's head hung limp. "I'll answer any question you ask."

The general waved the guard off and demanded of Lina, "Well?"

"I've been assigned to 8341 for almost three years."

"What are your duties in Zhongnanhai?"

The blood drained from Lina's face, and she looked as if she were about to faint. She gripped the sides of the seat and seemed to draw strength from the comforting feel of the wood. "I'm part of the detail that guards Madame Song Qingling."

The general was set back on his heels. And I was impressed. In a society in which law is far less important than one's relationship to powerful people, Lina had played a trump card. Song Qingling was a legend of modern China. She was the second-born of the three famous American-educated Song sisters. Her younger sister, Meiling, who had married Chiang Kai-shek, became more famous in the West than did she; but in China, Song Qingling was revered as the widow of Sun Yat-sen, and later, for having thrown her lot in with the Communists. My brain was beginning to work again. Did the general know with whom Madame Song's sympathies lay in the power struggle? What side was he on? Would any of this matter for the four of us?

"When were you born?" The general proceeded carefully, his tone calmer than before.

"1948, February 26."

"Where?"

"I don't really know," Lina said. "Some say Shaoguan in Guangdong. Others say Yenan. Still others claim that I was born in Shanghai. I was an orphan. All I know for certain is that I was raised by foster parents in Shaoguan."

"Who are your father and mother?"

"They're dead now. My father was an official in the Guangdong provincial Party apparatus, and my mother was a teacher at the Party school in Shaoguan."

"No, I need to know the identity of your biological parents."

"I never knew them. They were killed during the war."

"And it never occurred to you to ask why you, of all the war orphans in China, should be so lucky as to be raised by two prominent Guang-dong Party officials?" the General said with some of his earlier bluster. "Wasn't your stepfather the second cousin of Madame Zhou Enlai?"

Lina could manage only a feeble "yes." I could feel fear starting to surge in me again. I had to fight to control my face.

"What were you and your husband doing in the company of an American spy?"

"My husband," Lina said, "is a special agent at the Ministry of Public Security. He was assigned to report on the whereabouts of the American Bryan Paton."

"And you? What were you doing in the Forbidden City this afternoon?"

"I . . . uh . . ."

"You were helping your husband communicate with the American spy! And both of you were using your official status to disguise your traitorous acts! I demand to know who you are working for or your daughter will suffer!"

Lina sprang up from her chair and cried out, "No! Please don't hurt my daughter!"

One of the guards grabbed her and slammed her back in her chair.

"I am not a spy," I said. *I couldn't help it.*

The general whirled to face me. "Shut up!" He motioned to one of the guards, who wrenched my arms behind my chair, handcuffed my wrists to the rungs, and then did the same to Lina. Liaoping was left slumped over in his chair.

"So you say you're not a spy. Then what are you doing in Beijing?"

My wrists and shoulder joints were beginning to ache. "I've come on behalf of my employer to bring the body of his daughter back to Hong Kong for burial."

"And who is this phantom employer of yours?"

"Li Dak-chung," I said, emphasizing each syllable as much as I dared.

"The renegade capitalist oppressor of Hong Kong's workers and peasants? The criminal Chinese financier who in 1949 ran into the arms of the Americans and their British lackeys rather than remain in China and reconstruct the Motherland? Are we talking about the same Li Dak-chung?"

I did not bother to answer.

"The daughter of Li Dak-chung is a Chinese citizen," the general snapped.

"Then why didn't the Chinese government protect her after she came to China?" I said.

The general seemed genuinely surprised. "How do you know she is dead?"

"She isn't. The Bank of China office in Hong Kong confirmed her death to her father about two weeks ago," I said, "but the body in Capital Hospital isn't Fiona Li's."

"Bank of China . . ." Liang mused. "Does she have a Chinese name?"

Before I could respond, Lina said, "Li Guangmei. My husband has information about her. Please, he desperately needs medical attention."

The general ignored her and turned back to me. "Who is your China Travel Service guide?"

"Pan Bingqing," I replied reluctantly.

"Comrade Rong," the general said to Lina, "do you know a Pan Bingqing?"

Lina hesitated. "Yes, I know her." She was clearly uncomfortable with this fishing expedition, and so was I.

The general paced the floor of the small interrogation room, mulling over what he doubtless now saw as an even larger conspiracy. He paused several times to stare at Lina. Finally, he asked, "Where was your daughter born?"

"Shaoguan"

"Has she been with you all along?"

"No, until recently she was with my step-aunt in Shaoguan."

Abruptly turning to one of the guards, the general said, "Return the child to her mother at once. See that Rong Liaoping receives medical attention immediately." The tension ebbed from Lina's face, and she dropped her head in relief.

The guard saluted. "Yes, sir."

The general went to a phone on the wall and lifted the receiver. "This is General Liang. Get me General Zhu." Then he turned to the wall and muffled his voice.

General Zhu? The Long March veteran? I was in far deeper water than I had realized. And Liang. General Liang. I wouldn't soon forget him.

• • •

"Who did you say is calling?" the housekeeper asked.

Li Gwei-yu's housekeeper had been with her for nearly thirty-eight years, and she was going deaf. She was a Mainlander and so, despite her lowly station, looked down on any and all of the native Taiwanese she encountered. She was certain that the caller had a trace of a Taiwanese accent. Not welcome. Besides, it was after ten at night.

"My name is Harry Chen. Could I please speak to Madame Li Gwei-yu?"

"How do you know she wants to talk to you? State your business, or I'll hang up."

"Well, it's none of yours." His voice was loud enough now to be heard in the room.

"Who is it?" Li Gwei-yu said.

"Please wait." The housekeeper put a hand over the receiver.

"Madame, he says his name is Mr. Harry Chen, but he refuses to state his—"

"Give me the phone and leave." Li Gwei-yu held her hand over the receiver until the housekeeper had gone. Certain that her servant would listen in the hallway, she shouted, "And close the door behind you!" The housekeeper shuffled into view and sullenly closed the door.

Gwei-yu nestled her Chanel-clad body into the desk chair. Fiona's death had been serendipitous, indeed. A heaven-sent opportunity for a power grab. No doubt Chen was calling to report on his mission, but he was already violating her no further contact rule. Besides, she already knew about the meeting in Hong Kong. Control was everything, and she meant to hold on to it.

She removed a jade earring, carefully pushed back her expensively coiffed hair, and put the phone to her ear. "How dare you call me here? I told you to fence your pearls of wisdom through that attorney in Hong Kong . . . Mac something . . . you know, my brother's hired gun."

"Aidan MacKinnon?"

"Yes, that's him."

"Your brother, MacKinnon, and I are real tight. We had a strategy session and—"

"Bullshit. My brother wouldn't have anything to do with the likes of you!"

"Listen, you foul-mouthed bitch, if you want to find out what happened to your niece, you'll deal with me. You and I, we figure things the same. Now, if you want to hear what I have to say, you'll meet with me, and at a time of my choosing."

Of course, he was right. They did think alike. She prided herself on always being two moves ahead of any adversary, but she needed the information that only Chen could get for her. She did not care a whit that the silly cow had gone off and got herself killed. But control of Nan Hwa and Adair, Jameson . . . well, control them and you controlled Hong Kong. That was a role best played by Taiwan, and that would be the legacy that would forever enshrine her name in Chinese history: Li Gwei-yu, the one who delivered Hong Kong to the successors of Chiang Kai-shek.

"You're quite right." Gwei-yu began to fondle the pearl-handled derringer she had received as a hostess favor two years ago at a dinner party for the KMT ruling elite. Although she never went anywhere except in her armored limousine and with a full detail of motorcycle security, she carried the pistol everywhere. "I apologize, but you see I am not planning to be in Hong Kong any time soon." She was not about to tell him that her brother had called and demanded that she come to Hong Kong posthaste.

Chen chortled girlishly. "That's okay. I'm right here in Taipei. In fact, at this very moment I'm right down the street from you. I bought this house special because I wanted to be in your neighborhood."

Gwei-yu gripped the derringer so hard that one of her manicured fingernails snapped, and the pistol fell to the floor. "Damn!"

"Did I say something wrong?"

"No, it's nothing," she said. "Something . . . uh . . . something just slipped off my desk." Fortunately the derringer had not gone off when it hit the floor. That would have been hard to explain. "When would it be convenient for you to get together?"

"How about right now?"

"Excellent. I'll put my housekeeper on so that you can arrange to have your car admitted at the gate." She put the phone back in its cradle and consulted her Rolodex. Then she carefully replaced her jade earring, picked up the phone again, and rang her friend, the chief of the KMT secret police.

• • •

The boat ride from Taitung, a town on Taiwan's inhospitable and sparsely populated east coast, to the forbidding KMT prison bastion of Green Island twenty-five miles offshore was more harrowing than usual, thanks to a tropical rainstorm. The Pacific swells were so massive that the small craft's bow pitched violently upward then plunged downward into seemingly bottomless troughs.

Aboard that day was the usual complement of soldiers and KMT secret police, as well as two prisoners shackled to a bulkhead in the hold. Two soldiers assigned to guard the prisoners chatted and smoked in a corner.

One of the two prisoners whispered, "My name is Lu Shuibian. What's yours?"

One of the guards whirled around. "You two shut your—"

He was cut off by the boat suddenly pitching hard to one side. The soldiers fell clumsily against the hull as their rifles, leaning against the wall, clattered to the floor. The cigarette one soldier was holding burned the other on the arm, and the two fell to arguing, oblivious to the prisoners.

"Look," Lu whispered. "It's very important that we know as much about each other as possible. People have a way of never coming back from Green Island. Chances are, no one even knows where we are." The other prisoner maintained a stony silence, staring blankly into the distance.

"It's okay. You rest, and I'll speak." Lu glanced at the two soldiers, who were still arguing. "I'm from Kaohsiung. I'm a lawyer, a human rights lawyer. We'll probably be put directly into solitary confinement as soon as we land. It's extremely important that you at least tell me your name."

The other prisoner looked at Lu. "That filthy bitch double-crossed me. Nobody double-crosses Harry Chen and gets away with it. When my associates find out what she's done to me, I'll be on this scow's return trip to Taitung. Why, right this minute, I bet they're already—"

Lu tried to signal to Chen to stop talking. One of the soldiers walked across the hold and hammered Chen across the jaw with the butt of his rifle.

• • •

It was after 11:00 p.m. when General Zhu was finally able to relax over a glass of Scotch in his apartment. Earlier that day, he and his staff had gone over and over the plans for the National Day operation at the Great Hall of the People. They had scrubbed them, worst-cased them, and war-gamed them until Zhu was satisfied that all exigencies had been addressed. Now it was full speed ahead to victory on October 1 and triumph over the lingering savagery of the Cultural Revolution.

The one outstanding obstacle, his daughter's freedom, ostensibly had been resolved by General Liang's call from the Ministry's detention center saying that he had found her—in Beijing. The news had floored him. Colonel Peng had been sworn to secrecy and could be trusted to honor his pledge. And although Liang's revelation that he had turned up evidence of a daughter was unnerving, he thought he had successfully passed it off as gossip. Apparently Liang was not convinced and had pursued his suspicions. Who had he turned up—and why? To curry favor? Or was it something more unsavory? Liang had always been mercenary, which was why he had to be kept at arm's length.

He would have to sort out all of this later. Liang and several of the detention center guards were at that moment bringing the young woman to his apartment. Zhu smiled. It was sublime irony that his daughter, if it was his daughter, should be held in the same detention center where, two days hence, Jiang Qing would be brought after her arrest.

And what of this American who had penetrated the Ministry? Why were Chinese government agents with him? Zhu had ordered Liang to keep the American spy in custody until he could question him personally.

There was a knock at the study door.

"Come," Zhu said as he rose from his seat at the map table.

General Liang and two guards entered. They were followed by three more guards and a young woman carrying a child who was fast asleep on her shoulder. There was an uneasy silence while the guards stationed themselves around the perimeter of the room. The woman appeared hesitant, not sure what to expect.

Zhu was stunned at the sight of her and found himself staring. Struggling to retain his composure, he asked, "What is your name?"

"Rong Lina, sir, and this is my daughter Liming.

"Perhaps the child would be more comfortable sleeping on the sofa," Zhu said.

Lina laid the child down. Zhu took off the jacket of his uniform and covered the sleeping child. He then motioned the woman to a chair at the map table. Zhu and Liang remained standing in the shadows at the other end of the room.

"Tell me, General Liang," Zhu asked, "where is my daughter?"

The blood drained from the face of the intelligence chief. "General Zhu, that is your daughter sitting at the table. My intelligence apparatus confirms it beyond any doubt."

Zhu glared at his aide. *How could Liang have made such a fundamental mistake?* Disappointment welled up.

"General," Liang said, "perhaps you would like to question her."

"Yes," Zhu said, "but first explain to me what the American was doing in the company of two Chinese agents."

"The American spy," Liang said, "claims to be the attorney for a bourgeois Hong Kong capitalist on a mission to China to recover the remains of the capitalist's daughter. As I understand it, the husband of Rong Lina told the American spy that he had information about how the daughter died."

"And why did the three of them enter the tunnel?"

"Although my investigation is not yet complete, General," Liang said, "it seems that the husband Rong Liaoping and the American spy were meeting this afternoon at about two o'clock at a deserted site at the northern edge of the Forbidden City when they came under rifle fire."

"Wait . . . rifle fire?"

"Yes, sir. My investigators found bullet fragments at the site."

"That could only mean official involvement of some sort."

"I'm afraid so, sir. Interrogation of the woman and other preliminary evidence suggests that the shooters were Red Army political commissars."

"It is absolutely critical, General Liang," Zhu said, "that you complete your investigation into what happened to these three before the night is over."

"Yes, sir, General Zhu."

"Now," Zhu said, "why did they enter the tunnel?"

"It seems that, when they came under fire, your daughter . . . uh . . . the woman over there led them to the tunnel in order to escape. She claims to know of the tunnels because of her assignment to Detachment 8341. The American spy apparently carried Rong Liaoping to safety."

"What are the woman's duties in Zhongnanhai?"

"She claims to be part of the detail that guards Madame Song Qingling, sir."

"Impressive, if true. I assume you're checking. Let me know the minute you hear. The woman and the child can rest here as long as they like, then someone should see to it that they are returned home safely. Now, take me to the American."

• • •

I was alone except for three surly guards who stood near the door of the unheated basement cell. One of them had taken my watch, so I had no way of knowing how long I had been inside the Ministry. No one knew I was here—not Aidan, not Hugh or Emma, not even Miss Pan. I had quite simply never been so frightened in my life.

I tried to sit on my hands to warm them, but the guard nearest me grabbed my wrist and jerked it so hard that I nearly toppled from the chair. Just then the door swung open. The guard who had grabbed me whipped to attention as the other two guards straightened and clicked their heels. An older man in a general's uniform decorated with three stars swept through the door followed by two guards and General Liang, the officer who had interrogated Lina and me earlier that day.

I had no idea who the older man was. I did not recognize him from any magazine photographs, but given the deference paid, he had to be powerful. He turned to one of the guards and said, "Get an English translator down here right away."

Before the guard could react, Liang said, "That won't be necessary, General Zhu. The American spy speaks excellent Mandarin."

So this was the famous General Zhu. The plot was thickening, and I didn't like it one bit.

Zhu turned to me, "Do you speak *putonghua* and, more important, are you a spy?"

"Yes," I said, "I do speak Mandarin. And no, I'm not a spy."

General Zhu sat down in a chair pulled up for him by one of the guards. He crossed one knee over the other and lit a cigarette. A guard placed a small table and an ashtray next to him. He stared at the wall and smoked for a few minutes. "Where did you learn to speak our language?" he asked. I found it mildly disconcerting that he did not look at me.

"I began to study in the United States. Then I was a teacher for three years in Taiwan."

Zhu raised his eyebrows. I braced for the perfunctory "Taiwan is a renegade province of China enslaved by the hegemonic American military and their bourgeois KMT lackeys," but he simply said, "I understand that you saved the life of Rong Liaoping today."

I managed to stammer, "Yes . . . well, no . . . actually, he—"

"Rest assured, young man, that you can speak truthfully. No one is going to harm you so long as you do so."

I breathed a little easier. "I acted on instinct. After all, he did save my life two nights ago."

"I applaud your instinct. But tell me, exactly how did Rong Liaoping save your life?"

I described our midnight encounter with a Mercedes limousine in front of the old Austro-Hungarian Legation. I told him of the damage to the car, the incident with the hood ornament, and that someone had stolen the ornament from my hotel room that morning.

Zhu turned to Liang. "Have someone investigate this immediately." Zhu started to turn back to me but stopped and said to Liang, "Oh, and tell them also to check on the condition of all limousines in the fleet. Start with those assigned to Zhongnanhai." Then he said to me, "And what were you doing so late at night in such a place?" His distaste was obvious from his reluctance even to utter the words "Legation Quarter."

"As odd as it must appear, I was restless and wanted to take a walk. A friend had recommended the Legation Quarter."

"What friend?"

"A friend in Hong Kong," I replied. I couldn't implicate Hugh and Emma.

Liang stepped forward and whispered in Zhu's ear. I could only make out "attorney for" and "the capitalist's daughter." Zhu suddenly looked ill. Despite the cold, his face flushed. Then, just as quickly, it went white as a sheet.

Liang was alarmed. "General Zhu, can I get you anything? Some tea, perhaps?"

Zhu waved him off and seemed, by sheer force of will, to collect himself. He turned to me and, in a manner that conveyed that he would brook no delay or obfuscation, said, "I want two pieces of information from you: the name of the person you represent and the name of his daughter."

"I'm the attorney for Li Dak-chung, and his daughter's name is Fiona."

"Fiona is the daughter's English name," Liang said quickly. "Her Chinese name is Li Guangmei."

Without saying another word, General Zhu rose and strode out of the room.

• • •

Although it seemed an eternity, a few hours later I was hustled out of the Ministry of National Defense and taken back to the Beijing Hotel by a Major Wang, an amiable army officer who introduced himself as an aide to General Zhu. He was, I guessed, in his thirties, good-looking, and fairly tall, suggesting Manchu ancestry. On the way to the hotel we had a lively chat from my position under a blanket on the backseat floor. Wang had insisted on this for my safety, and presumably, his. He seemed genuinely interested in my background and told me of his beginnings in the PLA during the Cultural Revolution and mentoring by General Zhu. He was clearly in awe of his boss. Wang had arranged beforehand for a hotel employee to smuggle me in through a back door and up to my room. Before we parted company, he admonished me to say nothing about what had happened at the Forbidden City or at the Ministry and said he would contact me later about a subsequent meeting with General Zhu. When I finally reached my room, I collapsed on the bed and, for the first time since arriving in China, fell immediately into a dreamless sleep.

CHAPTER 18

Thursday, September 30, 1976

Colonel Peng stood in the aisle with the other passengers as the train neared Beijing's main central station. He felt refreshed after a night's sleep on the train, but he worried about how Zhu was taking the news that he had come up empty-handed in the search for Zhu's daughter.

The train lurched to a stop, rocking Peng and the other passengers hard to the right. The woman standing next to him was juggling a baby in one arm and a steaming mug of tea in the other. The tea cascaded over Peng's uniform and onto his shoes. Fearing the rage of a Red Army officer, the woman began to *ke tou* and swipe at Peng's sleeve with the edge of the blanket swaddling her now wailing baby. Nearby passengers, unwilling to witness the expected retribution, silently shrank back or slipped back to their compartments, closed the doors, and drew the curtains.

Peng tried to reassure the woman that he was not angry, but nothing he said allayed the woman's terror. He finally withdrew to his own compartment to await his greeter. By that time the aisle was empty except for the woman and her baby. Even the rail car's attendant, usually officiously omnipresent, had disappeared. Peng had just sat down again when the train lurched forward, and the last of the north China plain gave way to the outskirts of the capital. It was time to report on his failure.

Major Wang was on the platform to meet him. Wang said that General Zhu needed him at the Ministry as quickly as possible and, on the way, briefed him on the next day's military operation at the Great Hall.

As their car sped west on Chang An Jie, crews were out in full force hanging banners over the boulevard saying "Long Live the Glorious Chinese Communist Party!" and "Warmly Celebrate the Founding of the People's Republic of China!" Other crews were festooning lampposts with lanterns; and in Tiananmen, the Great Hall had been draped in massive swaths of red and gold cloth.

"There will be a glorious victory tomorrow," Wang said. Peng did not respond. "—a victory for socialism, China, and the masses." Peng remained silent. Wang did not try again.

When they arrived at the Ministry, Peng was out of the car and through the door before Wang could gather his overcoat around him. Wang hurried into the building after the now out-of-sight colonel and bolted up the stairs two at a time to General Zhu's apartment. One of Zhu's servants directed him to the general's study, the door to which stood open.

"Major," Zhu said to his young aide, "you look winded. Please, don't stand there in the doorway. Come in and join us." Zhu and Peng were sitting on the sofa. Wang crossed the room and sat in a straight-backed chair directly facing them.

"Colonel Peng," Zhu said, "was just briefing me on his trip to Lingkou. Colonel, please continue."

"I'm afraid that's the sum total, sir," Peng said. "The army intelligence officials whom General Liang said I could trust knew nothing of an unauthorized compatriot in the area. I ran down a few leads but came up empty."

"Unfortunate," Zhu said, "but not surprising, considering what I have learned during the last twelve hours."

Zhu related Liang's story of the events in the Forbidden City and the Ministry basement. On his orders, Liang's investigators had confirmed overnight that Rong Lina was, indeed, assigned to Detachment 8341 and that her husband, Rong Liaoping, was a special agent at the Ministry of Public Security. The report that Rong Liaoping had filed at his Ministry the night of the Legation Quarter incident verified the American's account. Finally, the investigators had discovered extensive damage to Jiang Qing's Mercedes limousine and corresponding scars on the gatepost at the Austro-Hungarian Legation. The limousine's hood ornament was missing.

"I had the American released from detention, and Major Wang, here, returned him to his hotel. Colonel Peng, I think it's time you had a talk with the Rongs. It is now unavoidable that they be brought in."

"On everything?" Peng asked.

"Everything. Oh, and include the American's Travel Service handler as well. The name is Pan."

• • •

Major Wang appeared unannounced at my room at the hotel before ten. Famished and exhausted by two, or possibly three, brushes with death within 24 hours, I had only just made it to breakfast before the dining room closed at 9:00. I was in the bathroom washing my hands when I noticed out of the corner of my eye a figure standing in the doorway. "What the—"

The Major put a finger to his lips. He was holding my jacket in one hand and, with the other hand, motioned for me to come with him. I took my jacket and followed him to the door, which was being held open by my hall monitor. She looked up and down the hallway and then waved us forward. With Wang leading the way, the two of us slipped through the door to the service staircase, down the stairs, and out of the hotel to a back alley. A car, engine idling, was waiting to take us, I assumed, to the promised second meeting with General Zhu.

As we clambered into the backseat, I caught my foot on the Shanghai's unusually high frame and splayed out on the floor, half of my body inside the car and half out. Thinking we were safely in the car, the driver accelerated. I desperately groped for anything that would keep me from sliding feetfirst onto the asphalt.

A hand jerked on my collar, and the Major barked, "Stop, you fool! Do you want to kill him?"

The driver slammed on the brakes, sending the car into a skid. When it stopped, the driver, without turning to face us, mumbled an unconvincing apology. With Major Wang's help, I scrambled up onto the seat.

Wang growled "okay," and the car once again tore down the narrow alley. When we reached the corner of the hotel building, the driver made a sharp left, then a sharp right onto Chang An Jie, hurtling onto the sidewalk and scattering a crowd of pedestrians.

"Slow down!" Wang said as he slid forward and gripped the back of the front seat. "The last thing I want is to attract attention!" I tried to look at the driver's face in the rearview mirror, but he spotted me and twisted it away.

Wang slid back into his seat. "Sorry, new driver. Well, not new. Our regular driver is sick, and this one is a temporary fill-in for today."

We were just passing Tiananmen and the heavily guarded entrance to Zhongnanhai when the driver turned right onto the boulevard that led north toward the Ministry of National Defense. After completing the turn, the car suddenly accelerated.

"I *said* slow down!" Wang shouted. "If it happens again, I'll take the wheel myself and you'll—"

The driver abruptly turned the steering wheel hard to the right, sending me sliding across the seat and up against Major Wang, who was pressed against the door. The car sped across another sidewalk, through an opening, and into a courtyard. The car's hood dipped as the driver slammed on the brakes, and the car skidded to a stop on the dirt-and-gravel surface. Two massive, ten-foot gray metal gates slammed shut behind us. *Oh, damn.*

We were immediately surrounded by soldiers, who, from their duck-billed hats, I recognized as Red Army political commissars. One of them jerked open the door, and Major Wang tumbled onto the gravel. Several other commissars opened the other door, grabbed my arm, and pulled me out onto the gravel as well. I caught a glimpse under the car of Major Wang being punched and clubbed by several of the commissars. Then another yanked me to my knees by my left arm—I was sure he had dislocated my shoulder—and somebody punched me in the stomach, doubling me over at the waist. Gasping for breath, I knew what the next punch would be. The upper-cut to my jaw threw me onto my back. Just before I passed out, I glimpsed the person who delivered this blow and realized why he had tilted the rearview mirror askew so I could not see his face. He was the driver who had been assigned to Miss Pan and me.

• • •

"What do you mean he can't be found, Hugh?" MacKinnon bellowed into the phone. It was midmorning, and with a few hours free between appointments, he had settled in to tend to his China stamp collection. He had started collecting soon after arriving in Hong Kong as a means to improve his recognition of Chinese characters, particularly the simplified system newly adopted by the Communists. It had quickly become a passion. Three years prior, his acquisition of one of the PRC's rarest stamps, "The Whole Country Is Red," had propelled him into the presidency of the Hong Kong branch of the China Stamp Society, a position he prized above all others he had held both inside and outside the legal profession.

Miss Chao, standing beside MacKinnon's desk, gingerly closed the stamp album he had been perusing, as much to protect the stamps as to acknowledge that his, and her, free time had ended.

MacKinnon shifted the phone to his other hand. "Bryan should be halfway back to Hong Kong by now." He scowled at the phone, then turned to Miss Chao, shrugged his shoulders, and waved to her to take the album.

"Emma went to his room," Hugh said, "but there was nobody there. The hall monitor, who Emma says was terrified, pulled her aside and whispered that Bryan had left that morning with a Chinese army officer."

Click.

"Perhaps he was on his way to the train station," MacKinnon said. "Did he check out of the hotel?"

"Emma says the hall monitor told her Bryan went out without his luggage. His room is still occupied. And Aidan, there's something else . . ."

MacKinnon bit his tongue at the hesitation. They both knew the line was bugged, but only Hugh could judge the sensitivity of what he was about to say.

"The hall monitor told Emma that she knows the officer with Bryan," Hugh said at last. "He's actively working on behalf of the moderates and Deng Xiaoping."

Click.

"Damn!" MacKinnon said. He agreed with Hugh's unspoken decision. They had to talk openly on a bugged phone line if they were to have any hope of saving Paton's life. "Did the hall monitor say Bryan went willingly?"

"Yes, Bryan did," Hugh said. "In fact, the hall monitor said she helped Bryan and the officer leave the hotel on the sly by a back stairway."

Click.

"Any clue as to where they were headed?"

"Emma got the impression that they were on their way to a meeting of some sort. But no, the hall monitor didn't know the details."

"What has that boy stumbled into?"

"There's more," Hugh said. "Emma is certain that the hall monitor is involved, and a good many others as well. It looks as if Bryan is hopelessly caught up in the post-Mao power struggle—and for that matter, Li Dak-chung and Fiona are, too. It's a real hornet's nest. And Aidan, I'm now convinced that Fiona is still alive. I suggest you ask Li . . . hello? . . . hello? . . . Aidan, are you still there?" The line had suddenly gone dead.

"Miss Chao," MacKinnon shouted, "we've been cut off!"

"I'm on now with the telephone company," Miss Chao said. "They say the Chinese have cut the line, and there's nothing they can do about it. Shall I try again in fifteen minutes to get through to Mr. Highgrove?"

MacKinnon thought a moment then said, "No, see if the governor is available."

"Certainly. Right away."

• • •

The Chinese army officer sitting in an office in Zhongnanhai took off the headphones with which he had been listening to the schemes of the enemies of socialism. He turned to his aide. "I'll brief Comrade Jiang Qing. You notify the hall monitor's work unit that she is terminated."

"Yes, sir." The aide turned to leave.

"Just a minute. I'm not finished," the officer said. "Terminate the hall monitor with extreme prejudice. Make her and her family socialist examples of what happens when you betray the Party and the masses."

"Yes, sir."

After his aide departed, General Liang rose from his desk and crossed the hall to Jiang Qing's office.

. . .

In the few minutes it took Miss Chao to call Government House, MacKinnon thought about Paton's fate. He also realized that he would need to tell Dak-chung that Hugh believed Fiona might still be alive. He used his private line to call Li and pass on this latest information. As he was hanging up, Miss Chao appeared in the doorway. "The governor can see you in fifteen minutes."

MacKinnon's driver pulled into the Upper Albert Road entrance to Government House barely ten minutes later. The guard was expecting them and waved their car through the gate. The servant who opened the door for MacKinnon directed him to the drawing room. As MacKinnon made his way there, he found the governor walking toward him.

"Sir Geoffrey, good of you to see me on such short notice," MacKinnon said as he and the governor shook hands and entered the drawing room.

Prime Minister Edward Heath had appointed Sir Geoffrey Lugard Governor in 1973, shortly after Lugard retired from the Diplomatic Service following a posting as British Ambassador in Beijing. A Mandarin speaker, Lugard had spent most of his diplomatic career in the Far East. He was thought of so highly that when Labour defeated the Conservatives in 1974, Harold Wilson kept Lugard on in the sensitive Hong Kong post.

"I'm always available for Hong Kong's foremost barrister," the governor said as the two old friends sat down. "I assume you're here to ask what can be done for your chap in Beijing."

"Well, yes. How did you—?"

"Don't be surprised. We just had a cable from our embassy there. Unfortunately, Her Majesty's government has no options, formal or otherwise. Especially since your chap is not a British subject."

"I thought as much," MacKinnon said, "but I felt I owed it to Paton and Dak-chung at least to take a run at some sort of official intervention."

"How is Dak-chung holding up?"

"A roller coaster of emotions, I'm afraid," MacKinnon said. "Elation at the prospect that Fiona may be alive. Rage about where she might be and how she's being treated."

Lugard shifted in his chair, uncrossed his legs, and looked intently at MacKinnon. "Aidan, what I'm about to say can never leave this room. On a personal level, I'm naturally as distressed as you are over what's happening to Dak-chung. But officially, I must be concerned only with what happens to the Li family conglomerate. Nan Hwa and Adair, Jameson are far too important to the Colony's stability to risk doing anything that might unsettle markets. London is aware of the situation, and the best minds at the Foreign Office have struggled with it. They have sadly concluded that it can only be a watching brief for us because we have neither leverage with the Chinese nor assets inside that benighted country. I'm afraid it's all now on the shoulders of your American chap in Beijing."

"I see. Thank you for your honesty."

During the drive back to Hutchison House, MacKinnon's ears were ringing with Sir Geoffrey's words, and he had a foul taste in his mouth so disagreeable that even the Havana cigar he was smoking could not expunge it. He didn't have the luxury of a mere "watching brief" and was nearly back to Bishops when it dawned on him what he had to do. He had to utilize Chen and his Triad network. It was then that MacKinnon identified the foul taste in his mouth.

• • •

"Kai-kui?" MacKinnon said into the phone. "Aidan MacKinnon, here."

Dai Kai-kui was Hong Kong's most important Communist union boss and had the best contacts on either side of the ideological divide, with the exception of Harry Chen. And MacKinnon desperately needed those contacts again.

"Aidan," Dai said, "what a pleasure to hear from you twice in one week. How have you been? And Glynis? I trust she's well."

"Oh, she gets ample exercise running in and out of the shops on Queen's Road," MacKinnon said.

Dai laughed. "Ah, false laments. Tell me, are you still the lap dog of Hong Kong's biggest *taipan*?"

MacKinnon knew that his old friend Dai was joking, but given the purpose of his call, hearing Li Dak-chung referred to in such terms irritated him.

"As a matter of fact," MacKinnon said, "Li family business is the reason I'm calling you."

Hearing MacKinnon's somber tone, Dai responded in kind, "How can I help you?"

"I'm trying to get in touch with Harry Chen," MacKinnon said. "I've called him several times, but I can't seem to raise him."

"Funny you should mention that scoundrel. Word on the street today is that he tangled with Li Gwei-yu and ended up with the short stick. She had Harry clapped into a very small cell on Green Island."

"Bugger! How on earth am I to contact him?"

"You'll have to go through the dragon lady."

"I'm sorry, what did you say?"

"I said you'll have to deal with Li Gwei-yu herself if you're to have any hope of springing Chen. She's apparently determined that Harry will never leave the island alive."

MacKinnon thanked Dai and hung up. He knew that a direct appeal from him to Gwei-yu would fail. Gwei-yu believed that he exercised too much control over Li family affairs and called him, even to his face, "my brother's keeper." No, MacKinnon knew that only her brother could persuade Gwei-yu to give up her Green Island catch. There would be an opportunity for that tomorrow.

. . .

In the basement of the Ministry of Public Security, General Liang's aide, Major Zhang, strode confidently into a room in which several dozen people had been assembled. He mounted a low wooden stage and asked, "What punishment do the masses demand?"

A woman dutifully rose and shouted, "Execute her!"

Zhang paced across the stage scowling until another woman shouted, "Execute all the vermin in her rat hole!"

Zhang smiled broadly. "The wisdom of the masses is never wrong. Bring in the prisoners."

To catcalls from the audience, a soldier led in the Beijing Hotel hall monitor, her fifteen-year-old son, her grown daughter and son-in-law, and her four-year-old grandson and three-year-old granddaughter, both of whom were wailing in terror. All had their hands tied behind their backs except for the young children, who each held fast to a corner of their mother's coat.

The hall monitor took a step forward. "Untie my family at once! Can't you see my granddaughter is terrified? I'm a Party member! You can't treat us like—"

A soldier stepped from the shadows and coldcocked her. She staggered backward, blood spilling from her mouth, and collapsed on the stage. The three-year-old screamed louder, and her four-year-old brother began to tremble uncontrollably. Their mother, attempting to comfort and quiet her children, knelt down on one knee. A soldier sprang at her, pulled a leather belt tight around her neck, and jerked upward with such force that her neck snapped. As she lay gasping at her children's feet, the soldier released the belt and pulled his pistol from its holster. Kicking her to one side so that blood would not splatter on his freshly polished boots, he delivered one shot to her forehead.

The woman's husband covered her body with his, then went limp as Zhang put a bullet in his back. Announcing that he could not bear to watch the children suffer, Zhang shot both in the head as they wept on their mother's lifeless body. A few in the audience gasped but quickly fell silent when Zhang swung around and glared at them, the pistol still in his hand.

The fifteen-year-old boy attempted to break his guard's hold on his neck but succeeded only in knocking off his thick glasses, which tumbled noisily to the stage. The soldier tightened his grip.

"No, wait," Zhang said, "don't kill him yet!"

The teenager gasped for air as the soldier loosened his arm then ground his heel into the teenager's glasses.

Zhang holstered his pistol. "Take him into the hallway." He gestured toward the bodies. "And get those vermin out in the hallway too. They're stinking up the room."

The soldiers grabbed the legs of the bodies and dragged them away. The head of the semiconscious hall monitor bounced from the stage to the floor with a sickening thud. The woman groaned but did not revive. A soldier hefted the bodies of the two children, carrying them over his shoulders like rag dolls. In the hallway, the soldiers covered each body with a sheet.

"Comrades, follow me." Zhang led the assemblage to the adjacent room, which contained an empty surgical gurney. "That's right," Zhang said when his men brought in the shrouded body of the hall monitor. "Put it here on the gurney. Nurse, could you please move the gurney under the light so everyone can see. That's right. Just there. Perfect."

"Permit me to introduce Dr. Song." Zhang motioned to a man in a white smock standing in a corner of the room. He bowed obsequiously to Song, who halfheartedly bowed back. "Dr. Song is the administrator and chief of surgery at Capital Hospital, and our country's foremost authority on the theory and practice of socialist medicine. He has been, I might add, a loyal Party member for nearly forty years. The good doctor will now demonstrate the extraction of human organs to you, the representatives of the socialist masses, for whose profit this bounty is harvested."

Dr. Song waved to his nurse to remove the sheet covering the body then turned to a small table against the wall on which lay his surgical instruments. As the other members of the team prepared for the procedure, Zhang nodded to the soldier guarding the door. The soldier opened the door, went into the hallway, and brought in the teenager.

The nurse at the gurney screamed, "Doctor, it's your wife! She's still alive!"

"Father!" the teenager shouted. The soldier guarding the boy abruptly silenced him with several punches to the face.

As Dr. Song lunged forward to protect his son, Zhang stepped forward and blocked his path. "Don't ever presume to interfere with a soldier in the lawful exercise of his duties!"

Dr. Song looked at his barely conscious wife whose breathing had become labored. "Please, let somebody take her and my son to the hospital."

"No," Zhang said. "You have a demonstration to present." He glared at the doctor. "And you shall *not* deprive the masses of their just retribution. Now, you will extract the organs from this traitor, or you and your son will die."

The doctor looked around at those gathered in the room. Some looked away; others stared back defiantly, aware that the doctor and his son were already dead men. Dr. Song fixed his gaze on the face of a woman standing among the observers, her eyes sad, her cheeks streaked with tears, her expression inconsolable. He smiled weakly at the woman then turned to the instrument table. After a few moments of deliberation, he picked up a knife with a long scimitar-like curve at the tip of the blade and balanced it in the palm of his hand. Satisfied with his selection, he took a deep breath and turned back to the assemblage. His son was staring plaintively at him.

Song turned and bent over the gurney. "Could you please step back a bit," he said to Zhang, who had crowded in at his elbow. "I need more space to . . . uh . . . to do what I must do."

"Certainly." Zhang stepped back. "And Doctor, please explain what you are doing so that the comrades present will not fail to learn the lesson of today's proceedings."

"Of course," Dr. Song mumbled. "This scalpel is used to extract the eyes from their sockets, as you would a succulent oyster from its shell. It is necessary to do this first because the corneas must be—" The nurse fell to her knees, her hands covering her eyes.

A woman at the rear vomited on the man standing next to her. As the man recoiled and cried out, the soldiers and the rest of the audience turned toward the commotion. Dr. Song, using both hands, plunged the scalpel into Zhang's jugular and pulled downward with all the force he could muster. Zhang, his chest cavity exposed and blood cascading on the floor, froze like an insect trapped in amber, then toppled over.

The soldiers reacted with greedy vengeance. One split the teenager's head open by ramming it into the masonry wall. To be certain the boy was dead, the soldier pulled his Ministry-issue garrote out of his pocket, wrapped it around the boy's throat, and strangled him with such force that he nearly severed the boy's head from his body.

Another grabbed a scalpel from the table and slit the wife's wrists, leaving her blood to drain on the floor. As her life ebbed away, she groaned several times but never regained consciousness.

A third soldier sprang at Song and began beating him savagely. He yanked on the doctor's hair, pulling his head erect and forcing him to watch as his wife and son were murdered. "I am now in charge," he said. "We will complete the exhibition."

He turned and, with his arm fully extended at his side, flicked his finger. The other soldiers immediately came to attention. One of them broke ranks and slid an S-shaped abattoir-like hook out from the wall along the overhead pipe to which it was attached. He positioned the hook directly above the doctor and, taking care not to lacerate his hands on the razor-sharp lower tip, pulled downward to ensure that it would not give way.

"Sergeant," he said, "the apparatus is ready for use."

"Proceed," the sergeant ordered.

Two soldiers approached the doctor, who, groggy and disoriented, was on the floor slumped forward on his knees. They grabbed him under the armpits and hoisted him to his feet. Gasps rippled through the audience when they saw the effect of the beating the doctor had suffered. His face was pulpy and bleeding profusely. Both eyes were purple and swollen shut, and he was drooling from the gaping hole of a mouth that was now grotesquely lopsided.

The two soldiers hoisted the doctor over their heads while a third soldier stood on a chair and steadied the meat hook. When the two holding the doctor thrust him onto the hook, it impaled him through the back of his head and neck. A gurgling sound came from Dr. Song's throat before the tip of the hook exited through the front of his neck and severed his vocal chords. Dangling for an instant, he went limp, then motionless.

A soldier approached the doctor's body and drove the butt of his truncheon into the doctor's stomach. Satisfied that he was dead, the soldier nodded to the sergeant.

"Comrades," the sergeant said, "I know you will want to thank the comrade soldiers for their work today under extremely difficult circumstances." There was halfhearted applause from among the observers.

"I remind you that you are forbidden to speak of these events with anyone, not even among yourselves. Anyone guilty of doing so will incur the same penalty that was paid by these traitors today. You will feel content only when you erase this episode from your memory. By doing so, you will follow the Party line and serve the masses."

• • •

Zhu looked up from his desk when Colonel Peng rushed in. He was not accustomed to seeing his closest aide so agitated.

"General," Peng said, "Major Wang and the American have disappeared. Their car and driver are missing as well."

Zhu pushed back from his desk, thought for a moment, and said, "Get General Liang up here right away."

National Day was tomorrow. Everything was poised for the military operation at the Great Hall. Major Wang knew everything about the plan—the timing, the troop movements, the leaders' involvement, and where Jiang Qing would be taken after her arrest. Even now, the radicals were probably torturing him to find out what he knew. For the moment, Zhu pushed thoughts of his daughter to the back of his mind.

Liang walked into the office followed by Colonel Peng. Zhu said to Liang, "Major Wang and the American have disappeared. They were on their way here from the Beijing Hotel. Needless to say, we have to find them right away. If we don't, tomorrow's operation will be in jeopardy. I want you to find them, General. Can you do it?"

"I'm not sure that will be possible," Liang answered. "Anyway, the major is a small fish."

Zhu was dismayed but not surprised by this response. When he heard that the Lingkou officials Liang recommended had turned out to be ineffectual, his suspicion had grown that the moderates had a spy in their midst. He would have to buy time—a few hours, not more—to consider what to do with the traitor Liang.

"General Liang," Zhu said quietly, "you underestimate your considerable talent and that of your intelligence apparatus. Please try." Peng coughed and shifted in his seat.

Liang took longer than normal to draw a cigarette from his pocket and light it. He exhaled a cloud of smoke, picked a speck of tobacco off his lip, and brushed imaginary dust from his trousers. "Of course, General Zhu, but you—"

"Good, good," Zhu said. "Now, if you will excuse me, I have a busy afternoon ahead of me."

"Of course, sir." Liang rose to leave.

"Oh, and one more thing, General," Zhu said as Liang was almost through the door. "Find them today."

Liang nodded and left.

Peng closed the office door. "So he's the one."

"As usual," Zhu said, "you read my thoughts. And unfortunately for Major Wang, it doesn't matter now whether they break him or not."

Peng knew Zhu was not writing Wang off, but if Liang knew the moderates' plans, then Jiang Qing knew them as well.

"I have to get word to Deng right away," Zhu said.

"Yes, sir. But what will you say? There's really only one thing you can—"

"That's right. There is only one thing I can tell him—that we'll have to call off tomorrow's operation. And why."

"All of it?" Peng asked.

"All of it."

• • •

The throbbing in my left shoulder woke me. In the darkness, I tried to look at my watch, but a jolt of pain in my shoulder stopped me. Even if I could have raised my arm, I could see nothing. I did not know how long I had been wherever I now was.

I tried to sit up, but my head struck something as hard as concrete. I felt above me with my hand. It was indeed concrete. I felt the floor. Also concrete. A wave of panic gripped my throat, nearly choking me. *Where was I?*

I tried to calm myself by doing something purposeful. I thrust my leg out to test the length of my prison. Something large and soft inside my trouser leg suddenly moved. I jerked my leg up, cracking my knee-cap against the ceiling. I felt a rat scurry down my trouser leg.

A faint sense of relief came over me. If the rat had a way in and out, maybe I did too. I maneuvered myself into a low crouch, the only position my prison's dimensions would allow, and crawled forward. I met concrete a few feet away. I heard the rat run to the opposite end of what I now knew to be a concrete box. I took a deep breath to control my panic.

I felt around for an opening. There was none. I ran my fingers around the edge of the ceiling. There was a narrow slit that ran the entire width and length of my box, as though the ceiling was actually some sort of lid. I tried to lift it, but with my weak shoulder I could only get enough leverage to budge it slightly. At least it wasn't bolted down. I lay on my back and pulled my knees tight to my chest. It took several tries, but I was finally able to slide the lid open with my feet. Spent by the effort, I lay motionless in the bottom of the box.

When my strength returned, I raised myself up and stood. The box sat in a damp cell that resembled Dr. Song's morgue in the basement of Capital Hospital. There was a metal door at one end and, at the opposite end, a tiny slit of a high window through which a faint glimmer of light entered.

I put one foot outside the box. As I did so, the rat leapt to the floor and ran through the crack under the door to freedom. I took stock of my predicament. It would be an understatement to say I had few options. With nothing to lose, I pounded on the cell door and called for help.

A guard pushed the door open so quickly that I had to jump backward. "Shut up! What are you doing? How did you get out?"

"I need medical attention," I said.

"Medical attention? You piece of pig shit. I'll give you all the medical attention you're ever going to get!"

He punched me in the stomach then in the jaw. I fell to the floor. The guard was about to punch me again when a voice from the open door stopped him.

"That will be enough."

The guard stopped, and then stood at attention as an officer entered. He was the same officer who had interrogated Lina and me the day before: General Liang.

"It seems we have use for Mr. Paton after all," he said. "Regrettably, we won't have the pleasure of executing him today."

I was still on the floor. Liang circled me once, then said, "Get up. Come with me."

As Liang left, the guard jerked me up by my bad arm and pushed me after him down a dark hallway lined with more cells. A small retinue of political commissars fell in behind us. We passed a guard station and climbed a short staircase to a well-lit hallway. While Liang and his retinue continued down the hallway, the guard pulled me into a side room. He slammed me down in the room's only chair then left, bolting the door behind him. The room had a single window. Outside, I could see that the day was waning. A gaunt, leafless tree seemed to be struggling to remain upright against a gathering gale. I shivered at the cold that set my shoulder throbbing. And at more than just the cold.

CHAPTER 19

Friday, October 1, 1976

Zhu arrived at his office early, despite having called off the afternoon's operation. The day before he had contacted Deng and explained everything. As Zhu knew he would, Deng had agreed to the postponement, given the circumstances; but no amount of dissembling could mask his disappointment. Deng ordered Zhu to develop a plan immediately for an operation the following week and to vet it with others in the moderate leadership.

Zhu was to meet with Minister Ye at 10:00 a.m. to present the new plan. He knew all too well that they had to act quickly. He was also painfully aware that, through whatever Major Wang might have divulged and the unwitting inclusion of the traitor Liang in the planning, he himself was at least partially responsible for having given the radicals the upper hand. Zhu buzzed Colonel Peng and asked him to step into his office.

"Good morning, General Zhu," Peng said. "Did you see Major Wang?"

"Yes, I did," Zhu said. "Considering what he's been through, I think he'll be fine."

As Zhu knew he would, General Liang had located Major Wang and the American, Bryan Paton. Liang had Wang taken to Capital Hospital rather than to the hospital reserved for the PLA, utterly at variance with required procedure. Paton was moved initially to an intelligence corps detention facility. Suspicious of Liang's motives, however, Zhu ordered Peng to transfer Paton to the Ministry's holding facility to be held under his personal control. Zhu was not yet ready to confront Liang, but neither was he prepared to let him have his way.

"I am quite concerned about what's going on at Capital Hospital," Zhu said. "Major Wang is still unconscious and too badly injured to be moved. But what really has me worried is the hospital's new administrator, Dr. Tang. He's a known radical sympathizer."

"Dr. Song is no longer there?" Peng said.

"Apparently not. When the new administrator welcomed me this morning, he said he didn't know why he'd been appointed or where Dr. Song was."

"Sir," Peng said, "Dr. Li should know what happened."

For twenty-two years, Li Zhisui had been Mao's personal physician. Thoroughly nonpolitical, he was nonetheless suspect because he had been educated in the United States. On occasion, therefore, Li had found it prudent to consult with prominent China-trained physicians before making a diagnosis or prescribing medication for Mao. Dr. Song had been foremost among Li's consultants.

"Yes, you're quite right. Li will know where Song has gone. And I'd feel better if he were to look in on Major Wang. Please contact him."

"Yes, sir."

"Now," Zhu said, "let's see what you've done on the new plan."

"Yes, sir." Peng spread several pieces of paper on the desk in front of Zhu. "Now, what I thought was that the units—"

"Sorry to interrupt. Are you sure no one on the staff has seen your plan, especially General Liang?"

"No, sir. No one has seen it."

• • •

In the fading light, the aging Greek bent closer to the papyrus on which he was writing. He squinted, rubbed his tired eyes, and then resumed recording the several pages of equations and diagrams so vital to explaining the proof he had developed over the past eighteen months.

The oil lamp next to him sputtered. Anxious to finish his work that night, he laid down his quill, picked up his knife, and teased out more of the lamp's wick. Newly revived, the lamp illuminated the room.

The old man thought of a phrase he had heard. He could not remember where or when, or even if he himself had authored it. Perhaps he had read it when he was a student in Egypt. All he was sure of was that it had resonated over the years and always comforted him: "The flame burned low on the wick, shadows of blue rather than glaring breaches of yellow, fragments of dusk rather than the ferocity of noon."

The daydreamer lying on the sofa all too briefly savored the reason why Archimedes, the greatest mathematician and scientist of antiquity, was the trigger to another, far more profound personal memory.

Violent pounding on the door and the sound of it crashing off its hinges abruptly interrupted his reverie. He opened his eyes just as he was jerked to the floor.

• • •

MacKinnon was pacing and fidgeting, something he rarely did. "You'd think that nowadays Asia's busiest air corridor would be flyable in any weather."

"Aidan," Li said, "your faith in technology is admirable, but fortunately, the heavens will never be governed by man."

"That's all well and good, but—"

Just then the airport loudspeaker crackled to life. "Cathay Pacific announces the arrival of flight 321 from Taipei."

The attendant crossed the first-class waiting room and approached. "Mr. Li, your arriving guest will be directed to this room, as you requested."

"Thank you." Li looked at MacKinnon.

"What will you say to her?" MacKinnon asked.

The look of bewilderment with which Li responded said more than words could about the unpredictability of Li Gwei-yu. MacKinnon knew that Dak-chung and his sister had not been close since they fled Shanghai in 1949. Moreover, although widowed, childless, and with no other living relatives, Gwei-yu not only did not dote on her brother's children but went out of her way to ignore them. In a Chinese family this was unheard of. MacKinnon had often wondered about the basis for her hostility to her niece and nephew. Dak-chung spoke fondly of their life together as children, but now he seemed barely able to tolerate her and was clearly wounded by her indifference to his offspring. Something had happened, some dark secret thing that Dak-chung would not reveal even to him. Given the siblings' relationship, MacKinnon was eager to learn why Gwei-yu would now be willing to involve herself in the search for her niece.

He did not have to wait long. Li Gwei-yu swept grandly through the waiting room door, enveloped in a cloud of Chanel, which she regarded not as a luxury but as a prudent prophylaxis against the odors that afflict the common man. She was followed by a gaggle of airline attendants who seemed drawn to her like a flock of gulls stealing scraps from a trawler. One was carrying her fur wrap, another was grappling with the weight of the case in which she kept her jewelry, and a third was carrying her makeup case. As he did whenever they met, MacKinnon marveled at how little Gwei-yu had changed over the years. Considered a beauty in her youth, she was still a handsome woman. He was sure this was due, at least in part, to the time she spent pampering herself. Unlike her brother whom she clearly resembled, she had grown a bit plump. This was not unattractive, however, even on her petite frame. MacKinnon did think that she wore too much jewelry in the daytime.

"You!" she barked at the attendant carrying her makeup case. "I need more perfume. Bring that here."

MacKinnon scowled but held his tongue. Li Dak-chung, standing directly in front of his sister, stood expressionless. MacKinnon could see the jaw muscles clench in Li's cheeks, belying his outward calm.

When Gwei-yu finished spraying herself liberally with perfume, she seemed genuinely surprised to see her only sibling standing in her path.

"Elder Brother," she said, "I do hope you brought your own limousine." She stared at MacKinnon, conveying that a Bishops car would not do. "If not, the hotel will send one of theirs for me."

"Younger Sister," Li said, "how nice to see you again after so long. It's clear that you haven't changed. Thank you for coming."

"Stop that!" she shouted at the person holding her fur. "That won't survive being twisted around your arm!" The waiting-room attendant hurried across the room, took the fur from the man, and turned toward the closet to hang it up. "That won't be necessary. We won't be here that long." Gwei-yu turned to her brother. "Well?"

"I came in my car, and Aidan came in his. However, if you'd prefer one of the hotel's . . ."

"Nonsense. Yours will be quite adequate." She glared at MacKinnon, conveying unequivocally that she hoped he would not accompany them to the hotel.

MacKinnon, having deciphered Gwei-yu years ago, understood immediately. "Dak-chung, you'll doubtless want some time alone with your sister. Do you need me any longer today?"

He knew the answer. Li had specifically asked him to come along in order to "manage" his sister. "An impossible task," he had said.

"Aidan," Li said, "Gwei-yu and I would be disappointed if you didn't join us for tea at the hotel."

"As always, I am your humble servant," MacKinnon said, largely for Gwei-yu's benefit.

They arrived at the Peninsula Hotel half an hour later. Never one to let humility or sensitivity dampen her sense of privilege, Gwei-yu immediately began to vent her spleen on the hotel staff. Housed in the premier suite of one of the world's finest hotels, she nonetheless found fault with everything—the closets were too small, the fresh orchids arrayed in vases throughout her suite were wilting, the complimentary champagne was too sweet. After Gwei-yu was finally placated and the manager had departed, she settled down to tea in her suite with her brother and MacKinnon.

"This tea is only lukewarm," Gwei-yu complained to no one in particular over her steaming cup.

"Younger Sister," Dak-chung said, "I need your help to contact Harry Chen."

"Who?" Gwei-yu replied unconvincingly.

"Chen came to me claiming to have contacts that could be useful in finding out what happened to Fiona. He said his offer to help was at your behest. I believe you know where Chen is and how I can contact him."

"Who told you such ridiculous nonsense? I don't know any Harry Chen."

Now it was Dak-chung's turn to bristle. With face flushed and fists clenched, he stood up so quickly and menacingly that MacKinnon momentarily thought he might actually hit her.

"Fiona is my daughter and your niece." Dak-chung carefully enunciated each word. "She has disappeared and—"

"Niece? She's no relative of mine after that—"

"Gwei-yu, hold your snake's tongue!"

MacKinnon had rarely seen his friend so angry. Dak-chung slowly unclenched his fists and color gradually returned to his face. When the muscles in his wiry frame relaxed sufficiently to allow him to move, he turned back to his chair. "I . . . uh . . . I apologize. My actions . . . my actions . . . are . . ."

MacKinnon sprang to his feet and took Dak-chung's arm. Looking down at MacKinnon's hands, Dak-chung regained his composure and allowed MacKinnon to guide him to his seat. Gwei-yu, pallid and trembling, remained silent.

MacKinnon swung around to face Gwei-yu. "Where is Chen?"

Bewildered, Gwei-yu looked at her brother for the help he had lavished on her when they were children. Dak-chung, however, was in no mood to be forthcoming. He merely stared blankly at her, preferring instead to let MacKinnon take the lead.

Looking at MacKinnon and then her brother, Gwei-yu said, "Green Island. He's on Green Island. I'll arrange for his immediate release and have him contact you at once."

• • •

It was now 9:45 p.m. Since before six that morning Lina had been keeping watch at her husband's bedside in the dimly lit communal ward of the dingy people's hospital on the northern outskirts of Beijing. Had she not been there, she was sure that Liaoping, still lapsing in and out of consciousness, would have received no nursing care at all. She was deeply suspicious of why Liaoping had been brought to a run-of-the-mill People's hospital rather than to the special facility reserved for Ministry of Public Security employees and other Party cadre. And it was certainly odd that there was only one other patient on this twenty-bed ward.

Lina bent over her husband and said softly, "Liaoping, please try to drink." She held the cup to his lips and cradled his head slightly off the pillow. "It's broth. You haven't had anything today. You need to build up your strength."

Liaoping managed a sip and was making an effort to take another when, in the bed closest to the door on the opposite side, the only other patient in the ward began to scream for the doctor. Startled, both Lina and Liaoping stared, trying to make out what was happening. The screaming continued then grew even louder.

After a few minutes, the double swinging doors at the far end of the ward opened, and the only other person Lina had seen in the hospital that day walked the few steps to the bed of the noisy patient. It was the same woman who had directed Lina to the ward that morning. She had called herself a barefoot doctor then, but Lina had her doubts. So far as Lina could make out in the dim light, the woman rearranged the covers on the patient's bed but did nothing more. The two spoke for a while in low voices—Lina could not make out the words—then the woman walked down the empty ward toward them. On the way, she grabbed a tall metal-framed cloth hospital screen and began dragging it toward Liaoping, who had slipped back into unconsciousness.

"Comrade," she said to Lina, "please help me to extend this screen alongside your husband's bed. It will give you more privacy."

"Of course," Lina said, although she failed to see how much more privacy she and Liaoping needed. "I do hope that other patient has someone to look after him."

"Oh, don't worry about him. He's not so sick."

Lina was wary. Why would a doctor, even a barefoot doctor, be so dismissive of a patient's distress? Unless, of course, the woman wasn't really hospital staff at all . . . or the man a patient.

After the two of them finished extending the screen, Lina decided to test her suspicions by soliciting the woman's help in tending to

Liaoping. She needed to return to the neighbor's house where she had left Liming for the day. She was more than surprised when the woman cheerfully agreed. While Lina prepared to leave, the woman busied herself moving the objects on Liaoping's bedside table like the pawns on a chessboard.

Lina put on her jacket and said good-bye to the woman. As she rounded the screen, she thought she saw the other patient, fully clothed, quickly slip back into bed.

"The bad light must be playing tricks on me," Lina mumbled.

"What?" the woman said.

Lina had not realized she had spoken aloud. "I'm sure it's nothing. I thought I just saw that other patient out of bed. I guess I'm more exhausted than I thought."

The woman giggled. "I'm sure it's just your imagination. You must go home and get a good night's sleep. Your husband will be fine. I'll be here all night."

By now Lina's internal security alarm, that personal quality that made her so valuable to Detachment 8341, was sounding clearly. *The woman had already been here for twelve hours and was volunteering to be here twelve more?* Lina knew that if she suddenly reversed course and stayed, it might put the woman on her guard, or worse. No, whatever she decided to do, she had to make the woman believe that she had left the hospital.

Lina pulled on her gloves and wrapped her muffler around her neck. She walked slowly to the door while carefully watching the other patient. As she drew abreast of the man, he raised his head slightly off the pillow and squinted. As she turned to look at him, Lina caught a glimpse of a collar. She knew it well. She wore the same uniform when on duty—that of a soldier. *And probably a political commissar.* Lina smiled at the man, who slumped back on his pillow and closed his eyes.

Now on full alert, Lina knew what she had to do. Her plan depended on the man following her. She needed to get him to the vestibule just inside the main door to the hospital, one floor below. She left the ward and made her way to the staircase at the end of the hall. She could just make out hurried whispering inside the ward behind her. When she reached the stairs, she stepped loudly on each step as she descended to the ground floor.

In the reception area at the bottom of the stairs, the only light came from the moon shining through the transom above the main door. *Perfect.* Feeling her way along the wall, Lina made her way to the small table lamp she remembered having seen that morning. She grabbed it with both hands and raised it, gently but firmly coaxing the plug from the wall socket. Grasping the lamp in one hand and the cord in the other, she tugged, separating the cord from the lamp.

Lina heard the upstairs wood floor creak. Someone was in the hallway. With cord in hand, she slipped into the vestibule, opened the heavy main door, and then, still remaining inside, let the door slam. As she pressed her body out of sight against the vestibule wall, she heard someone on the staircase stop momentarily then descend the stairs two at a time down into the reception area. The man rushed through the reception area and into the vestibule toward the main door. Lina wound the lamp cord between her hands. As the man reached for the door handle, Lina lunged at him from behind, wrapping the garrote twice around his neck and jerking backward with all the force she could muster. Death came wordlessly.

Lina dashed back up the stairs to the second-floor hallway. She knew that what the man wanted to do to her in the street, the woman was preparing to do, or may already have done, to Liaoping. She crept noiselessly to the ward and slowly cracked open the swinging door. The woman was still behind the screen. Lina slipped into the ward and crept down the aisle that separated the two rows of beds. Halfway to Liaoping and with eyes still fixed on the screen, Lina stopped, transferred one end of the lamp cord to her empty hand, and again wound the cord into a garrote.

As she moved forward, the wood floor beneath her feet creaked loudly. Lina froze. There was movement behind the screen. Lina braced for attack.

Just then, the ancient, rusting radiator against the wall near the head of Liaoping's bed began to vent steam and let out a horrendous clanking noise. Under cover of the sound, Lina rushed the screen and pushed it hard down on top of Liaoping. There was a groan. Lina ran around the bed, grabbed the screen, and threw it onto the bed next to Liaoping's. The woman, grazed by the metal frame, was on the floor. A pillow covered Liaoping's face. Lina flipped it off. Liaoping gasped, and his chest heaved as he fought for air. The woman groaned again, but before she could move, Lina knelt down, wrapped the garrote around her neck, and pulled it tight. Eyes bulging with terror, the woman struggled briefly then went limp.

Lina jumped up and bent over her semiconscious husband. "Liaoping, we have to get out of here. Please try to help me as much as you can."

Groggy, Liaoping nodded. Lina helped him to his feet and threw one of his arms over her shoulder. As they struggled through the swinging doors and into the hallway, Liaoping seemed to revive, as though movement had breathed new life into his body. At the staircase, he was able to grasp the banister and steady himself as he and Lina descended to the ground floor. They exited the building into the chill night air.

"No, not that way," Lina whispered as the two approached a major road. "If someone's looking for us, they'll come that way. Let's stick to the lanes. It'll take longer, but it's much safer."

For the next hour, Lina and Liaoping struggled through the dark narrow-walled lanes in which most of Beijing lived. The warren of pathways afforded them virtually unseen flight from the hospital, except for the watchful eyes of Communist Party neighborhood wardens. When they encountered the infrequent pedestrian, Liaoping leaned on Lina while she loudly scolded him for drunkenness.

When they reached the road fronting their house, Liaoping pulled Lina flat against a wall. "The street's crawling with agents," he whispered. "We'll have to wait until they've gone."

Several cars were parked in front of their house. About a dozen agents, apparently having just finished a search, were getting back into their cars. The man in charge, whom Liaoping recognized as a colleague from the Ministry of Public Security, was still talking to the neighborhood warden. After a few minutes, he got into the lead car and the detail drove off.

The warden looked up and down the street then set off in the direction of her own house. She stopped suddenly in midstride, paused, and did a quick about-face. She began walking toward Lina and Liaoping while squinting into the shadows. When she was about eight meters away, she put her index finger to her lips and hurried toward them. Lina and Liaoping turned and began to run. Liaoping suddenly stumbled and fell hard on the packed earth.

"Don't run," the warden stage-whispered. "I have a message for you."

Lina helped Liaoping to his feet as the warden caught up to them.

"It's all right," the warden said between gulps for air. "You're among friends."

Lina was still wary. "How do we know?"

The warden took one final gulp of air. "Well, you really don't have much choice, do you?"

"What's this message of yours?" Liaoping said.

"You have to get to the safe house right away. It's in the—"

"What safe house?" Liaoping said.

"If you'll give me a chance, I'll tell you. The moderates have set up a safe house in the Legation Quarter, in the old Beijing Club. A jeep will pick you up as soon as I give the signal."

The warden turned her back to walk away.

"Wait!" Liaoping shouted. "How did you know we were here?"

"How do you think?" she said. "I heard your heart pounding in your chest."

• • •

The iron door to the tiny cell swung open, and light from the hallway flooded in. General Liang sauntered in followed by three PLA political commissars. He approached the bed, a pallet of wooden planks, and kicked one of its legs. "Wake up!"

Lying in the frigid cell fully clothed but without a blanket, Zhu was already awake. He sat up on the edge of the bed and rubbed his hands together to warm them.

"Certainly," Liang said, "the great General Zhu, the Long March veteran able to survive any hardship, certainly one so illustrious isn't cold."

Zhu stared at Liang. It was a stare he had perfected over the years for dealing with insubordinate underlings.

Liang broke off eye contact and abruptly turned away. "You won't be surprised to learn that nothing happened tonight at the Great Hall reception. Tell me, what does Deng now have in mind for Jiang Qing? You obviously abandoned your National Day plan. Did you conclude it was hopeless? All your subversive plots are doomed to fail. It's still not too late to change sides. Let me help you."

Liang was rambling, and he and everyone in the room knew it. One of the political commissars lowered his head and coughed.

"You know," Zhu said evenly, "the way you were swaggering just now, the way you keep slapping your gloves into the palm of your hand, even the way your cape is draped over your shoulders reminds me of one of those KMT generals in our propaganda films."

Liang slapped Zhu twice across the face. *Violence, the last refuge of the powerless.*

"You're clearly intent on being uncooperative!" Liang yelled. "So be it. You'll be treated accordingly. Now, what were you mumbling when I came to arrest you?"

General Zhu's arrest had occurred several hours earlier, after his morning meeting with Marshal Ye. He could not now remember what had been in his mind.

"I don't know what you're talking about," Zhu said.

"Advanced age and senility have blurred your already failing memory," Liang said. "It's a thin reed, indeed, on which to rest the hopes of Deng and his supporters. Allow me to assist you. It sounded like '*ya . . . ke . . . mi . . . zi.*' What does this signify? Perhaps it's the code name for Deng's newest plan to usurp the succession from Jiang? Well?"

An avalanche of memory overwhelmed Zhu. He was carried back over forty years, transported to a happier time—a time of optimism and hope, not only for China but also for himself and for his beautiful young bride.

"Answer! What does it mean?" Liang leaned in barely an inch from Zhu's face. "Answer!"

Zhu took a handkerchief from his pocket and wiped the spittle from his face. "I must remind you that you are dealing with a superior officer."

"Answer!" Liang began flailing at Zhu with his fists. "You are no longer a PLA officer. You're nothing but a traitor to the masses and the Party." He dealt a vicious blow to Zhu's already bleeding mouth. "Now," Liang said, his fists clenched at his sides and his face contorted with rage, "you . . . will . . . ANSWER!"

Zhu's face was badly bruised, and his right eye was beginning to close. He daubed at his mouth with his handkerchief. "It's nothing. Just a personal matter, that's all."

"Does it have anything to do with your daughter?" Liang said.

"Only indirectly," Zhu said.

The light in the hallway, the only illumination in the grimy subterranean chamber, suddenly flickered, went brown, then failed entirely.

In the dark, Zhu could hear the three commissars drawing their pistols from their holsters. When the light came back on, three pistols were trained at his head.

"Just a precaution," Liang said. "You were saying?"

"It's a personal memory. Nothing more."

"In the New China, we're in the business of creating collective memory. Nothing is personal anymore." Liang leaned in on Zhu, rested his fists on the bed frame, and enunciated as though Zhu was hard of hearing, "Does it have anything to do with your daughter?"

"No."

"What do you mean 'no'?" Liang punched Zhu in the mouth. The commissar who had restrained Liang before again took several steps toward him. Liang backed off, with both arms raised above his head. After a moment, he said, "Where is your daughter?"

"I don't know."

Liang glared at Zhu in disbelief. "I'll ask you once again. Where are Rong Lina and her husband . . . uh . . . what's his name?"

"Rong Liaoping," one of the commissars said.

"Yes, Rong Liaoping," Liang said. "Where are they?"

"Rong Lina is not my daughter."

Liang stopped and backed away. He paced around the cell for several minutes. "Give me that photograph," he said to one of the commissars then swung around to face Zhu.

"Who does that look like?" he said, thrusting the photograph in Zhu's face.

"It's Rong Lina."

"I know, but does Rong Lina resemble anyone else?"

"No," Zhu replied while carefully studying the photograph. *But it was all too familiar.*

"Keep it," Liang said, striding toward the door. "Perhaps you'll recognize her after you've been here for twenty years . . . if you live that long."

CHAPTER 20

Saturday, October 2, 1976

Marshal Ye Jianying and General Wang Dongxing acted quickly. Within minutes of learning that General Zhu had been arrested, Ye deployed additional forces to key military installations surrounding Beijing and placed the Beijing-based units of the PLA Air Force on alert. Wang assigned additional soldiers to the safe house the moderates had set up at the old Beijing Club in the Legation Quarter, and he put scores of security agents on the streets to scour the neighborhood warden network for leads on where the radicals were holding Zhu.

That accomplished, Ye convened an emergency meeting of the moderate leadership to deal with the challenge posed by Jiang Qing's orchestration of General Zhu's trial. Such a trial, coupled with control of China's propaganda apparatus, would allow her to destroy him. The masses would clamor for Zhu's execution, and she would obey.

Colonel Peng, whom Ye directed should temporarily take Zhu's place, briefed the leadership on the abduction of the American Bryan

Paton and his detention at the safe house. Some among the leadership demanded that the American be killed. They reasoned that by disposing of one of Jiang's most powerful accusations against General Zhu, they could blunt her argument for executing him.

Others countered that not only would this fail to save Zhu, but the death of the American would become known to the U.S. government and could precipitate a crisis in the Taiwan Strait or over Jinmen or Mazu. The Americans might use the execution of one of their citizens as a pretext to launch an invasion of the Mainland from the many U.S. military bases on Taiwan.

Deng, still in Guangzhou, came down on the side of those against execution. That decided, the discussion moved to the important questions of how to stop Jiang Qing before she seized power, how to seize power themselves, and how to save Zhu. Peng proposed a well-received plan that won Deng's endorsement, and he was put squarely in charge of its implementation.

• • •

"Mr. Paton," a voice said.

I opened my sleepy eyes. Someone had pulled off the blanket that covered me. I was freezing. I sat on the edge of the bed and whined, "Where am I?"

"Please, keep your voice down. You're in the Ministry of National Defense. We have to get you out of here."

Like a cold shower, the phrase "out of here" revived me. In the gloom, I saw that the voice belonged to Colonel Peng, the man who the day before had brought me to this place.

I stood up. "What's going on?"

"Listen very carefully. General Zhu has been arrested. This morning's intelligence report announced that he will be put on trial in one week. The charges will include harboring an American spy. That can mean only one thing. They plan to kill him. I don't intend to let that happen." Peng grabbed my good shoulder and shoved me through the door ahead of him. "If they can't find you it may buy us some time."

I was under no illusion that Colonel Peng gave a damn what happened to me. But if helping him kept me alive for the moment, I was game. The hallway dead-ended, and I took a left. Peng grabbed me and shoved me down the right-hand corridor. We saw no one. The cell doors on either side of the hall were closed. The hall led to a staircase, and as there was no place else to go, I started taking the stairs two at a time.

"Slow down," Peng whispered. "There's a guard station at the top."

I waited. When he caught up to me, he whispered in my ear, "Put your hands behind your back." He grabbed my elbow as if he had me in custody.

We came into sight of the guard, who was looking straight at the staircase. The guard went for his pistol. I closed my eyes, lowered my head, and braced for a bullet's impact. Nothing happened. I slowly raised my head. Peng nodded at the guard, who returned his pistol to its holster and waved us forward through the door behind him. Outside was a small enclosed portico in front of which a car idled. Peng pushed me into the backseat. "Lie down and stay there."

I heard the driver's door open and close. The engine gunned. The car jerked forward, gained speed, and bumped over an obstacle that I took to be the sidewalk. I tipped my head up slightly and saw the glimmer of dawn beginning to dispel the night.

After about ten minutes of fast driving, the car slowed and turned left. Peng gunned the car forward a short distance and then abruptly stopped. I heard metal gates crash shut and thought about Major Wang. The same sound had preceded our abduction.

"Get out," Peng said.

When I emerged from the car, I could see that we were inside the grounds of a Western-style mansion whose spacious lawn, once manicured but now gone to seed, was surrounded by a ten-foot metal wall. About three dozen PLA soldiers carrying rifles were positioned at intervals along the wall and elsewhere throughout the compound. We had to be somewhere in the Legation Quarter.

Peng hustled me into the small, two-story mansion, which was largely devoid of furniture. We climbed the stairs to the second floor. Peng pointed to one of the rooms and said, "Stay in there until we figure out what to do with you."

Just then a door down the hall opened, and Rong Liaoping emerged followed by an older man carrying a stethoscope. I heard the man say that Liaoping would be fine.

When he spied me, Liaoping smiled broadly and approached me with hand extended. "How are you?"

"I'm fine." My eyes remained fixed on the older man, who was ashen-faced and trembling.

"It's all right, Dr. . . . uh . . ." Peng said.

"Cai, from Capital Hospital," the doctor said.

Peng eyed the doctor warily and positioned his hand so that he could quickly grab his pistol from its holster. "Do you know why Dr. Song has been replaced? Where did he go?"

The doctor laughed nervously. "I . . . uh . . . I really don't know."

"Who sent you?"

"Why, Dr. Tang, of course." His voice became increasingly shrill. "If you don't want me here, just say so. I'll go." His eyes dropped to Peng's pistol.

I thought that the doctor was unconvincing, and Colonel Peng apparently agreed. He drew his pistol and motioned the doctor toward the stairs.

The doctor cursed under his breath and slowly walked to the

staircase and down the stairs. Peng followed him. I heard Peng say something in a low voice to one of the PLA soldiers guarding the compound. There was the sound of a scuffle, then nothing. The front door closed.

I turned to Liaoping. "I'm glad to see you . . . and in better health. How did you get here? Where is Lina?" There was so much I wanted to know. The questions flowed in a torrent.

"Lina and I made our way here from the hospital. It's a long story. She's not here right now. She's gone to see to Liming. We couldn't risk bringing her with us."

"And how is Major Wang? Do you know him?"

"No, I don't; but Colonel Peng told me his story. He had a bad time of it at the hands of the commissars, but thanks to General Zhu, he is recovering in hospital under the care and watchful eye of Li Zhisui."

"Wasn't Li Chairman Mao's physician?" I asked.

"Yes, and walled off from politics because of it. No one is likely to interfere with his patients."

"Unfortunately," I said, "for me there still remains the matter of Fiona Li . . . Li Guangmei. What were you going to tell me that day in the Forbidden City?"

"Well, first, that my brother Chenli talked to Dr. Song just after Pan Bingqing telephoned that you were coming to the Ministry. Chenli had already agreed that the fingerprints should go to Hong Kong but couldn't say so in the presence of the woman you brought with you. His position requires him to be circumspect in his dealings with diplomatic personnel, including family members who enjoy embassy protection. Second, and the purpose of the meeting in the Forbidden City, was to tell you that the results of the forensic investigation had come in the previous day and declared that the body you saw was not your client's daughter."

"I wouldn't have been surprised," I said. Liaoping raised his eyebrows. "You see, I had received the same news from my employer in Hong Kong."

I told Liaoping of my meeting with General Zhu and of my gratitude for his protection. "I was hoping that General Zhu could help now that he knows who I am," I said, "but according to Colonel Peng, I've become a threat to the general's life. What a mess I've made of things."

"The enemies of General Zhu are the enemies of all Chinese," Liaoping said. "They fail to understand that, to survive, China must seek a new direction. They care only about power and, if allowed to consolidate it, will continue to torment us with one political struggle after another."

"But what can be done?" I asked.

"Why, we plan to put a stop to it—and soon."

· · ·

Pan Bingqing was trying not to attract attention even as she fled for her life. She hurried south on Wang Fu Jing toward Chang An Jie. Just north of the *People's Daily* headquarters, she crossed the street to avoid the crowd reading the day's issue. She knew that the subject consuming the entire paper was the upcoming trial of the Beijing Military Region Commander, General Zhu Fangguo. Jiang Qing's cohorts at the paper were already manipulating the masses with tales of Zhu's supposed betrayal of them.

Pan stopped at a shop doorway to catch her breath. She had been running for almost an hour. Rong Liaoping's brother, Chenli, had come to her apartment to warn her that political commissars were on their way to arrest her. In doing so, he had blown his cover, exposing him as one of several pro-Deng moles in the Ministry of Public Security. Like Pan, Rong was at that very moment attempting to reach the moderates' safe house, but by a different route. Pan feigned study of the meager wares displayed in the shop window, glancing back to catch a glimpse of any would-be pursuers. Seeing no one and with her head down, she again set out south on Wang Fu Jing.

A car screeched to a halt at the curb ahead of her. The driver, a uniformed political commissar, leaped from the car and began running up the sidewalk toward her, scattering several dozen pedestrians. The pedestrians stared, relieved that they were not his target but anxious to see who was. Pan froze. To have done otherwise would be like waving a red flag.

The commissar, however, knew exactly who he was looking for and ran straight to Pan. "Get in the car!" He grabbed her arm and shoved her so violently that, after managing a few stumbling steps in the direction of the car, she fell down on the sidewalk.

He turned his wrath on the onlookers. "Who wants to be next?"

The crowd quickly dispersed, forming a barricade line behind which hundreds of other gawkers gathered like a flood pressing against a weakening dam. Pan, her coat torn and one elbow bleeding, struggled to her feet. The commissar pushed her along to the car, shoved her inside, and the two drove off.

Once they were moving, Pan pressed her handkerchief against her bleeding elbow. "Did you have to push me quite so hard?"

"Sorry, but I didn't think you'd recognize me in this uniform. Besides, you should count yourself lucky that Rong Chenli made it to the safe house and alerted us so that I could find you before the goons did."

"Of course I recognized you," Pan said as the gates of the old Beijing Club swung open to let the car driven by Colonel Peng enter the safe house compound.

• • •

Liang was in the radicals' headquarters in Zhongnanhai, seething with rage. The commissars had bungled the Forbidden City operation. The attempt to dispatch the Rongs had left two of his operatives dead. Major Wang and the American had slipped from his grasp. And today Pan Bingqing had eluded the commissars. He would have to explain these failures to Jiang Qing, and she would not be pleased. What he could tell her about Zhu would be her only comfort.

Liang had known about Zhu's old Whampoa Military Academy connection to Li Dak-chung since the days of his assignment to the Guangzhou Military Region. He had ordered his intelligence agents on both sides of the Hong Kong border to collect information on Li, then as now, Hong Kong's wealthiest tycoon. At first, Liang's agents brought him newspaper clippings. Furious at their incompetence, he executed a few of them as a warning to the others. He then brought in a Bank of China team from Beijing to train the remaining agents to track any large transfers of cash. He specifically charged them with finding the origin of the millions that Li had needed to complete Nan Hwa's take-over of Adair, Jameson.

Liang initially suspected that the funds had come from KMT coffers on Taiwan and that the takeover was part of an attempt by Chiang Kai-shek to seize control of Hong Kong. The information the agents eventually uncovered astounded him: the monies originated from a secret Hong Kong account controlled by the then commander of the Shenyang Military Region, General Zhu Fangguo.

Until now, Liang had remained silent, holding this crucial information in reserve for future use. He knew that Zhu was on the fast track to the top of the Chinese Communist hierarchy. He, on the other hand, was buried in the middle ranks of the general officer corps and unlikely to rise any higher, either in the military or, far more important, in the Party. If he were to advance, he would have to draw on his considerable private supply of intelligence to blackmail Zhu . . . or to bring him down, if it came to that.

Liang knew that Jiang Qing, once she seized power in China, would be receptive to waging war against Western colonialism. He meant not only to suggest this strategy to Jiang but also to provide her with the ammunition she would need to wage that war. After that, with his loyalty proven, he expected her to consider him indispensable. If she did not, he was perfectly willing to blackmail her with the intelligence information he had collected on her over the years, especially the records of her purchases of luxury goods from Hong Kong.

But before he used the Nan Hwa and Adair, Jameson information to polish his credentials with Jiang, he needed to clear up some mysteries. What was the significance of "*yakemizi*"? And why did Li Dak-chung's daughter keep coming up in relation to Zhu? Liang knew that Rong Liaoping had something to tell Li's American attorney about Li Guangmei, but what? And Zhu had denied that Rong Lina was his daughter. Why?

And then there was the American, Paton. Liang knew that he was not a CIA spy, but that accusation was always plausible enough to be useful. He had already dispatched the traitorous hall monitor who helped Paton and Wang escape from the Beijing Hotel. But why hadn't Paton left China when he had the chance? And why had Paton's friend at the British Embassy implied to Paton's employer, MacKinnon, that Li Dak-chung was somehow linked with China's power struggle?

"Highgrove mentioned that Li's daughter was also mixed—" Liang said aloud. That was it. The recognition of his own fallibility stunned him. For all of his adult life, he had been able to rely on his considerable intelligence skills to survive. Why, this time, had he failed until now to grasp the truth? He grabbed the phone on his desk and ordered a commissar to have Zhu brought to him.

• • •

As Zhu entered Liang's office, he blinked back the afternoon sunlight streaming through the window. He walked straight to a chair and slumped down heavily. Liang was absently rubbing his knuckles, sore no doubt from the beating he had suffered at Liang's hands the day before.

"Was it really necessary to throw me into solitary?" Zhu asked haltingly, his jaw aching.

"I'm afraid it was." Liang walked to the window. "You see, I know you. To break you, I had to impress on you that I was serious."

Liang stroked his heavily pomaded hair, which, like the majority of Chinese men of his age, was dyed jet-black. He took a cigarette from his pocket, lit it, and held it somewhat effetely with the tips of his fingers as he drew greedily and savored the nicotine. "Where are my manners? Would you care for a cigarette?"

Notwithstanding the irony of the offer, Zhu took a cigarette, which Liang lit for him. The two smoked for a while, seemingly enjoying the macabre respite that smoking afforded from their roles of captor and captive. Liang cut the interlude short.

"Who or what is yakemizi?"

Zhu scowled. He had hoped that Liang had forgotten the subject. "He was a person important in the life of my wife. She's now dead, and so is he."

"Was he a relative? A comrade? How do you know he's dead?" Liang shot back.

"Neither a relative nor a comrade," Zhu replied dryly. "He lived and died about 2000 years ago. The name is pronounced Ar . . . kuh . . . mee . . . dees."

Liang turned away and stared out the window. "Do you really expect me to believe there's nothing more?"

"I really don't care whether you believe me or not."

Liang swung around and glared at Zhu. He circled Zhu's chair and stood behind him. "I quite understand your reluctance to talk about memories that may be painful for you and your family, but in this case you have no alternative but to tell me everything about Archimedes."

"Clearly, you won't give up on this until I convince you that Archimedes has absolutely nothing to do with Jiang Qing. May I?" Zhu gestured to a sofa, far friendlier to his aging body than the straight chair in which he was sitting.

"Of course." Liang joined him on the sofa.

"Archimedes," Zhu said, "had fascinated my wife ever since she was a very young girl, long before I knew her. Back then, mathematics and science were all she thought about, and she excelled at them in school. For some reason Archimedes, an early Western mathematician, Greek I believe, came to symbolize her passion for these subjects. My father-in-law even bought her a small bust of a bearded Westerner and told her it was Archimedes, although I think it was a nineteenth-century Russian composer. How she treasured that bust."

"Your wife's name," Liang said, "was Ye Guangrong, wasn't it?"

"Yes." Zhu had not heard his wife's name spoken out loud for nearly thirty years. On Liang's lips it sounded profane.

"Her father," Liang said, now with a vaguely accusatory tone in his voice, "was a bourgeois capitalist, wasn't he? Didn't he own a factory?"

"Yes."

The Ye family of Tianjin was among China's wealthiest, and his wife's father had been the country's most honored progressive industrialist. Before 1949, even the Communist Party hailed him as a model employer. Nonetheless, the family was persecuted by the Communists when they seized power. The Ye family tragedy became both prologue to and example of how other Westernizing Chinese would be treated. Zhu's only consolation was that his wife had not lived to see her family murdered.

"Please, continue with your wife's story." Liang had a self-satisfied look on his face, which Zhu found repellent. He knew Liang was finding sadistic pleasure in forcing him to relive his wife's life and her premature death in 1948.

"Her parents naturally encouraged her interest," Zhu said. "You may recall that at that time China couldn't get enough of Western science and technology. Everyone who was educated and lived in a large city wanted his son or daughter to grow up to become an engineer or a scientist or some such thing.

"As a teenager my wife became interested in playing the *erhu* and violin and in poetry. She regarded these pursuits as a natural outgrowth of her extraordinary childhood aptitude for mathematics. She continued these interests into—"

"Did she find it necessary to study the *erhu* out of guilt?" Liang interrupted. "I mean, wasn't she really only interested in the violin, which isn't at all common in China? That is except outside of the bourgeois class in the large cities?"

Zhu restrained himself from taking the bait.

"She continued these interests into adulthood. In Yenan after the Long March, she put on many impromptu *erhu* and violin recitals for Mao, Jiang, and others in the leadership. My wife became a favorite of Mao's, and Jiang Qing grew increasingly jealous of her. Those were complicated and dangerous days."

Zhu had no need to explain to Liang what he meant. Mao's womanizing was well-known among the Party elite, as was Jiang's hatred of the women her husband favored. In his wife's case, her love of music and poetry and the intelligent discussion of both proved fatal. Zhu knew how she had died, and he now meant to settle the score with Jiang. It was that as much as anything else that motivated him to survive this ordeal—that and rescuing his daughter.

"There are only curves in the universe," Zhu continued. "It's something my wife used to say when she thought I needed cheering up. When we were first married, we had long discussions about many things, but mostly about mathematics, music, and poetry. The phrase was her way of summarizing the unity she saw among these subjects. I didn't understand much about the connection between them, so she hit upon that phrase as a way to help me remember.

"After that, each time she repeated the phrase was an occasion for much laughter and happy recollection of our younger married days. The phrase had private meaning for the two of us, much like the bust of Archimedes that she kept all those years as a way of remembering her father. She carried that bust throughout the Long March, and it arrived safely in Yenan. Mao in particular was enchanted by that story and had her retell it often in the caves."

"What did the phrase mean?"

Zhu smiled, memory transporting him to a happier time and place. "It meant, if I remember correctly, that nature is fundamentally lyrical, as is poetry, and that, mathematically, motion in nature always happens on a curve, never at angles. She used to say that birds in flight may appear to dart at angles, but they actually move on a slope. As a child, she also noticed that carp swimming in her family's pond always seemed to keep time with whatever music she happened to be listening to or playing. Flying birds did too. So, she found a bond among those three subjects. Because I loved her, I found it too."

"Your wife died in 1948. Is that correct?" Liang probed.

"Yes. I don't like to remember."

"What happened to your daughter? Why isn't she with you?"

"At that time, in Yenan," Zhu said, "the struggle against the KMT was entering the final phase. Victory was by no means certain, and I had to . . . uh . . . make arrangements for her safety."

"Go on."

"My concern was to find someone to care for her, and fortunately, I found just the right couple in . . . in Guangdong province. The woman wet-nursed my daughter after my wife died."

"And she grew up there?"

"Yes."

Liang remained silent, apparently lost in thought. Zhu thought he had dodged a bullet, several in fact. But he was exhausted from the strain of the interrogation and the feints necessary to avoid serious, potentially fatal, mistakes.

Suddenly Liang rose from the sofa and stood in front of him. "And you expect me to swallow that story? Guangdong province, you say. Wasn't it Shanghai? And wasn't it your old Whampoa crony Li who took her in? And didn't they flee to Hong Kong?"

Zhu felt his jaw clench but said nothing. Liang waited. Finally he said, "Well, I have my answer."

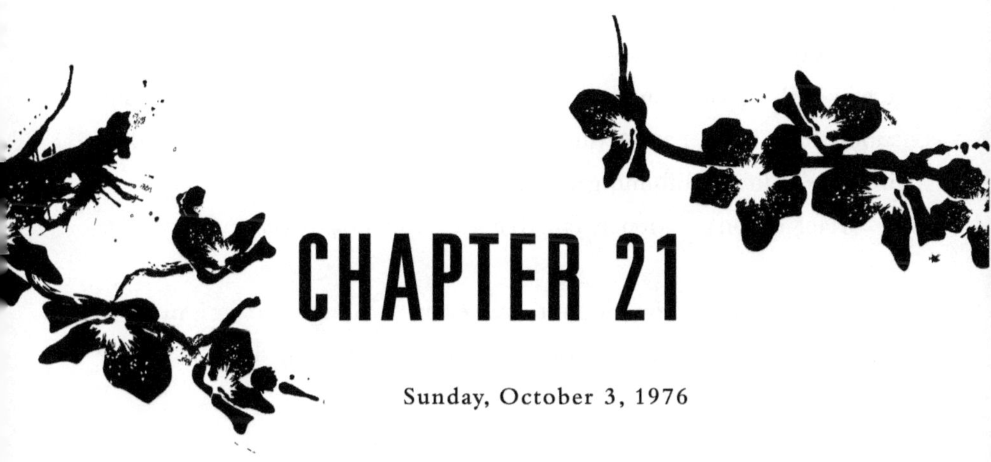

CHAPTER 21

Sunday, October 3, 1976

"Now," the officer said, "let's run through it again. When was the last time you saw Fiona Li?"

Harry Chen, MacKinnon, and a Special Branch officer were in an interrogation room at the Central District Police Station in Hollywood Road. Chen had been taken into custody as soon as he stepped off the plane from Taipei. He was being held at the station, ostensibly for his own safety, until he divulged the information the Hong Kong authorities sought.

The Special Branch officer had long ago taken off his suit coat and rolled up his sleeves. He was sitting backward on a chair directly facing Chen, arms dangling off the chair back, pen and pad in hand. MacKinnon paced the room in full lawyerly regalia of the same summer-weight wool that he had worn since the day he arrived in Hong Kong.

Chen shot a disgusted look at the officer. "I've already told you a thousand times. I've never met the lady. Never means never. I don't know how else to say it."

"Who do you know who's seen Fiona Li during the preceding three weeks?" the officer asked.

"I don't exactly run with her social set, if you know what I mean," Chen said. "That is, unless I happen to have made the lady's acquaintance at the races. Let me think." He looked at the ceiling, as if pondering one of life's profound mysteries.

MacKinnon's patience failed him. "You know very well you've never—"

"Mr. Chen, if you do not answer in a straightforward manner, you will be placed in solitary confinement until you do," the officer interrupted.

"I don't know anyone who's seen the Li broad," Chen said.

"Mr. Chen—"

Chen blurted something so rapidly that neither the officer nor MacKinnon could understand him.

"Please repeat that," the officer said.

"I said," Chen replied slowly, "I know who has the Li broad but not where they have her."

• • •

Locks. Damn it. I twisted the knob harder, as if doing so would somehow magically open the door. It did not budge. The rifle fire that had begun shortly before dawn was getting closer to the house. I heard people running up the stairs and others firing from the upstairs windows. In fact, it sounded like a pitched battle was going on around me.

I scanned the room for something to use to pry open the window. Nothing. I grabbed the blanket off the bed, wrapped it around my hand, and punched out the lower pane. Gunfire drowned the sound of the tinkling glass falling onto the roof below. At least I could finally see outside the confines of my room.

Directly outside the window, a section of the roof sloped gently downward. It was edged with a badly rusted rain gutter whose roof-to-ground downspout was attached to the house with brackets, some of which had pulled loose from the wall. So far as I could see, inching my way down the downspout was my only chance to escape.

The decision was made for me by loud banging on the door and a voice shouting, "Come out! We know you're in there! Open the door!" I heard the knob rattle several times then another voice shouted, "Break it down!"

By then, I was out the window and nearly across the roof to the downspout. When I heard the door in my room crash open, I flattened my body against the roof and watched the window. One of the people searching my room stuck his head out. A political commissar. He looked directly down instead of across at me. I lay flat, praying that he would not look in my direction or hear my heart pounding hard against the roof. After a few seconds, he withdrew back into the room. I heard the voices grow faint and then vanish entirely. I breathed for the first time in what seemed like an eternity. Only then did I notice that the gunfire had stopped.

I lifted my head and took stock. I had to assume that the commissars were now in control of the compound. I had no idea whether Colonel Peng, Liaoping, Lina, and the soldiers were still alive. My immediate concern was how to get myself off the roof and to safety outside the Legation Quarter.

About ten feet separated the rear of the house from the concrete wall that enclosed the compound. The branch of a tree growing just outside the wall hung into the compound. If I could get to ground, I could use the branch to get over the wall. Fortunately the house was only two stories high. If I fell, I still had a chance to make good my escape. But would the gutter and downspout support my weight? I gave in to the inevitable.

I edged forward and grabbed the gutter. Part of it crumbled, but the remaining section felt solid. I slid on my stomach across and off the roof, dangled perilously from the gutter for a few seconds, then began losing my grip. Suddenly, the gutter broke away. As it fell, I lunged for the downspout and grabbed it with both hands. As I slid down, the brackets gave way, and the downspout clattered to the ground.

I hit hard, rolled, and started for the branch about three yards away when my ankle gave way. I fell hard on my left hand, and intense pain shot up my arm to my injured shoulder. I heard footsteps running along the house.

I got up, limped to the branch, and started to climb. Just when my shoulder would not lift me any farther, a hand darted suddenly out of the tangle of branches and pulled me up into the tree and over the wall. I fell hard on the other side. Gunfire from inside the compound peppered the tree.

I found myself on the street behind the compound, but before I had a chance to lick my wounds, two PLA soldiers, whom I recognized as part of the safe house guard detail, hustled me a short distance to a waiting jeep. We went directly to the former Austro-Hungarian Legation, where Liaoping had pulled me from in front of the Mercedes limousine twelve days before. It was now an armed camp protected by two tanks and several machine-gun nests. Colonel Peng was waiting for us.

"Congratulations," Peng said to the soldiers when the jeep braked to a stop, "you found him."

"Sir," the driver said, "we didn't have to find him. He was already escaping when we got there."

"You still rescued him, didn't you?" Peng seemed annoyed, but the expression on his face telegraphed grudging respect for my courage.

"Sorry I had to leave you locked up there temporarily," he said to me, "but we had to get out rather quickly to avoid any further . . . uh . . . unpleasantness."

Out of the corner of my eye, I saw Liaoping and Lina approaching. Rong Chenli was with them. I'd like to hear Chenli's story, I thought to myself. They all nodded "hello" to me and smiled.

"Colonel, we must get Mr. Paton to a place where our opponents can't exploit him," Liaoping said.

"Yes," Lina said, "if we are to save General Zhu from a trial, the best way to do that is to deny Jiang Qing access to Mr. Paton."

Amen to that. I knew that I was not their principal concern, but anything that enhanced my chances of survival was welcome.

"What do you suggest?" Peng said.

"An embassy," Lina said. "That way, even if they find out where he is, they can't get their hands on him."

"That's true, but there's no American Embassy here," Chenli said.

"He has two friends at the British Embassy," Lina mused, "but that's the first place they'd expect him to go. Jiang and her rabble certainly wouldn't be reluctant to sack the embassy again to get at him. No, we have to be more creative."

Liaoping turned to me. "Who was the other person you were having lunch with that day in the Beijing Hotel? You were with Mr. Highgrove and another man."

"He's Danish." I was reluctant to mention Knud's name, much less to involve him in my problem.

"Wait here. I'll find out who he is," Liaoping said and ran inside the legation. It seemed that a decision had already been made.

While Colonel Peng, Lina, and Chenli were chatting, my thoughts strayed to Hugh and Emma. To Li Dak-chung and MacKinnon, too. How were they coping with my disappearance? And Fiona. Was she still alive and caught up in the power struggle?

"His name is Knud Ascanius," Liaoping said when he returned. "He's the First Secretary at the Danish Embassy."

Gunfire rang out in the distance. Lina turned to Peng. "How can we get Mr. Paton inside the Danish Embassy quickly without being detected?"

"Well, the soldiers guarding the embassy gate may or may not be Deng supporters," Peng said. "We can't be certain. The only thing we can count on is that the guards will recognize everyone who works at the embassy. They're required to memorize all employee photographs. So we have to convince the guards that Paton is a visiting Danish official who's just arrived in Beijing. That means a Travel Service handler whom all the guards recognize."

"Or if they don't," Lina said, "at least they'll recognize a CITS identification card. Pan Bingqing is the obvious choice."

So Miss Pan was still alive. I was relieved.

"The only potential problem," Peng said, "would be that the guards who happen to be on duty are in fact Jiang supporters and have been warned to watch for an American and Pan, particularly if they're together. We'll just have to take that chance."

"Is Pan well enough to do it?" Liaoping asked. "She was wounded when the commissars took over the safe house." *Oh no, not Miss Pan.*

"Let's ask her." Lina went back inside the legation and returned with Miss Pan. It was the first time that I had seen her in almost a week— since her Greta Garbo performance in the hotel lounge. I smiled at her, and she smiled back.

"Colonel Peng," Miss Pan said, "I understand you need me to get Mr. Paton through the gate to the Danish Embassy. I'll do whatever you ask."

"It could be dangerous. Are you sure you're up to it?"

Miss Pan shrugged. "Lina said it was necessary in order to save General Zhu. That's more than enough reason for me. We'd better get moving."

As Miss Pan got into the jeep, I noticed that the right sleeve of her jacket had a blood stain that seemed to be spreading. "Are you okay?" I asked. "We should get that treated when we get to the embassy."

"It hurts, but I'll be all right," she said. "Just a minor war wound."

"Get in," Peng said as he shoved me toward the jeep. "I'll drive. You three, wait here," he said to Lina, Liaoping, and Chenli. He gunned the jeep in a circle and back down the driveway out of the compound.

The Legation Quarter was eerily deserted. When we turned onto Chang An Jie, the bustle was jarring. Didn't those people on the bus know there was a titanic power struggle under way? Weren't those bicyclists concerned about the gunfire in the vicinity? I marveled yet again at the brute power of a Communist dictatorship to hide from its citizens things that they needed to know.

After passing through the diplomatic enclave of Jianguomenwai, we continued a short distance to Sanlitun, Beijing's other diplomatic district and the site of the Danish Embassy. We braked to a stop in front of the modern structure, which was guarded by two soldiers. One of them approached the jeep.

Peng did not wait for the soldier to address us. "We have a Danish government official to take into the embassy. Comrade Pan, please show the soldier your ID card."

The soldier rounded the jeep to inspect Miss Pan's credentials. He did not notice her wince with pain when she reached for her card. He did, however, notice the spreading bloodstain on Pan's sleeve. He shot a quick look at the other soldier blocking the embassy entrance. Peng saw the soldier's glance and slid his hand down to the pistol holster on his belt. I braced for a violent confrontation.

The soldier at the car looked back at Miss Pan and took the ID card from her hand. Peng raised his hand from his holster and placed it back on the steering wheel. After a few seconds, the soldier handed the card back to Pan and waved the jeep forward through the embassy gate.

My elation at the prospect of finally being safe inside the embassy was short-lived. The gate guard did not move and shot a questioning look at the soldier who had checked Miss Pan's ID.

That was it. One was an ally, one was an enemy. I hunched down in my seat.

"You should never let a vehicle carrying Chinese citizens into an embassy," Peng shouted at the soldier still standing by the car. "Your fellow guard over there obviously knows how to deal with such situations." Peng gestured to the soldier barring the gate. "Soldier, explain the procedure."

The soldier snapped to attention. "Sir, the proper procedure is to order all passengers out of the vehicle. They may only enter a foreign embassy on foot. The vehicle driver, if he or she is a Chinese citizen, is in no case permitted to enter a foreign embassy."

"And?" Peng said.

The soldier's shoulders slumped and he looked bewildered.

"Isn't it the case that only China Travel Service personnel are permitted to enter an embassy and only when absolutely necessary?" Peng said.

"Yes, sir!" the soldier shouted.

Peng turned back to face the soldier who had checked the ID card and whispered, "Well done. They're in."

• • •

"Find her and bring her here!" Jiang Qing screamed as she pointed a rapier-like finger at Liang. "Alive!" She turned and stormed out of the room.

General Liang was in the private quarters of Jiang Qing's villa in Zhongnanhai. He had just told Jiang that Li Guangmei was the daughter of General Zhu. She reacted as he had expected: a show trial for Zhu paled in comparison to the possibilities that this relationship offered.

Liang needed to act quickly to get his hands on Guangmei. He hoped she was still alive. Fortunately, he had the means to find out and, if so, where she was being held and by whom. If she was dead, he was doomed.

He left the room and hurried down two flights of stairs. Brushing by the commissar standing guard in the anteroom, he went directly to his office and picked up the phone.

"Get me General Yang," he barked. Yang was head of the intelligence staff of the Shanghai Military Region, the base of operations of the four radical leaders. Although Jiang Qing had personally selected Yang for this position, he reported to her through Liang.

"Yang? Liang here."

"General! Congratulations on smashing the plot of the enemies of socialism!"

"Yes. Zhu Fangguo's arrest put an end to that. Listen, I need your help. A while ago, I sent you one of Zhu's lackeys, a Colonel Peng. Do you remember him?"

"Yes, as instructed, we were not helpful."

"Well, I can't be sure, but I think he was there searching for Zhu's daughter."

"You're correct. At least, that's what he told local police who, of course, reported the conversation to us. The woman is here—I think she's the one he was looking for . . . a foreigner—in the village of Lingkou about 60 miles northwest of the city. How do you know she's Zhu's daughter?"

"Well, about a week ago there was a breach of security at the Defense Ministry by two Deng loyalists and an American lawyer from Hong Kong. On that day, our operatives were closing in on a counterrevolutionary mole in the Ministry of Public Security. We'd had him and his cell under surveillance for a month. They tailed him to Tiananmen, where he happened to be meeting the American. The bloody incompetents bungled the operation; and the target, along with his wife and the American, escaped down into the tunnels. During the interrogation, the American—Paton—claimed to represent Li Dak-chung. You know of him, of course."

"Yes. Notorious."

"Paton said he came to China to claim the body of Li's daughter, Li Guangmei, but the body he was shown for identification wasn't hers. When I told Zhu about it, he insisted on interrogating the American himself and was visibly upset when he heard the names. Afterward, he placed the American under his protection."

"I knew that Zhu and Li had been classmates at Whampoa and discovered that Li had taken care of Zhu's daughter during the war and then fled with her to Hong Kong. After Zhu's arrest, I confronted him with this information. He denied none of it. Now this is where you come in. Jiang Qing wants the woman brought to Beijing."

"Why?"

"Leverage. She thinks Zhu could be useful in the return of Hong Kong to the Motherland. Can you get her here . . . as soon as possible?"

"That will be difficult. The Triads won't willingly turn her over to me."

"What? What are the Triads doing with her?" Liang shouted. "Who—?" He held the phone away from his ear and breathed deeply, unable to think clearly.

Yang's voice came through tinny and distant. "I suggest that what we need now is a cool head."

"Well, we've dealt with the Triads before," Liang said. "How much ransom will they want from us?"

"They want nothing from us. And they're after more than just money," Yang said. "They want power and influence in Hong Kong. One of the players is a guy who uses the name Harry Chen."

"Who the hell is Harry Chen?"

"He's a Hong Kong–based Triad boss with connections in Taipei."

"What's his angle?" Liang asked.

"Well, his father was Du Yuesheng. Chen aims to resurrect the Green Gang's fortunes in a Hong Kong eventually controlled by the KMT."

"Never!" Liang said. "And how would that be possible anyway? He would have to have an ally very high inside the KMT establishment."

"He has one," Yang said, "and she's second only to Song Meiling in—"

"Ah . . . of course. Li Gwei-yu, the puppet master. Well, that certainly ties the loose ends together into one nice, neat bundle. Li Gwei-yu pays a ransom to Chen to spring Guangmei and deliver her into the loving arms of Li Dak-chung. Or maybe . . . maybe she has Chen and his Triad compatriots dispose of the girl. That way, Guangmei simply vanishes, and Li Gwei-yu steps in to console the grieving father. Either way, Li Dak-chung incurs a debt to his sister, which she and her KMT cronies will find a way for him to repay. Chen merely waits until his ally is successful to revive the Green Gang in Hong Kong."

After Liang hung up, he felt calm return. Now he knew where he stood and was satisfied with the plan he had just launched. He would let the ransom money from Li Gwei-yu pass through Chen to Guangmei's kidnappers. Yang would pounce before the kidnappers had a chance to surrender or murder the girl, and then he would bring her to Beijing. Soon thereafter, Chen would suffer a fatal car crash on a busy Hong Kong boulevard, a warning to Li Gwei-yu not to meddle with Communist designs on Hong Kong. Liang estimated that the entire process—except for Chen's tragic accident, which he did not regard as urgent—would take less than two days. Then the heir to Li Dak-chung's financial empire would be in Jiang Qing's hands.

• • •

She has a morbid fear of the untidy. Not filth, mind you—people the world over are quite properly disgusted by squalor—but the merely unkempt, things in disarray, objects out of alignment. Those things send her into paroxysms of fury. That, for example, is the reason that her sort abhors modern art. Things do not line up. Perspective is distorted. Paint wanders outside the lines. Her sort has that in common with the Nazis. Both groups—the so-called ultra-left Communists and the ultra-right Nazis—are, in short, identical. As with all perfectionists, they mean to force the world to stand crisply at attention.

Hugh was working late in his office at the embassy reading a psychological profile of Jiang Qing prepared by MI6. It was part of the detailed analysis of who might succeed Mao that the Foreign Office had sent to the embassy in recent days.

He threw his reading glasses on the desk and rubbed his eyes. He was having difficulty concentrating on Deng Xiaoping and Jiang Qing. The dispatch he had received that morning from London instructed the embassy to discontinue any efforts to locate Fiona or Bryan and concentrate on defending British sovereignty over Hong Kong. Resources, the Foreign Office cable had read, were scarce. The embassy should do nothing further to find an American citizen or the remains of a person whom the PRC government considered to be a Chinese citizen. *Short-sighted buggers.*

The phone on Hugh's desk rang. He plucked the receiver from its cradle. "Highgrove, here."

"Hugh, it's Aidan. I tried to reach you earlier at the apartment, but Emma said you'd gone to the embassy to catch up on reading."

"Yes. Any further news?"

"Indeed there is," MacKinnon said. "The Hong Kong political adviser has just fired off a cable to London laying out what we've learned in the last twenty-four hours. You should be getting your copy at the embassy at any moment."

Click.

Hugh was well aware that someone was recording their conversation, and he was certain that MacKinnon realized this as well. But he had to be sure. "Aidan, do you remember the saying 'Little pitchers have—"

"—big ears,' yes. I'm just calling to give you a heads-up."

"I'll look out for the cable. Aidan, on another matter, I'm deeply worried about Emma's mental state. She is taking Fiona's disappearance harder than even a best friend should. I was thinking that a long visit in Hong Kong with you and Glynis might do her a world of good."

"She's of course always welcome here," MacKinnon said, "but . . ."

"But?" Hugh said after a moment.

"I was just thinking," MacKinnon said, "about how to put this."

Hugh thought he was about to hear the objection that Emma was too unwell to travel alone. He had already decided that Emma's health came first, even at the risk of his career, and that he was going to accompany her to Hong Kong.

"Before you make a decision," MacKinnon said, "it's imperative that you first read the cable from Hong Kong and share the gist of it with Emma. I think you'll both find the information most . . . encouraging."

An hour later, Hong Kong's cable arrived at the embassy. Hugh skimmed quickly through to the meat, which he read with a greedy eye. When he finished, it was obvious why MacKinnon could not reveal more over the phone. Fiona was alive.

CHAPTER 22

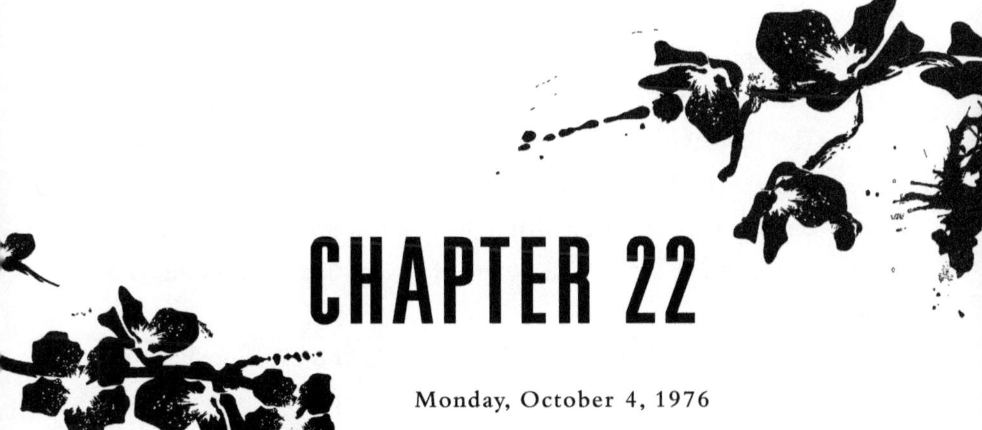

Monday, October 4, 1976

It took a moment to register that I was no longer under threat. The day before, the Danish Embassy doctor had seen to Miss Pan's wound, given her a tetanus shot, and had her back out the embassy gate to Peng and the jeep before anyone could become suspicious. He put my arm in a sling, looked at my sprained ankle, and gave me painkillers for both. The Danes settled me in an apartment used for visitors, and the doctor ordered me to go to bed early that evening. As soon as my head hit the pillow, I fell into a deep sleep.

I was to meet with Hugh and Knud later that morning. Knud had called Hugh the day before to let Emma and him know where I was. I got out of bed and organized myself before eating the breakfast delivered to my room on a tray. Eventually I made my way to Knud's office.

"Why is your arm in that sling?" Hugh said as I walked in.

"Actually, it's my shoulder." I took a seat next to Hugh in front of Knud's desk. "A burly commissar with a rotten attitude dislocated it when he and a crowd of his friends kidnapped Major Wang and me last week."

Knud, who knew that my injuries were not serious, roared with laughter. Hugh, who did not, was not so sanguine. "Kidnapped? Did you say kidnapped? And who is Major Wang?"

"I guess I'd better bring you up to date," I replied, and proceeded to relate in detail what had transpired since the day I left the hotel to meet Liaoping in the Forbidden City. For what it was worth, I also passed on the scraps of information that I had overheard in the intervening days concerning the power struggle between Deng Xiaoping and Jiang Qing.

When I finished, Hugh said, "What a gold mine of intelligence! The Foreign Office hasn't had this much on the power struggle since . . . since ever! I have to get back to the embassy and fire off a cable to London."

"Wait a minute," I said as he got up to leave. "How is your beautiful wife, Emma?"

"She went to Hong Kong early this morning." Hugh's demeanor grew somber. "I'm worried about her, but for the time being she's better off outside China. She's been on such an emotional roller coaster. She felt she wanted to be near her parents and the Lis now that we know Fiona is still alive."

I sat bolt upright in my chair. "What? Alive?" I had suspected as much, but this meant there had been some confirmation.

"Yes. At least that's what we heard from Hong Kong yesterday," Hugh said. "Special Branch has been working around the clock on her disappearance."

"How is she? Where is she? Who has her?" My questions cascaded like an avalanche.

"Unfortunately," Hugh said, "we don't know where she is or in what condition. All we can be sure of right now is that the Triads are still holding her. Special Branch is pressing a local Triad hood for information on her whereabouts, but he isn't talking."

"Sounds to me like he's protecting someone," Knud said.

"Special Branch are proceeding on the same theory," Hugh said, "but so far they haven't turned up anything useful."

My spirits sank. Sure, it was my job to care about Fiona Li, but I had come to feel personally responsible for her welfare. And I wanted to know her more than ever.

"You're mistaken," I said quietly, "about the Triads." Hugh and Knud stared at me. "She is most probably in the hands of political commissars. I think Jiang Qing has Fiona . . . maybe even here in Beijing."

"Look here, Bryan, you had better spill everything you know," Hugh said testily.

I did so over the next hour. I finished: "Colonel Peng and the group at the safe house are bent on saving General Zhu. With me here, out of harm's way, Jiang Qing and her henchmen have one less accusation—harboring an American spy—to level at Zhu in a trial. Peng's group must be part of a larger effort to seize power for Deng and the moderates. Liaoping as much as admitted it to me. I still don't understand the reason why Fiona is important in all of this, but if Jiang has her file, it must be a lulu. I have to speak to Colonel Peng. Fiona has to be close by."

Hugh groaned. "For Christ's sake, Bryan, you just told us why he couldn't afford to have you around. You don't know that you're right, and how would you get hold of Peng anyway?"

"Miss Pan," I said. "Miss Pan will contact Colonel Peng."

After Hugh's obligatory lecture, he grudgingly telephoned the China Travel Service and requested that Miss Pan come to the embassy. I was ready to go home to Hong Kong he lied. When Miss Pan arrived, Hugh and Knud left us alone. I told her of my theory, and she assured me that she would relay it to Colonel Peng. I had done all I could.

• • •

"General Wang Dongxing is the key to getting us into Zhongnanhai," Peng said. "Without him, it will be much too risky getting to Jiang."

He had gathered Pan Bingqing, Lina, Liaoping, and Rong Chenli in a room at the old Austro-Hungarian Legation for a tactical run-through of the moderates' new plan. General Wang had ordered special agents onto the streets after Zhu was kidnapped, and they had turned up evidence that Jiang Qing had taken Zhu to her Zhongnanhai villa through an underground tunnel to which she alone controlled access. "It is also possible," Peng said, "that the general's daughter, Li Guangmei, is being held there as well." Pan smiled.

"Security detachment headquarters is inside Zhongnanhai," Peng said, "and so is General Wang's residence. We move on Thursday night, just three days from now. At 7:00 p.m. General Wang will leave Zhongnanhai, ostensibly heading to the Ministry of National Defense for a meeting. He'll take a jeep instead of his car. He sometimes does this. He'll have his usual driver so that the guards at the gate won't be suspicious when they don't see his car. He'll also have with him an aide and one bodyguard, for a total of four in the jeep.

"But instead of going to the Ministry, General Wang will come here. The meeting at the Ministry is scheduled to last two hours, until 9:00 p.m. At 9:15, General Wang will call the watch officer at detachment headquarters. He will tell him that the meeting will last longer than expected and to alert the Zhongnanhai gate guards to expect him back very late, possibly as late as 3:00 a.m.

"At about 2:45, General Wang, his driver, Liaoping, and I will leave here in the General's jeep and drive to Zhongnanhai. The aide and the bodyguard will stay here. At that hour, the city will be asleep, and so will everybody in Zhongnanhai except the guards."

"But won't the guards stop the jeep when they see that the aide and the bodyguard aren't there?" Lina asked. "They're trained to watch for anything out of the ordinary."

"That's why," Peng replied, "we're waiting until after midnight when the guards' shift changes. The guards who saw the general and his party leave at 7:00 won't be the same as those on the gate when the party returns." Lina nodded.

"When the four of us are in Zhongnanhai," Peng continued, "we'll drive to the watch officer house. General Wang will go inside to check on how things are. That's what he usually does before retiring for the night. But this time, his real purpose will be to ensure that everything is quiet at Jiang Qing's villa. If it is, we will all proceed there."

Peng paused for a moment, staring at each of them in turn. "This is where it could get dangerous. Jiang has her own round-the-clock security detail of political commissars. The plan is for the four of us, with General Wang in the lead, to enter the residence. Wang will tell the commissars on duty that he has an urgent message for Jiang from Premier Hua."

"Isn't it a little far-fetched to expect all the players to follow your script?" Pan asked.

"Actually, it isn't," Peng said. "Standard procedure dictates that when one senior leader sends a message at night to another, the watch officer notifies General Wang, who delivers the message."

"But what if one of the commissars insists that he himself take the message to Jiang?"

"He won't." Peng knew that Pan was just worst-casing the plan, but he was nonetheless irritated by her interruptions. "But if one of them varies from S.O.P., the general will simply pull rank and give him a good dressing-down." He cocked his head to one side. "You know the power of standard procedure."

"What if they want to see the message? The general won't have one. What then?"

"He'll have a message, all right. He'll have a warrant for Jiang's arrest."

"She'll challenge the warrant. What then?" Pan pressed.

"The warrant will be signed by Premier Hua," Peng said. "Even Jiang Qing won't defy the Premier."

"But surely the Premier won't sign an arrest warrant for a potential ally!" Pan turned to Lina and Liaoping for support then looked back at Peng.

"Marshal Ye agreed to my request that he approach Hua and get him to authorize the warrant," Peng said quietly. "This operation will happen."

CHAPTER 23

Wednesday, October 6, 1976

Liang danced a little hop-skip for glee, something he would have never done anywhere else. But he was safe in his office inside Jiang's villa, deep within Zhongnanhai. He could do anything he wanted to do.

The door opened, and a commissar walked in. "General, the prisoner is ready to be brought to your office."

"Bring her here at once."

At last the prize was his and his alone. Like rain falling on parched earth, it would be the salvation of a thousand generations of his descendants—once, that is, he had delivered it to Jiang Qing. When the commissar returned moments later with Li Guangmei, Liang was seated at his desk, all signs of glee deeply buried.

"Sit down," he said.

"My name is Fiona Li, and I've been kidnapped, presumably for some sort of ransom, which my father—he's very rich—will gladly pay. Perhaps you've heard of my father. His name is—"

"Shut up!" Liang shouted. "I already know your father's name. The question is, do you know your father's name?"

"Don't be stupid, of course I—"

"Shut your yap!" Liang stood up. "You may think your father is Li Dak-chung. Well, he's not."

Liang paused to allow his words to have maximum impact on the prisoner. He sat down again and studied her. He was sure that he had seen her before. She was wearing baggy green cotton pants and shirt and loose-fitting cotton shoes. She had no makeup on, and her hair, which had not been washed in weeks, hung limp in greasy clumps against her skull. Notwithstanding all of this, Liang still thought she was beautiful.

"Of course he's my father," she said presently. "And stop leering at me. Where's my coat? I'm freezing in this tomb."

Liang jumped up and began pounding on the desk. "You ungrateful capitalist swine! The Chinese masses have given you the clothes on your back, and still you complain like a spoiled child!"

Liang rounded the desk and struck her a vicious blow in the face. Her left cheek and eye began to swell. She bent double, dry-heaving several times, and then remained with her head between her knees. Liang stood towering over her, reveling in the moment. It was for this sort of power over spoiled capitalists that he had joined the Party.

Eventually, Liang moved away and sat down again at his desk.

Li raised her head slowly. "Don't do that again," she said in a steely voice.

Liang threw his head back and laughed. "Or you'll what? You don't seem to realize that you are in the People's Republic of China. You are completely within my control. Mine and mine alone. Do I make myself clear?"

Li just stared back at him.

"Your father's name is Zhu Fangguo," Liang said. "Have you ever heard that name?" Again Li did not respond.

Liang got up and went to a small side table on which sat a metal tray containing a clear flask of water. He poured himself a large glass, drank it in one continuous swallow, and turned back to Li.

"There is no reason you should have heard it," he said. "He's a very senior Chinese military officer. It is unfortunate that he has chosen to betray the Party by supporting the traitor Deng Xiaoping."

He noticed that Li was eyeing the water flask. "You can drink later. I assume that you would like to meet your father. Well, that might be possible." He leaned across the desk. "If you cooperate with us."

• • •

Fiona wiped blood from her upper lip, which was now red and swollen. She was terrified, but she refused to show her fear to Liang or let him manipulate it to his advantage. She knew now that Liang and Jiang Qing needed her, and she meant to parlay that need into survival, not only for herself but also for those she cared about. Liang had dismissed her as nothing more than a rich indolent child. But she had changed since she had been kidnapped, and her enemies were yet to find out just how much.

• • •

The plan would have to be reworked, and at the last possible moment. Peng was a professional military officer used to rolling with the punches, but nothing had prepared him for the news that Lina had smuggled to him from inside Zhongnanhai: Zhu and his daughter were both being held in Jiang Qing's villa, and Liang was planning to execute one or both of his prisoners that very night.

It was now shortly after 10:00 p.m. The warrant for Jiang's arrest had to be executed right away if they were to have any chance of saving

Zhu and Li Guangmei. General Wang had agreed when Peng reached him by telephone at the Ministry of National Defense and was now on his way to the Legation Quarter. He ordered Peng and Liaoping to be ready to leave immediately for Zhongnanhai when he and his driver arrived, which should be . . .

". . . at any moment," Peng said aloud as Liaoping entered the room wearing the uniform of a captain in the PLA. Peng had specified this disguise to minimize the risk to the team in case the guards in Zhongnanhai became suspicious.

"General Wang is here," Liaoping said.

The two hurried outside to the waiting jeep. Like Liaoping, General Wang's driver was dressed in the uniform of a PLA captain. The jeep sped out of the Legation Quarter and west on Chang An Jie to Zhongnanhai. At the red pagoda-style gate, the jeep slowed briefly to allow the guards to recognize it as General Wang's vehicle then accelerated through the gate, zigzagging carefully around the obstacles designed to protect the entrance from breach by even the heaviest tank.

Once inside the compound, the driver slowed to minimize engine noise and proceeded to Jiang's Guanyuan villa, the most palatial of the numerous residences in Zhongnanhai. Satisfied that the jeep was General Wang's, the sentries posted along the way waved it on.

When the jeep stopped at the gate to Jiang's villa, the two sentries standing guard came to attention. General Wang, followed by the other three passengers, got out of the vehicle and swept past the sentries up the short walkway and into the residence. The only light shone from a small alcove off the lobby from which two commissars emerged to confront the visitors. General Wang addressed the most senior of the two. "I have an urgent and sensitive message from Premier Hua to deliver personally to Jiang Qing," he said.

The commissar laughed nervously. "What's so urgent that it can't wait until morning?"

"Stand at attention," General Wang shouted, "and wipe that smirk off your face!"

The two commissars snapped to attention. General Wang glared at them. "You two will remain here while my aides and I deliver the Premier's message and take down Comrade Jiang's reply. Is that understood?"

"Yes, sir," the two said in unison.

"At ease," General Wang said as he motioned behind him for Peng, Liaoping, and his driver to follow him. He bounded up the darkened stairs to the first-floor landing out of sight and earshot of the two commissars.

"Colonel," General Wang said to Peng, "it's all yours now."

"Yes, sir." Peng led the general up the stairs two at a time to the top floor of the villa. Liaoping and the driver followed.

"Which one is Jiang's bedroom?" Peng whispered.

"Last on the right," General Wang said.

The only light came from the commissars' alcove two flights below, but it was enough to permit the four of them to negotiate the hallway. Once at the bedroom door, Peng pressed his ear against it. All was quiet. He turned to check that the others had reached the door then twisted the knob and threw the door open.

The sound woke Jiang instantly. She leapt out of bed. "How dare you wake me!"

Liaoping switched on the light. The power at the helm of the largest Communist state in the world was wearing a lacy nightgown that provided little protection from the night chill.

Jiang gaped at the four intruders and then fixed an imperiously withering gaze on General Wang. "Chairman Mao is barely gone and you have the nerve to mount a coup!"

"Jiang Qing," Colonel Peng said, "you are under arrest by order of Premier Hua!"

The tyrannical megalomaniac, the person who ten years prior had loosed the Cultural Revolution and the Red Guards on a supine China, the person who struck terror and loathing into the heart of every Chinese—that person now slid to the floor and wept uncontrollably.

A commotion erupted downstairs. Shouts and sounds of scuffles gained in intensity, reached a peak, and then died out, all in the space of about two minutes. Footsteps pounded on the stairs. Peng already had his pistol drawn; the other three drew theirs and watched the open door as the footsteps approached the bedroom.

Two soldiers appeared in the doorway. One of them said, "General Wang, as you ordered we have neutralized the commissar guard force and surrounded the villa."

"You miserable traitors," Jiang said.

"Hold your tongue," Peng said.

Jiang began to weep again. Peng holstered his pistol and pulled her to her feet.

"Don't touch me!" She wrested her elbow free of his hand. "Don't touch me!"

"Where are General Zhu and his daughter?" Peng said.

"I have no idea where Zhu is, and I don't know anything about any daughter."

"Don't worry about that now, Colonel Peng." General Wang motioned to the two soldiers. "Take the prisoner Jiang Qing to the truck."

"Yes, sir," one of them said as they flanked Jiang and led her away.

"My soldiers," General Wang said, "are now searching the house for General Zhu and his daughter and for General Liang. If they're here, the soldiers will find them."

• • •

Lina, assigned to the company of soldiers securing Jiang's villa, proceeded straight to the basement. There, she began searching the rooms on either side of a narrow corridor. These were the only rooms in the basement as far as she knew, but she remembered about the catacomb of tunnels beneath the Forbidden City, Zhongnanhai, and Tiananmen. The rooms were empty except for one, which was a kind of workshop and storage room. She entered and switched on the light. Unlike the other rooms, this one had a closet. Suspicious, she removed the brooms, mops, and pails to get a better look. Nothing out of the ordinary. With her truncheon she tapped on the wooden floor, walls, and ceiling. They all seemed solid, but she was sure there had to be something about the closet that was the key to locating General Zhu.

With the palm of her hand, she went over every inch of the floor and walls for evidence of a panel that might open. Using an overturned pail to add to her height, she checked the ceiling again. Still nothing.

Dejected, she slumped against the wall. There had to be a reason why this room had a closet and the others didn't. She began running the possibilities through her mind as she absentmindedly moved the brooms, mops, and pails back and forth. She picked up a mop and hung it on a protruding nail.

Suddenly the light-switch plate next to the door slid open, revealing a hook-like lever. She crossed the room, carefully inspected the lever, and gently pulled it. The entire left wall of the closet slid open, and the light-switch plate closed.

From the opening, a staircase led downward. Lina descended the stairs, which made a sharp right turn, then led further downward into the subterranean void. A faint light filtered up from below. At the bottom, a long curving hallway led to an open space from which the light was emanating. She could hear muffled voices. She crept silently down the hallway until she could better see and hear.

Lina recognized General Liang, who stood talking to a woman seated at a table spread with papers. She shuddered at the memory of her interrogation at the hands of this man. Lina could not see the woman clearly. Zhu sat blindfolded and tied to his chair to the left of Liang, his head hanging limp to one side.

"So you see," Liang was saying to the woman, "transferring your Hong Kong assets to the Motherland by signing this document will relieve your conscience and save you and your father. You both will live in luxury in China as the guests of a grateful nation."

The woman began to weep into the palms of her hands. "Are you sure," she said between sobs, "that my fath . . . uh . . . Li Dak-chung died three days ago?"

"I showed you the Hong Kong newspaper, didn't I?"

The woman nodded but continued crying. Liang sat down and idly tapped a pen on the table.

Lina knew that it would be easy for a man as powerful as Liang to arrange printing of a single copy of a newspaper. She also knew that she had to make her move before Liang made an example of General Zhu. But she did not know how many guards might be in the room.

"Either you sign," Liang said, "or I'll finish your father off right in front of you. Your real father, that is. And then, it'll be your turn. I have in mind to turn you over to my men. Quite possibly, you'll never be seen again. But I'll let them decide your fate."

The woman had stopped crying and was glaring at Liang.

"Perhaps you think I'm joking. Maybe watching your father suffer will persuade you."

Liang raised his arm over his head and motioned to someone behind the woman. Two commissars came into view. One rolled up Zhu's sleeve. The other, holding a dripping hypodermic needle poised over Zhu's bare arm, looked at Liang.

Two guards. There were at least two. Lina could not take them without help.

"This is your final chance to save your father," Liang said. The woman's look of defiance turned to distress and then to rage. "So, you cling to your childish obstinacy. So be it."

As Liang turned toward the man holding the needle, the woman grabbed the pen from the table and vaulted at Liang's back. The help she needed. Truncheon in hand, Lina rushed into the room and swung at the man holding the needle. With a sickening crack the man's arm shattered, and the needle fell to the floor. While he screamed in pain, Lina dispatched the second guard with a hard kick to the groin and, as he doubled over, a blow to the back of the head. Then Lina spun on Liang. The woman was clinging to Liang's back, trying to plunge the pen into his neck, but he had her arm in both of his hands. He twisted the woman's arm, tearing her off his back and driving her to her knees. With her truncheon, Lina dealt a savage blow to Liang's kidneys. He screamed, loosed his hold on the woman, and crumpled to the floor.

Suddenly, the woman jumped to her feet, grabbed the truncheon out of Lina's hand, and beat repeatedly at Liang's head. Lina, numbed by the woman's frenzy, could only watch as Liang's skull was crushed to a pulpy, bloody mass, brain tissue oozing onto the concrete floor. When she was sure Liang was dead, the woman dropped the truncheon, fell to her knees, and wept.

Lina heard a commotion in the hallway behind her. The room was soon flooded with soldiers, Colonel Peng and Liaoping among them. Peng rushed to General Zhu and immediately ordered that the unconscious general be taken to the hospital at the Ministry of National Defense. Liaoping saw to it that Lina was all right and then helped the still-weeping woman to her feet.

Lina went to the woman to comfort her. "Are you really the daughter of General Zhu?"

The woman raised her face from the palms of her hands and was about to reply when, suddenly, she gasped. Lina hesitated, mystified, then she, too, gasped. The two stared at each other and fell into each other's arms.

"Seeing you is like looking into a mirror!" Fiona Li said.

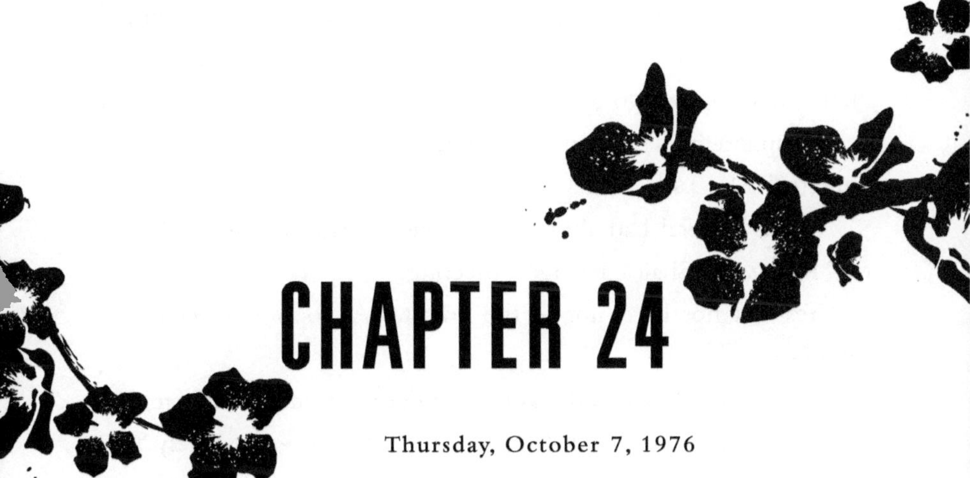

CHAPTER 24

Thursday, October 7, 1976

"Hah! They got her! Deng and Marshal Ye got her before she could get us. And even the Premier had a hand in it! What good news! What good news, indeed!"

Zhu laughed as he tossed the morning's People's Daily on the table beside his hospital bed. He had been reading with relish the special announcement to the Chinese people of the arrest of Jiang Qing, despite having been briefed on the entire operation by Colonel Peng the previous night.

"What was that name the propagandist pinned on the radical leadership?" Zhu asked Peng, who was sitting at his bedside.

"The article labeled them the 'Gang of Four,' General," Peng said.

"Gang of Four," Zhu chuckled. "How appropriate. It ropes them all together, labels them as criminals, and even foreshadows the trial that Comrade Deng has in mind."

"The label has many advantages."

Peng wondered why Zhu had not raised the subject of his daughter now that Jiang was in custody. He could understand that the general might feel a certain trepidation, even reluctance, to meet an adult woman last seen as a tiny baby almost thirty years ago. But she was, after all, the other of his two preoccupations.

"I suppose you're wondering why I haven't asked to meet my daughter," Zhu said.

Ah, the general had always been able to read his mind. "Yes, sir, I am," Peng said. "Shall I arrange a meeting?"

"Yes, but not here, not in the hospital. As soon as I get back to my office."

Zhu got out of bed and was preparing to put on his uniform when a nurse rushed in. "General Zhu, get back into bed immediately. You're much too sick to go anywhere."

"Comrade," Zhu replied, "I appreciate your concern, but I'm much too busy to lie about in bed all day. Besides, I have an important family matter to attend to."

• • •

It was midmorning, and the weather outside was foul. The rain had begun shortly after 3:00 a.m. with a thunder and lightning spectacular that put to shame even Hong Kong's Chinese New Year fireworks.

"Good news!" Hugh said as he walked into Knud's office.

"I couldn't agree more," I replied. "Jiang's arrest spells the end of the Cultural Revolution and all this madness."

"Oh, yes, that too." Hugh said, turning to Knud, "but I was talking about our chance to finally get rid of this man." He walked up behind my chair and started massaging my good shoulder.

"I had no idea you were so anxious for me to leave," I said in mock surprise.

Hugh tossed his overcoat onto an empty chair and sat down beside me. "If this rain ever stops, I'll personally chuck you in the Grand Canal and let you float out to sea and back to Hong Kong."

"What, you won't even let him stop to visit Hangzhou?" Knud said.

"Not a chance!" Hugh said. "With his record of going missing, I won't even let him stay in Beijing long enough to welcome Emma back."

"She's well?" I asked.

"Yes. At least she seemed right as rain when I talked to her on the telephone this morning. She was elated at the news that Fiona has been found."

"Where? How did you find out?" Why hadn't he told me right away? I was weary of the diplomatic habit of playing everything close to the chest.

Hugh held up his hands. "Let me start from the beginning because you two will have masses of questions, and the whole story will answer most of them. This morning about 7:00 a.m., the China Travel Service—your Miss Pan—rang me at my flat to say that the authorities were deporting to Hong Kong, quote, 'the First Secretary's friend, Bryan Paton,' close quote. They were also expelling, quote, 'to the place from which she arrived in the People's Republic of China, the Chinese citizen named Li Guangmei,' close quote. Because that 'place' was Hong Kong, which incidentally she referred to as 'China's sovereign territory temporarily and illegally occupied by Britain,' the authorities were notifying the British Embassy."

"That'll be the first time they've ever notified one of the embassies in advance," Knud said.

"Or deported someone they claim as a citizen," Hugh said.

"How did you know that the caller was Miss Pan?" I asked.

"Well," Hugh bent forward and rested his elbows on his knees, "first, Jiang Qing was arrested last night. That means the moderates are in control of China, at least temporarily, so Pan's side wins the first scrimmage.

Second, the caller knew the names Bryan Paton and Li Guangmei. Only someone like Pan would be familiar with both."

"That makes sense," Knud said.

"And third," Hugh said smiling, "she immediately identified herself as Pan Bingqing." I gave Hugh a sheepish look.

"Where's Fiona now, and what's her condition?" I asked. "Can we see her? Has she been injured?"

"I asked those very questions, as well as many others," Hugh said. "Pan wouldn't say anything other than that Li Guangmei—that's what she insisted on calling Fiona—was to be expelled. No date, no method of travel, nothing about Fiona's condition. The only information she would give me was your deportation date." When I did not respond, he said, "Sorry, that was a lame attempt at taking your mind off Fiona. Look, nobody can do anything until she appears back in Hong Kong."

"You're right, of course," I said, "but I just can't shake the feeling that, in the end, I failed Mr. Li and Simon."

"Oh, don't talk rot," Hugh said. "If you hadn't followed every lead that turned up, no matter how dangerous, we might never have got our girl back."

Hugh was being generous, but I was feeling better. Fiona was alive and both of us were going home. "When do I leave?"

"Pan pointedly said that I should tell you to be ready to go at 7:00 a.m. tomorrow morning. She will collect you and take you to the hotel to pack your bags and pay your bill."

"They could have chucked you across the border in your skivvies!" Knud chortled.

"Yes, and if Deng and his moderates had not seized control, General Liang would have . . . I shudder to think."

"Was General Liang the one who interrogated you and the others?" Hugh asked.

"One and the same. And what a vicious, sadistic bastard he is."

. . .

It was midafternoon, and Zhu was standing at the window of his study. He had just returned from a meeting of the moderate leadership, chaired at long last by Deng Xiaoping. The rain had cleared the smog, and the sun was shining. It was a rare afternoon in Beijing, clear and luminous.

As Peng entered the study, Zhu turned from the window. "Thank you for coming so quickly, Colonel Peng," Zhu said. "Please, have a seat. Deng and Marshal Ye are delighted with the outcome of your operation last night at Zhongnanhai."

"Sir," Peng said, "as I told you this morning, General Wang was in charge."

"Yes . . . well," Zhu said, "your modesty is commendable, but Rong Liaoping's report made clear that General Wang gave operational control to you. When the report found its way to Deng, your role last night caught his attention. He was very pleased."

"Thank you, sir, but—"

"Now enough of that," Zhu raised his hand. "Let's change the subject, shall we? I'm most anxious to meet my daughter and get to know her."

"Yes, sir." Peng started to turn toward the door then stopped. "General Zhu, I think you should prepare yourself for a shock."

"She's all right, isn't she?" Zhu said.

"She was badly beaten by General Liang, sir," Peng said. "That would be bad enough, but there's more. It seems that another woman is also claiming to be your daughter. Could that be possible?"

Zhu smiled and mulled the best way to proceed. Clearly Peng knew that it was not only possible but true.

"Did this woman tell you why she thought this was true?" Zhu asked.

"General Zhu," Peng said, "once again I find myself in the disagreeable position of having to insist that you tell me all the facts about your family . . . if I am to be of any help."

It was an audacious move and one which, in a different context and with a different senior officer, would have at a minimum earned Peng an immediate dressing-down. But Peng was right to ask, and Zhu would honor that request.

"I didn't know all the facts myself," Zhu said, "until just over a week ago when Liang brought Rong Lina to my apartment. That's when I was struck by her astonishing resemblance to my daughter."

"But General, you've never actually seen your daughter."

"That's right," Zhu said, "but I have seen a recent photograph of her. I thought that Rong Lina was a carbon copy." He took a deep breath. "So I managed to locate the one person in the world who would know the truth—the midwife who was present at the birth of my children in Yenan in 1947 and 1948. She confirmed what I now consider to be my very good fortune."

Peng waited, expecting Zhu to continue, but Zhu fell silent, put his hands together as if in prayer, and touched the tip of his nose. After a few minutes he said, "Please forgive me. I was just thinking how happy their mother would be if she were here. She never had a chance to know them."

"General, would you like to meet the two women . . . your daughters . . . now?" Peng asked.

Zhu's pensive expression gave way to a mischievous smile and then to a chuckle. "Yes . . . yes, I would like to meet my daughters. Could you please get them for me?"

"Gladly, sir," Peng replied and left the room.

Zhu walked to the window. Never before had he appreciated so much the grand vista stretching over North Lake and the Forbidden City just beyond. Now he reveled in its glory in the brilliance of the afternoon.

Peng returned and closed the study door behind him. "General, they're right outside. Would you like me to bring them in?"

"Yes, yes of course," Zhu said. "No, I should greet them myself. You wait here. No, you'd better come in case . . . in case something goes wrong." He stopped halfway to the door. Wrong? What could possibly go wrong? After all, they are just two small— No, they are not small girls. They are young women. And they are your daughters.

"General," Peng said, "might I suggest that you wait here, and I'll bring the two young ladies in to you?"

"Thank you." Zhu sat down on the sofa. Commanding armies and dealing with daughters were two different skills.

When the door opened again, Lina entered the study, followed by Guangmei and Colonel Peng. Zhu stood ramrod straight until all three had filed in.

Lina, eyes downcast and respectful, stared at the carpet. Guangmei looked straight at Zhu, her eyes portraying wariness and caution. Her face bore witness to the beating she had suffered at the hands of General Liang.

When Zhu saw Guangmei's wounds, he went to her to help her to the sofa. Lina, too, grasped her elbow and helped her sister sit down.

"Thank you," Guangmei said, "thank you both." She had an expression of amazement on her face, as if she had not expected such kindness. And that, more than anything, showed Zhu what she had been through.

"That's what families are for . . . to help each other," Zhu said.

"Father is right." Lina patted Guangmei on the knee. "You have nothing to fear now."

Guangmei stared at Lina and then at Zhu. In a barely audible voice, she said, "Thank you."

The housekeeper and another servant entered the study, each carrying a tray. They laid out the tea service on the map table and left.

"Guangmei," Zhu said, "are you able to come to the table, or shall I bring your tea to you?"

"No, you don't have to bring me my tea. I can come to the table."

Zhu led Guangmei to the table with Lina on her other arm. Peng held back, assuming he was no longer needed, and waited for Zhu to excuse him.

"Join us." A smile on his face, Zhu motioned Peng to the table. He turned to Guangmei and Lina. "I want you to know, my daughters, that there is no one I trust more than Colonel Peng. If anything ever happens to me, do not rely on anyone but him."

"I'm grateful for your trust, General Zhu." Peng pulled his chair a short distance from the table and sat down.

"You must have many questions," Zhu said to Guangmei and Lina, "and I have so much to tell you."

The three of them were silent, no one knowing quite where to begin.

"General Zhu," Peng said, "perhaps your daughters would like to hear about their mother and the circumstances of their birth."

"Yes." Zhu was grateful for Peng's help.

Lina leaned forward and said, "Please tell us about our mother. Please."

Guangmei nodded. After she drank some of her tea, she settled back in her chair, her shoulders signaling that her body had relaxed.

"Your mother's name," Zhu said, "was Ye Guangrong. She was born in Tianjin in 1919 to one of China's richest capitalists. Her childhood was unusually privileged, but her father was also unusually progressive, especially for China in the 1920s. Whenever he visited one of his factories, he took Guangrong along to teach her about the workers who gave her such fine things. She learned the lesson well."

Zhu stopped and sipped his tea. He took a pack of cigarettes from his pocket, offered them to Guangmei and Lina, who both declined, and lit one himself.

"As a child, your mother was an excellent student—she was especially proficient in mathematics—and a talented musician."

"How lovely," Lina said. "Which instrument did she play?"

Zhu was now warming to the task. "She played the violin and the *erhu*. She even serenaded Chairman Mao in Yenan!"

For the next several hours, Zhu told Guangmei and Lina about their mother's privileged childhood; her fascination with Archimedes as a symbol for her love of mathematics, poetry, and music; their participation in the Long March; how they met, courted, and married; and the joy of their life together in a cave in Yenan. He also told them about his life since their mother's death.

By the time he finished, it was late in the afternoon, and the sun was setting. Zhu stood up and walked to the window. Peng and Lina followed.

"The morning rain has been good to us. It washed the soot from the sky and gave us this fine day."

"Yes, Father, it did," Lina said, "and the ducks on the lake—"

Guangmei exploded. She stood up and rounded the table to face her father, both fists clenched at her waist. "You're talking about the weather when all you've told us about our mother is facts. I could probably go to a decent library and look those up. Did you ever think to tell us what she was really like? Like why she had to become a goddamn Communist anyway!" Tears welled up in her eyes and began coursing down her face. "And who is Li Dak-chung . . . really? Until recently, I thought he was my father."

She began sobbing and laid her head on Zhu's chest. He put his arms around her and felt her tremble. "And I need to know how my mother . . . our mother . . . how our mother died."

"You're right, Guangmei, you're absolutely right," Zhu said. "Come, sit down."

He led her back to the sofa and sat down beside her. Lina sat next to Guangmei, and Peng sat on a chair he moved from the map table.

"The year your mother was born, 1919," Zhu said, "was the year of the Treaty of Versailles. China wasn't involved in World War I but suffered damage and, more important, great humiliation at the hands of that treaty. That humiliation continues to this day to be a powerful unifying force for Chinese patriots all over the world."

"But what does this have to do with our mother?" Guangmei asked, now a bit calmer.

"I suspect that's why she became a Communist," Lina said. "Every Chinese child learns in school of the shame the Treaty brought down on China. And every child is taught never to let such shame happen ever again to the Motherland."

"But what did the Treaty do that was so bad?"

"The Treaty treated China like carrion," Zhu said, "to be scavenged and torn apart at will by Japan and the West. Germany already had part of Shandong province. That was bad enough. But then the Treaty not only failed to give sovereignty back to China, it ceded it to Japan. The Chinese nation was humiliated, as it had been several generations before when, in 1842, Britain grabbed Hong Kong after the Opium War.

"Word of the Treaty reached China on May 4, 1919, and the nation erupted in protests and boycotts of Western goods. University students, the pride and hope of China and the leaders-in-training of the next generation, led the protest movement, which was soon dubbed the 'May 4th Movement.' On that one date, more Chinese patriots and national-ists became Communists than at any time before or since. China had been dealt a brutal shock by the West, one that it would never forget. Faith in Western governments was destroyed."

Zhu stood up and again walked to the window. It was now early evening and dark outside. The only light visible was from the Beijing Hotel and that part of Chang An Jie around Tiananmen Square. And even that was only a pallid glimmer.

"So, when your mother learned about Communism as a young woman," Zhu said, "it grew naturally out of her childhood study of the May 4th Movement. It was the same for me. We wanted to keep China from being dismembered by the West, and Communism was the only way to do it. Your mother believed this."

The room was eerily silent. Zhu took out a cigarette and lit it. He smoked a moment to collect his thoughts, then walked back to the sofa and sat down. This was the hard part.

"Before I tell you, Guangmei, about how Li Dak-chung became involved in your life and the life of my son, Guoliang—"

"Simon, you mean?" Guangmei interrupted. "We call him Simon."

"Yes, Simon . . . Guoliang. Before I tell you about Li Dak-chung's involvement, I want to tell you how Guangrong died."

Zhu paused. Even after nearly thirty years, it was painful to remember. But his children had to know the truth.

"Your mother was murdered. She was murdered by an insanely jealous Jiang Qing on the very night the two of you were born."

Lina gasped, but all Guangmei said was, "That certainly doesn't surprise me."

"The masses will take care of her at the trial," Zhu said, "but I want to be sure you two and Guoliang know the details. That's important to me because I've never told this to anyone, not even to Colonel Peng, here." Zhu stopped to light another cigarette and gather himself.

"It was February 10, 1948, and your mother wasn't due to give birth until March. A party including Mao, Liu Shaoqi, and myself left Yenan for a five-day visit to the front. When we left Yenan the sun was shining brilliantly, but the weather was raw with wind and cold. By the time we made camp that night, we were bogged down in a blizzard.

"In Yenan, where the blizzard was also raging, your mother suddenly went into labor. The midwife managed to get her to the infirmary where she gave birth prematurely to the two of you. It was a long and difficult labor. Immediately after giving birth, your mother began to have seizures and convulsions and lapsed into unconsciousness.

"The doctor who attended the birth was terrified that the wife of someone on Mao's personal staff might die while under his care. He panicked and summoned Jiang Qing to make the decision as to what to do. Jiang promptly ordered everyone out of the delivery room. The doctor made a token protest but then fled the room behind his nurse and the midwife.

"No one knows what occurred in the delivery room that day. Jiang emerged later to say that Guangrong was dead. She refused to permit an autopsy and ordered that Guangrong's body be cremated as soon as the snowstorm lifted. The snow ended the next day. I never saw her again." Zhu took out his handkerchief and wiped his eyes and mouth.

"Did any of them ever say whether she could have survived?" Lina asked. "Before Jiang got there, that is."

"The midwife told me she thought that Guangrong could have been saved had the doctor been allowed to stay, but that may have been wishful thinking or guilt speaking. The doctor and the nurse died many years ago. Only Jiang knows the truth."

"What happened to the two of us?" Lina said.

"That's the part of the story that I learned from the midwife only last week," Zhu replied. "According to her, Jiang was enraged that your mother had given birth to twins. At the same time, one or both of you were wailing, which only made Jiang angrier. She apparently stormed out of the infirmary shouting, 'Get rid of those screamers! I told the Party we needed a one-child policy!' The midwife didn't know if Jiang would come back later and kill you two, but she wasn't taking any chances. She took one of you—from what we know now, it was

Lina—to a woman who had also just given birth. The woman—your foster mother, Lina,—was leaving Yenan the next day to travel south to Hunan to join her husband, a major in the PLA serving with our forces there."

"But wouldn't Jiang have wanted to kill us both?" Guangmei asked. "After all, including Simon . . . uh . . . Guoliang, we were now three children."

"I don't know. Perhaps she wanted you for herself. Perhaps I returned before she found out you were still alive. In any case, when I got back to Yenan, I was able to protect you and Guoliang, at least for a while. The midwife said that, at the time, she was too terrified of Jiang to tell me about Lina."

"Father," Guangmei said, "what did you mean when you said you were able to protect us for a while?"

"One sweltering afternoon in the summer, about six months after your mother died, I took you to the infirmary because you had developed a rash. Jiang happened to be there, too, and was just leaving when she stopped to dote on you. I knew she was pretending to be interested, that she really had another motive. When it finally came out, however, it shocked even me.

"She said that you and Guoliang were fortunate to have avoided being raised by a mother who harbored capitalist principles. Then she said—I'll never forget it—that the Party and the masses would observe my children as they grew for the slightest sign that they were infected with the dangerous capitalist virus. I knew then that I had to get you and Guoliang out of Jiang's reach, that she would always be a threat to you.

"I remembered an old classmate of mine at the Whampoa Military Academy. It had been years since we'd seen each other, but I felt sure he would help me. More important, he owned a shipping company, which meant that he had means to smuggle two small children to safety. He lived in Shanghai, which in 1948 was controlled by the KMT. I had difficulty getting a message to him, but I finally succeeded. We worked out how to smuggle the two of you from Yenan to Shanghai. That was in March of 1949, and you left in April. When our forces liberated Shanghai at the end of May, I was, of course, overjoyed. But I was also terribly worried that perhaps you and Guoliang had been caught up in the confusion that reigned in those days. Had you in fact made it to Shanghai? Months passed with no word. Finally in December I received a message from my old friend Li saying that he had taken you to Hong Kong and that you were both safe and well.

"I longed to see you and Guoliang, but hostility to the West led Mao to seal off China to outside influence. I despaired of ever seeing you again. Then four years ago, Mao welcomed the American president, Nixon, to China. The Cultural Revolution was still under way, and life was hard, but at last I could hope for a reunion someday.

"Over the years, Li Dak-chung became the richest and most powerful capitalist in Hong Kong. Interest in Li was extremely high here, and the intelligence service was ordered to keep the Li family under surveillance. I received routine reports on what you, Guoliang, and Li Dak-chung were doing. When I read you were opening an antique shop, I saw an opportunity and arranged for you to be offered a consignment of the finest Chinese antiques. I personally authorized a Hong Kong compatriot visa for you.

"But what I could not have foreseen, Guangmei, was your abduction and my sudden transfer from Shenyang to Beijing following Mao's death. After that . . . well, that's when all our struggles began."

There was a long, pregnant silence. Then Guangmei walked over and put her arms around her father.

"Thank you," she said. "Thank you for all you've done."

For Zhu, the weight of memory eased at last.

CHAPTER 25

Friday, October 8, 1976

"Why does he want to see me?" I asked.

Miss Pan gave me her most withering look and a harrumph of exasperation at my stubborn refusal to learn the mores of a Communist dictatorship. "Mis . . . ter . . . Paton," she said, "when the Beijing Military Region commander summons you, you do not question his motive."

We were in the backseat of a 1949 Ford—no, Shanghai—en route to the meeting, the location of which Miss Pan had not shared. I had only heard about it earlier that morning when Miss Pan came to fetch me at the Danish Embassy. I was to depart Beijing by train that evening.

The morning was still less than half gone, and unlike the day before when the morning rain washed the afternoon sky to a sparkling azure blue, the Beijing sky resembled sooty brown gauze. Things were back to normal.

The driver went by a circuitous route that I did not recognize. Eventually, however, we turned onto the side street that Emma and I had crossed on the morning we walked from the hospital to the Ministry of Public Security. We passed the old Beijing Club, my first safe house and the scene of my escape from a second-story window, and turned into the now familiar Austro-Hungarian Legation. When we entered through the gate, I saw that the compound was deserted. What had been an armed camp bristling with tanks and machine guns five days ago was now eerily silent. The building itself was closed and shuttered. There was no evidence of anyone about. The driver pulled the car behind the building and stopped.

"We're here," Miss Pan announced unnecessarily as she got out of the car. "Come. General Zhu may already be inside."

She led me through the unlocked back door and small scullery to the kitchen. "Wait here," she said and disappeared through the kitchen's swinging door.

Presently, I heard voices. Miss Pan swung the door open and gestured to me. "Please come in here, Mr. Paton," she said in her most pleasant barbarian-handling manner.

I walked into the dining room, dark except for a single small glowing bulb in the cut-glass Austrian chandelier and the faint glimmer of sunlight around the edges of the shutters. General Zhu and Colonel Peng were seated at one end of the dining table. Peng motioned me to one of the empty chairs near them. Miss Pan chose to sit some distance from the three of us. I began to wonder if this proceeding was to be as benign as Miss Pan had said it would be, a feeling heightened by the taciturn expressions on the faces of the two army men. I sat down not knowing what to expect.

General Zhu went straight to the point. "Mr. Paton," he said, "I promised my daughters Guangmei—Fiona—and Lina that I would meet with you again before you left China. They seem to think that you need some answers for Li Dak-chung."

I was floored. Fiona . . . was Zhu's . . . daughter? And Lina, too? How? I could barely take it in.

"What questions do you have?" Zhu said. He waited barely a second before he jumped up. "No? Well, I'll tell Guangmei that—"

I was still reeling from the general's revelation, and my voice shook as I spoke, but I knew that I would never get an opportunity like this again. I wouldn't be able to look at myself in the mirror or face Li Dak-chung if I blew it. "General," I sputtered, "I actually do have questions."

Zhu already had his right arm in the sleeve of his overcoat. "Like what?" He now had his overcoat on and was buttoning it.

"Like, for example, what . . . uh . . . that is, whose body was that in the hospital morgue, the body the authorities wanted me to accept as Fiona's . . . uh . . . Guangmei's?"

Zhu stood motionless for a moment then sighed. When he began taking his overcoat off, I felt the tension ebb from my body.

"Colonel Peng, could you please open those shutters. It's very dark in here." Zhu threw his coat over the back of a chair, sat down, and lit a cigarette. Peng opened the shutters, and the noontime light flooded into the room.

"You have five minutes, young man," Zhu said.

"Whose body was it?" I asked.

"I don't know," Zhu said. "That is, I don't know her identity. As I understand it, the criminals who kidnapped Guangmei wanted to put pressure on Li Dak-chung by making him think his daughter had been murdered. So they found a dead woman of roughly her age and arranged to have Guangmei's identity documents associated with the woman's corpse. They planned to reveal to Li later that Guangmei was alive in the hope of a ransom, but events overtook them." Zhu looked at his watch but made no move to leave.

"General, I still have some questions about—"

"Get on with it then." Zhu took out another cigarette, lit it, and then stubbed it out. "I apologize, young man. I'm afraid this old man is used to moving things along with military precision. Are you as uncomfortable sitting in these chairs as I am? Of course you are." He turned to Peng. "Colonel, would you and the other comrade please excuse us for about half an hour?"

"Of course, General," Peng said. He and Miss Pan disappeared into the kitchen while Zhu and I moved to the living room.

Zhu pointed to the sofa. "Please, sit. These old legs need stretching, so I'll stand for a while." He lit another cigarette and opened the shutters facing the front of the house.

I was now reasonably certain I would get the answers to my questions. I also suspected that there was something else that Zhu wanted me to know.

"Mr. Paton, you can be sure that your activities in China these past three weeks will never be known," he said. "Your involvement with me, Colonel Peng, the Rongs, Major Wang, and your kidnap and subsequent rescue—these things never happened. No one in the People's Republic of China will ever speak of them. Do I make myself clear?"

"Yes, perfectly." I realized that Zhu had just given me leave to delve more deeply.

"General, where were Guangmei's kidnappers holding her?" I asked.

"In Lingkou, a village near Shanghai," he said. "The criminals were themselves Triads. They're not nationalists or Chinese patriots, just remnants of Chiang Kai-shek's old ally, the Green Gang."

"She was not in the hands of political commissars?" I asked.

"Not originally," Zhu said. "Colonel Peng had her under his protection briefly, after the police rescued her in Guangzhou. But when they were on their way to Beijing," Zhu continued, "she was taken off the train at gunpoint. The men who took her were dressed as soldiers, but I have my suspicions."

"Surely the Triads wouldn't have brought her here," I pressed.

"It's doubtful, but that is Guangmei's story and hers to tell . . . or at least as much of it as she wants you to know."

"Thank you. Do you know why Guangmei came to China?"

"Antiques," Zhu replied without hesitation. "The New China is full of warehouses stacked to the ceiling with all manner of Chinese and Western antiques that we impounded after the war. The Red Guards tried to destroy them, but fortunately, cooler heads in the Party prevailed. When I heard that Guangmei was opening a shop, I dangled the prospect of a consignment of our best wares and arranged for a visa—quietly, of course. After all, I had been waiting for nearly thirty years to see her again."

It crossed my mind to ask about the derelict turn-of-the-century hotel in the Legation Quarter and the treasures that it and other buildings in the abandoned quarter must contain, but I thought better of it. I was determined to keep Zhu focused.

"Did you often help Guangmei and her brother after they went to Hong Kong?"

"No!" Zhu shot back.

I sensed that I had touched a raw nerve, perhaps one reflecting embarrassment or the guarding of a secret. I decided to risk pressing the point. "They were just babies and so defenseless," I ventured. "You must have trusted Mr. Li a great deal."

"I knew Li to be a good man. Besides, I had no choice but to trust him."

"But surely you had family money to provide for them."

"My wife's family was wealthy, but the Party confiscated their property in 1950," Zhu said. "Anyway, Li was well-off and willing to help." Zhu looked uncomfortable.

"You must have been very worried when Nan Hwa teetered on the verge of bankruptcy," I said. "After all, a collapse of Li's finances would have had repercussions for Guangmei and Simon."

"I wasn't worried. I knew that . . . I thought that Nan Hwa would survive." Zhu got up and began to pace around the room. He was clearly still burdened by something, and I had to encourage him to unload it.

"General Zhu, as you said, I am not here. Nothing you tell me will ever leave this room."

Zhu sat down again and lit a cigarette. He sighed and looked directly into my eyes.

"Young man, because you are my children's attorney, I will tell you something very important: Nan Hwa and Adair, Jameson are theirs, not Li's."

Oh, my. I knew Fiona had a share in Nan Hwa. MacKinnon had let it slip. But half? And for Simon, too.

"I seem to have surprised you," Zhu said. "I was surprised, too, when shortly after my wife died my father-in-law told me what he had done with his fortune. My father-in-law was more than a wise businessman. He was also a far-sighted investor who saw which way the winds of change were blowing. As far back as 1946 he knew that we Communists were going to emerge the victors; so he liquidated most of his assets, and as a measure of security against the new Chinese government confiscating the funds, he transferred the money to a bank in Hong Kong. He put the money in trust for his minor grandchildren, with my wife serving as trustee, until they reached adulthood. When my wife died, my father-in-law told me about the money and that the trusteeship had passed to me.

"At that time, I was thinking only about how to get the children safely away from Jiang Qing. I never thought they would end up in Hong Kong, so I never gave the money a second thought . . . that is, until years later when I found out that Nan Hwa was in trouble. Fearing for my children's livelihood, I transferred a good portion of their funds to Li. In the end, it saved Nan Hwa from bankruptcy and facilitated the takeover of a British company ready to pounce."

"Did Li know where the money came from?"

"He did. But he also realized how dangerous it would be for me if he ever divulged the source. Unfortunately, General Liang discovered my secret. To keep him at bay, I let it be known that I was investigating the embezzlement of Party funds in Guangdong where Liang was posted at the time. Then I had my agents debit the Guangdong Party account by an amount equal to the sum that I'd secretly put into Nan Hwa and transfer it to central Party coffers in Beijing. Liang reported none of this to the Party. I knew then that he would keep quiet—until he wanted something. Now my secret has died with him."

"Liang is dead?" I was ashamed of my feeling of satisfaction.

"Yes . . . killed during the arrest of Jiang Qing."

"And Jiang is soon to stand trial," I said. "You must feel relieved."

"Yes, I do," Zhu said. "I know that Jiang, if given the chance, would have used the information as a dagger against my throat and the throats of my children. She's been a vengeful person her entire life. Her spectrum has no colors, only black and white."

Zhu grew pensive. He turned to the window, cigarette held at the tips of long, arthritic fingers, his black-dyed hair shining in the light. He continued in a soft voice, almost as if he were alone. "I understand such people. I just can't empathize with them. Totally devoid of curiosity, wonder, and—a word I heard on Voice of America—whimsy. Such a wonderful word. Tell me, Mr. Paton, do you realize how lucky you are to have been born American?" He turned abruptly and stared at me. "Well, do you?"

Miss Pan and Colonel Peng stepped cautiously into the room. "General Zhu," Peng said, "Comrade Pan informs me that Mr. Paton must leave now so that he can check out of the hotel and make his train to Guangzhou."

I stood up and offered my hand to General Zhu. Wordlessly, Zhu took it and laid a hand on my shoulder. He smiled.

"Thank you, sir" was all I could think to say.

• • •

Later, as we were driving along Chang An Jie heading toward the Beijing Hotel, Miss Pan asked, "What did the general say to you?"

"That, as far as he's concerned, he doesn't know me," I replied.

"That is the usual procedure in such cases," Miss Pan said matter-of-factly. I would miss her.

When we arrived at the hotel, Miss Pan and I said our good-byes. Then I went straight to the elevator bank to go to my room. As I passed the reception counter, the surly clerk who had been asleep the night I arrived called out to me, "Mr. Paton, it is the policy of this hotel to charge guests for meals not taken," she said. "I informed you of this policy when you checked in. You will see it on your bill."

I thought about what I had been through in the previous three weeks. I had been shot at, nearly impaled by a car, kidnapped, shut up in a concrete box, and interrogated by a psychopath.

So I had to pay for uneaten meals. All I could do was throw my head back and laugh.

EPILOGUE

Fiona and I were each placed in a closed train car under armed guard for the 39-hour journey to Guangzhou. We were not permitted to see each other or anyone else except our guards. After an overnight in Guangzhou—for which I was billed—we proceeded on to Lo Wu, where we walked across the bridge demarcating the border between the People's Republic of China and the British Crown Colony of Hong Kong. We arrived back at the Kowloon station on Monday, October 11. Li Dakchung, MacKinnon, and Simon were there to welcome us home.

As I watched the emotion-filled reunion, I wondered what the years would bring to those of us who had shared so much in the past few months. Fiona had learned the truth about her family, a history that must have transformed her. And I could only imagine the impact of her kidnapping and subsequent ordeal, the details of which I never learned.

In the months and years that followed, I came to admire Fiona immensely. Her Beijing father, as she referred to Zhu, made good on his commitment for the consignment of antiques. The shipment arrived in Hong Kong in time for the January 1977 grand opening of the Hollywood Road shop. Emma, who came down from Beijing for the occasion, insisted that the *feng shui* master approve the final physical arrangement of the shop. This time Fiona was sympathetic.

Over the years, the shop was able to turn a handsome profit. With Emma's enthusiastic support, Fiona plowed the majority of its earnings into a shelter she established for newly arrived refugees from the PRC. After the shop was firmly on its feet, Fiona hired a woman she met at the shelter to manage it. The woman was a 1946 Qinghua University graduate in architecture, but after the Communist takeover in 1949, she was forced onto a reform-through-labor farm, where she spent twenty-six years spreading night soil on the rice paddies. She finally escaped from the farm and fled to Hong Kong in 1975.

Fiona devoted much of her spare time to the shelter. With the help of Li, she established a free medical clinic there and hired a seventy-year-old Harvard-educated former Shanghai doctor to run it. Only a year before, after being freed from prison, the doctor had escaped to Hong Kong, where he was reunited with his wife and three adult children whom he had not seen for over twenty years.

Simon made his family proud, too. Under MacKinnon's guidance, he became Hong Kong's foremost authority on admiralty law. The revenue he generated for Bishops enabled him to devote significant time to pro bono work, especially among Hong Kong's large population of boat people. They showed their gratitude by electing Simon to be their representative to the Legislative Council, the city's governing body.

MacKinnon continued to prosper inside and outside the legal profession. He was elected to several more corporate boards and to the presidency of the Hong Kong Law Society. Bishops also made him managing partner of their worldwide operation. In June of 1980, the Queen conferred a knighthood on him in the birthday honors list. He and Glynis traveled down to London from Scotland, where they were on home leave, for the ceremony.

But the prize MacKinnon ultimately coveted finally fell into his hands shortly after he and Lady MacKinnon returned to Hong Kong that next September: the Hwai-nan 20-cent red—a pre-Revolution Communist-area issue, perhaps the rarest of all Chinese stamps. The wife of a member of Li Dak-chung's tai chi group had died, and her husband was selling her stamp collection. Li brought MacKinnon and the husband together.

Li Dak-chung gradually withdrew from the day-to-day management of Nan Hwa and Adair, Jameson, preferring to let several longtime subalterns run the conglomerate while still exercising oversight. With so much free time, he took up golf and joined the country club at Fanling. Gwei-yu took to visiting her brother more frequently, about which Li had mixed emotions.

In Beijing, Deng Xiaoping consolidated his hold on power. He eliminated his rivals—the Gang of Four—by means of a show trial that convicted Jiang Qing and her cohorts. With his rivals in jail, Deng began to dismantle gradually the PRC's socialist command economy and move it toward a market system. With their energies unleashed for the first time since 1949, the Chinese people began the arduous task of rebuilding an economy and a society devastated by the disastrous Maoist economic policies and the Cultural Revolution.

For Miss Pan, the change was initially confusing and frustrating. But once she got her sea legs, she proved an adept participant in the new Dengist economy. In 1984 she left CTS for a job at an English translation service and was eventually promoted to manager. In late 1988 she founded her own company to provide bilingual guides for China's burgeoning tourism industry.

Lina and Liaoping fared as well as Miss Pan in negotiating the shoals of the new regime. In the spring of 1981, Madame Song Qingling passed away. After the funeral, her security detail was disbanded and its members offered other assignments. Rather than accept one of these, Lina elected to leave government service in order to spend more time with Liming and to get to know her father better. Liaoping resigned from the Ministry of Public Security in 1982 and, in concert with the economic transformation under way, accepted the position of head of security at the Jianguo Hotel, the first new hotel built in the People's Republic of China in nearly thirty years. Rewarded for his loyalty to the moderates, Chen Li remained at the Ministry. He rose steadily and in 1989 became a vice minister.

Zhu's prediction about Colonel Peng's prospects came to fruition earlier than expected. In 1978 after Deng consolidated his hold on power, he promoted Peng to general. At the same time, Deng refused Zhu's request to be relieved of his command and allowed to retire, pending completion of the trial of the Gang of Four. In January 1981, the Gang of Four defendants were found guilty. A month later, Deng permitted his old friend to step down.

As for me, I stayed on at Bishops and was all but adopted by the MacKinnon and Li families. I saw Hugh and Emma during their sojourns in Hong Kong until Hugh was posted back to the Foreign Office in London in 1981.

In 1989, Simon decided that political conditions in China had improved sufficiently for him to make the long-awaited pilgrimage to meet his biological father. I had been in no particular hurry to return to the Mainland, but when Simon asked me to accompany him, I agreed. We took the train to Lo Wu at the end of March, a bare two weeks before Hu Yaobang's death set off a chain of events in China that riveted the world and profoundly altered the course of the Middle Kingdom.

But that is another story.

ABOUT THE AUTHOR

Bruce Gray was born in Santa Monica, California, and grew up in Los Angeles and Frankfurt, Germany. He earned his B.A. and J.D. at the University of California, Berkeley, and was for twenty-six years a career U.S. diplomat specializing in Chinese Affairs. He speaks six languages, including both Mandarin Chinese and Cantonese, and lived in Beijing, Hong Kong, and Taiwan on official postings for eight years. His Foreign Service career ended prematurely when he was diagnosed with Lou Gehrig's disease. He lives with his wife and former diplomat, Kaarn Weaver, in Naples, Florida, where he continues to write.